HONOR HARRINGTON
The Short Victorious War

DAVID WEBER

THE SHORT VICTORIOUS WAR

This is a work of fiction. All the characters and events portrayed in this book are fictional, and any resemblance to real people or incidents is purely coincidental.

A Baen Books Original

Baen Publishing Enterprises
PO Box 1403
Riverdale, NY 10471

ISBN: 0-671-87596-5

Cover art by Laurence Schwinger

First printing, April, 1994
Third printing, October 1996
FourthPrinting, October 1997

Distributed by Simon & Schuster
1230 Avenue of the Americas
New York, NY 10020

Printed in the United States of America

TOUCHDOWN!

"I'm not sure what it is, Ma'am," Admiral Chin's operations officer said. "I'm picking up some very small radar targets at about seven million klicks. They're not under power, and they're too small to be warships, even LACs, but they're almost exactly on our base course. We're overtaking them at about five-five-niner-four KPS, and—*Jesus Christ!*"

✧　　　✧　　　✧

Admiral Mark Sarnow's task group had completed its turn, presenting its broadsides to the oncoming enemy, and the missile pods streamed astern like lumpy, ungainly tails.

"Stand by," Honor murmured, and data codes flashed as each division of battlecruisers and cruisers confirmed acquisition of its assigned target. She waited two more heartbeats, then—

"Fire!" she snapped, and Task Group Hancock-Zero-One belched fire.

Nike and *Agamemnon* alone spat a hundred and seventy-eight missiles at the Peeps, almost five times the broadside of a *Sphinx*-class superdreadnought. The other divisions of her squadron had fewer birds, but even Van Slyke's cruiser divisions had twice a *Bellerophon*-class dreadnought's broadside. Nine *hundred* missiles erupted into Admiral Chin's teeth, and every ship's drive came on line in the same instant. They swerved back onto their original heading, redlining their acceleration, and deployed decoys and jammers to cover themselves as they raced ahead down the Havenites' base course at gravities.

BAEN BOOKS by DAVID WEBER

Honor Harrington:
On Basilisk Station
The Honor of the Queen
The Short Victorious War
Field of Dishonor
Flag in Exile
Honor Among Enemies

Mutineers' Moon
The Armageddon Inheritance
Heirs of Empire

Path of the Fury

Oath of Swords

with Steve White:
Insurrection
Crusade

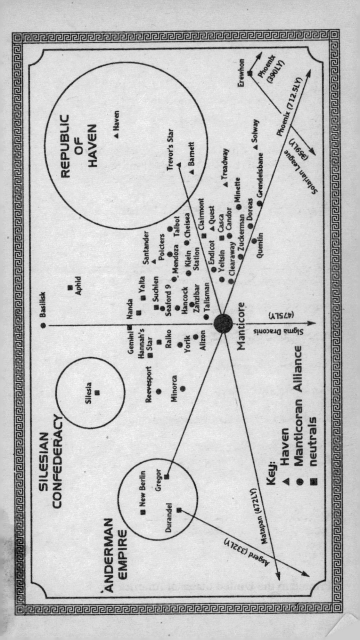

"What this country needs is a short, victorious war to stem the tide of revolution."

V.K. Plehve, Russian Minister of the Interior to General A.N. Kuropatkin, Minister of War, 200 Ante-Diaspora (1903 C.E.), on the eve of the Russo-Japanese War

"The belief in the possibility of a short decisive war appears to be one of the most ancient and dangerous of human illusions."

*Robert Lynd
(224-154 Ante-Diaspora)*

• PROLOGUE

Hereditary President Sidney Harris watched the long cortege wind out of sight along the Promenade of the People, then turned his back upon it. The conference room's two-hundredth floor height had transformed the black-draped vehicles into mere beetles crawling harmlessly along an urban canyon, but their implications showed only too clearly in the grim faces that looked back at him.

He crossed to his chair and sat, propping his elbows on the long table and leaning his chin into his palms while he rubbed his eyes. Then he straightened.

"All right. I've got to be at the cemetery in an hour, so let's keep this short." He turned his eyes to Constance Palmer-Levy, Secretary of Security for the People's Republic of Haven. "Anything more on how they got to Walter, Connie?"

"Not specifically, no." Palmer-Levy shrugged. "Walter's bodyguards stopped the gunman a bit too permanently. We can't question a dead man, but we've identified him as one Everett Kanamashi . . . and what little we have on him suggests he was a fringe member of the CRU."

"Wonderful." Elaine Dumarest, the secretary of war, looked ready to chew splinters out of the table edge. She and Walter Frankel had been adversaries for years—inevitably, given the budgetary conflicts between their ministries—but Dumarest was an organized individual. She preferred a neat and tidy universe in which to make and execute her own policies, and people like the Citizens' Rights Union were high on her list of untidy individuals.

1

"You think the CRU leadership targeted Walter?" Ron Bergren asked, and Palmer-Levy frowned.

"We've got our moles as deep into them as we can," she told the secretary of foreign affairs. "None of them suggested the leadership was contemplating anything drastic, but there's been a lot of rank-and-file anger over Walter's BLS proposals. They're getting more security conscious, too. I'm seeing signs of a real cellular organization, so I suppose it's possible their action committee authorized it without our finding out."

"I don't like the sound of that, Sid," Bergren murmured, and Harris nodded. The Citizens' Rights Union advocated "direct action in the legitimate interest of the people" (meaning a perpetually higher Dolist standard of living) but normally limited itself to riots, vandalism, occasional terrorist bombings, and attacks on lower-level bureaucrats as object lessons. The assassination of a cabinet minister was a new and dangerous escalation . . . assuming the CRU had, indeed, authorized the attack.

"We ought to go in and clean those bastards out," Dumarest growled. "We know who their leaders are. Give the names to NavSec and let my Marines take care of them—permanently."

"Wrong move," Palmer-Levy disagreed. "That kind of suppression would only make the mob even less tractable, and at least letting them go on meeting lets us get a read on what they're up to."

"Like this time?" Dumarest asked with awful irony, and Palmer-Levy flushed.

"If—and I emphasize *if*—the CRU leadership did plan or authorize Walter's murder, then I have to admit we dropped the ball. But as you just pointed out, we've been able to compile lists of members and sympathizers. Drive them underground, and we lose that capability. And, as I said, there's no direct evidence Kanamashi wasn't acting on his own."

"Yeah, sure." Dumarest snorted.

Palmer-Levy started to answer hotly, but Harris' raised hand stopped her. Personally, the President tended to agree with Dumarest, but he could see Palmer-Levy's point as well. The CRU believed the Dolists had a God-given right to an ever higher Basic Living Stipend. They blew up other people (including their fellow Dolists) to make their point, and it would have done Harris' heart good to shoot every one of them. Unfortunately, the Legislaturalist families who ran the People's Republic had no choice but to permit organizations like the CRU to exist. Quite aside from the potential for even greater violence inherent in any open move against them, they'd been around for so long, become so deeply entrenched, that eliminating one would only make room for another, so it made sense to keep an eye on the devil they knew rather than rooting it up for a devil they knew nothing about.

Yet Walter Frankel's assassination was frightening. Dolist violence was almost legitimized, part of the power structure which kept the mob satisfied while the Legislaturalists got on with the business of running the government. Occasional riots and attacks on expendable portions of the Republic's bureaucratic structure had become a sanctioned part of what passed for the political process, but there was—or *had* been—a tacit understanding between the Dolist leaders and the establishment that excluded cabinet-level officials and prominent Legislaturalists from the list of acceptable targets.

"I think," the President said finally, his slow words chosen with care, "that we have to assume, for the moment at least, that the CRU did sanction the attack."

"I'm afraid I have to agree," Palmer-Levy conceded unhappily. "And, frankly, I'm almost equally worried over reports that Rob Pierre is sucking up to the CRU leadership."

"*Pierre*?" Surprise sharpened the President's voice, and the security chief nodded even less happily. Robert Stanton Pierre was Haven's most powerful Dolist manager. He not only controlled almost eight percent of the total Dolist vote but served as the current speaker of the

People's Quorum, the "democratic caucus" which told the Dolist Managers how to vote.

That much power in any non-Legislaturalist's hands was enough to make anyone nervous, since the hereditary governing families relied on the People's Quorum to provide the rubber-stamp "elections" which legitimized their reign. But Pierre was scary. He'd been born a Dolist himself and clawed his way from a childhood on the BLS to his present power with every dirty trick ambition could conceive of. Some of them hadn't even occurred to the Legislaturalists themselves, and if he followed their instructions because he knew which side his bread was buttered on, he was still a lean and hungry man.

"Are you certain about Pierre?" Harris demanded after a moment, and Palmer-Levy shrugged.

"We know he's been in contact with the CRP," she said, and Harris nodded. The Citizens' Rights Party was the political wing of the CRU, operating openly within the People's Quorum and decrying the "understandable but regrettable extremism to which some citizens have been forced." It was a threadbare mask, but accepting it gave the Quorum's managers an often useful pipeline into the CRU's underground membership.

"We don't know exactly what they've been talking about," Palmer-Levy went on, "and his position as Speaker of the Quorum means he could have any number of legitimate reasons for meeting with them. But he seems to be getting awful chummy with some of their delegates."

"In that case, I think we have to look very seriously at the possibility that he knew the assassination was coming," Harris said slowly. "I'm not saying he had anything to do with planning it, but if there was official CRU involvement, he could have known—or suspected—what they were up to. And if he *did* know and didn't tell us, it could have been because he saw a need to cement his own relationship with them, even at our expense."

"You really think things are that bad, Sid?" Bergren asked, and the President shrugged.

"No, not really. But we can live with being overly pessimistic, whereas if the CRU did okay it—and if Pierre knew something about it but chose not to tell us—and we assume they didn't, we could talk ourselves into a serious domestic policy error."

"Are you suggesting that we abandon Walter's BLS proposals?" George De La Sangliere asked. The portly, white-haired De La Sangliere had succeeded Frankel as secretary of the economy . . . not without strenuous efforts to decline the "honor." No one in his right mind wanted to take responsibility for the Republic's decrepit fiscal structure, and De La Sangliere's expression was unhappy as he asked the question.

"I don't know, George." Harris sighed, pinching the bridge of his nose.

"I hate to say it, but I don't really think we can," De La Sangliere replied. "Not unless we can cut military spending by at least ten percent."

"Impossible," Dumarest snapped instantly. "Mr. President, you *know* that's out of the question! We *have* to maintain our fleet strength at current levels—at least—until we deal with the Manticoran Alliance once and for all."

De La Sangliere frowned without looking at her while he kept his eyes almost pleadingly upon his president, but the hope faded from them at Harris' expression.

"We should have hit them four years ago," Duncan Jessup grunted. The secretary of public information was a stocky, perpetually disheveled man who cultivated the public image of a grumpy but golden-hearted uncle. Public Information was the official government spokesman, its main propaganda pipeline, but it had also wrested the Bureau of Mental Hygiene away from the Ministry of Public Health twenty years before. Jessup employed the Mental Hygiene Police with a cold and ruthless dispatch which sometimes frightened even Harris, and his personal control of the MHP made him the most powerful member of the cabinet, after the President himself.

"We weren't ready," Dumarest protested. "We were overextended digesting our new acquisitions, and—"

"And you got too fucking fancy," Jessup interrupted with a rude snort. "First that screw-up in Basilisk and then the disaster in Yeltsin and Endicott. All we've done is let them build their 'alliance' while *our* military potential held steady. Are you seriously suggesting we're in a stronger relative position now than we were then?"

"That's enough, Duncan," Harris said quietly. Jessup glowered at him for a moment, then lowered his eyes, and the President went on more calmly than he felt. "The entire cabinet endorsed both operations, and I'll remind all of you that however spectacular those failures were, most of our other operations have succeeded. We may not have prevented the Manticorans from building up their alliance, but we *have* secured countervailing positions. At the same time, I think we all know the showdown with Manticore is coming." Heads nodded unhappily, and Harris turned his eyes to Fleet Admiral Amos Parnell, CNO of the Peoples' Navy, who sat at Dumarest's elbow. "How do the odds really stack up, Amos?"

"Not as well as I'd like, Sir," Parnell admitted. "The evidence suggests Manticore has a considerably greater technical advantage than anyone thought four years ago. I've personally debriefed the survivors from the Endicott-Yeltsin operation. None of our people were involved in the final action there, and we don't have any hard data to support our analyses of what happened, but it's pretty clear the Manties took out a *Sultan*-class battlecruiser with only a heavy cruiser and a destroyer. Of course, the Masadans crewing *Saladin* were hardly up to our standards in terms of training and experience, but that's still a disturbing indication of our hardware's relative capabilities. On the basis of what happened to *Saladin* and reports of survivors from the earlier actions, we're estimating that, ton-for-ton, their technical superiority probably gives their units a twenty to thirty percent edge over our own."

"Surely not *that* much," Jessup objected, and Parnell shrugged.

"My personal gut feeling is that that's conservative, Mr. Secretary. Let's face it, their education and industrial systems are much better than ours, and it's reflected in their R&D establishment."

The admiral allowed his eyes to angle towards Eric Grossman as he spoke, and the secretary of education reddened. The catastrophic consequences of the "democratization of education" in the People's Republic were a sore point between his ministry and the ministries of economics and war alike, and the exchanges between him and Dumarest since the superiority of Manticore's technology had become evident had been acid.

"At any rate," Parnell went on, "Manticore has a definite edge, however pronounced it may actually be. On the other hand, we have something like twice their absolute tonnage, and forty percent of their wall of battle consists of dreadnoughts. RMN dreadnoughts may be bigger than our own, but ninety percent of our wall are *super*dreadnoughts. Added to that, we've got a lot of combat experience, and their alliance partners don't add much to their actual fighting power."

"Then why are we so worried about them?" Jessup demanded.

"Because of astrography," Parnell replied. "The Manties already had the advantage of the interior position; now they've built up a defense in depth. I doubt it's as deep as they'd like—in fact, it's barely thirty light-years across at Yeltsin—but now that they've closed the gap at Hancock, they've got an entire network of interlocking fortified supply and maintenance bases all along the frontier. That gives them the advantages of forward surveillance, and each of those bases is a potential nexus from which they can raid our supply lines if we advance against them, as well. Their patrols already cover every axis of approach, Mr. Secretary, and it's only going to get worse once the actual shooting starts. We'll have to fight our way through them, taking out the bases in our path as we go to protect our flanks and rear, and that means they're going to have advance notice of our line of attack and be able to deploy their strength to meet us head on."

Jessup grunted and leaned back, lumpy face set in a frown, and Parnell went on levelly.

"At the same time, we've established our own bases to cover theirs, and as the attacker, we'll hold the advantage of the initiative. We'll know when and where we actually intend to strike; *they*'ll have to cover all the points we *might* choose to attack, and do it with a numerically inferior fleet, to boot. I don't think they can stop us if we commit to an all-out offensive, but they're going to hurt us worse than anyone else has."

"Are you saying we should attack them, or not, then?" Harris asked quietly. Parnell glanced sideways at the secretary of war, who gestured for him to go ahead and answer, and cleared his throat.

"Nothing is ever certain in a military campaign, Mr. President. As I've said, I have serious reservations about the inferiority of our hardware. At the same time, I feel we currently have a decisive quantitative edge, and I suspect the gap in our technical capabilities is only going to get worse. I'll be perfectly honest with you, Sir. I don't *want* to take Manticore on—not because I think they can defeat us, but because they can *weaken* us— but if we have to fight, we should probably do it as soon as possible."

"And if we do, how should we go about it?" Jessup asked sharply.

"My staff and I have drawn up plans, under the overall operational code name of 'Perseus,' for several possible approaches. Perseus One envisions the capture of Basilisk as a preliminary in order to allow us to attack Manticore directly via the Manticore Wormhole Junction with simultaneous assaults down the Basilisk-Manticore and Trevor's Star-Manticore lines. It gives us the best chance to attain surprise and win the war in a single blow, but runs the greatest risk of catastrophic losses if we fail.

"Perseus Two is more conventional. We would assemble our forces at DuQuesne Base in the Barnett System, far enough inside the frontier that Manticore couldn't tell what we were up to. From there, we'd attack southwest against Yeltsin, the thinnest point in their perimeter. With Yeltsin in our hands, we would advance directly against Manticore, taking out the bases on our flanks to protect our rear as we went. Losses would be higher than a successful Perseus One, but we'd avoid the risk of the total destruction of our forces which Perseus One entails.

"Perseus Three is a variant of Perseus Two, directing two prongs from Barnett, one against Yeltsin and a second striking northwest, against Hancock. The intention is to present Manticore with two axes of threat, forcing them to split their forces against them. There's some risk of their concentrating their total strength to defeat one attack in detail, but the odds are against it because of the risks it would force *them* to accept against the other arm of our offensive. In my staff's opinion, our exposure to that sort of attack would also be offset by our own ability to dictate the pace of operations by choosing when to push with either prong.

"Finally, there's Perseus Four. Unlike the others, Four envisions a limited offensive to weaken the Alliance rather than take Manticore completely out with one blow. In this instance, we would attack northwest once more, toward Hancock Station. There are two possible variants. One is to reinforce our forces at Seaford Nine and attack Hancock directly, while the other is to send a separate force out from Barnett, take Zanzibar, then hook up to the north while our Seaford Nine forces attack southwest to take Hancock in a pincer. The immediate objective is to destroy the only major Manty base in the area and conquer Zanzibar, Alizon, and Yorik, after which we should offer to negotiate a ceasefire in place. The loss of three inhabited star systems—especially in an area only recently added to the Alliance—would have to shake the Manties' other alliance partners, and possession of the region would position us quite nicely for a later activation of Perseus One or Three."

"And if Manticore chooses to continue operations rather than accept our peace terms?" Palmer-Levy asked.

"In that case we could proceed with Perseus Three—unless we've been hurt far worse than I expect—or retreat to our pre-war positions and negotiate a ceasefire from there. The second option would be far more disadvantageous, but it would still be available if military operations blow up in our faces."

"And do you have a preference for one of the four attack plans, Amos?" Harris asked.

"My personal preference is for Perseus Three, if we want a permanent decision, or for Perseus Four, which substantially lessens our overall risk, if our objectives are more limited. Exactly what our actual objective is, of course, is a political decision, Mr. President."

"I see." Harris pinched the bridge of his nose again, then looked around the table. "Comments, ladies and gentlemen?"

"We've *got* to continue expanding our economic base if we're going to maintain the Basic Living Stipend payments," De La Sangliere said heavily. "And if the CRU did take Walter out, I think we have to be very cautious about curtailing the BLS."

Harris nodded somberly. Two-thirds of Haven's homeworld population was now on the Dole, and rampant inflation was an economic fact of life. Faced with a treasury which had been effectively empty for over a century, desperation had driven Frankel to propose limiting BLS adjustments to the inflation rate, maintaining its actual buying power without increase. The carefully phrased "leaks" Jessup had arranged to test-flight the idea had provoked riots in virtually every Prole housing unit, and, two months later, Kanamashi had put twelve explosive pulser darts into Frankel's chest, requiring a closed-coffin state funeral.

It was, Harris reflected grimly, one of the less ambiguous "protest votes" on record, and he understood the near panic thoughts of actual BLS cuts woke in his cabinet colleagues.

"Given those considerations," De La Sangliere went on, "we've got to gain access to the systems beyond Manticore, especially the Silesian Confederacy. If anyone knows some way we can grab them off without fighting Manticore first, I, for one, would be delighted to hear of it."

"There isn't one." Palmer-Levy looked around the table, daring anyone to disagree with her flat assertion. No one did, and Jessup endorsed her comment with a sharp nod. Bergren looked far more unhappy than either of his colleagues, but the dapper foreign minister also nodded unwilling assent. "Besides," the security minister went on, "a foreign crisis might help cool off the domestic front, at least in the short term. It always has before."

"That's true." There was an almost hopeful note in De La Sangliere's voice. "Traditionally, the People's Quorum's always accepted a freeze in the BLS for the duration of actual military operations."

"Of course they have." Dumarest snorted. "They know we're fighting for more slops for their trough!"

Harris winced at her caustic cynicism. It was just as well Elaine was in charge of the war ministry and not something with more public exposure, he reflected, but he couldn't fault her analysis.

"Exactly." Palmer-Levy's smile was cold as she glanced at Parnell. "You say we may take losses against the Manticorans, Admiral?" Parnell nodded. "But would operations against them be extended?"

"I don't see how they could be too extended, Ms. Secretary. Their fleet simply isn't large enough to absorb the kind of losses we can. Unless they somehow managed to inflict an incredibly lopsided loss ratio, it would have to be a fairly short war."

"That's what I thought," Palmer-Levy said in a satisfied tone. "And it might actually work in our favor to take a certain number of casualties. I'm sure you could put the right spin control on it and use the deaths of our gallant defenders to mobilize public opinion in our time of crisis, couldn't you, Duncan?"

"I could, indeed." Jessup almost licked his chops—and *did* rub his hands—at the prospect of such a propaganda coup, oblivious to the sudden, angry glitter in Parnell's eyes. "In fact, we can probably build up a balance of support for future need, if we handle it right. It would certainly be a far cry from the kind of growing unrest we're seeing now, anyway."

"There you are, then," Palmer-Levy said. "What we need is a short, victorious war . . . and I think we all know where we can find one, don't we?"

• CHAPTER ONE

Dame Honor Harrington dropped her long, rolled bundle and removed a hat someone on Old Earth of two millennia past would have called a fedora. She dried the sweatband with a handkerchief, then sat on the weather-worn rock outcrop with a sigh of relief, laid the hat beside her, and looked out over the magnificent panorama.

Wind cold enough to make her grateful for her leather jacket ruffled sweat-damp hair that was longer than it had been before her convalescence. It was still far shorter than current fashion decreed, but she ran her fingers through it with a curiously guilty sensuality. She'd worn it cropped close for helmets and zero-gee for so long she'd forgotten how satisfying its curly, silken weight could feel.

She lowered her hands and stared out over the endless reaches of the Tannerman Ocean. Even here, a thousand meters above its wrinkled blue and silver, she smelled salt on the chill wind. It was a smell she'd been born to, yet it was perpetually new, as well. Perhaps because she'd spent so little time on Sphinx in the twenty-nine T-years since joining the Navy.

She turned her head and looked down, down, down to where she'd begun her climb. A small splash of bright green stood out boldly against the red-gold and yellow of autumn-touched grass, and she twitched the muscles of her left eye socket in one of the patterns she'd learned in the endless months of therapy.

There was a moment of disorientation, a sense that she was moving even while she sat still, and the green splash was suddenly much larger. She blinked, still not fully accustomed to the effect, and reminded herself to get more practice with her new eye. But the thought was distant, almost absentminded, as the prosthesis' telescopic function brought the sprawling, green-roofed structure and the greenhouses clustered about it into sharp focus.

That roof rose in a steep, snow-shedding peak, for Sphinx lay so far from the G0 component of the Manticore binary system that only an exceptionally active carbon dioxide cycle made it habitable at all. It was a cold world, with huge icecaps, a year sixty-three T-months long, and long, slow seasons. Even here, barely forty-five degrees below the equator, its natives measured snowfall in meters, and children born in autumn—as she herself had been—learned to walk before spring came.

Off-worlders shuddered at the very thought of a Sphinx winter. If pressed, they might agree that Manticore-B IV, otherwise known as Gryphon, had more violent weather, but it was also warmer, and its year was much shorter. At least whatever happened there was over three times as quickly, and nothing could change their considered opinion that anyone who voluntarily lived on Sphinx year-round had to be crazy.

Honor smiled at the thought as she studied the stone house where twenty generations of Harringtons had been born, but there was an edge of truth in it. Sphinx's climate and gravity made for sturdy, independent inhabitants. They might not be crazy, but they were self-sufficient and stubborn—one might even say obstinate.

Leaves rustled, and she turned her head as a fast-moving blur of cream-and-gray fur snaked out of the pseudo-laurel behind her. The six-limbed treecat belonged to the crown oak and picket wood of lower elevations, but he was at home here in the Copper Walls, as well. Certainly he'd spent enough time wandering their slopes with her as a child to become so.

He scampered across the bare rock, and she braced

herself as he leapt into her lap. He landed with a solid thump, his nine-plus standard kilos working out at almost twelve and a half here, and she oofed in reproach.

He seemed unimpressed and rose on his haunches, bracing his mid-limbs' hand-paws on her shoulders to gaze into her face with bright, grass-green eyes. Near-human intelligence examined her from those very unhuman eyes, and then he touched her left cheek with a long-fingered true-hand and gave a soft sigh of satisfaction when the skin twitched at the contact.

"No, it hasn't stopped working again," she told him, running her own fingers over his fluffy fur. He sighed again, this time in unabashed pleasure, and oozed down with a buzzing purr. He was a limp, heavy warmth across her thighs, and his own contentment flowed into her. She'd always known he could sense her emotions, and she'd wondered, sometimes, if she could truly sense his or only thought she could. A year ago he'd finally proven she could, and now she savored his content like her own as her fingers stroked his spine.

Stillness gathered about her, perfected rather than marred by the crisp, sharp breeze, and she let it fill her as she sat on the rock shelf as she had in childhood, mistress of all she surveyed, and wondered who she truly was.

Captain Dame Honor Harrington, Countess Harrington, Knight Companion of the Order of King Roger. When she was in uniform, her space-black tunic blazed with ribbons: the Manticore Cross, the Star of Grayson, the Distinguished Service Order, the Conspicuous Gallantry Medal with cluster, the blood-red stripe of the Monarch's Thanks with two clusters, two wound stripes . . . The list went on and on, and there'd been a time when she'd craved those medals, those confirmations of achievement and ability. She was proud of them even now, but they were no longer the stuff of dreams. She'd learned too much about what those bits of ribbon cost.

Nimitz raised his head and kneaded the tips of his

claws through her trousers to register his discontent with the direction of her thoughts. She stroked his ears in apology, but she didn't stop thinking them; they were the reason she'd spent the last four hours hiking up here to the refuge of her childhood. Nimitz studied her for a moment, then sighed in resignation and laid his chin back on his true-hands and left her to them.

She touched the left side of her face and clenched her cheek muscles under her fingers. It had taken over eight Sphinxian months—almost a full T-year—of reconstructive surgery and therapy for her to be able to do that. Her father was one of Manticore's finest neurosurgeons, yet the damage the disrupter bolt had wreaked had taxed even his skill, for Honor was one of the minority of humans who did not respond to regeneration therapies.

There was always some loss of function in neural repairs without regen. In her case, the loss had been unusually severe and complicated by a stubborn tendency to reject natural tissue grafts. Two complete nerve replacements had failed; in the end, they'd been forced to use artificial nerves with powerful boosters, and the unending surgery, the repeated failures, and long, agonizing therapy as she struggled to master the high-tech substitutes had almost defeated her. Even now there was an alien, sharp-edged strangeness to reports from her synthetic nerves. Nothing felt quite *right*, as if the implants were an ill-tuned sensor array—a sensation the undamaged nerves on the other side of her face only made worse by comparison—and she doubted she would ever truly become accustomed to it.

She returned her gaze to the distant house and wondered how much of her melancholy stemmed from the months of strain and pain. There'd been no fast, simple way through them, and she'd wept herself to sleep more than once as the unnatural fire crackled in her face. There were no scars to reveal the massive repairs—no visible ones, anyway—and her face was almost as sensitive, its muscles almost as responsive, as they'd ever been. But only almost. She could tell the difference when she watched herself in a mirror, see the slight hesitation when the left side of her mouth moved, hear the occasionally slurred words that hesitation produced, even as she felt the skewed sensitivity when the wind kissed her cheek.

And deep inside, where no one else could see, there were other scars.

The dreams were less frequent now, but they remained cold and bitter. Too many people had died under her orders . . . or because she hadn't been there to keep them alive. And with those dreams came self-doubt. Could she face the challenge of command once more? And even if she could, should the Fleet trust her with others' lives?

Nimitz roused again and rose on his haunches once more, bracing his true-hands against her shoulders. He stared into her chocolate-brown eyes—one natural, the other born of advanced composites and molecular circuitry, and she felt his support and love flow into her.

She scooped him up and buried her wind-chilled face in his soft fur, embracing its physical warmth even as she treasured that deeper, more precious inner one, and he purred to her until she lowered him once more and drew a deep, deep breath.

She filled her lungs with crisp air, sucking the early fall chill deep until her chest ached with it, and then she exhaled in one long, endless breath that carried away . . . something. She couldn't put a name to that something, yet she felt it go, and something else roused in its place, as if waking from long sleep.

She'd been planetbound too long. She no longer belonged here on this beloved mountain, looking down on the place of her birth through its chilled crystal air. For the first time in far too long she felt the call of the stars not as a challenge she feared she could no longer meet but with the old need to be about it, and she sensed the change in Nimitz's emotions as he shared her feelings.

"All right, Stinker—you can stop worrying now," she told him, and his purr turned brisker and louder. His prehensile tail twitched as he touched her nose with his, and she laughed as she hugged him close once more.

It wasn't over. She knew that. But at least she knew where she had to go, what she had to do, to lay the nightmares to rest at last.

"Yeah," she told the treecat. "I guess it *is* about time I stopped feeling sorry for myself, isn't it?" Nimitz twitched his tail more strongly in agreement. "And it's time I got back on a command deck, too," she added. "Assuming, of course, that The Powers That Be want me back." This time there was no fresh flash of pain at the qualifier, and she smiled in gratitude.

"In the meantime," she said more briskly, "it's also time the two of us got airborne."

She stood, set Nimitz on the rock, and bent over her long bundle. She unfastened the straps that held it closed, and alloy clicked as she assembled the tubular frame with deft, practiced fingers. She and Nimitz had discovered the wild joy of riding the Copper Walls' glorious winds before she was twelve T-years old, and the 'cat bleeked in encouragement as she stretched the infinitely tough, gossamer thin fabric into place.

It took less than half an hour to assemble the hang-glider and double-check every joint. She slipped into the harness with the specially modified safety straps for Nimitz, and he scampered up her back and clung to her shoulders as she adjusted them about him. She felt his delight and anticipation bubbling with her own exuberance, and her natural eye sparkled as she clipped the harness leads to the glider and gripped the hand bar.

"All right, hang on!" she told him, and launched herself over the edge of the long, lofty drop with a whoop of sheer delight.

The sun was a fading rim of red-orange beyond the Copper Walls' peaks as Honor made the final turn. She floated like a Sphinx albatross, five kilometers off-shore, and her eyes slitted with amusement as she saw the bright splash of light against the deep twilight at the mountains' feet. The Harrington homestead's brilliant exterior lights blazed in the darkness, for her steward—who obviously thought a four-hour hike followed by a three-hour glide was a bit much for a recent invalid—was taking no chances with his captain's landing.

She grinned and shook her head fondly. Hang-gliding was a planetary passion on Sphinx, but Senior Chief Steward MacGuiness was from the capital world of Manticore. She suspected that he believed all Sphinxians (herself included) were more than a bit mad and needed looking after. He certainly did his level best to rule her life with an iron hand, and while it would never do to admit that she enjoyed the way he fussed over—and at—her, she had to admit (privately) that this time he had a point. She'd been an expert glider for over thirty T-years. As such she should have had the sense to get herself home when she had good light for the landing, which meant she was going to have to endure his ever so respectful reproaches with meek acceptance.

She swept in from the sea, adjusting her weight with finicky precision, smoothing her angle of descent, and the ground rushed up toward her with suddenly breathtaking speed. Then the brilliant light was right in front of her, her dropping feet reached out, and Nimitz chittered with delight as she raced forward, absorbing her velocity with an exultant laugh of her own.

She lost the last of her speed and went down on one knee, resting the glider frame on the red-gold grass before the house, and a cold, whiskered nose caressed her right ear as Nimitz radiated his own content. She unfastened his safety straps, and the 'cat dropped lightly to the ground and sat up to watch her unlatch her own straps and rise, stretching until her shoulders popped and grinning at him like a schoolgirl. Then she collapsed the glider with a few practiced motions—not completely, just into a halfway convenient burden—and tucked it under her arm as she headed for the house.

"You left your com home again, Ma'am," a respectful, gently reproving voice said as she stepped up onto the glassed-in storm porch.

"Did I?" she asked innocently. "How careless of me. It must have slipped my mind."

"Of course it did," MacGuiness agreed, and she turned her head to give him a brilliant smile. He smiled back, but there was an edge of carefully hidden regret behind his eyes. Even now the left side of the Captain's mouth was less expressive and responsive, giving her smile a lopsided quality that was more sensed than seen. "The fact that someone might have called you in earlier had nothing at all to do with it," he added, and Honor chuckled.

"Not a thing," she said, crossing the porch to stand the collapsed glider in the corner.

"As it happens, I *did* try to com you, Ma'am," MacGuiness said after a moment, his voice more serious. "A letter from the Admiralty arrived this afternoon."

Honor froze for just one moment, then adjusted the glider's position with careful precision. The Admiralty used electronic mail for most purposes; official letters were sent only under very special circumstances, and she schooled her face into calm and made herself fight down a sudden surge of excitement before she turned and raised an eyebrow.

"Where is it?"

"Beside your plate, Ma'am." MacGuiness glanced pointedly at his chrono. "Your supper's waiting," he added, and Honor's mouth quirked in another smile.

"I see," she murmured. "Well, let me get washed up and I'll deal with both of them, Mac."

"At your convenience, Ma'am," MacGuiness said without a trace of triumph.

Honor forced herself to move without haste as she walked into the dining room and felt the quiet old house about her like a shield. She was an only child, and her parents had an apartment near their medical offices in

Duvalier City, almost five hundred kilometers to the north. They were seldom "home" except on weekends, and her birthplace always seemed a bit empty without them. It was odd. Somehow she always pictured them here whenever she was away, as if they and the house were a single, inseparable entity, like a protecting shadow of her childhood.

MacGuiness was waiting, napkin neatly folded over one forearm, as she slid into her chair. One of the perks for a captain of the list was a permanently assigned steward, though Honor still wasn't entirely positive how MacGuiness had chosen himself for that duty. It was just one of those inevitable things, and he watched over her like a mother hawk, but he had his own ironclad rules. They included the notion that nothing short of pitched battle should be allowed to interfere with his captain's meals, and he cleared his throat as she reached for the anachronistic, heavily embossed envelope. She looked up, and he whisked the cover from a serving dish with pointed emphasis.

"Not this time, Mac," she murmured, breaking the seal, and he sighed and replaced the cover. Nimitz contemplated their human antics with a small, amused "bleek" from his place at the far end of the table, and the steward replied with a repressive frown.

Honor opened the envelope and slid out two sheets of equally archaic parchment. They crackled crisply, and her eyes—organic and cybernetic alike—opened wide as they flicked over the formal printed words on the first page. MacGuiness stiffened at her shoulder as she inhaled sharply, and she read it a second time, then glanced at the second sheet and looked up to meet his gaze.

"I think," she said slowly, "that it's time to open the good stuff, Mac. How about a bottle of the Delacourt '27?"

"The Delacourt, Ma'am?"

"I don't think Dad will mind . . . under the circumstances."

"I see. May I assume, then, that it's good news, Ma'am?"

"You may, indeed." She cleared her throat and stroked the parchment almost reverently. "It seems, Mac, that BuMed in its infinite wisdom has decided I'm fit for duty again, and Admiral Cortez has found a ship for me." She looked up from the orders with a sudden, blinding smile. "In fact, he's giving me *Nike!*"

The normally unflappable MacGuiness stared back at her, and his jaw dropped. HMS *Nike* wasn't just a battlecruiser. She was *the* battlecruiser, the fiercely sought after, most prestigious prize any captain could covet. There was always a *Nike*, with a list of battle honors reaching clear back to Edward Saganami, the founder of the Royal Manticoran Navy, and the current *Nike* was the newest, most powerful battlecruiser in the Fleet.

Honor laughed out loud and tapped the second sheet of parchment.

"According to this, we go aboard Wednesday," she said. "Ready for a little space duty again, Mac?"

MacGuiness' eyes met hers, and then he shook himself, and a huge, matching smile lit his own face.

"Yes, Ma'am. I think I can stand that—and this certainly *is* a night for the Delacourt!"

• CHAPTER TWO

The intra-system shuttle settled into the docking buffers of Her Majesty's Space Station *Hephaestus*, and Honor tapped the save key on her memo pad and rose from her seat just inside the hatch.

Her face gave no hint of her inner excitement as she drew the white beret of a starship's commander from under her left epaulet. She grimaced mentally as she adjusted it, for she hadn't worn it in over a T-year, and she hadn't allowed for the way her hair had grown. It was considered bad luck for an RMN officer to replace her first white beret, which meant she either had to get her hair clipped or the beret re-sized, she thought, and held out her arms to Nimitz.

The 'cat swarmed up onto her padded shoulder and settled his weight with a soft bleek, then patted the soft, white beret with a proprietary air. Honor hid a grin that would never have suited the probity of a senior grade captain, and Nimitz snorted in amused tolerance. He knew how much that symbol meant to her, and he saw absolutely no reason she shouldn't show it.

For that matter, Honor had to admit there was no real need to assume her "captain's face" so soon, since, aside from MacGuiness, no one on the shuttle knew who she was or why she was here. But she needed the practice. Even the shuttle felt strange after so long off a command deck, and few things were more important than starting a new command off on the right foot. Besides—

She brought her mental babbling to a stern halt and admitted the truth. She didn't feel just "strange"; she felt *worried*, and under her joy at getting back into space, butterflies mated in her midsection. She'd put in all the simulation hours she'd been allowed between bouts of surgery and therapy, but that wasn't as many as she would have liked. Unfortunately, it was hard to argue with your physician when he was also your father, and even if Doctor Harrington had allowed all the sim time she wanted, simulators weren't the same as reality. Besides, *Nike* would be her biggest, most powerful ship yet—eight hundred and eighty thousand tons, with a crew of over two thousand—which was enough to make anyone nervous after so long dirt-side, simulators or no.

Yet she knew her long medical leave wasn't the only reason for her anxiety. Being picked for *Nike* was an enormous professional compliment, especially for a captain who'd never before held battlecruiser command. Among other things, it was an implicit approval of her performance in her last command, whatever her own mixed feelings, and a clear indication the Admiralty was grooming her for flag rank. But there was another side to the coin, as well. With opportunity came responsibility . . . and the chance to fail.

She inhaled deeply, squaring her shoulders, then touched the three gold stars embroidered on her tunic, and deep down inside something laughed at her own reactions. Each of those stars represented a previous hyper-capable command, and she'd been through almost exactly the same internal cycle with each of them. Oh, there were differences this time, but there were always differences, and the underlying truth never changed. There was nothing in the universe she wanted more than command . . . and nothing that scared her worse than the thought of failing once she had it.

Nimitz bleeked again, softly, in her ear. The sound was comforting yet scolding, and she glanced over at him. A delicate yawn showed needle-sharp white fangs in the lazy, confident grin of a predator, and humor narrowed her eyes as she rubbed his ears and started for the hatch with MacGuiness at her heels.

The personnel tube deposited them at a slip on the extreme rim of *Hephaestus'* hull. The space station seemed larger every time Honor saw it . . . probably because it was. *Hephaestus* was the Royal Manticoran Navy's premiere shipyard, and the Navy's steadily accelerating building programs were mirrored by an equally steady growth in the station's size. It was over forty kilometers long, now—a lumpy, ungainly, immensely productive amalgamation of building and repair slips, fabrication shops, deep-space foundries, and living quarters for thousands of workers that never stopped growing.

She glanced through the armorplast wall of the spacedock gallery as she and MacGuiness headed for the docking tube, and it took all her will power not to gawk like a middy on her first deployment, for the sleek, powerful shape floating in the building slip's mooring tractors cried out for her to stop dead and stare hungrily through the armorplast.

HMS *Nike* was all but completed. Yard dogs and their remotes floated about her and crawled over her like tiny, furiously laboring ants, and the double-ended, flattened spindle of her battle steel hull looked mottled as it awaited its final coating of skin-fused pigment. But the hollow throats of missile tubes and the ominous snouts of lasers and grasers crouched in her opened weapon bays, and mechs were already closing up the plating around her last drive nodes. Another two weeks, Honor thought, three at the most, till the acceptance trials. Only twenty T-years ago, the process would have been far more extended, with builder's tests followed by pre-acceptance trials before she was turned over for the Navy's own evaluation, but there was no time for that now. The tempo of construction was almost scary, and the *reason* for the endless hurry was enough to frighten anyone.

She turned a bend in the gallery and the Marines

manning the outboard end of *Nike's* docking tube stiffened and snapped to attention as she crossed to them with a measured stride. She returned their salutes and handed her ID to the sergeant in charge, who scrutinized it briefly but closely before he returned it with another salute.

"Thank you, Milady," he said crisply, and Honor's upper lip quivered. She was still getting used to being a peer of the realm—although, in truth, that wasn't *exactly* what she was—but she suppressed the temptation to smile and accepted her ID folio with a grave nod.

"Thank *you*, Sergeant," she said and started to step into the tube, then paused as she saw one hand twitch towards his communicator. He stiffened into immobility, and this time she did let herself smile. "It's all right, Sergeant. Go ahead."

"Uh, yes, Milady." The sergeant blushed, then relaxed and responded with a slight smile of his own. Some captains preferred to catch their new crews by surprise, but Honor had always thought it was rather pointless—and foolish. Unless an executive officer had managed to completely alienate her crew, they were going to flash a warning to her as soon as the new captain's back was out of sight anyway. And there was no way a crew would leave *Nike's* exec in the dark.

She grinned at that thought as she crossed the scarlet zero-gee warning stripe and launched herself into a graceful free-fall glide.

A full side party waited in the entry port. The side boys came to attention, electronic bosun's pipes twittered in archaic ritual, and the spotlessly uniformed commander at the head of *Nike's* assembled senior officers snapped a salute that would have done Saganami Island proud.

Honor returned it with equal formality and felt Nimitz sitting perfectly still on her shoulder. She'd worked hard at impressing the need for proper decorum upon him, and she was a bit relieved to find her efforts paying off.

He was choosy about familiarity, but he was also demonstrative about greeting those he admitted to the select circle of his friends.

"Permission to come aboard, Ma'am?" Honor asked very formally as she lowered her hand from the salute.

"Permission granted, Milady," the commander replied in a soft, furry contralto, and stepped back to clear the entry port.

It was an oddly gracious gesture on a subordinate's part. Not consciously so, but on an almost instinctive level, and Honor hid another smile. She stood a good fourteen centimeters taller than the other woman, but she'd never had the same presence, the same easy ability to dominate the space about her, and she doubted she ever would.

The Manticore Colony, Ltd., had drawn its original settlers primarily from Old Earth's western hemisphere, and five hundred T-years had gone far towards pureeing the original colonists' genetic heritages. There were exceptions—such as Honor herself, whose emigrant mother was of almost pure Old Earth Asian extraction by way of the ancient colony world of Beowulf—but by and large it was difficult to estimate anyone's ancestry at a glance.

Her new exec was an exception, however. Through whatever trick of genetics, Commander The Honorable Michelle Henke was a throwback to her first Manticoran ancestor's genotype. Her skin was barely a shade lighter than her space-black uniform, her hair was even curlier than Honor's . . . and there was no mistaking the cleancut, distinctive features of the House of Winton.

Commander Henke said nothing as she escorted Honor up-ship to the bridge. Her face was admirably grave, but a twinkle lurked in her eyes, and Honor was relieved to see it. The last time they'd seen one another had been over six T-years ago, and Henke had been senior to her at the time; now she was not only two full ranks Honor's junior but her executive officer and immediate subordinate, as well, and Honor hadn't quite been able to rule out the possibility of resentment over the change.

They reached the bridge, and Honor looked around appreciatively. Her last ship had been just as new as *Nike* when she assumed command, and she knew how lucky she'd been, even in the expanding Manticoran Navy, to win two brand new ships in a row. Yet marvelous as the heavy cruiser *Fearless* had been, her bridge paled beside *Nike's*, and the hugely expanded tactical section made her mouth water. Battlecruisers were Manticore's ship of choice, ideally suited to the fast, slashing tactics the Navy had embraced for over four T-centuries, and she could practically feel her new command's lethality quivering about her.

She shook off the moment of almost sensual enjoyment and crossed to the captain's chair. She started to shoo Nimitz off her shoulder to the chair's back, then stopped herself. This was his moment, as well as hers, and she decided to let him be as she reached out and touched a stud on the chair arm.

The clear, sharp chimes of an all-hands announcement sounded from every speaker on the ship, and com screens blinked alive with her face as she reached into her tunic and withdrew the stiff parchment. She looked straight into the pickup, forcing herself not to clear her throat and wondering, with a corner of her mind, why she felt so nervous. It wasn't as if she'd never done this before!

She pushed the thought aside and unfolded her orders, the sound of the paper loud in the stillness, and began to read in a calm, clear voice.

"'From Admiral Sir Lucien Cortez, Fifth Space Lord, Royal Manticoran Navy, to Captain Dame Honor Harrington, Countess Harrington, KCR, MC, SG, DSO, CGM, Royal Manticoran Navy, Twenty-First Day, Sixth Month, Year Two Hundred and Eighty-Two After Landing. Madam: You are hereby directed and required to proceed aboard Her Majesty's Starship *Nike*, BC-Four-One-Three, there to take upon yourself the duties and responsibilities of commanding officer in the service of the Crown. Fail not in this charge at your peril. By order of Lady Francine Maurier, Baroness Morncreek, First Lord of Admiralty, Royal Manticoran Navy, for Her Majesty the Queen.'"

She refolded the document slowly and carefully, feeling once more the thrill of the moment, then looked at Commander Henke.

"Madam Exec, I assume command," she said.

"Captain," Henke replied formally, "you have command."

"Thank you," Honor said, and looked back at the pickup that connected her to her so-far anonymous crew. "This is a proud moment for me," she said, and her quiet sincerity deprived her words of the trite formality she feared infused them. "Very few captains have the honor of commanding a ship with this one's battle record. Even fewer are privileged to assume command straight from the builder's hands, and none of them ever have the opportunity to do both of those things more than once. As keel plate owners, we have a great deal to live up to as we build on the tradition entrusted to our keeping, but I know that when the time comes for me to pass this ship into another captain's keeping, he or she will have even more to live up to than we do now."

She paused, her eyes very level, then smiled almost impishly.

"You're going to feel overworked and underappreciated while we work up, people, but try to remember that it's all in a good cause. I'm sure I can rely on all of you to give me your very best. I promise you'll get *my* best in return." She nodded at the pickup. "Carry on," she said, and killed the circuit and turned back to Henke.

"Welcome aboard, Captain." The commander extended her hand in the traditional welcoming handclasp, and Honor gripped it hard.

"Thank you, Mike. It's good to be here."

"May I present your senior officers?" Henke asked, and then waved the waiting officers forward at Honor's nod.

"Commander Ravicz, Ma'am, our engineer."

"Mr. Ravicz," Honor murmured. The engineer's deep-set eyes were frankly curious as he nodded courteously to her, and she shook his hand before glancing back at Henke.

"Commander Chandler, our tac officer," her exec said.

"Ms. Chandler." The diminutive tactical officer's flaming red head didn't reach even to Honor's shoulder, but she had a tough, no-nonsense look to her, and her blue eyes were as firm as her handshake.

"I believe you know Surgeon Commander Montoya, our doctor," Henke said, and Honor smiled hugely as she took Montoya's hand in both of hers.

"Indeed I do! It's good to see you again, Fritz."

"And you, Skipper." Montoya studied the left side of her face for a moment, then nodded. "Especially to see you looking so good," he added.

"I had a good doctor—two of them, in fact," Honor said, and gave his hand another squeeze before she turned to the next officer on Henke's list.

"Lieutenant Colonel Klein, commanding our Marine detachment," Henke said.

"Colonel." The Marine bobbed a sharp, respectful nod as he took Honor's hand. His was the sort of face that revealed very little, but the ribbons on his black tunic were impressive. Which they ought to be. *Nike* carried a full battalion of Marines, and the Admiralty wouldn't have picked their commander's name out of a hat.

"Lieutenant Commander Monet, our com officer," Henke continued down the order of seniority.

"Mr. Monet." The com officer was the antithesis of her new tac officer: a tall, thin, almost colorless man with humorless features. His handclasp was firm enough, but almost mechanical.

"Lieutenant Commander Oselli, our astrogator." Henke's bland voice laid just a hint of emphasis on the word "astrogator," and Honor's lips twitched, for her own astrogation skills were less than outstanding.

"Ms. Oselli." Honor shook her astrogator's hand, pleased with what she saw. Oselli's hair and eyes were as dark as Honor's own, and her thin, almost foxy features looked both confident and intelligent.

"And last but not least, Lieutenant Commander Jasper, our logistics officer."

"Mr. Jasper." Honor gave *Nike's* supply officer a small smile that mingled conspiracy and sympathy. "I imagine you and I will be seeing a lot of one another over the next week or so, Commander. I'll try not to ask the impossible of you, but you know how captains are."

"Yes, Milady, I'm afraid I do." Amusement colored Jasper's deep baritone. "At the moment, I know almost exactly where we are and what we still need. Needless to say, that's subject to change without notice until the yard turns us loose."

"Needless to say," Honor agreed, and folded her hands behind her as she surveyed the entire group. "Well, ladies and gentlemen, we've got a lot to do, and no doubt I'll get to know you all in the process. For now, I'll let you get on with whatever you were doing before my arrival interrupted, but you're all invited to dine with me at eighteen hundred, if that will be convenient."

Heads nodded as agreements were murmured, and Honor chuckled mentally. It was a rare officer who *wouldn't* find it "convenient" to dine with a new captain on her first day in command! She nodded a courteous dismissal, and they began to move away, but she held up a hand as Henke started to leave.

"Wait a moment, Exec. I'd appreciate it if you could join me in my quarters. We've got a lot to discuss."

"Of course, Milady," Henke murmured, and looked across the bridge. "Ms. Oselli, you have the watch."

"Aye, aye, Ma'am. I have the watch," Oselli responded, and Henke followed Honor into the intraship car. The doors slid shut behind them, and the commander's formality vanished in a face-splitting grin.

"Damn, but it's good to see you again, Honor!" She flung an arm around her superior and squeezed tightly, then reached up to Nimitz. The treecat buzzed a happy purr and extended a true-hand in a handshake all their own, and she laughed. "Good to see you, too, Stinker. Still extorting celery out of your hapless companions?"

Nimitz bleeked smugly and flirted his fluffy tail, and Honor smiled back at her exec. As a rule, she disliked easy embraces, and despite her own recent elevation, she was still uncomfortable with those from the rarefied heights of the aristocracy, but Mike Henke was a rule unto herself. She never presumed upon her family's position as a cadet branch of Manticore's ruling dynasty, yet she had an unaffected ease with people and public situations Honor could only envy. They'd been roommates at Saganami Island for over three T-years, and Henke had spent hours trying to beat the fundamentals of multi-dimensional math into her shy, towering roommate, and even more hours unveiling the mysteries of etiquette and social interaction. Honor's yeoman ancestry hadn't prepared her for interaction with the nobility, and she'd often wondered if that was one reason the Academy adjutant had paired her with Henke, but whether it had been intentional or not, she knew how much Michelle's easy, breezy confidence had helped her.

"It's good to see you, too, Mike," she said simply, squeezing back briefly, then straightened as the lift stopped. Henke grinned at her, then twitched her face into properly formal lines as the door hissed open and the two of them walked down the passage to Honor's quarters.

The Marine sentry outside the captain's cabin came to attention at their approach, immaculate in green and black. Honor nodded courteously to her, then opened the hatch and waved Henke through it, only to pause as she saw her new quarters for the first time.

They were huge, she thought with a touch of awe. Her belongings had come up the day before, and MacGuiness was fussing over the treecat-sized life-support module mounted on a bulkhead. He turned and started to come to attention as he realized his captain wasn't alone, but Honor gestured for him to stand easy.

"Mac, meet Commander Henke. Mike, Senior Chief MacGuiness—my keeper." Henke chuckled, and MacGuiness shook his head resignedly. "Go on with what you're doing, Mac," Honor continued. "Commander Henke and I are old friends."

"Of course, Ma'am." MacGuiness bent back over the module, and Nimitz leapt lightly from Honor's shoulder to the module's top to watch him while Honor looked around and shook her head. Her personal gear had filled her last set of quarters to the point of crowding; here, it looked almost spartan. Expensive carpet covered the decksole, and a huge painting of the original *Nike*'s final action in the Battle of Carson dominated one bulkhead, faced from across the cabin by a state portrait of Elizabeth III, Queen of Manticore. A portrait, Honor noted, which bore a striking resemblance to her own exec.

"BuShips really spoils its battlecruiser captains, doesn't it?" she murmured.

"Oh, I don't know." Henke looked around and quirked an eyebrow. "I'd say it's about right for one of your eminence, Dame Honor."

"Yeah, sure." Honor crossed to the padded seat under a view port and leaned back, staring out at the space station's irregular flank. "This," she said, "is going to take some getting used to."

"I'm sure you'll adjust," Henke replied dryly. She crossed to Honor's desk and reached out to a heat-warped golden plaque on the bulkhead. The sailplane etched into its metal had lost a wing tip, and the commander reached out to touch it gently. "This happen in Basilisk?" she asked. "Or Yeltsin?"

"Basilisk." Honor crossed her legs and shook her head. "Just missed Nimitz's module, too. We were lucky."

"Sure you were. Skill didn't have a thing to do with it," Henke agreed with another grin.

"I wouldn't go quite that far," Honor said, surprised by how easily it came out, "but honesty compels me to admit that luck *did* enter into it."

Henke snorted and turned back to the plaque,

straightening it carefully, and Honor smiled at her back. They hadn't seen one another in far too long, and their relationship had changed, for their roles were different, but her earlier concern that the change might make them awkward with one another seemed as silly as it had been unfounded now.

The exec gave up on getting the warped plaque to hang square and turned one of the comfortable chairs to face the view port. She draped herself across it with a loose-limbed casualness that was the antithesis of Honor's economical movement and cocked her head.

"It really is good to see you again—especially looking so fit," she said quietly. "I'd heard it was a rough convalescence."

Honor made a small, throwing-away gesture. "It could have been worse. Given that I lost half my command, I sometimes think it was actually easier than I deserved," she said, and Nimitz looked up from the life-support module, ears half-flattened, as bitterness shadowed her voice despite herself.

"Now how did I know you'd say something like that?" Henke murmured with a headshake. "Some people don't change a lot, do they?"

Honor glanced at MacGuiness. "Mac, could you bring us a couple of beers?"

"Of course, Ma'am." The steward gave a last punch at the module keyboard and vanished into his pantry, and Nimitz jumped from its top to the couch beside Honor.

"All right, Madam Exec. You might as well give me your version of the pep talk," she sighed as the pantry hatch closed, and Henke frowned.

"I don't think a 'pep talk' is exactly what you need, Honor. Maybe a lick or two of common sense wouldn't hurt, though." Honor looked up, startled by her friend's suddenly astringent tone, and Henke gave her a crooked smile.

"I realize a commander isn't supposed to tell a senior grade captain she's got her head up her ass, but blaming yourself for what happened to your people—or to Admiral Courvosier—is stupid." Honor winced at Courvosier's name, and Henke's voice softened. "Sorry. I know how close you were to the Admiral, but, damn it, Honor, *no one* could have done better with the information you had. And didn't Admiral Courvosier always tell us no officer's performance can be accurately measured except in terms of what she knows at the moment she makes her call?"

Her eyes were stern, and Honor's mouth quirked as she remembered other lectures in a dormitory room long, long ago.

She started to reply, then paused as MacGuiness returned with their beers. He served both officers, then withdrew again, and Honor turned her stein in long fingers, staring down into it. She sighed.

"You're right, Mike. The Admiral would kick my backside up between my ears if he knew how much I blame myself for what happened to him, and I know it. Which—" she looked back up "—doesn't make it a lot easier to stop doing it. But I'm coping with it. Really."

"Good." Henke raised her beer. "Absent friends," she said softly.

"Absent friends," Honor whispered back. Glass clinked, and both women sipped, then lowered their steins almost in unison.

"In case I haven't already mentioned it," Henke went on more briskly, gesturing at the four gleaming gold rings on Honor's cuff, "I must say a captain's uniform becomes you."

"Makes me look less like an overgrown horse, you mean," Honor said wryly, relieved by the change of mood, and Henke laughed.

"If you only knew how lesser mortals envy your centimeters," she teased. "But I hope you realize I expect you to do wonderful things for my career."

"Oh? How's that?"

"Well just look at it. Both your last two execs got their own ships, and from what I hear, Alistair McKeon's getting his fourth ring next month. I just got a letter from Alice Truman, too, and *she* just got her first heavy cruiser. You think it's just a coincidence they all served with you? Hell, Honor—I'm not going to be satisfied with anything less than a cruiser of my own at the end of this commission!" She grinned and took another long pull at her beer, then leaned back with an expansive air.

"And now, Ma'am, before we dive into the kilometers of paperwork we both know are waiting for us, I want to hear *your* side of everything that's happened since the last time I saw you."

● CHAPTER THREE

Rain beat on the double-paned window, and the crackling fire behind Hamish Alexander, Earl of White Haven, danced as wind sucked over the chimney top. It was an archaic, even a barbaric, way to heat a room, but then, that wasn't the real reason it had been lit. The dreary chill of an early winter not yet ready for snow had settled over White Haven, seeping into bones and spirits, and the bright, popping hiss of an open fire still worked the ancient magic at need.

The thirteenth earl leaned back in the oversized wooden chair built to the eleventh earl's special orders and studied his guest. Sir James Bowie Webster, First Space Lord of the Manticoran Admiralty, wore the black and gold of a fleet admiral, but White Haven was in mufti.

"So it's official, is it?"

"Yep." Webster sipped hot coffee, then shrugged. "Can't say he's the man I'd have chosen, but my tenure ends in two months."

White Haven gave a little grimace but nodded. It was irritating, to say the least, when someone with Webster's talent had to step down as First Space Lord, but given the long careers the prolong anti-aging treatments produced, the Navy had long ago developed a policy of rotating its senior admirals regularly to keep them current with operational realities.

Webster grinned at his friend's expression, but his eyes were serious as he continued. "*Someone* has to replace me, and whatever else he may be, Caparelli's got a backbone. That may be important in the next year or so."

"A real *thick* backbone—to match the one in his head," White Haven muttered, and Webster snorted.

"You still haven't forgiven him for kicking your ass all over the soccer field at Saganami Island, have you?" he challenged.

"Why should I?" White Haven demanded with a gleam of humor. "It was a classic example of brute force over technique, and you know it."

"Besides, it pisses you off to lose."

"And it pisses me off to lose," the earl agreed wryly, then shrugged. "Well, as you say, he's got guts. And at least he won't have to put up with Janacek."

"Amen," Webster said fervently. The recently replaced civilian head of the Navy was very low on both officers' lists of favorite people.

"But," White Haven went on after a moment, "somehow I don't think you came all the way out here just to tell me Cromarty and Baroness Morncreek have picked Caparelli."

"Perceptive as usual." Webster set his cup aside and leaned forward, bracing his forearms on his knees. "The fact is, Lucien Cortez is staying on as Fifth Space Lord, but Caparelli's going to want to put his own personnel policies in place, and I'm here to get your input before I sign a few midnight command assignments." He waved a hand at White Haven's raised eyebrow. "Oh, it's his prerogative to make his own personnel decisions. I certainly wanted the same thing when I took over. But he's going to be feeling his way into things for a couple of months. Given the current situation in the PRH, I want him to have a solid team in the field during the transition."

"Makes sense," White Haven acknowledged.

"Glad you think so. At any rate, I'm fairly comfortable that I've got all the round pegs in the round little holes . . . with a few exceptions."

"Such as?"

"Hancock Station's the most important one. That's why I wanted to talk to you," Webster said, and White Haven grunted in understanding, for he had just returned from an inspection tour of the Royal Manticoran Navy's newest and, just possibly, most critical Fleet station.

The Hancock System's barren red dwarf had absolutely nothing to recommend it . . . except its location. It lay directly to galactic north of Manticore, ideally placed as an advanced picket for the systems of Yorik, Zanzibar, and Alizon, all members of the Kingdom's anti-Haven alliance. Perhaps more to the point, it was less than ten light-years from the Seaford Nine System, and Seaford Nine was one of the People's Republic of Haven's largest frontier bases. Which was very interesting, since Haven had absolutely nothing worth protecting within a good fifty light-years of it.

"Leave it to Mark Sarnow," the earl said, and Webster groaned.

"Damn it, I *knew* you were going to say that! He's too junior, and we both know it!"

"Junior or not, he's also the man who talked Alizon into signing up with the Alliance," White Haven countered, "not to mention having set Hancock up in the first place. And if you've read my report, you know what kind of job he's been doing out there."

"I'm not questioning his competence, only his seniority," Webster shot back. "No one admires the job he's done more than I do, but now that the yard facilities are coming on-line we're upgrading the station to a full task force. That means we need at least a vice admiral out there, and if I put a rear admiral—and a rear admiral of the red, at that!—in command, I'll have a mutiny on my hands."

"Then promote him."

"Lucien already bumped him from commodore at least two years early." Webster shook his head. "No, forget it, Hamish. Sarnow's good, but he just doesn't have the seniority for it."

"So who *are* you thinking of putting in?" White Haven demanded, then paused with an arrested expression. "Oh, no, Jim! Not me!"

"No." Webster sighed. "Mind you, there's no one I'd rather have out there, but even with the upgrade, it's only a vice admiral's slot. Besides, I want you closer to home if the fecal matter hits the rotary air impeller. No, I was thinking about Yancey Parks."

"Parks?" One of the earl's mobile eyebrows rose in surprise.

"He's almost as good a strategist as you are, and he's one hell of an organizer," Webster pointed out.

"Why do you sound like you're trying to convince yourself of that?" White Haven asked with a small smile, and Webster snorted.

"I'm not. I'm trying to convince *you* to agree with me."

"I don't know, Jim. . . ." The earl rose, clasping his hands behind him, to take a quick turn around his study. He gazed out into the wet night for a moment, then wheeled to stare down at the crackling flames.

"The thing that worries me," he said without turning his head, "is that Yancey's too much of a thinker."

"Since when has that been a liability? Weren't you just objecting to Caparelli because he's *not* one?"

"*Touché*," White Haven murmured with a chuckle.

"Not only that, he's been working with BuPlan on the general buildup in the sector. He knows it backward and forward, and the first priority has to be getting Hancock fully operational."

"That's true." The earl frowned down into the fire, then shook his head. "I don't know, Jim," he repeated. "There's just something about the idea that . . . bothers me." His hands fisted and opened behind him a time or two, then he wheeled to face the First Space Lord. "Maybe it's just that he doesn't have enough fire in his belly. I know he's got guts, but he second-guesses himself. Oh, he's got good strategic instincts when he listens to them, but sometimes he over-analyzes himself right into indecision."

"I think an analyst may be exactly what we need," Webster argued, and White Haven frowned a moment longer, then snorted.

"Tell you what—give him Sarnow as a squadron commander, and I'll give you my blessings."

"Blackmail!" Webster grumbled around a grin.

"So don't pay. You don't really need my approval, Your Lordship."

"True." Webster rubbed his craggy chin, then gave a sharp nod. "Done!" he said crisply.

"Good." The earl smiled and sat back down behind his desk before going on in an unnaturally casual tone. "By the way, Jim, there was something else I'd like to speak to you about while you're here."

"Oh?" Webster sipped coffee, regarding his friend levelly over the cup's rim, then lowered it. "What might that be? No—let me guess. It wouldn't be your newest protégée, Captain Harrington, would it?"

"I'd hardly call her that," White Haven objected.

"Oh? Then it must have been someone else who's been badgering Lucien and me to get her back into space," Webster said ironically.

"She was Raoul's protégée, not mine. I simply happen to think she's one hell of an outstanding officer."

"Who happens to have gotten herself shot up so badly it's taken a T-year or so to put her back together."

"Oh, for God's sake!" White Haven snorted. "I haven't been monitoring her medical condition, but I've met the woman. She beat the hell out of a Peep battlecruiser that out-massed her damn nearly three-to-one *after* she'd been wounded! And I also know a bit about traumatic injuries, thank you." His mouth tightened, then he shook himself. "If she isn't back at a hundred percent physically by now, I'll eat my beret!"

"I can't argue with you there," Webster said pacifically, but behind his calm eyes he was surprised by the genuine anger in the earl's voice. "And as you're perfectly well aware, it's BuMed that's been throwing up the 'hold' signals. I want her back in space, Lucien wants her back in space, and you want her back in space, but they're concerned about the possibility of putting her back too quickly. They just think she may need more time."

"Get her back up on the horse, Jim," White Haven said impatiently.

"And if the Commanding Officers Board has a few reservations?"

"Reservations?!" White Haven half rose, and his eyes were dangerous.

"Will you please sit down and quit looking like you want to assault me?" Webster said with some asperity. The earl blinked, as if only then aware of his own expression, and twitched his shoulders. Then he resumed his seat and crossed his legs with a faint smile.

"Thank you," the First Space Lord said. "Look, Hamish, it's the psycho-babblers who're worried about her." White Haven started to say something quick and angry, but a raised hand stopped him. "Just hold your horses, will you?" Webster waited for his friend to settle back again, then continued.

"As you know perfectly well, even Lucien and I have to have a damned compelling case before we can override BuMed, especially for commanding officers, and Harrington's had a rough convalescence. I don't have all the details, but there were some fairly serious complications with her treatment, and as you yourself just said, you know better than I do how that can wear someone down."

He paused, holding the earl's eyes steadily, and White Haven's face tightened. His own wife had been a near-total invalid for years, and he bit his lip for a moment before he nodded.

"All right. From what I can make out, all the complications and therapy had her pretty low for a while, but she's bouncing back from that. What worries the psych types is all the people she lost in Grayson. Then there's Raoul. He was damned near a second father to her, from all I can make out, and he died when she wasn't even there. There's a lot of room for pain—and guilt—in something like that, Hamish, and she hasn't exactly been forthcoming in discussing it with anyone."

White Haven started to reply, then frowned. Harrington had lost nine hundred dead, with another three hundred wounded, stopping the battlecruiser *Saladin*, and he remembered the anguish he'd seen in her face when her defenses crumbled for just one moment.

"What do the evaluations show?" he asked after a moment.

"They're within acceptable limits. But don't forget her treecat," Webster said, then snorted. "BuMed certainly hasn't! I got a long, involved memo from Captain Harding about how that telempathic link can throw the testing parameters out of kilter."

"But it might also explain why she hasn't cried on the psychs' shoulders, too," White Haven said thoughtfully. "And without doubting Harding's sincerity for a moment, you know the head-shrinkers have never been happy about their inability to figure out just how that link works. But even they have to admit it can be a powerful stabilizing influence, and she's as stubborn as they come. If she can fight her way through something on her own, there's no way she's going to ask for help."

"Granted, but BuMed doesn't want to put her in a situation where she has to make the same sorts of decisions if she's hanging by her fingernails out of stubbornness. Too many lives could depend on her judgment—and putting her in that sort of crunch situation would be totally unfair to *her*, too."

"Agreed." White Haven plucked at his lip, then shook his head. "It's not going to happen, though. She's stubborn, yes, but she's not stupid, and I don't think she even knows how to lie to herself. If she were in real trouble, she'd tell us. Besides, both her parents are doctors, aren't they?"

"Yes." Webster's surprise that White Haven knew that showed in his voice. "In fact, her father's been in charge of her treatment. Why?"

"Because that means they're probably as aware of the potential for problems as BuPsych, and if there were one, they'd push her into getting help. People who raised a daughter like that don't lie to themselves, either. And unlike Harding, they've known her—and her relationship with the 'cat—since she was a child, now haven't they?"

"True," Webster agreed, and White Haven raised an eyebrow as he saw the First Lord's small smile.

"Something funny?" he growled, and Webster shook his head.

"No, no. Just go on with what you were saying."

"There's not a lot more *to* say. She's an outstanding officer who needs to get a deck back under her feet again, and BuMed is full of crap if they think she can't handle it." White Haven snorted derisively. "If they're so worried about her, why don't you give her something fairly sedate to ease back into command?"

"Well, you know, Lucien and I considered that," Webster said slowly, "but we decided against it." White Haven stiffened, and his friend looked back levelly for several seconds, then startled him with a rolling belly laugh. "Oh, hell, Hamish! You're too damned easy!"

"What?" White Haven blinked in confusion, then frowned. "What d'you mean, 'easy'?" he growled, and Webster shook his head and grinned.

"Put *Harrington* into something 'sedate'? Lord, she'd be chewing the bulkheads inside a week!" He laughed again at the earl's expression and leaned back in his chair. "Sorry," he said, not sounding particularly sorry, "but I just couldn't pass up the opportunity to twist your tail after all the grief you've given me over her. As a matter of fact, Lucien and I, um, overruled BuMed while you were out at Hancock. We figure she's up to snuff whatever the psycho-babblers think, so we're throwing her right back into the deep end."

"Deep end?"

"Indeed. We gave her *Nike* last week."

"*Nike?*" White Haven sat bolt upright, jaw dropping, then recovered and glared at his friend. "You bastard! Why didn't you just tell me?!"

"I told you you're too easy." Webster chuckled. "Got a bit of a God complex when it comes to faith in your own judgment, too." He cocked an eyebrow. "What made you assume I didn't share your opinion of her?"

"But last month you said—"

"I said we had to go through channels, and we did. Now we've done it. But it was certainly worth it to see you hot and bothered."

"I see." White Haven leaned back in his own chair, and his lips quivered. "All right, so you put one over on me. Next time it's my turn."

"I await the event with trepidation," Webster said dryly.

"Good, because I'm going to catch you when you least expect it." The earl tugged at an earlobe for a moment, then snorted. "But since you're putting her back on a bridge, why not—"

"You never quit, do you?" Webster demanded. "I've just given her *the* plum command slot in the entire Fleet! What more d'you want from me?"

"Calmly, Jim. Calmly! I was just going to say, why don't you send *Nike* out to Hancock Station as Sarnow's flagship when she commissions?"

Webster started to reply, then stopped with an arrested expression. He played with his coffee cup for a moment, and then he began to grin.

"You know, you might just have something there. Lord, won't all our other junior flag officers just howl if Sarnow cops *Nike!*"

"Of course they will, but that wasn't my point. I assume that the fact that you're giving Harrington *Nike* means that despite your 'tail twisting' you share my estimate of her capabilities?"

"Of course I do. She needs more seasoning before we start talking about flag rank, but she's definitely on the fast track."

"Well, she could learn a lot from Sarnow, and the two of them'd get along like a house on fire," White Haven said. "More than that, frankly, I'd feel a lot better if Parks had a pair like them to keep him on his toes."

"Um. I think I like it," Webster said slowly. "Of course, Yancey will have a fit. You know what a stickler for protocol and proper military courtesy he is. The way

Harrington busted that asshole Houseman's chops in Yeltsin is probably going to stick in his craw."

"Let it. It'll be good for him, in the long run."

"All right, Hamish." The First Lord nodded crisply. "I'll do it. And I only wish I could be there to see Yancey's face when *he* finds out!"

• CHAPTER FOUR

"All right, Helm, take us to eighty percent," Honor said quietly.

"Aye, aye, Ma'am. Coming to eighty percent power." Master Chief Coxswain Constanza's skilled hands brought up the strength of *Nike*'s impeller wedge, and Honor watched the command chair repeater displays as her ship's acceleration rose to the Navy's normal maximum power settings. *Nike* charged towards the outer reaches of Manticore-A's family of planets and asteroids, the bright star chip of Manticore-B glaring dead ahead in the visual display, as the drive readings peaked.

"Eighty percent power, Ma'am," Lieutenant Commander Oselli announced. "Three-point-niner-four-one-four KPS squared."

"Thank you, Charlotte." Honor's soprano was coolly courteous, but her satisfaction was unmistakable. That was bang on the builder's estimate, and she touched a stud on her chair arm.

"Engineering, Commander Ravicz," a voice replied instantly.

"This is the Captain, Commander. How does it look down there?"

Ivan Ravicz glanced at the builder's rep at his elbow, and the woman raised a circled thumb and index finger in the ancient gesture of approval.

"Looking good, Ma'am," the engineer told his CO. "We're getting a tiny kick in the telemetry from Fusion Three, but the drive's dead on the green."

"What sort of kick?"

"Nothing major, Ma'am, just a little bottle fluctuation.

47

It's well within tolerances, and the power room systems don't even show it. That's why I think it's in the telemetry, but I'm keeping an eye on it."

"Good, Ivan. Stand by for our full power run."

"Standing by, Ma'am."

Honor cut the circuit and looked back across at Constanza.

"Take us to maximum military power, Helm."

"Aye, aye, Ma'am. Coming to maximum military power."

There was a hint of suppressed excitement in the helmswoman's voice, and Honor hid a smile. Coxswains didn't get many opportunities to really open their ships up—nor, for that matter, did captains, since BuShips could be remarkably crabby over "unnecessary and undue strain on the propulsive systems of Her Majesty's starships"—but there was additional reason for excitement today.

Constanza adjusted her power settings slowly, eyes intent on her panel while Honor watched her own readouts with equal intensity. Her mind always tended to drift to the inertial compensator at moments like this. If it failed, *Nike's* crew would turn instantly into something gruesomely reminiscent of anchovy paste, and Honor's ship had been chosen to test BuShips's newest generation compensator. It was an adaptation of the Grayson Navy's, which hadn't been calculated to inspire confidence in all hands, given that Grayson's general technology lagged a good century behind Manticore's, but Honor had seen the Graysons' system in action. It had been crudely built and mass-intensive, yet it had also been undeniably efficient, and BuShips claimed not only to have exterminated every possible bug but to have tweaked the specs even further, as well. Besides, the Navy hadn't had a compensator failure in over three T-centuries.

Or, at least, not one anyone *knew* about. Of course, there'd been the occasional ship lost "to causes unknown," and since a compensator failure under max accel would leave no survivors to report it. . . .

She put the thought aside as the wedge peaked and Oselli spoke.

"Maximum military power, Captain." The astrogator looked up with an enormous smile. "Five-one-five-point-five gravities, Ma'am!"

"Very good!" This time Honor couldn't quite keep her delight out of her voice, for that was two and a half percent *better* than BuShips and the builders had estimated. It might be three percent less than her last ship had been capable of, but HMS *Fearless* had massed only three hundred thousand tons.

She touched the stud again.

"Engineering, Commander Ravicz."

"The Captain again, Ivan. Everything still green down there?"

"Yes, Ma'am. I wouldn't care to keep her here too long," Honor heard Ravicz's satisfaction warring with his professional caution, "but this ship is really built." The builder's rep grinned at the compliment, and he smiled back.

"We'll back off shortly," Honor told him, and leaned back in her chair as she released the stud. "Hold us at max for another thirty minutes, Helm."

"Aye, aye, Ma'am," Constanza replied crisply, and Honor felt her bridge crew's pleasure at their ship's performance.

She shared it, but her mind was already reaching ahead to the next phase. Once the sustained full power trial was out of the way, it would be time to exercise *Nike*'s armament. That was one reason for their present course, since the Beta Belt was the Navy's traditional gunnery exercise area. There'd be a few less asteroids shortly, she thought cheerfully, and reached up to scratch Nimitz's chin as he purred on the back of her chair.

James MacGuiness poured cocoa into Honor's mug, and she raised it to sniff the rich, chocolaty aroma. The steward watched the crown of her bent head with a hint of anxiety, then banished the expression instantly as she straightened.

"Do I detect something new, Mac?"

"As a matter of fact, you do, Ma'am. Try it."

She sipped cautiously, and her eyebrows rose. She took another, longer sip, then lowered the mug with a sigh.

"Delicious! What did you do to it?"

"I added a touch of almond to it, Ma'am. The Bosun tells me it's something of a favorite on Gryphon."

"Well, I certainly approve. And be sure you remind me to tell Dad about it next time I see him, would you?"

"Of course, Ma'am." MacGuiness tried unsuccessfully to hide his pleasure at her reaction, then straightened as the admittance signal chirped and Honor pressed a button.

"Yes?"

"Executive Officer, Ma'am," her sentry announced.

"Thank you, Corporal." Honor touched another key to open the hatch, and Commander Henke stepped through it.

"You wanted to see me, Ma'am?"

"I did, indeed, Mike. Sit down." Henke obeyed, her "on-duty" manner softening at the welcoming, informal tone, and Honor glanced up at MacGuiness. "The Exec is one of those barbarian coffee-drinkers, Mac. Could you get her a cup?"

"Of course, Ma'am." MacGuiness vanished, and Henke shook her head at Honor.

"Still sucking up the calories, I see. No wonder you spend so much time working out!"

"Nonsense," Honor said comfortably. "Some of us have active metabolisms, which allow us to indulge our taste for the finer things in life without fear of the consequences."

"Yeah, sure." Henke snorted.

MacGuiness reappeared with a coffee cup on a gold-rimmed saucer, and the commander's eyebrows rose. The cup bore *Nike*'s crest, the winged goddess of victory hurling thunderbolts from a raised hand, but the hull number under the crest was BC-09. Which made the cup over two Manticoran centuries—almost five hundred T-years—old. It was part of the captain's service from the second ship of her name and, as such, reserved for formal occasions.

"To what do I owe the honor?" she asked, and Honor chuckled.

"Two things, actually. One, I happen to remember that it's your birthday." Henke grimaced, and Honor chuckled again. "Now, now! You're not getting older, just better."

"Maybe. But if I know you, you ratted to the rest of the wardroom about it—probably through your faithful minion here—didn't you?" Henke demanded with a wave at MacGuiness. Honor looked innocent, and the commander groaned. "Yes, you did. And that means they're waiting to pounce with that stupid song! Damn it, Honor, you *know* I've got perfect pitch! Have you ever heard Ivan Ravicz try to sing?" She shuddered, and Honor turned a laugh into a hasty cough.

"I'm sure you'll survive," she soothed. "On the other hand, that's only one of the things I'm celebrating. We've got our orders, Mike."

"Oh?" Henke straightened in her chair and set her cup aside, levity vanquished by sudden interest.

"Indeed. Being in all respects ready for deployment, HMS *Nike* is directed to Hancock Station, there to take aboard Rear Admiral of the Red Mark Sarnow as flagship of Battlecruiser Squadron Five."

"Hancock Station as a squadron flagship—and a newly formed squadron at that, hey? Well, well, well," Henke murmured, and her dark eyes gleamed. "Not too shabby. And from what I hear, Sarnow should keep things lively."

"If he lives up to his reputation," Honor agreed. "I've never met him, but I've heard good things about him. And I know at least one member of his staff quite well."

"Oh? Which one?"

"His communications officer was my com officer in Basilisk. Lieutenant Commander Webster."

"Webster," Henke repeated thoughtfully. "Would that be Sir James's cousin, or his grand-nephew?"

"Nephew. He's young, but he doesn't owe his rank to his relatives. I think you'll like him."

"If he does his job as well as his uncle, I probably will," Henke agreed, then smiled. "And, speaking of relatives, *I've* got one serving in Hancock, too."

"Really?"

"Yes. My cousin—fourth cousin, actually—is the repair base's exec." Henke cocked her head for a moment, regarding Honor with a quizzical expression. "As a matter of fact, you've met him."

"I have?" Honor was surprised. She'd met several of Henke's relatives—mostly exalted personages who'd dropped in to visit her on free days at Saganami Island—but she doubted any of them would be serving as an orbital base's executive officer.

"Uh-huh. You met him in Basilisk. Captain Paul Tankersley."

Honor tried—almost successfully—to keep her mouth from tightening in repugnance. Not, she told herself after the instant initial shock, that she had anything against Tankersley himself. To be honest, she hardly even remembered him. She tried to recall what he looked like, and frowned at the image's vagueness. Short, she thought, but square and solid looking. That was all that came to mind—that and his obvious discomfort at the situation he'd found himself in at the time.

"Paul told me about it," Henke said after a moment, breaking into her thoughts. "Or some of it, anyway. I think he'd have said more if he hadn't thought it would sound disloyal to an ex-CO. He's funny that way, even when the CO in question was Pavel Young."

This time Honor couldn't keep the cold, bleak hatred off her face, and her hand tightened about her cocoa mug in poisonous memory.

"You know," Henke went on, her voice carefully light, "you never did tell me what really happened that night."

"What?" Honor shook her head and blinked.

"I said, you never told me what really happened that night."

"Which night?"

"Oh, don't be silly, Honor! You know perfectly well which night." Henke sighed as Honor looked at her without expression. "The night," she explained, "when you beat the holy living hell out of Mr. Midshipman Lord Pavel Young. You do remember that night?"

"He fell down the stairs," Honor said almost automatically, and Henke snorted.

"Sure he did. That was why I found you hiding under the covers with Nimitz ready to go rip someone's face off!" Honor winced, remembering a time when Nimitz had done just that, but Henke didn't seem to notice. "Look, Honor, I know the official story. I also know it's bullshit, and in case no one's ever told you, there are all sorts of rumors floating around about it—especially since Basilisk."

"Rumors?" Honor set her mug down, feeling a sort of distant surprise as she saw the tremors in her fingers. "What rumors? I haven't heard anything about them!"

"Of course not. Who's going to breathe a word about them around *you?* But after the way he tried to stab you in the back at Basilisk, there aren't too many people who doubt them."

Henke leaned back, eyes steady, and Honor shifted uncomfortably under their weight. She'd done her level best never to reveal any hint of what had actually happened, and she'd hoped—more desperately than realistically, she thought now—that the story had finally died a natural death.

"All right," Henke said after a moment, "let me tell you what *I* think happened. I think the bastard tried to rape you, and you kicked his balls up between his ears. Yes?"

"I—" Honor stopped and took a sip of cocoa, then sighed. "More or less," she said at last.

"Well, for God's sake, why didn't you say so at the time?! Lord knows *I* tried to get it out of you, and I'm sure Commandant Hartley did, too!"

"You're right." Honor's soprano was uncharacteristically

soft, almost inaudible, as she stared down into her mug. "I didn't realize it at the time, but he must have known. Or guessed. But I was just—" She broke off and inhaled deeply. "I felt so *dirty*, Mike. Like he'd soiled me somehow, just by touching me. I was . . . ashamed. Besides, he was an earl's son, and I wasn't even pretty. Who would have believed me?"

"I would have," Henke said quietly, "and so would Hartley. So would anyone who knew both of you and heard both sides of the story."

"Oh?" Honor's smile was crooked. "You would have believed the Earl of North Hollow's son tried to rape a hatchet-faced overgrown horse like me?"

Henke flinched inside at her friend's bitter tone but bit her tongue against a quick reply. She suspected very few people guessed how ugly Honor had thought she was at the Academy. And, in truth, she *had* been on the homely side then, but her sharp-planed face had matured into a clean-cut beauty in the years since. She *wasn't* "pretty," and she never would be, Henke thought, but she also had no idea how other women envied her unique bone structure and dark, exotically slanted eyes. Her face had a mobile, expressive aliveness, despite the slight stiffness of its left side, and she didn't even know it. Yet the pain in her eyes now wasn't for her supposed homeliness. It was for the girl she had been, not the woman she was. And, Henke knew, for the way she'd betrayed that girl by not seeking justice for her.

"Yes," she said softly. "I would have believed you. As a matter of fact, that was pretty much what I thought had happened at the time. That's why I went to Hartley."

"You went to Hartley?!" Honor's eyes widened, and Henke shrugged uncomfortably.

"I was worried about you—and I was fairly sure you weren't going to come forward with the truth. So, yeah, I told him what I thought happened."

Honor stared at her, and her memory replayed the agonizing scene in the commandant's office, the way he'd almost begged her to tell him what had really happened, and she wished—again—that she had.

"Thank you," she said softly. "You're right. I should have spoken up. They might've have broken him if I had . . . but I didn't think about all that then, and it's too late now. Besides—" she squared her shoulders and inhaled again "—he finally got his."

"Yes and no," Henke countered gently. "His reputation's shot to hell, and he knows it, but he's still in the service. And he's still on active duty."

"Family influence." Honor gave a ghost of a smile, and Henke nodded.

"Family influence. I guess none of us who have it can really help using it, whether we want to or not. I mean, everyone knows who we are, and there's always someone who wants us to owe them a favor, even if we never asked for it. But North Hollow—" She shook her head distastefully. "People like him make me sick. Even if you weren't my friend, I would have *loved* to see Young busted. Hell, with a little luck, he might even have drawn brig time, but—" Henke's mouth quirked "—I forgive you. It's hard, you understand, but I guess I'm just naturally big-hearted."

"Gee, thanks," Honor said, relieved by the lightening tone of the conversation, and Henke grinned.

"Don't mention it. But I think you should know that Paul never did like Young, and he likes him a lot less now. As far as I can tell, it's mutual, too. Something about Paul's helping the brass deliberately sabotage his refit so *Warlock* didn't get back to Basilisk in time to keep you from making him look like the stupid sack of shit he is."

"What? I never knew that was deliberate!"

"Paul never said it was, but he sure did *something* Admiral Warner liked. They pulled him out of *Warlock* and transferred him to *Hephaestus* before you were even back from Basilisk, and he's been playing yard dog ever since. He's up to captain junior grade now, and Daddy tells me they're probably going to sneak him onto the list sometime soon. But don't you dare tell him I told you that!" Henke said with a sudden, ferocious frown. "He'd be madder than hell if he thought someone was pulling strings for him."

"Is someone?"

"Not as far as I know. Or, at any rate, not any more than they do for anyone they think is good at his job. So don't breathe a word to him."

"My lips are sealed. Not that I expect to have much opportunity to exchange confidences with him."

"No?" Henke cocked her head again, then grinned. "Well, just remember to keep mum if you do get the chance," she said. "Now, about those orders—"

● CHAPTER FIVE

"—so we're on schedule for our construction projects, and the yard is fully operational for local repairs," Commander Lord Haskel Abernathy concluded.

The commander shut his memo pad down, and Vice Admiral of the Green Sir Yancey Parks nodded in approval.

"Thank you, Hack," he said to his logistics officer, then raised his eyes to the staff officers and squadron commanders in the flag briefing room of the superdreadnought HMS *Gryphon*. "And well done," he went on. "That goes for all of you, and especially for Admiral Sarnow's people. Between you, you've put the yard a good month ahead of projections."

Abernathy smiled at the compliment, and Sarnow gave a silent nod. It was a courteous gesture, yet Parks felt an instant stir of irritation.

He stepped on it quickly, castigating himself for feeling it at all, but it was hard. There was always a certain awkwardness when an officer relieved a junior who stayed on under him, and Parks resented being put in such a position. Knowing the situation couldn't be any easier for Sarnow didn't help much, either. Parks had been in Hancock for barely a T-month, and the rear admiral would be more than human if a part of him weren't gauging Parks' successes against what *he* might have achieved if he'd retained command. To his credit, he'd never let a sign of it show, but that didn't prevent the new station commander from feeling challenged by his very presence.

Parks pushed the thought aside and cleared his throat. "All right, ladies and gentlemen. That brings us up to date on what *we're* doing. What do we think the Peeps are up to, Zeb?"

Commander The Honorable Zebediah Ezekial Rutgers O'Malley, Parks' staff intelligence officer, was a tall, rangy man with mournful eyes whom everyone but his admiral knew as "Zero." He also had a lively sense of humor (fortunately, given the burden of his initials) and a memory like a computer, and he didn't even bother to key his memo pad.

"At this moment, Sir, Seaford Nine has been reinforced to two squadrons of superdreadnoughts, one dreadnought squadron, and one understrength battlecruiser squadron, with half a dozen cruiser squadrons and three full destroyer flotillas as escorts."

He paused, as if inviting comment, but there was none.

"That means, of course, that we've got an edge of about forty percent in ships of the wall," O'Malley went on, "and once we have the rest of Admiral Sarnow's squadron on hand, we'll have sixteen battlecruisers to their six, though we have reports a third superdreadnought squadron may be *en route* to Admiral Rollins. That would give *him* the edge, but, according to ONI, he's sticking with the same basic activities—drills and maneuvers, never more than a light-year or two out from Seaford—and there's no sign of any particular increase in preparedness on his part.

"There is one item in my latest download which concerns me, however." He raised an eyebrow at his admiral, and Parks nodded for him to continue.

"Our attaché on Haven has expressed a belief that the assassination of the Peeps' finance minister represents a significant increase in domestic instability. His analysis of the situation—which differs somewhat from that of ONI's analysts back home—is that the Harris Government might welcome some sort of foreign crisis to defuse Dolist tensions."

"Excuse me, Commander," Mark Sarnow's melodious tenor interrupted politely, "but how, exactly, does the attaché's analysis differ from ONI's?"

"I'd say it was more a matter of degree than of kind, Sir. ONI agrees the domestic front is giving Harris and his stooges grief and feels Harris probably wouldn't be heartbroken by an opportunity to posture and view with alarm where we're concerned, but their analysts think his hands are too full for him to actively seek a confrontation. Commander Hale, our attaché, thinks they're wrong. That the pressure Harris feels might push him into seeking just that as a diversion from economic problems which are fundamentally insoluble."

"I see." Sarnow rubbed one thick eyebrow, his dark face intent. "And do you have any feeling for which of them is correct?"

"That's always difficult to say without access to the raw data, Sir. Having said that, I happen to know Al Hale, and I don't think he's an alarmist. You want my honest opinion?" O'Malley raised his eyebrows, and Sarnow nodded. "Under the circumstances, I'd give Al a seventy-thirty chance of being closer to right."

"And if they do decide to create an incident," Parks put in, "this region is certainly a logical place for them to do it."

Heads nodded around the table. The Basilisk terminus of the Manticore Wormhole Junction, which lay another hundred and sixty light-years to galactic north of Hancock Station, had become of constantly growing economic importance as the terminus drew ever more colonization and exploration to itself, but stars were sparse out here, and there was precious little of intrinsic worth *between* Manticore and Basilisk. Which meant, since the Star Kingdom had never been particularly interested in expansion for expansion's sake, that the Navy had developed virtually no bases to cover the region.

That might not have been a problem . . . except that the People's Republic had already made one try at seizing Basilisk. If the Peeps tried a second time and succeeded, Manticore would lose perhaps ten percent of its total out-system revenue. Worse, Haven already controlled Trevor's Star, which meant conquest of Basilisk would give it two termini, raising the specter of direct invasion of the Manticore System via the Junction, and leave the Royal Manticoran Navy no choice but to take it back at any cost.

Getting Basilisk back would be a grim task under any circumstances, but especially if the Peeps established a powerful fleet presence to block access from the home system. Seaford Nine was obviously the first step in creating that fleet presence, and until Manticore had gotten Alizon and (especially) Zanzibar to join the Alliance—and established Hancock Station—there had been nothing to counter it. As it was, the local treaty structure remained untested and quite possibly a little shaky, and Haven was doing all it could to prevent it from stabilizing. Their activities—including political recognition of the "patriots" of the Zanzibar Liberation Front—left Parks an unenviable strategic equation.

Given the disparity in capital ship tonnage and, even more, Manticore's technical edge, he had an excellent chance of crushing the Peeps' local forces. Unfortunately, he had three allies to defend, spread over a sphere nearly twenty light-years in diameter. As long as both sides stayed concentrated, he could handle anything the Peeps dished out. But if he divided his forces to cover all of his responsibilities and Haven chose to mass its full strength against a single target, they could overwhelm the detachment covering it and smash his units in isolation.

"I think," the admiral said at last into the quiet, "that we have to assume a worst-case scenario. I also know Commander Hale, and I've been impressed by his past work. If he's right and ONI is wrong, we could find ourselves looking at two particularly dangerous situations. First, the Peeps may try to engineer a crisis, even create an incident or two, solely for the consumption of their propaganda machine. That's bad enough, given the potential for an incident to get out of hand, but, frankly, it worries me less than the second alternative. They *could* have finally reached the point of being ready to pull the trigger on a real war.

"The question, of course"—there was no twinkle in Parks' blue eyes to match the whimsy of his smile—"is which they're up to. Comments?"

"I'm more inclined to think in terms of provocations and incidents," Admiral Konstanzakis said after a moment. The tall, big-boned commander of Superdreadnought Squadron Eight leaned slightly forward, looking down the table to meet Parks' eyes, and tapped her index finger on the folder of hardcopy before her. "According to these reports, the ZLF's activities are increasing, and if Haven wants a low-risk, cheap incident, the Liberation Front's their best bet. They're already providing the ZLF's raggedy-assed 'fleet' with sanctuaries. If they decide to back a major terrorist push against the Caliph's government, as well—" She shrugged, and Parks nodded.

"Zeb?" he asked.

"It's certainly a possibility, Sir, but getting significant support to Zanzibar through the Caliph's own navy and the light forces we've deployed to back them up would be a real problem. The Caliphate severed diplomatic relations with the Republic and embargoed Havenite trade when the Peeps recognized the ZLF, so they don't have any good covert channels to slip weapons in. If they try to run them in openly, they risk kicking off an escalation they can't control." It was the intelligence officer's turn to shrug. "Frankly, Sir, there are a dozen places they can engineer a confrontation. Zanzibar would be the most dangerous one from our viewpoint, but that very fact might cause them to look elsewhere, especially if their objective is to generate lots of noise but not an actual war."

Parks nodded again, then sighed and rubbed his right temple.

"All right, let's put the engineered crisis scenario on hold until we have some evidence of actual activities to guide us. Even if there is an incident, the bottom line will be how we respond to it, and that brings us right back to *our* options. What's the most effective thing we can do with our forces to protect our allies and insure the security of Hancock itself?"

Silence hovered as he looked around the table. No one spoke for several seconds, then Konstanzakis tapped her folder a second time.

"We should at least strengthen the pickets for Zanzibar, Sir. It might not be a bad idea to split one of the battlecruiser squadrons into divisions and spread its units across all three systems. We'd still be superior to Seaford's current capital ship strength, and, politically speaking, it would both reassure our allies and draw a line for the Peeps."

Parks nodded again, though the thought of parceling out battlecruisers in penny packets which couldn't possibly face a concentrated attack was hardly appealing.

He started to speak, but Mark Sarnow cleared his throat first.

"I think we should consider a forward deployment, instead, Sir," Parks' junior squadron commander said quietly.

"How far forward, Admiral?" The question sounded sharper than Parks had intended, but Sarnow seemed unfazed.

"Right on the twelve-hour limit from Seaford Nine, Sir," he replied, and feet shuffled under the table. "I'm not talking about a permanent presence, but an extended period of maneuvers out there would almost have to make Rollins nervous, and we'd still be outside the territorial limit. He wouldn't have a leg to stand on if he tried to protest our presence, but if he started anything, we'd be close enough to keep our force concentrated and stay with him all the way to his intended target—whatever it might be."

"I'm not sure that would be a good idea, Sir," Konstanzakis objected. "We've already got a light cruiser squadron keeping an eye on the Peeps, and they know it. If we move in with ships of the wall, we up the stakes all around. That sort of deployment makes excellent sense if they're really ready to push the button, but if all they want is an incident, we'd be giving them a golden opportunity to find one, territorial limit or no."

"We've just more or less agreed that if they want an incident we can't stop them from producing one, Dame Christa," Sarnow pointed out. "If we sit tight and wait to see what they're up to, we're only giving them the advantage of picking their own time and place. But if we pressure *them*, instead, they may decide the game isn't worth the risk. And if they don't see it that way and decide to push back, we'll be in position to do something about it. It's unlikely they'd actually attack us if we stay on their backs, and if they do, we'll have our full strength massed to cut them off at the knees."

"I'm inclined to agree with Dame Christa," Parks said in a carefully neutral voice. "There's no point helping them rattle their sabers at this point, Admiral Sarnow. Of course, if the situation changes, my view of the proper response will change with it."

He met Sarnow's eyes, and the rear admiral nodded after only the slightest of pauses.

"All right. In that case, Admiral Tyrel," Parks went on, looking at his other battlecruiser commander, "we'll split your squadron. Put two ships at Yorik and three each at Zanzibar and Alizon. Captain Hurston—" he nodded at his operations officer "—will assign appropriate screening elements."

"Yes, Sir." Tyrel looked unhappy, and Parks didn't blame him. Splitting his squadron would not only increase each unit's individual vulnerability but effectively reduce Tyrel from a squadron CO to a divisional commander. On the other hand, it would put a senior officer at Zanzibar, by far the most ticklish of Parks' responsibilities. And, he admitted to himself, it would leave *Sarnow's* battlecruisers, once they were all assembled, here in Hancock where he could keep an eye on their aggressive CO.

"I think that concludes our business for the morning, then," he said, rising to indicate the end of the conference, and started for the hatch.

It opened as he reached it, and a communications

yeoman recoiled as he found himself face-to-face with his admiral.

"Uh, excuse me, Sir Yancey. I have a priority message for Captain Beasley."

Parks waved the yeoman past him, and his staff com officer took the message board from him. She scanned the text, then made an irritated sound through her teeth.

"Problems, Theresa?" Parks asked.

"Perimeter Tracking picked up a new arrival about thirty minutes ago, Sir," Beasley said, and glanced across at Sarnow. "It seems your flagship's arrived, Admiral. Unfortunately, she's not exactly in fighting trim."

She handed the message board to the rear admiral, and went on speaking to Parks.

"*Nike*'s suffered a major engineering casualty, Sir. Her entire after fusion plant's off-line. According to her engineer's preliminary survey, there's a fracture clear through the primary bottle generator housing."

"Something must have gotten past the builder's scans," Sarnow agreed, still reading the message. "It sounds like we're going to have to pull the entire installation."

"Did they suffer any personnel casualties?" Parks demanded.

"No, Sir," Beasley reassured him.

"Well, thank God for that." The admiral sighed, then shook his head with a dry chuckle. "I'd hate to be her skipper about now. Imagine reporting for your first deployment with the Fleet's newest battlecruiser and having to tell your station commander you're reduced to two-thirds power!" He shook his head again. "Who is the unfortunate fellow, anyway?"

"Countess Harrington, Sir," Sarnow said, looking up from the message board.

"*Honor* Harrington?" Parks asked in surprise. "I thought she was still on medical leave."

"Not according to this, Sir."

"Well, well." Parks rubbed his chin, then looked back at Beasley. "Alert the yard to expedite their detailed survey, Theresa. I don't want that ship out of action any longer than necessary. If it's going to be faster to return her to *Hephaestus*, I want to know it soonest."

"Yes, Sir. I'll get right on it."

"Thank you." Parks rested his hand on Sarnow's shoulder for a moment. "As for you, Admiral, it would seem your transfer to your new flagship may be a bit delayed. For the moment, I'll hold *Irresistible* here for you. If *Nike* has to be sent home, I'm sure the Admiralty will send you a replacement before I have to release *Irresistible*."

"Thank you, Sir."

Parks nodded and beckoned for his chief of staff to join him as he left the briefing room. Commodore Capra fell in at his right side, and Parks glanced back to be sure they were out of earshot before he sighed.

"Harrington," he murmured. "Now isn't that just peachy?"

"She's an outstanding officer, Sir," Capra replied, and Parks' nostrils flared in a silent snort.

"She's a damned hothead with no self-control is what she is!" Capra said nothing, and Parks grimaced. "Oh, I know all about her combat record," he said testily, "but she ought to be kept on a leash! She did a good job in Basilisk, but she could have been more diplomatic about it. And that business about *assaulting* an envoy in Yeltsin—"

He shook his head, and Capra bit his tongue. Unlike Parks, the commodore had met The Honorable Reginald Houseman, Ph.D., and he suspected Harrington had let him off far more easily than he deserved. But that wasn't a viewpoint he could expect his admiral to share, and the two of them walked on in silence until Parks suddenly stopped dead and slapped his forehead.

"Oh, Lord! It was *Houseman* she attacked, wasn't it?"

"Yes, Sir."

"Great. Just wonderful! And now Houseman's cousin is chief of staff for the heavy cruiser element of *Sarnow's* screen. I can hardly wait for the two of them to meet up!"

Capra nodded without expression, and Parks went on,

more to himself than his companion, as they stepped into the lift and he punched their destination code.

"Just what we need." He sighed. "*Two* fire-eaters, one of them flag captain to the other, and the makings of an instant feud between her and a cruiser squadron's chief of staff!" He shook his head wearily. "Somehow I'm starting to think this is going to be a very *long* deployment."

● CHAPTER SIX

"There, Ma'am," Ivan Ravicz said unhappily. "See it?"

Honor studied the scanner display, then tightened her left eye socket to switch to microscopic mode. She bent closer to the housing and grimaced as she finally found it. The tiny, ruler-straight fracture line was almost invisible—even her cybernetic eye had trouble spotting it—but it ran clear across, cutting diagonally from corner to corner and extending almost down to deck level.

"I see it." She sighed. "How did the builder's scans miss it?"

"Because it wasn't there." Ravicz scratched his nose, deep-set eyes more mournful than ever, and gave the generator a disgusted kick. "There's a flaw in the matrix, Skipper. It looks like good old-fashioned crystallization to me, even if that isn't supposed to be possible with the new synth alloys. The actual fracture probably didn't occur until we went to a normal operational cycle."

"I see." Honor readjusted her eye to normal vision and straightened, feeling the gentle pressure of Nimitz's true-hand on her head as he balanced against her movement.

Like Honor's last ship, *Nike* had three fusion plants, yet her energy requirements were huge compared to a heavy cruiser's. HMS *Fearless* could have operated on a single plant, but *Nike* needed at least two, which gave her only one backup. She needed Fusion Three back before she could be considered truly operational, and from the look of things, getting it back was going to take far longer than Honor cared to think about.

Admiral Parks' greeting message had been perfectly

correct, but she'd sensed a coolness behind it, and, under the circumstances, she would have loved to blame this on *Hephaestus'* yard dogs. Deprived of a legitimate human target for his unhappiness, Parks might well decide *Nike's* captain ought to have known it could happen . . . and taken steps to see that it didn't.

"Well, in that case, I suppose we—"

She broke off and turned her head as boots sounded on the deck plates behind her, and her lips tightened ever so slightly as she saw the man at Mike Henke's side. He was short, the crown of his head just topping Honor's shoulder, but solid and chunky, and his dark hair, longer than current fashion decreed, was drawn back in a neat ponytail under his black beret. His cuffs bore the same four gold rings as her own, but his collar carried the four gold pips of a junior grade captain, not the single planet of a captain of the list, and Nimitz shifted on her shoulder as he sensed her sudden spurt of associative dislike—and her self-recrimination for feeling it.

"Sorry we're late, Ma'am," Henke said formally. "Captain Tankersley was tied up on another job when we docked."

"No problem, Mike." Honor's soprano was cooler than she would have preferred, but she held out her hand. "Welcome aboard *Nike*, Captain. I hope you can get her back on-line quickly for us."

"We'll certainly try, Milady."

Tankersley's voice was deeper than she remembered, rumbling about in his chest, and a trickle of someone else's feelings oozed into her brain. It was Nimitz, tapping her into Tankersley's emotions as he'd learned to do since Yeltsin. She was still far from accustomed to his doing that, and she reached up to touch him in a silent injunction to stop. But even as she did, she recognized the matching discomfort in the other captain, a sense of awkward regret over the circumstances of their first meeting.

"Thank you," she said more naturally, and gestured at

the scanner. "Commander Ravicz has just been showing me the damage. Take a look, Captain."

Tankersley glanced at the display, then looked again, more closely, and pursed his lips in a silent whistle.

"All the way across?" He cocked an eyebrow and grimaced at Ravicz's doleful nod, then smiled wryly at Honor. "These new alloys will be wonderful things, Milady—once we figure out exactly what we're doing with them."

"Indeed." Honor's lips twitched at his tone, and she tapped the generator. "Am I right in assuming we're looking at complete replacement here?"

"I'm afraid so, Ma'am. Oh, I could try a weld, but we're talking a bead a good twenty meters long just across the outer face. This stuff's not supposed to break in the first place, and according to The Book, patching should only be considered as a last resort. The fracture cuts right through two of the central load-bearing brackets *and* the number two hydrogen feed channel, too, I'm afraid. Odds are we'd have to pull it anyway, and I'd rather not leave you with a repaired unit that could crap out again without warning. My people can try to patch it once we have it in the shop. If they pull it off—and if it meets specs after they do, which I doubt it will—we can put it in stores for later use. In the meantime, we can get *Nike* back up and running with a new housing."

"You have one we can swap out?"

"Oh, yes. We're topped up with spares for almost everything." Tankersley's pride in his newly operational base showed, and Honor felt herself thaw even further at his obvious readiness to tackle the job.

"How long are we talking, then?" she asked.

"That's the bad news, Milady," Tankersley said more seriously. "You don't have an access way large enough to move the spare through, so we're going to have to open up the fusion room." He put his hands on his hips and turned slowly, surveying the huge, immaculate compartment, and his eyes were unhappy.

"If *Nike* were a smaller ship, we could disable the

charges and take out the emergency panel, but that won't work here."

Honor nodded in understanding. As in most merchantmen, fusion rooms in destroyers and light cruisers—and some smaller heavy cruisers—were designed with blow-out bulkheads to permit them to jettison malfunctioning reactors as an emergency last resort. But larger warships couldn't do that, unless their designers deliberately made their power plants more vulnerable than they had to. *Nike* was a kilometer and a half long, with a maximum beam of over two hundred meters, and her fusion plants were buried along the central axis of her hull. That protected them from enemy fire, but it also meant she simply had to hope the failsafes worked in the face of battle damage which did get through to them . . . and that there was no easy access to them from outside.

"We're going to have to go through the armor and a lot of bulkheads, Milady, and then we're going to have to put them all back again," Tankersley went on. "We've got the equipment for it, but I imagine it's going to take at least two months—more probably fourteen or fifteen weeks."

"Could *Hephaestus* knock that time down if we returned to Manticore?" She kept her tone as neutral as possible, but if Tankersley took any offense at the question it didn't show.

"No, Milady. Oh, *Hephaestus* has an edge in ancillary equipment, but I doubt they could shave more than a week off our time, and you'd spend twice that long in transit for the round trip."

"I was afraid of that." Honor sighed. "Well, it seems we're in your hands. How soon can we get started?"

"I'll get my own survey people over here within the hour," Tankersley promised. "We're still pretty busy with expansion work, but I think I can juggle my schedules a bit and start clearing away the control runs by next watch. I've got a tin-can in Slip Two with her after impeller ring wide open, and my exterior crews will need another day or so to button her back up. As soon as they're finished, *Nike* gets top priority."

"Outstanding," Honor said. "If I have to turn my ship over to someone, Captain, I'm glad it's at least someone who gets right to it."

"Oh, I'll certainly do that, Milady!" Tankersley turned back from his study of the bulkheads with a grin. "No mere yard dog wants a starship captain on his neck. Don't worry. We'll have you back up as quickly as possible."

Admiral Mark Sarnow looked up and touched a stud as the admittance chime sounded.

"Yes?"

"Staff Communications Officer, Sir," his sentry announced, and Sarnow nodded in satisfaction.

"Enter," he said, and smiled as the hatch opened to admit a tall, gangling redhead in a lieutenant commander's uniform. "So, Samuel. May I assume you bear word from the repair base?"

"Yes, Sir." Lieutenant Commander Webster held out a message board. "Captain Tankersley's estimate on *Nike*'s repairs, Sir."

"Ah." Sarnow accepted the board and laid it on his desk. "I'll read it later. Just give me the bad news first."

"It's not all that bad, Sir." Webster's formal expression turned into a smile of his own. "The housing's definitely shot, but Captain Tankersley figures they can have a replacement in place within fourteen weeks."

"Fourteen weeks, eh?" Sarnow rubbed his brushy mustache, green eyes thoughtful. "I hate to have her down that long, but you're right—it is better than I was afraid of." He leaned back, still stroking his moustache, then nodded. "Inform Admiral Parks I think we can allow *Irresistible* to depart on schedule, Samuel."

"Yes, Sir." Webster braced briefly to attention and started to leave, but Sarnow raised a hand.

"Just a minute, Samuel." The lieutenant commander paused, and the admiral gestured at a chair. "Have a seat."

"Yes, Sir." Webster sank into the indicated chair, and Sarnow let his own swivel slowly back and forth as he frowned down at his desk. Then he looked back up to meet his com officer's eyes.

"You were in Basilisk with Lady Harrington?" His tone made the question a statement, and memory darkened Webster's eyes. One hand rose to his chest, almost by reflex, but he snatched it back down and nodded.

"Yes, Sir. I was."

"Tell me a little about her." Sarnow tipped his chair back and watched the lieutenant commander's face. "Oh, I've read her record, but I don't have any sort of real feel for her personality."

"I—" Webster paused and cleared his throat at the unexpected question, and Sarnow waited patiently while he got his thoughts in order. RMN personnel were seldom invited to comment on their seniors—especially their ex-COs—and, as a rule, the admiral disliked officers who encouraged people to do so. But he didn't retract the request. Admiral Parks hadn't actually said anything, yet his reservations about Harrington were obvious in the *way* he hadn't said it.

Honor Harrington had more command combat experience than any two other officers her age. Nothing in Sarnow's download of her record seemed to justify any admiral's being less than delighted to have a captain of her proven ability under his command, yet Parks obviously was. Was that because he knew something Sarnow didn't? Something that wasn't in her official personnel jacket?

Of course, Parks always had been a nitpicker where military etiquette was concerned. No one could deny his competence, but he could be depressingly prim and proper—in fact, he was a pretty cold damned fish—and Sarnow had heard the gossip about Harrington. He also knew there were always stories, especially about officers who'd achieved what she had; the problem was knowing which were based in fact and which in fancy. What worried him were the ones that suggested she was hotheaded—even arrogant—and he more than suspected it was those same reports that concerned Parks, as well.

He could discount a lot of them as the work of those jealous of her achievements, and the Admiralty would hardly give any officer *they* had doubts about command of *Nike*. But there was always the specter of personal influence, and by all accounts, Admiral White Haven had decided to make Harrington's career some sort of personal project. Sarnow knew White Haven, if not well, and his obvious partisanship probably reflected his own belief that Harrington was every bit as good as her record indicated. It was an admiral's job to nurture outstanding junior officers, after all. But, in a way, White Haven's very reputation for refusing to play the influence game for *anyone* in the past made his present efforts on her behalf just the least bit suspect.

Yet whatever anyone else thought of her, she was now Sarnow's flag captain. He had to know the woman behind the stories, not just the "official" record. For that he needed input from someone who knew her, and Webster was hardly a typical junior officer. Despite his youth, Samuel Webster had probably seen more senior officers, both socially and professionally, than Sarnow had. He'd also been critically wounded under Harrington's command, which should counteract any tendency to idealize her. More than that, he was bright and observant, and Sarnow trusted his judgment.

Webster settled himself deeper in his chair, unaware of Sarnow's thoughts, and wished his admiral hadn't asked him. It felt disloyal to discuss Captain Harrington with her current superior. But he was no longer *her* com officer; he was Admiral Sarnow's.

"I'm not certain what you're asking for, Sir," he said finally.

"I know I'm making you uncomfortable, Samuel, but you're the only member of my staff who's actually met her, and—" The admiral waved his hand, unwilling to explain the reason for his concern, and Webster sighed.

"In that case, Admiral, all I can say is that she's the

best," he said finally. "We had some serious problems when they banished us to Basilisk, and the Captain— well, she *dealt* with them, Sir, and I never heard her raise her voice once while she did it. You know what Basilisk Station used to be like, and we weren't exactly the best crew anyone ever gave a captain, either. Not when we arrived. But, by God, Admiral, we were when we left!"

Sarnow leaned back, surprised by Webster's vehemence, and the com officer looked away before he went on.

"The Captain gets the best out of her people—sometimes more than they ever guessed they could give—and I don't really think it's anything she does. It's who she *is*, Sir. You trust her. You know she'll never let you down, and when the shit hits the fan, you know she'll get you out of it if anyone can. I'm a com officer, not a tac specialist, but I saw enough in Basilisk to realize how good she really is. I don't know if you've been briefed on just how BuShips butchered our armament, Admiral, but we were so far out of our league it was pitiful. We all knew that from the start, but the Captain took us in anyway. The Peeps smashed us into a wreck, Sir—three-quarters of our people were dead or wounded, but she kept right on coming, and somehow she took them out. I don't know if anyone else could have done it, but *she* did."

The lieutenant commander's voice was soft, almost inaudible in the quiet cabin, and he stared down at his hands.

"We blamed her for getting us sent to Basilisk when we first arrived. It wasn't her fault, but that didn't change the way we felt, and it showed. But by the time it all broke loose, we would have followed her into Hell. In fact, I guess that's just about what we did . . . and we'd do it again."

Webster blushed at his own intensity. "I'm sorry, Sir. I don't know if that's what you wanted to know, but—" He shrugged almost helplessly.

He met his admiral's gaze, blue eyes strangely vulnerable, and Sarnow looked back in silence for a long, long moment, then nodded.

"Thank you, Samuel," he said quietly. "That was exactly what I wanted to know."

Honor worked steadily, frowning in concentration as her fingers moved on her keyboard. She sometimes thought the Navy was *really* powered by reports and memos, not fusion plants. There was never an end to it, and BuShips was almost worse than BuPers—especially when one of Her Majesty's captains was so careless as to break the starship with which the Lords of Admiralty had entrusted her. Had some psych type convinced Their Lordships to generate so many forms as a none too subtle way to punish such miscreants for their sins?

She finished the final corrections and captain's endorsements to Ravicz's report, cross-referenced her own report to Captain Tankersley's, routed copies of all relevant documents to Admiral Sarnow, Admiral Parks, and Third Space Lord Danvers, with yet another copy to the attention of *Nike's* builders and one for the inspectors aboard *Hephaestus*, then dashed her signature with the electronic stylus and pressed her thumb to the scan panel with a sigh of relief. From here on out, it was in the yard dogs' hands, and she, for one, was profoundly grateful it was.

She leaned back and sipped the cocoa MacGuiness had left at her elbow. It was fresh and hot, though she hadn't even noticed his silent passage to deliver it, and she made a mental note to thank him later.

She sighed again. There was plenty more paperwork where the last lot had come from, and she was guiltily aware that she should get straight onto it, but the thought was unappealing. Part of her wanted to wander down to Fusion Three to rubberneck, instead, but Captain Tankersley's people would be less than delighted to have *Nike's* skipper hanging over their shoulders. On the other hand, she could feel herself developing a serious case of bulkhead fever, complicated by an allergic reaction to paperwork. Maybe what she ought to do was take herself off to the gym and spend an hour or so—

Her com chirped, and she pressed the button with something like relief.

"Captain speaking."

"Communications, Ma'am," Lieutenant Commander Monet's voice said. "I have a personal signal for you from *Irresistible*. It's Admiral Sarnow."

Honor set her cocoa mug hastily aside and ran her hands through her hair. It remained far too short to braid as most female officers did, but its new, longer length made it harder to keep tidy, and she wished fervently that she'd had some warning Sarnow might com. She winced as her hurried, ruthlessly grooming fingers caught in a snarled curl, then twitched her tunic straight. It was one of her older, more comfortable uniforms, a little worn, its braid just a bit frayed, and she dreaded MacGuiness' reaction when he discovered she'd greeted her new admiral for the first time wearing something so disreputable, but there was no time to change. A brand new flag captain didn't keep her admiral waiting when he finally got around to screening her at last.

"Put it through to my terminal, please, George," she said.

"Yes, Ma'am," Monet replied, and Admiral Mark Sarnow replaced the data on her screen. His complexion was darker than she'd expected, a darkness emphasized by his green eyes, chestnut hair, and the pronounced eyebrows, several shades darker than his hair or mustache, which met in a straight line above the bridge of his high-arched nose.

"Good evening, Dame Honor. I hope I'm not interrupting?" His tenor voice was gentler than his strong-jawed face, almost soft.

"Good evening, Sir. And, no, you're not interrupting. I was just wrestling with some routine paperwork."

"Good. I've had a chance to look over the yard report on your fusion plant, and it seems to confirm your engineer's assessment. I realize you'll be stuck in dock for quite a while yet, but under the circumstances, I'd like to release *Irresistible* to return to Manticore and shift my flag to *Nike* as soon as possible."

"Of course, Sir. At your convenience."

"Thank you." Sarnow's sudden smile gave his face an unexpected, almost boyish enthusiasm. "We'll try not to get in your way, Captain, but I want my staff to shake down with your officers as soon as possible. And, of course, *I* need to spend some time getting *you* involved."

"Yes, Sir." Honor kept her face calm, but she felt an undeniable satisfaction at his welcoming tone. Some admirals would have greeted an unknown flag captain with reserve—especially one who'd inconvenienced them by arriving with a lamed ship, whether it was her fault or not.

"Very well, then, Captain. With your permission, we'll come aboard at oh-seven hundred tomorrow."

"That will be fine, Admiral. If you wish, I'll have my steward contact your steward and arrange the transfer of your personal gear."

"Thank you. And, in the meantime, I'd like to invite you to join Captain Parsons, Captain Corell, and myself for supper aboard *Irresistible* at seventeen hundred, if that would be convenient."

"Of course, Sir."

"Good! I'll see you then, Captain," Sarnow said, and cut the connection with a courteous nod.

● CHAPTER SEVEN

"I'm impressed, Dame Honor. This is quite a ship you have here," Admiral Sarnow said as they walked down the passage, and Honor smiled.

"I'm a bit pleased with her myself, Sir," she said. "When she isn't broken, that is."

"I can understand that, but the base crews do excellent work, and I've noticed that they tend to consistently overestimate how long a job is likely to take." The admiral's mustache quivered as he grinned. "I don't think they've quite realized just how good they are."

"They're certainly the most efficient bunch of yard dogs I've ever dealt with," Honor agreed, and she meant it. The task the Hancock Station base staff faced was far more complex than Captain Tankersley's assessment might have suggested, but they were tearing into it with energy and efficiency.

The two of them reached the central lift, and she stood aside to let her senior precede her into it, then keyed their destination. The short trip passed in comfortable silence, and Nimitz sat relaxed on her shoulder, a sure sign he approved of her new squadron CO. She was inclined to agree with the 'cat. Mark Sarnow was young for his rank, only eight T-years older than she was, but he exuded an air of confident energy.

The lift delivered them to *Nike*'s flag bridge. It was smaller than Honor's command deck, but just as magnificent, and the master plot took up almost two-thirds of the deck space while repeater displays duplicated the critical readouts of her own bridge crew.

The admiral's staff was waiting, and Captain (Junior Grade) The Honorable Ernestine Corell, his chief of staff, looked up from a memo pad with a smile.

"I was about to send out a search party, Sir. You're cutting it awful close for Admiral Parks' conference."

Sarnow glanced at his chrono and grimaced. "We've got time, Ernie. Why don't you and Joe join us in the briefing room?"

"Of course." Corell and Commander Joseph Cartwright, Sarnow's operations officer, followed the admiral toward the briefing room hatch, and Honor paused only to smile at Samuel Webster before she joined them.

"Have seats, people," Sarnow invited, waving them into chairs around the conference table. He pulled off his beret, unsealed his tunic, and dropped into the chair at the head of the table; Honor took her own place, facing him up its length from the far end.

"We don't have time to get too deep into things," the admiral said, "but I want to hit the high spots for Dame Honor's benefit before we disappear to *Gryphon* again." He grimaced again. "One reason I'll be glad to get *Nike* operable again will be the chance to get away from the station flagship. I seem to be spending more time there than anywhere else."

Honor said nothing, but Sarnow's edge of exasperation wasn't lost on her, and she wondered just how tense things really were between him and the man who'd relieved him.

"And once we *are* operable, Captain Harrington," he continued, "we're going to be extremely busy working up the squadron. I'm afraid the Admiralty hasn't sent us out here on vacation."

His staff officers chuckled, and Honor smiled at his wry tone as he turned to Corell.

"What's our status, Ernie?"

"We got an updated ETA on *Defiant* and *Onslaught* while you and the Captain were below decks, Sir," the tall, delicate-boned chief of staff replied. "We can expect *Defiant* within another three days, but *Onslaught*'s been delayed. She won't be here until the twentieth of next month."

"Wonderful." Sarnow sighed. "Any explanation of why?"

"No, Sir. Just the revised ETA."

"Why am I not surprised? Oh, well. The yard won't be releasing *Nike* any time soon, either. Does Admiral Parks have that information?"

"Yes, Sir."

"Good." Sarnow rubbed his chin, eyes narrowed in thought, then looked at Honor.

"Basically, Dame Honor, what we have here is an entirely new squadron. There hasn't been a Fifth Battle Cruiser Squadron since the last major Fleet reorganization, and aside from *Achilles* and *Cassandra*, who transferred in from BatCruRon Fifteen together, none of our units have any experience as a team. We'll have to start building from the ground up, and time isn't on our side."

He held Honor's eyes, and she nodded.

"Every flag officer I've ever known," he went on, "had his own ideas on exactly what he expected from his flag captain, and I'm no exception. I expect your constant input, Dame Honor. If you see a problem, either fix it yourself or bring it to my attention—and if the problem is *me* or something *I'm* doing, tell me about it. Ernie and Joe do their best to keep me straight, but there are times I need all the help I can get. Understood?"

He smiled, but there was steel behind the smile, and Honor nodded again.

"You won't be the squadron's senior captain, but you *are* its flag captain. That may lead to problems when you have to deal with someone who's senior to you, but I expect you to deal with that—and to remember you're the flag captain. You're the woman who's going to be sitting in on staff meetings they can't get to, the one most familiar with my plans and intentions. I don't plan on passing any bucks to you, but I expect you to use your own discretion and initiative to deal with squadron matters, as well as *Nike*, whenever they come within your purview.

"In return for your slavelike devotion to duty," he went on, with another of his fierce grins, "I will back you right down the line. If at any time I am displeased with your actions, I will tell you so before anyone else hears about it. From your record, I expect you to be a major asset, especially to a brand new squadron. Don't do anything to change my mind."

"I'll try not to, Sir," Honor said quietly.

"I'm certain you will—and I expect you to succeed. Now, Joe," Sarnow turned to his ops officer, "what do we know about our mission parameters?"

"Not as much as I'd like, Sir," Cartwright said. "With Admiral Tyrel's squadron detached, we're obviously going to be Admiral Parks' primary screening unit, but the entire task force's operational posture seems to be undergoing a fairly radical reassessment." The bearded commander shrugged. "All I can tell you right now is that the Admiral apparently intends to retain us here for the immediate future."

"Could be worse," the admiral said, though he didn't sound especially convinced of it. "At least it'll give us time to work up." Cartwright nodded, and Sarnow rubbed his chin again, then looked back at his chrono and straightened in his chair.

"All right. Ernie, since *Achilles* and *Cassandra* have at least operated together before, we'll start building around them. I want you and Joe to get the available squadron set up for gunnery practice in the next day or two. Form them in two divisions—*Achilles* and *Cassandra* in one, *Invincible*, *Intolerant*, and *Agamemnon* in the other—to compete with one another. I'll ride in *Invincible*. Please warn Captain Daumier I'll be coming."

"Yes, Sir." The chief of staff made notes on her memo pad, and Sarnow glanced at Honor.

"Obviously, we can't take *Nike* along, Dame Honor, but I'd like you to ride with me. And don't worry about your presence bothering Captain Daumier. *Invincible*'s the current holder of the Queen's Cup, and she's almost as proud of her ship as you are of *Nike*. No doubt she'll enjoy showing you what kind of gunnery I'll expect my flagship to match." He flashed another grin, and she smiled in reply.

"When we get back, I'm going to start setting up the squadron command net, so please have your com officer sit down with Commander Webster to be certain everything's up and running before we leave. I'd like to run through some squadron-level sims ASAP to see where the roughest spots are."

"Of course, Sir."

"Thank you." The admiral inhaled, pushed himself to his feet, and gathered up his beret. "I suppose that's everything for the moment, then. Ernie, Joe—we have an appointment with the Admiral. Will you excuse us, Dame Honor?"

"Of course," Honor repeated, and Sarnow bustled through the hatch, staff officers in tow. The energy level in the compartment dropped dramatically with his departure, and she smiled as Nimitz sighed on her shoulder.

But even as she smiled, there was an edge of question deep within her. George Monet had receipted the original message setting up the conference aboard *Gryphon* because Webster hadn't been aboard yet, and every other admiral had been instructed to bring his or her flag captain along. Sarnow had not.

No reason had been given for excluding her, and there might be any number of causes. Certainly the fact that her ship was undergoing major repairs could have explained it. But by the same token, a captain whose ship was in yard hands had *more* free time, not less . . . and she was the only flag captain who wouldn't be there. Was there some other reason Admiral Parks hadn't invited her? She couldn't think of one, but that didn't mean one didn't exist. And if it did, was it something to do with Sarnow, or did it reflect on her?

She rose, folded her hands behind her, and walked

slowly from the conference room, and her mind was busy.

The sound of her breathing was loud in the hushed gym as Honor worked grimly through the reps. Of all forms of exercise, she was least fond of weight work, yet her convalescence had taken a lot out of her. Not enough to worry the BuMed, perhaps, but enough to dismay *her*. She was still rebuilding upper-body muscle, and weights were the fastest way to do it, even if they were mind-numbing. But once she got her edge back, she promised herself, releasing the grips with a gasp, she'd find any number of more enjoyable ways to keep it.

She touched the storage button, retracting the adjustable resistance cables silently into the bulkhead, and ran her hands through her wet hair. *Nike* had been designed from the keel out as a flagship, and unlike any of Honor's previous commands, she had a private gym for a flag officer and his staff. Honor wasn't sure she approved of that in principle, but she wasn't about to turn down Admiral Sarnow's invitation to use it. It was smaller than the main gym, but its privacy meant she could adjust the internal gravity to match that of her homeworld without either inconveniencing others or waiting until the middle of the night to get it to herself.

She braced both hands against the small of her back and arched in spine-popping relaxation as she turned away from the weight machine, and Nimitz looked up from his usual comfortable sprawl along the lower of the uneven parallel bars. He started to get up, but she shook her head.

"Oh, no you don't, Stinker. It's not time for frisbee yet," she told him, and he curled back down with a mournful sigh. She chuckled at him and stepped up onto the diving board, which was one thing she unequivocally approved of. Most spacers were perfectly happy "swimming" in a null-gee tank, but Honor preferred water, and *Nike*'s designers, in a burst of no doubt misplaced zeal, had provided a pool for the admiral's use. The water in it formed part of the battlecruiser's consumables storage system, which probably explained how the architect had convinced BuShips to buy it, and it was on the small side, but it was deep enough for diving.

She took three gliding steps along the board, arced gracefully through the air, and entered the water with no more splash than a fish, and Nimitz shuddered fastidiously on his perch. Humans, he'd long ago concluded, found pleasure in some very strange activities.

The water was warmer than Honor would have chosen . . . but then again, she was from Sphinx. She glided to the bottom, then curled briefly into a ball, straightened, and broke the surface with a gasp of delight. She shook her head to toss hair out of her eyes, got her bearings, and swam strongly over to the ladder. Principle, she decided, was a very fine thing, but there was something to be said for wallowing in the decadent privileges of rank, as well.

She grinned and started up the ladder, then paused, waist-deep in the water, as the hatch opened. Sarnow's staff was still aboard *Gryphon*, and she'd expected to have the gym to herself until their return.

The newcomer started through the hatch but stopped dead when he felt the cranked up pull of the grav plates. He wore a comfortably worn-looking exercise outfit, and he looked around quickly, his own surprise evident, then straightened his spine as he saw her standing in the water.

"Excuse me, Dame Honor," he said quickly. "I thought the gym would be unoccupied. I didn't mean to intrude."

"That's all right, Captain Tankersley." Honor finished climbing out of the pool. "And you're not intruding. Come on in."

"Thank you, Ma'am." Tankersley moved further forward to let the hatch close behind him, then looked around and whistled silently. "Admiral Sarnow wasn't joking when he said they'd given him his own playground, was he?"

"No, he wasn't," Honor agreed. "Just a second, and I'll turn the gravity back down."

"Don't bother, please. I often turn it up myself—when there's no one around to scream about it. That's one reason I was so grateful the Admiral invited me to drop by when I was off duty."

"It *does* make people a bit cranky," Honor agreed with a smile.

"Well, I can see their point, but I got into the habit at Saganami Island. I was on the unarmed combat team, and Chief MacDougal always had us Manticoran and Gryphon sissies work out under at least an extra quarter-gee."

"You were on the team?" Honor asked in surprise. "So was I! Which form did you train in?"

"The Chief's favorite," Tankersley said wryly. "*Coup de vitesse.*"

"Have you kept in training?" she demanded.

"Yes, Ma'am. Not as well as I'd like, but I've kept it up."

"Well, well, well," Honor murmured. "That's very interesting, Captain Tankersley. It just happens that I need a sparring partner. Interested?"

"Only if you promise not to hurt me," Tankersley said. Honor's eyebrows rose, and he grinned. "I've seen that footage from Grayson, Ma'am."

"Oh." Honor's cheeks heated, and she looked away. "I'd hoped people would forget about that."

"Good luck, Ma'am. It's not every day a Manticoran officer foils an attempt to assassinate a friendly head of state—and on camera, no less."

Honor shrugged uncomfortably. "It was really Nimitz's doing. If he hadn't felt their emotions and warned me, we'd all have been dead."

Tankersley nodded more soberly and glanced across the gym at Nimitz, who returned his gaze with all the hauteur of a holovid star.

"At any rate," Honor went on more briskly, "I still need a sparring partner, and if you're available . . . ?"

"Of course, Ma'am. I'd be honored."

"Good!" Honor held out her hand and he took it with a smile. She smiled back, but then she looked into his eyes and paused. There was something in them she wasn't accustomed to seeing. She couldn't quite put her finger on what that something was, but she was suddenly aware of how wet and clinging her thin unitard was. She felt her face heating again, and her own eyes fell as she released his hand with a sudden sense of awkwardness.

He seemed to feel it, too, for he looked away with a slight air of embarrassment. Silence hovered between them for a moment, and then he cleared his throat.

"By the way, Dame Honor," he said, an edge of strain shadowing his voice, "I've always wanted to apologize for what happened in Basilisk. I—"

"There's no need to apologize, Captain."

"I think there is, Ma'am," Tankersley disagreed quietly. He looked back into her face, his own expression serious.

"No, there isn't," she said firmly. "You happened to get caught in an old feud. *You* certainly didn't have anything to do with it, and there wasn't anything you could have done to prevent it."

"But I've always felt so dirty over it." Tankersley's eyes fell. "You see, I'd endorsed Captain Young's request for a refit before we knew anyone else had been assigned there. All his senior officers had."

Honor stiffened. She'd wondered why Young hadn't been relieved for leaving his station; now she knew. He must have learned of her assignment to Basilisk before she had, and he'd taken steps to cover himself when he abandoned the picket to her. A captain who arbitrarily pulled his ship off station for refit had better have a very compelling hardware problem to justify it. But if all of his department heads agreed his ship was in need of general overhaul, The Book authorized him to seek permission from his station's senior officer to return to the yard. As long as the senior officer in question approved, he couldn't be officially censured for abandoning his station . . . even if it later turned out the overhaul hadn't been necessary after all. And since Pavel Young had also been the senior officer on Basilisk Station, he could grant his own "request"—and leave Honor alone and unsupported—without ever quite violating the letter of the regs.

But his career couldn't have survived it when the station blew up in her face, family influence or no, if his officers hadn't signed off on his request as well.

"I see," she said after a moment. She picked up her towel and dried her hair, then wrapped it around her neck and draped its ends to cover her breasts. Tankersley stood silent, spine rigid, still looking away, and she reached out and touched his shoulder lightly.

"I see," she repeated, "but what I *don't* see, Captain, is any reason you should blame yourself for it." She felt his shoulder twitch and gave it a tiny squeeze before she removed her hand. "You couldn't have known what was coming when you endorsed his request."

"No," he said slowly, then sighed and turned back to her at last. "No, Ma'am, I didn't know what he was up to. As a matter of fact, I did know there was bad blood between you. I didn't know exactly why," he added hastily, "and, as I say, I didn't know you were coming when I signed off on his refit request. But I should have guessed he was up to *something*, and it never even occurred to me to wonder what. I suppose that's what I really blame myself for. I knew him, and I should have wondered, but to tell you the truth, all I wanted was to get away from Basilisk myself."

"Now *that*," Honor said with a grin that was only slightly forced, "I can understand! I was none too pleased to be sent there myself, and you'd already been stuck there for—what? A T-year?"

"Just about," he replied more naturally, and his mouth twitched in a grin of its own. "The longest year of my life, I think."

"I can imagine. But, seriously, I don't blame you or anyone but Young himself, and you shouldn't either."

"If you say so, Milady." The broad-shouldered captain surprised her with a formal bow that should have made her feel ridiculous as she stood looming a full head taller than him in her dripping unitard. But it didn't, somehow.

"Well, then!" she said. "You were on your way to exercise, and I've got to get back to my paperwork. When do you think you might be free for a match?"

"Tomorrow at twelve hundred would be good." He sounded relieved by the change of subject. "I've got a work crew scheduled to start pulling the outer hull plates under Fusion Three during the first watch, and I want to be there, but I should be clear by lunch."

"Fine! I'll see you at twelve hundred, then, Captain Tankersley," Honor said with a nod, and headed for the showers with Nimitz padding along at her heels.

• CHAPTER EIGHT

The battlecruiser *Invincible* accelerated toward her assigned target area. Captain Marguerite Daumier sat in her command chair, outwardly relaxed as she led her temporary division's firing run, but Honor suspected she was less calm than she looked, for the atmosphere on *Invincible*'s bridge was prickly with tension.

She rubbed Nimitz's ears, her own face carefully expressionless, as she stood at the back of the bridge, silently comparing Daumier's command crew to her own. Daumier had commanded *Invincible* for over a T-year, and her people worked with a smooth precision *Nike*'s bridge crew had yet to attain—not that Honor intended to admit that to a living soul. But whatever *Invincible*'s internal command team was like, the performance of her division had been sadly substandard.

It wasn't Daumier's fault. Nor, for that matter, was it anyone else's, really. None of the three ships had ever worked together before, and there was an undeniable hesitancy to their coordination. *Intolerant* had actually missed a course change and maintained three hundred and eighty gravities acceleration on her old heading for over ninety seconds before Captain Trinh realized what had happened. Honor was just as glad she hadn't been on his bridge to witness his reaction when he did, and she'd half expected Sarnow to com the unfortunate offender for the express purpose of ripping his head off. But the admiral had only winced and stood watching the display in silence while Trinh fought to get back into formation.

That had been the day's most spectacular error, but it

certainly hadn't been the only one. Most of them might not have been apparent to someone simply watching the exercise, but they were painfully evident to the people trying to carry it out. Despite their size, battlecruisers were far too lightly armed to oppose a wall of battle ship broadside to broadside. They had to rely on bold, perfect handling to outmaneuver larger opponents, and the same qualities were required to catch the smaller ships which were their rightful prey, for cruisers and destroyers could pull higher accelerations and were faster on the helm. Unhappily for Sarnow's captains, their ability to act and react as a unit was far below the Navy's usual standards, however good they might be as individuals.

Except for *Achilles* and *Cassandra*, that was, which must make Captain Daumier even more unhappy, Honor thought sympathetically. Commodore Isabella Banton's veteran division had operated as a team for over two T-years, and it showed as she whipped them around in obedience to Sarnow's signals. They moved as if they were a single ship, performing with a precision which brutally underscored the other ships' clumsiness. Had it come to an actual fight, Banton's two ships could probably have whipped Daumier's three, which couldn't make Daumier a very happy woman just now.

"Entering firing range, Ma'am." *Invincible*'s tac officer sounded a bit tense, and his spine was taut, as if he were physically resisting the urge to look over his shoulder at Admiral Sarnow.

"Pass the word to the division, Com," Daumier said. "Request confirmation of their readiness."

"Aye, aye, Ma'am." The com officer bent over her panel. "All units confirm readiness, Captain," she reported after a moment.

"Thank you."

Daumier leaned back, arms folded. There was something almost prayerful in her attitude, and Honor tried hard not to smile in sympathy lest someone misinterpret her expression. She knew Daumier would have vastly preferred to slave *Agamemnon*'s and *Intolerant*'s weapons to *Invincible*'s fire control, but that wasn't the purpose of the exercise. Sarnow already knew Daumier's was a crack gunnery ship; he wanted to see how the division performed in a high-speed, short-range, short-notice firing pass without the squadron tac net, and Honor suspected the answer was going to be not very well.

"Coming to final firing bearing," the tac officer said. "Beacon search initiated. Searching . . . searching . . . contact!" He waited one more moment, eyes glued to his display as the asteroid-mounted beacons mimicking hostile warships blinked at him. "Beacon ID confirmed! I have lock, Captain!"

"Fire," Daumier replied sharply, and *Invincible*'s waiting broadside fired in instant response.

Honor's eyes turned almost automatically to the visual display. It was useless for battle control, but at such a short range—

A terrible, silent tornado erupted across the display as lasers and grasers tore at the inoffensive nickel-iron of Hancock's asteroid belt. Some of the smaller asteroids simply vanished, vaporizing in explosive spits of fury; others flashed like tiny stars as the beams ripped into them, and then the first missiles began to glare like small, dreadful suns, and Honor felt something almost like awe.

She'd seen more destruction unleashed in a single broadside. Indeed, she'd unleashed it herself long ago, as HMS *Manticore*'s tac officer. But *Manticore* was a superdreadnought, huge, slow, and ponderous, clumsy with her own power and designed to survive the crushing embrace of the wall of battle. This was different, somehow. There was a sense of fleetness fused with power, an awareness of the squadron's graceful lethality.

Or, she amended with a glance at the tracking display, its *potential* lethality, at any rate, for someone had screwed up big time.

She kept her eyes on the display, carefully not looking at Sarnow, as the ships completed their firing pass and CIC analyzed the results. One of the ships—it looked like the unfortunate *Intolerant* yet again—had locked her batteries on the wrong set of target beacons.

Had that been an enemy squadron out there, one of its units would have been left totally unengaged. Not only would it have escaped any damage of its own, but its fire control crews, unhampered by the threat of incoming fire, would have been free to reply as if *they* were engaged in target practice. Which meant one of Sarnow's ships would have taken a terrible beating.

Captain Daumier's shoulders tightened, and the silence on the bridge stretched out endlessly until Sarnow cleared his throat.

"It would appear we have a problem, Captain," he observed, and Daumier turned her head to meet his gaze. "Who was it?" he asked after a moment.

"I'm afraid *Intolerant* targeted *Agamemnon's* beacons, Sir." Daumier's level reply was equally devoid of apology or any condemnation of Trinh's ship, and Honor gave a mental nod of approval.

"I see." Sarnow folded his hands behind him and walked slowly over to the tactical section to study the detailed readouts, then sighed. "I suppose it's still early days. But we'll have to do better than this, Captain."

"Yes, Sir."

"Very well. Bring the division about, please, Captain Daumier. Put us at rest relative to the belt while Commodore Babcock makes her run. I want to see how her division does."

"Aye, aye, Sir. Plot it, Astro."

"Aye, aye, Ma'am." The astrogator's voice was as uninflected as his captain's, but Honor knew neither of them was looking forward to the Admiral's wordless object lesson.

The squadron and division commanders of BatCruRon Five and its attached screening elements came to attention as Admiral Sarnow walked into the briefing room aboard *Nike*. Honor followed at his heels with Captain Corell, and the assembled officers' wariness was like a visible cloud. It was the first time Sarnow had gathered them all together, and Commodore Prentis, CO of Division 53, had arrived with HMS *Defiant* less than six hours before. He hadn't been around to participate in the last few days' exercises, but that was a mixed blessing. He might not have any blots on his copybook, but it made him very much the new kid on the block, and he must have realized by now that the rest of the squadron expected their admiral to pitch a tantrum over their recent performance.

"Be seated, ladies and gentlemen," Sarnow directed, taking his own chair at the head of the table while Honor and Corell sat to his right and left. Most of the others looked uncomfortably straight ahead of themselves, but an immaculately groomed commander seated beside Commodore Van Slyke, CO of Heavy Cruiser Squadron Seventeen, glanced sharply at Honor before he looked away. He looked vaguely familiar, though she was certain they'd never met, and she wondered who he was.

"Well, people," the admiral went on after a moment, "it seems we have our work cut out for us. Fortunately—and I use the word advisedly—Admiral Parks isn't going to expect us to do anything difficult any time soon."

His tone was light, almost whimsical, but something like an invisible mental wince ran around the table, and Captain Trinh flushed.

"I realize no one person can be blamed for our present shortcomings," Sarnow continued. "Unfortunately, all of us bear the responsibility for overcoming them. From this moment, we start with a clean slate, but everything that happens from here out gets written down. Understood?"

Heads nodded, and he gave one of his fierce smiles.

"Good! Understand, ladies and gentlemen. I don't look for scapegoats and I don't hold *past* mistakes against people, but I can also be the worst son-of-a-bitch you never want to meet. And the fact that Admiral Parks is watching every move we make isn't calculated to put me in a better humor. Any new squadron has its problems. I know that, and Admiral Parks knows it. The extent of our sympathy for those problems, however, will be dictated by the efforts made to overcome them. I'm sure you won't disappoint us."

Heads nodded again, a bit more emphatically, and he leaned back.

"In that case, let's begin by examining what went wrong. Captain Corell and Captain Harrington have prepared a critique of the recent exercises, and I'm sure we'll all find their presentation fascinating."

Murmuring voices filled the compartment, and crystal clinked gently as stewards refilled empty glasses. Admiral Sarnow's guests stood clumped in small knots or circulated like slowly swirling water, and Honor made herself smile and nod whenever the Brownian movement brought someone into interaction range.

It wasn't easy, for she disliked social gatherings. She always had, but at least she'd learned to counterfeit the air of comfort required of a host.

She plucked a celery stick from a tray of canapes and reached up to hand it to Nimitz. The cat gave a soft chitter of delight and clasped the delicacy in a true-hand, balancing himself on her shoulder with his four rear limbs while he chewed, and her eyes twinkled as she felt his epicurean bliss. She scratched his chest idly while she watched MacGuiness move unobtrusively among the commodores and captains, watching over *Nike's* other stewards, and thanked God she had him. And while she was at it, a prayer or two of gratitude for her exec might not be amiss. Commander Henke glided about with the grace of a Sphinx albatross, and her junior rank was more than offset by her poise. And, of course, her lineage, Honor thought with a smile.

Commodore Stephen Van Slyke emerged from the crowd to engage Sarnow in a low-voiced conversation. Honor didn't know Van Slyke, but what she'd seen of him looked good. He was built like a wrestler—bull-necked, black-haired, and brown-eyed, with eyebrows even heavier than Sarnow's—but his movements were quick, and if his comments during the COs' meeting hadn't been marked by brilliance, they'd been both pragmatic and to the point.

The same gorgeously-tailored commander who'd looked her way at the conference table followed in Van Slyke's wake and paused with an almost pained expression as the two flag officers stepped aside without him. He looked about for just a moment, and then his hazel eyes settled on Honor and narrowed.

She returned his gaze levelly, wondering what his problem was. He was a slender, wasplike man who moved with the languid, studied grace a certain segment of the aristocracy affected—and which Honor had always disliked. She'd served with officers who were even more languid and drawling, and some of them had been among the sharpest people she'd ever met. She had no idea why they chose to hide their competence behind such irritating, foppish facades, and she wished they wouldn't.

The commander continued to look at her—not quite staring, but more fixedly than was courteous—then crossed the deck to her.

"Captain Harrington." His voice was cultured, with a polished veneer that reminded her instantly of someone, though she couldn't think who.

"Commander." She nodded. "I'm afraid we haven't been introduced," she continued, "and with so many new officers to meet, I didn't catch your name."

"Houseman," the commander said flatly. "Arthur Houseman, chief of staff to Commodore Van Slyke. I believe you've met my cousin."

Honor felt her smile stiffen, and Nimitz stopped chewing his celery. No wonder he'd seemed so familiar. He was shorter than Reginald Houseman, and his complexion was fairer, but the family resemblance was pronounced.

"Yes, I have, Commander." Her cool soprano struck his rank with just an edge of emphasis, and he flushed faintly at the reminder of her seniority.

"I thought you had . . . Ma'am." The pause was deliberate, and her lips tightened. Icicles formed in her eyes, and she stepped closer to him, pitching her voice too low for anyone else to hear.

"Understand something now, Commander. I don't like your cousin, and he doesn't like me, but that doesn't concern you. Unless, of course, you *want* it to, and I really don't think you do." Her smile showed her teeth, and something like alarm flickered in his eyes. "But regardless of your personal feelings, Commander Houseman, you will observe proper military courtesy, not simply to me but to anyone on my ship." Houseman's gaze avoided hers, flitting to Sarnow and Van Slyke, and Honor's smile turned even colder. "Don't worry, Commander. I won't involve Admiral Sarnow—or Commodore Van Slyke. But, then, I don't think it will be necessary, will it?"

His eyes darted angrily back to her, and she held them coldly. Then he swallowed, and the moment of confrontation passed.

"Was there anything else, Commander?" she asked softly.

"No, Ma'am."

"Then I'm certain you have somewhere else you need to be," she said. His face tightened again for just an instant, but then he nodded curtly and turned away. Nimitz quivered with anger on Honor's shoulder, and she reached up to stroke him reassuringly while she watched Houseman vanish into the crowd.

She could have handled that better, she told herself, though the man's sheer arrogance appalled her. A commander, whatever his family influence—and the Houseman clan, she admitted, had plenty of that—who picked a quarrel with a captain of the list deserved whatever grief it bought him, yet she knew her own response had confirmed his enmity, and she regretted that. There probably hadn't been much chance of avoiding it, but she was Sarnow's flag captain. It was part of her job description to defuse matters that might hamper the squadron's smooth operation, and she hadn't even tried. Worse, it hadn't even occurred to her that she *ought* to have tried until it was all over.

She sighed silently and listened to Nimitz crunch his celery. One of these days she was going to have to learn to control her own temper.

"Penny for your thoughts, Dame Honor," a tenor voice murmured. She looked up quickly, and Admiral Sarnow smiled at her. "I was wondering when you and Commander Houseman would meet. I see he survived the experience."

Honor's cheeks heated at his ironic tone, and his smile turned wry.

"Oh, don't worry about it, Captain. Arthur Houseman is a liberal bigot with an ego problem. If you stepped on him, he undoubtedly needed it, and if I'd thought you'd step too hard, I would have warned you about him." Honor's blush faded, and he nodded. "Exactly. As I told you, Dame Honor, you're my flag captain, and I expect you to act the part. Which includes not taking any crap from a junior officer who's also a stuck-up prig and resents your having proved his cousin is a coward. Unfortunately, he really is good at his job. That, I imagine, is the reason Commodore Van Slyke tolerates him, but it's no reason *you* have to."

"Thank you, Sir," she said quietly.

"Don't thank me, Captain." He touched her elbow lightly, his eyes twinkling with curiously mingled amusement and warning. "When you're right, you're right. When you're not, I'll cut you off at the knees."

He smiled again, and she felt herself smile back.

• CHAPTER NINE

Captain Mark Brentworth surveyed his spacious bridge with intense satisfaction. The heavy cruiser *Jason Alvarez*, the most powerful ship ever built in the Yeltsin System—at least until the battlecruisers *Courvosier* and *Yanakov* were commissioned next month—was the pride of the Fleet. She was also all his, and she'd already won her spurs. The pirates who'd once infested the region were rapidly becoming a thing of the past as local Manticoran units and the rapidly expanding Grayson Navy hunted them down. *Alvarez*—and Brentworth—had two independent kills and four assists to their credit, but prey had gotten progressively scarcer over the last few months, and, in a way, the captain was almost grateful for the boredom of his present assignment. Picket duty just beyond Yeltsin's Star's hyper limit was unglamorous, but his people needed the rest after the wearing concentration of pirate-hunting. Not that he wanted them to feel *too* relaxed, he thought with an inner smile.

The latest convoy from Manticore was due within six hours, and it ought to arrive inside *Alvarez's* sensor envelope, but he and his exec hadn't mentioned that to the rest of his crew. It would be interesting to see how quickly his people detected the convoy's arrival . . . and how quickly they got to battle stations until it was positively IDed.

In the meantime, however, there were—

"Unidentified hyper footprint at three-point-five light-minutes, Sir!"

"Plot it!" Brentworth snapped, and looked at his exec. "Battle stations, Mr. Hardesty!"

"Aye, aye, Sir!"

Alarms began to whoop even as the exec replied, and Brentworth looked down at the displays deploying about his chair with a frown. If this was the convoy, it was much earlier than it ought to be. On the other hand, it seemed improbable anything else would come in this close to its scheduled ETA.

The captain rubbed the tip of his nose, then turned to his tac officer. Lieutenant Bordeaux's eyes were intent as he studied the data. It would be a while yet before his light-speed sensors picked up anything at this range, but CIC's analysis of the FTL gravitic readings coalesced before him while Brentworth watched.

"It's a singleton, Sir," Bordeaux reported, never looking away from his display. "Looks like a freighter. Range six-three-point-one-six million kilometers. Course zero-zero-three by one-five-niner. Acceleration two-point-four KPS squared. Present velocity point-zero-four-eight Cee."

Brentworth started to nod, then snapped upright. The course was right for a least-time vector to Grayson, but that velocity was all wrong. The freighter must have been burning along at a full sixty percent of light-speed to carry that much vee across the alpha wall. That was well outside the safe hyper velocity envelope for a ship with commercial grade anti-rad and particle shielding, and the physiological stress of a crash translation at that speed was brutal. For that matter, she must be riding the ragged edge of compensator burnout to maintain her present acceleration with a freighter's drive!

No merchant skipper would maneuver like that—not if he had a choice—and the captain's stomach tightened. There were supposed to be three freighters, escorted by a pair of destroyers, but *Alvarez* saw only one impeller source. Coupled with the freighter's crash translation and accel. . . .

"Astrogation, plot me an intercept course! Communications, get off an immediate contact report to Command Central!"

He hardly noticed the taut responses as he waved

Hardesty in close beside his chair. The exec's face was as worried as his own, and Brentworth forced his voice to remain very level.

"Who else is out here, Jack? Anyone closer to them than us?"

"No, Sir," Hardesty said quietly, and Brentworth's mouth tightened, for *Alvarez* was currently at rest relative to Yeltsin's Star. His ship's acceleration was twice that of the unknown freighter, but the freighter was headed almost directly away from her at over 14,000 KPS, and she was far beyond missile range . . . as anyone following her would also be.

"Where's that course, Astrogation?" he snapped.

"Sir, we can't intercept short of Grayson orbit if she maintains her current acceleration," the astrogator replied. "At max accel, we'll take over eighty-eight minutes just to match velocity with her."

Brentworth's hands clenched on the arms of his chair, and his nostrils flared as he inhaled sharply. He'd been afraid of that. The only real hope for an interception now was that someone closer to Grayson had a convergent vector. But the freighter wouldn't be running this hard unless something was chasing her, and it was remotely possible he *could* get into range of that something.

"Put us on her track anyway," he said coldly.

"Aye, aye, Sir. Helm, come zero-one-three degrees to port."

"Aye, aye, Sir. Coming zero-one-three to port."

"Sir, I have a transmission from the freighter!"

"Put it on the main screen."

"Aye, aye, Sir."

A face appeared on the main view screen. It was a woman's face, damp with sweat and lined with strain, and her voice was harsh and tight.

"—ayday! Mayday! This is the Manticoran merchant ship *Queensland*! I am under attack by unknown warships! My escort and two other freighters have already been destroyed! Repeat, I am under attack by unknown war—"

"Captain! I've got another footprint!" The tactical officer's report slashed across the unknown woman's frantic message, and Brentworth's eyes snapped back to his repeater. A new impeller source burned within it, hard upon the freighter's heels. No, there were two—*three!*— of them, and the captain swallowed an agonized groan. These were no merchantmen—not with those power curves—and they were streaking in pursuit of the freighter at over five KPS^2.

"—any ship," the Manticoran captain's voice spilled from the com. It had taken over three minutes for her words to reach *Alvarez*. They'd been transmitted before she could have seen her executioners transit behind her; now they echoed in the back of Brentworth's mind like some curse from the dead as he watched the grav signatures of impeller drive missiles spit towards her ship. "Any ship who can hear us! This is Captain Uborevich of the *Queensland*! I am under attack! Repeat, I am under attack and require assistance! Any ship who can hear me, please respond!"

Alvarez's com officer stared at his captain almost pleadingly, but Brentworth said nothing. There was no point in responding, and every man on the bridge knew it.

The missile specks drove after the freighter, accelerating at almost 90,000 gravities, and Brentworth watched sickly as they overtook their target. They merged with the freighter's larger impeller signature . . . and *Queensland* vanished from the face of the universe.

"—respond!" Uborevich's voice still called from the com. "Any ship, please respond! I require assi—"

"Turn it off," Brentworth grated, and the dead woman's voice died in mid-word. He stared at his display, watching *Queensland*'s killers arc away, knowing they would recross the hyper limit and vanish long before he could bring them into range, and frustration— and hate—burned in his eyes.

"Readings, Henri?" he asked in a deathly quiet voice, and his tac officer swallowed.

"Nothing positive, Sir. They're regular warships—they have to be to pull that accel and fire that many missiles. I'd guess a light cruiser and a pair of tin-cans, but that's about all I can tell you."

"Make sure everything you can get goes on the chip. Maybe Intelligence or the Manties can get more from an analysis than we can."

"Yes, Sir."

Brentworth sat silently, glaring at his display until the trio of murderers swept back out across the limit and disappeared, then leaned back with a weary, defeated sigh.

"Keep us on our intercept, Astro," he said tiredly. "Maybe she at least got her lifeboats away before they killed her."

Lieutenant Commander Mudhafer Ben-Fazal yawned and sipped more coffee. The G4 primary of the Zanzibar System was a brilliant pinprick far behind his light attack craft as it swept slowly along the edge of the outermost asteroid belt, and he treasured the coffee's warmth as an anodyne against the cold loneliness beyond its hull. He would have preferred to be elsewhere—almost *anywhere* elsewhere—but he hadn't been consulted when his orders were cut.

The leaders of the ZLF had been driven from the soil of their homeworld, yet they still got infrequent weapon shipments into their adherents' hands somehow. They were coming from out-system, and though whoever supplied them was very careful to remove all identifying marks before turning them over, the People's Republic of Haven was the only interstellar power which had recognized the ZLF. Intelligence was virtually certain the PRH was doing more than merely providing sanctuary in ports like Mendoza and Chelsea for the terrorists' decrepit "navy."

But whoever was funding and arming the ZLF, they still had to get the guns and bombs to Zanzibar, and Intelligence's best guess was they were using miners for their conduit. The Zanzibar system was rich in asteroids, and no one could stop and search every battered work boat. Nor could they hope to patrol the belts themselves in any meaningful way, Ben-Fazal thought tiredly. The area was simply too huge for the Navy's limited strength to search, but there was always the chance that someone might happen across something, which explained why *al-Nassir* was out here, depriving one Lieutenant Commander Ben-Fazal of his hard earned leave time.

He chuckled and tipped his chair back as he took another sip of coffee. *Al-Nassir* was a child's toy compared to real warships like the division of Manticoran battlecruisers orbiting Zanzibar, but her weapons would more than suffice for any of the ZLF "Navy's" rag-tailed ships. And, his chuckle faded, it would be sweet to catch some of the animals whose bombs and "liberation offensives" had killed and maimed so many civilians.

"Excuse me, Captain, but I'm getting something on my passive arrays."

Ben-Fazal cocked an eyebrow at his tactical officer, and the lieutenant shrugged.

"It's not much, Sir—just a little radio leakage. Could be a regular prospector's beacon, but if it is, it's pretty badly garbled."

"Where's it coming from?"

"That cluster at two-seven-three, I think. As I say, it's very faint."

"Well, let's take a look," Ben-Fazal decided. "Bring us to two-seven-three, Helm."

"Yes, Sir."

The tiny warship altered course, heading for the elusive signal source, and the tac officer frowned.

"It really *is* garbled, Sir," he reported after a moment. "If it's a beacon, its identifier code's been completely scrambled. I've never heard anything quite like it. It's almost like—"

Lieutenant Commander Ben-Fazal never learned what it was almost like. The lean, lethal shape of a light cruiser swam into sight, drifting from the clustered asteroids like a shark from a bed of kelp, and he had one fleeting instant to realize the signal had been a lure to suck him in and to recognize the cruiser's Havenite emissions signature before it blew his ship apart.

"They're definitely crossing the line, Commodore."

Commodore Sarah Longtree nodded acknowledgment of her ops officer's report and hoped she looked calmer than she felt. Her heavy cruiser squadron was a powerful formation, but not as powerful as the Peep force coming at her.

"Time to missile range?"

"A good twelve hours yet, Ma'am," the ops officer replied. He scratched his nose and frowned at his display. "What I don't understand is why they're making an n-space approach. They've taken out a dozen sensor platforms, but even with light-speed limits, they have to know we got full downloads before they did—and they're ignoring a dozen others that have them in range right now! That makes taking the others out completely pointless, and if they really want to hit us, the logical move was to get at least to the hyper limit before they translated down. Why let us see them coming from so far out?"

"I don't know," Longtree admitted, "but, frankly, that's the least of my concerns just now. Have we got class IDs on them yet?"

"Perimeter Tracking's still refining the data from our intact platforms, Ma'am, but the ones they've already hit got pretty good reads on their lead element, and there are at least two battlecruisers out there."

"Wonderful." Longtree pushed herself deeper into the cushions of her command chair and made her mind step back a bit.

The ops officer was right about the strangeness of their approach. The Zuckerman System's outer surveillance platforms had picked them up well short of the twelve-light-hour territorial limit, and letting that happen was an outstandingly dumb move on someone's part. If they'd just stayed in h-space to the hyper limit, they'd have been on top of Zuckerman—and Longtree—before she even knew they were coming. As it was, she'd had plenty of time to get a courier away to Fleet HQ; even if they wiped out her entire squadron, Manticore would know who'd done it. As acts of war went, that made this one of the most pointless and stupid on record.

Which wasn't particularly comforting to the people who were going to get killed in the course of it.

"Update from Perimeter Tracking, Ma'am," her com officer announced suddenly. "Enemy strength now estimated at six battlecruisers, eight heavy cruisers, and screening elements."

"Acknowledged." Longtree bit her lip at the new information and watched them close. Her own ships would have stood a better than even chance without the battlecruisers, but they made the odds impossible.

"Still no reports of any other incursions?"

"No, Ma'am," her ops officer replied. "We're receiving continuous updates from all other sectors, and this is the only one."

"Thank you." She leaned back again and chewed delicately on a knuckle. What in Hell's name were these people up to? Both sides had been so careful to avoid overt violations of the other's territory for years—now the Peeps were sailing boldly in in front of God and everyone to attack a Fleet base that wasn't even very important anymore? It made no sense at all!

"Status change!" The commodore's head snapped around, and her ops officer looked up at her with an utterly incredulous expression. "They're reversing course, Commodore!"

"They're what?!" Longtree couldn't keep the surprise out of her own voice, and the ops officer shrugged.

"It doesn't make any more sense than anything else they've done, but they're doing it, Ma'am. Perimeter Tracking reports they've altered course by one-eight-zero degrees and gone to four-zero-zero gees acceleration. They're heading right back where they came from!"

Longtree sagged about her bones in disbelief . . . and relief. She and her ships weren't going to die today after all, and, even more importantly, the war all Manticore dreaded wasn't going to begin in the Zuckerman System.

Yet even through her relief, her confusion only grew.

Why? What in God's name had it all been about? They had to know they'd been seen and identified, and all they'd managed was the destruction of a dozen easily replaced sensor platforms. So why had they committed what could be construed as an act of war—especially such a sloppy one—and then not even bothered to carry through and attack?

Commodore Longtree didn't know the answer to her question, but she knew that answer was of vital importance. For some reason, the People's Republic of Haven had committed a deliberate violation of Alliance territory, and if the destruction of sensor platforms was hardly a life-or-death fight to the finish, it was still a provocation the Star Kingdom of Manticore couldn't possibly ignore. There *had* to have been a purpose behind it.

But what?

• CHAPTER TEN

Honor Harrington floated on her back, one toe hooked under a rung of the pool's ladder to hold her in place, and let welcome relaxation soak through her.

The last five weeks had been more than merely hectic. She'd never served as a flag captain before, but she'd held squadron command in her own right, and she'd thought she'd known what to expect.

She'd been wrong. Of course, her "squadron" had been a more or less *ad hoc* affair, thrown together by the Admiralty for a single operation, whereas the Fifth Battlecruiser Squadron was a permanent formation. It also dwarfed any force she'd ever commanded, and Admiral Sarnow's unending drive to correct its defects accounted for her present weariness.

The fact that she'd had to feel her way into her new role hadn't made things any more restful, and she'd been leery, at first, of stepping on Captain Corell's toes. The relationship between any chief of staff and flag captain was critical, but the Royal Manticoran Navy drew a clear distinction between staff and line responsibility. It was Corell's job to plan, organize, and advise—even to make policy decisions in Sarnow's absence—but it was *Honor's* job, as his flag captain, to serve as Sarnow's tactical and executive deputy.

It was also up to her to decide which decisions were hers to make and which had to be passed to her admiral and his staff, and in a way, she was almost glad *Nike* had been disabled. When the squadron's operable units weren't engaged on actual maneuvers, they spent at least four hours a day tied together by their computers, carrying out *simulated* maneuvers. From Honor's viewpoint, that was all to the good. However wearing, it had given her a chance to discover exactly what Sarnow expected of her, knowing he was watching every move but without the added strain of actually throwing seven battlecruisers (now that *Defiant* had joined) around in space.

On the whole, however, she was deeply pleased with her new position. Aside from Houseman, she'd had no problems with any of the admiral's subordinates, despite the occasional need to act as his hatchet woman when some outstanding snafu blew up in everyone's faces. And Sarnow himself was a genuine pleasure to work with. Serving under him could be exhausting, for he was like a fusion plant—crackling with energy and bristling with ideas—and he expected his officers to keep up with him. Some of his captains seemed to find that irritating, at least initially, but it was fine with Honor, who held flag officers to the high standards Raoul Courvosier had instilled into her.

Mark Sarnow met those standards. He was one of the finest tacticians she'd ever met, but she'd known other good tacticians and many of them never learned what was perhaps the hardest lesson of all: when to stand back out of the way.

Honor had seen graphic proof of what could happen when an admiral didn't learn that lesson. HMS *Manticore* had been Home Fleet's flagship when she served aboard her, and *Manticore's* captain, one of the best Honor had ever served under, had been driven into requesting a transfer from his prestigious post by an admiral who'd insisted on controlling every detail to an extent which had made him little more than a passenger in his own ship. But once Mark Sarnow had given an order, he left it up to Honor to execute it. They'd only worked together in the sims so far, but his style was already becoming clear, and he relied upon her in a partnership that freed him to consider *future* tactics while she and his other captains executed the ones he'd already formulated.

He was also an able administrator, always fully informed yet capable of delegating with an ease and confidence Honor could only envy. She'd learned more about squadron command from him in five weeks than in her entire previous career, and she knew it.

Of course, there was another side to him, as well. Honor smiled wryly and stretched in the water. The admiral radiated charisma, but she wouldn't want to be the person who failed his standards. He didn't rant or rave; he simply looked at the sinner with disappointed eyes and spoke softly, almost gently, as if to some raw middy he shouldn't have *expected* to get it right. He wasn't even sarcastic, but she'd never seen anyone make the same mistake twice.

Something plopped into the water near her, and she frowned. There was another, closer plop, and she opened her eyes . . . just as the third tennis ball hit her squarely in the midriff.

Honor *oofed*, and her toe lost its anchorage. Her head went under with a splutter before she could spin upright and tread water, and a chitter of delight echoed in the gym. She turned indignantly to face it, and Nimitz hopped back and forth on his hand-paws and true-feet on the end of the diving board and launched a fourth fuzzy sphere at her.

The ball splatted into the water in front of her nose, and she shook a fist at the furry bombardier as he picked up yet another.

"Throw it and you're bedroom shoes!" she told him. He only chittered and bounced a ball off the crown of her head, and she went under again with a fresh splutter as she snatched at the rebounding missile. She managed to catch it and kicked her way back to the surface, and it was Nimitz's turn to *oof* as she pegged a quick, straight shot back at him. The ball caught him dead center, and his *oof* became a squeal as he went over the edge of the board and hit the water in a sprawling splash.

He bobbed to the surface like an Old Earth otter, but treecats were arboreals. They disliked swimming, however good at it they were, and Nimitz's disgusted expression wrung a peal of laughter from his person. He ignored her unseemly delight and swam quickly to the edge of the pool, then climbed out of the water with a bedraggled, splattering flip of his normally fluffy tail. It was rat-tailed and dripping, and he sat with a sniff of disdain for her unbecoming snickers, gathered it in true-hands and hand-paws, and began to wring it dry.

"Serves you right," she chuckled, swimming to the side with a few brisk strokes, and he gave her a baleful look as she heaved herself easily over the edge. "Oh, don't worry! You won't shrink. Here."

She sat on the pool's raised lip and picked up her towel. He took the cue and hopped up into her lap, and his disgust quickly gave way to purrs as she dried him.

"There, Stinker. All better now?"

He looked up at her consideringly, then flipped his ears in agreement and patted her thigh with a true-hand, and she laughed again, more softly, as she gathered up a double armful of still-damp 'cat and hugged him.

"Am I interrupting?" a voice asked, and she looked up quickly. Paul Tankersley stood just inside the gym hatch, smiling faintly.

"No, not really." She gave Nimitz one last swipe with the towel and shooed him out of her lap so she could stand.

"Fell in, did he?"

"Not exactly." Honor gave another chuckle as the 'cat flirted his tail in fresh disdain and headed for his perch on the parallel bars. "He decided to play ground attack with tennis balls, and the dastardly enemy's return fire shot him down." She pointed at the balls still floating in the pool, and Tankersley followed her finger in brief puzzlement, then laughed out loud.

"I never realized treecats could be such devils."

"There's no limit to the deviltry *he* can get up to." Honor grabbed a fresh towel to dry her own short hair. "You ought to see him with a frisbee," she went on through its enshrouding folds. "There's not enough room for him to show his true mastery in here, but join us in the main gym some day when he's at the top of his form. Only don't forget a helmet."

"I'd like to. Mike tells me she still doesn't believe the things he can do with one of them."

"Neither do I," Honor said darkly. She finished drying her hair, draped the towel around her neck, and changed the subject. "How are we coming on Fusion Three? I just got back from the Admiral's latest exercise, and I haven't really checked in with Mike yet."

"We're doing better than I thought we would, actually," he told her with a satisfied air. "Commander Ravicz's suggestion that we come up from below is going to chop at least a couple of weeks off my estimate. We have to cut through more decks, and repairing all the circuit and service runs we're breaking is going to be a nightmare, but avoiding the armor's really speeding things up." He shook his head. "I know The Book insists on coming in from the side to avoid the control runs, but that part was written before the new alloys came in. I imagine we'll see some quiet procedure changes once BuShips digests our reports, because this is not only faster, but it's going to let us put things back together more quickly, even with the need to rewire."

Honor nodded in agreement. The R&D types' latest armor—a complex ceramic and metal alloy unbelievably light for its volume and toughness—was formed in place as part of the basic hull matrix, not added on later. That gave it vastly improved integrity against damage but meant there were no convenient sections to pull in the event of repairs. On the other hand, armor, however light, still used mass. No warship had that to waste, and since a warship's impeller wedge protected it against fire from above or below, BuShips' designers armored the inner areas of its top and bottom lightly or not at all in order to maximize protection elsewhere.

Nike was no wall of battle ship, but leaving her top and bottom unarmored let her flanks carry twelve centimeters of side armor over more critical areas and as much as a meter over her vitals—like her fusion rooms.

That much battle steel could stand up to a near-miss from a megaton-range nuke . . . and sneered at the best efforts of a standard laser cutter. Indeed, getting through it was a nightmare job even with chem-catalyst gear.

All of which explained why she'd been delighted by Ravicz's suggestion, and she was equally, if quietly, pleased by Tankersley's reaction to it. Yard dogs weren't noted for responsiveness to recommendations from shipboard officers. As a rule, they were too concerned with keeping interfering busybodies out from underfoot while they got on with their jobs to consider whether or not a suggestion had merit, but Tankersley had embraced the idea enthusiastically. He'd praised Ravicz generously in his reports, too, and that couldn't hurt the engineer's chance for promotion down the line.

"How did the exercise go?" Tankersley asked after a moment.

"Quite well, actually." Honor frowned thoughtfully. "We're getting the rough edges smoothed off, at least, but I don't think Captain Dournet was too pleased when Admiral Sarnow announced his intention to form *Agamemnon* with *Nike* as the first division."

"Too close to the flag?" Tankersley chuckled, and Honor's frown turned wry as she shook her head.

"No. I think he's more concerned over the way *Nike*'s missed all the live-fire exercises. We're doing well in the sims, but he's afraid we're going to get rusty and make him look bad once we join the rest of the squadron."

"Fat chance with you and Mike running things!" Tankersley snorted.

His tone was so sharp Honor glanced at him in surprise. She'd decided weeks ago that she'd been utterly unfair to regard Paul Tankersley with reservations simply because he'd once been Pavel Young's exec, but he was still a yard dog. A ship was a work project for yard people, not a living, breathing entity. Very few of them ever identified personally with the vessels they worked upon, yet he sounded almost angry at the thought that Dournet might have any reservations about *Nike*.

Or was it because Dournet might have reservations about her *captain*?

Her face felt suddenly hot at the thought, and she raised her towel to burnish her almost dry hair. She and Tankersley had been sparring partners for five weeks now, and she'd come to regard him as a friend, as well. It hadn't hurt any that they were surprisingly well matched. She had the advantage in reach and reaction speed, but his chunky body was surprisingly powerful, especially for a native Manticoran. The capital world's gravity was barely three-quarters that of Sphinx, and Honor was accustomed to the advantage that normally gave her against its denizens, but the first time she'd taken a liberty with Tankersley, he'd thrown her clear across the mat.

She'd sat flat on her backside, looking up at him in such astonishment he'd burst into laughter. She'd found herself laughing right back at him—and then she'd gotten up and shown him a little trick she'd picked up aboard her last command from a Marine sergeant-major with more experience in the *coup* than she and Tankersley had between them. He'd gasped in surprise, then whooped in shock as he landed belly-down on the mat with her kneeling on his spine, and the final awkwardness had gone out of their relationship from that moment.

But she hadn't realized what might be replacing it, and she examined her own feelings with care and no small amount of shock.

"Well, we'll just have to show Captain Dournet he's wrong, won't we?" she said at last, her tone light, and lowered the concealing towel as she felt her flush fade. She smiled at him. "Which, of course, we can't do until you yard dogs get us put back together."

"Ouch!" He threw up a hand like a fencer acknowledging a hit. "We're doing the best we can, Ma'am. Honest. Cross my heart."

"Well, for a bunch of idle lay-about yard types, you aren't doing *too* badly," she allowed with a grin.

"Why, *thank* you! And while I'm thinking about it, you wouldn't happen to have time for a little sparring match with an idle lay-about, would you?" He smiled menacingly, and she shook her head.

"Sorry. I didn't even check in with Mike when I came back aboard. I just headed down here to soak, and now that I've done that, I've got about three megs of paperwork waiting in my cabin computer."

"Chicken."

"Merely industrious," she assured him. She gave him an airy wave and turned to leave, but he reached out and touched her shoulder.

"If you don't have time to spar," he said, his voice suddenly devoid of all teasing, "would you care to join me for supper tonight?"

Honor's eyes widened. It was a small thing, barely noticeable, but Nimitz sat up abruptly on the parallel bar, and his ears twitched.

"Well, I don't know—" she began almost instinctively, then stopped herself. She stood there, feeling awkward and uncertain, and looked into his face intently. She'd gone to some lengths to convince Nimitz not to link her to others' emotions without warning, but just this once she longed for the 'cat's ability to read the feelings behind Tankersley's expression. For that matter, she wished she understood her own feelings, for her normal cool detachment seemed frazzled about the edges. She'd always avoided anything that even looked like an intimate relationship with a fellow officer—partly because it was a professional complication she could do without, but even more because her experiences in general had been less than happy—yet there was something in his eyes and the set of his mouth. . . .

"I'd be delighted to," she heard herself say, and fresh surprise washed through her as she realized she meant it.

"Good!" His smile wreathed his eyes in laugh wrinkles, and Honor felt a strange, answering bubble of silent laughter deep within her. "May I expect you around eighteen hundred, then, Lady Harrington?"

"You may, Captain Tankersley." She gave him another smile, then stepped across to the parallel bars, scooped Nimitz up, and headed for the dressing rooms.

• CHAPTER ELEVEN

Admiral of the Green Sir Thomas Caparelli, First Space Lord of the Royal Manticoran Admiralty, was a barrel-chested man with a weight-lifter's torso grafted onto a sprinter's legs. Although he was going just a bit to fat these days, the athlete whose bruising, physical style had run Hamish Alexander's soccer team into the mud of Hopewell Field—repeatedly—was still recognizable. Yet his face was taut, the unabashed swagger which had characterized him as both captain and junior flag officer in abeyance, for the First Space Lord was a worried man.

He and his fellow officers rose as Allen Summervale, Duke of Cromarty, leader of the Centrist Party and Prime Minister to Her Majesty Queen Elizabeth III, entered the conference room. The PM was tall and slim, like all the Summervales, and, despite prolong, his hair was silver and his handsome face deeply lined. Cromarty had spent over fifty T-years in politics and headed Manticore's government for fifteen of the last twenty-two, and every one of those years had cut its weight into him.

The Prime Minister waved his uniformed subordinates back into their seats, and Caparelli's jaw tightened as he saw who'd walked into the room behind Cromarty. Lady Francine Maurier, Baroness Morncreek, had every right to be here as the civilian First Lord of Admiralty. So did Chancellor of the Exchequer Lord William Alexander, the Government's second ranking member. But Alexander's older brother didn't—officially, at least—and the First Space Lord tried not to glower as the Earl of White Haven found a chair of his own.

115

"Before we begin, Sir Thomas, I'd just like to mention that Earl White Haven is here at my request, not his." Cromarty's expressive, whiskey-smooth baritone had always been a potent political weapon, and his gentle announcement drew Caparelli's eyes to him. "As you know, he recently completed a survey of our frontier stations' readiness states for Admiral Webster. Under the circumstances, I felt his input might be of value."

"Of course, Your Grace." Caparelli knew he sounded grudging. It wasn't that he *disliked* the earl, he told himself. It was just that, athletics aside, Alexander—or White Haven, as he now was—had always had a knack for making him feel he was competing out of his class, and the earl's succession to his father's titles, coupled with the prestige of his year-old conquest of the Endicott System, only made it worse.

"Thank you for your understanding." Cromarty's smile was so winning Caparelli actually felt much of his resentment seep away. "And now, Sir Thomas, may I hear your conclusions?"

"Yes, Sir." Caparelli gestured at Second Space Lord Patricia Givens, head of the Bureau of Planning, under whose control the Office of Naval Intelligence fell. "With your permission, Your Grace, Admiral Givens will brief us on the high points."

"Certainly." Cromarty nodded and turned his attention to Admiral Givens as she stood and activated the holo wall behind her, bringing up an enormous star map of the frontier between the Manticoran Alliance and the People's Republic of Haven. She stood with her back to the display, facing the people around the table, and drew a light wand from her pocket.

"Your Grace, Lady Morncreek, Lord Alexander." She nodded courteously to each of the civilians and smiled briefly at White Haven, but she didn't greet him by name. They were old colleagues and friends, but Patricia Givens had a strong sense of loyalty. She was on Caparelli's team now, and, despite the Prime Minister's explanation, the earl was an interloper today.

"As you know, reports are coming in of incidents all up and down our frontier." She pressed the remote built into her light wand, and a sparkle of blood-red lights—a dangerous, irregular line of rubies that arced around Manticore in a complete half-circle—glittered in the display behind her.

"The first incident reported," Givens went on, turning and using her light wand to pick out a single red spark, "was the destruction of Convoy Mike-Golf-Nineteen, here at Yeltsin. It was not, however, the first incident to *occur*. We simply heard about it first because the transit time from Yeltsin to Manticore was shorter than for the others. The first known incursion into Alliance territory actually occurred here—" the light wand moved southeast from Yeltsin "—at Candor. Nineteen days ago, a light cruiser squadron, positively IDed by our sensors as Havenite despite its refusal to respond to our challenges in any way, violated the Candor System's territorial limit. Our local mobile forces were unable to generate an intercept vector, and the Peeps passed through the outer system, well within missile range of one of our perimeter com centers, without firing a shot, then departed, still without a word."

She cleared her throat and moved the wand again, first to the north, and then back to the southwest of Yeltsin.

"The same basic pattern was followed here, at Klein Station, and again here, in the Zuckerman System." The wand touched each star as it was named. "The only substantive differences between any of these incursions was that the force employed at Zuckerman was much heavier than either of the others, and that it destroyed approximately ninety million dollars worth of remote sensor platforms as it came in—after which it, like the others, turned around and withdrew without saying a word.

"There have also been more serious incidents, on the same pattern as the attack on Mike-Golf-Nineteen," she continued into the intense quiet, "but in these cases we cannot definitely assert that the Peeps were responsible.

In Yeltsin's case, for example, the Grayson cruiser *Alvarez* got readings on the raiders. They were surprisingly good, considering *Alvarez*'s limited tracking time, and our analysts have studied them carefully."

She paused and gave a small, almost apologetic shrug.

"Unfortunately, we don't have anything we could take to a court of law. The impeller wedge signatures were definitely those of a light cruiser and two destroyers, and their drive's gravitic patterns match those of Haven-built units, but their other emissions do *not* match those of the People's Navy. My own belief, and that of a majority of ONI's analysts, is that they were, in fact, Peeps who had deliberately disguised their signatures, but there's no way to prove that, and the Peeps have 'sold' enough ships to various 'allies' to give us a whole crop of other potential suspects."

Givens paused again, hazel eyes hard, then tilted her head.

"The same is true of the incidents at Ramon, Clearaway, and Quentin. In each case, we or our allies lost shipping and lives to the 'raiders' without getting a close enough look to positively ID the responsible party. The timing of the raids, coupled with the intelligence work it must have taken to plan and execute them so smoothly while denying us any interceptions, certainly suggests Havenite involvement, but again, we can't prove it. Just as we can't prove the recent heavy losses among the Caliphate of Zanzibar's picket and patrol ships are not the work of the ZLF. For that matter, we can't *prove* there's any connection at all between these episodes—except, of course, for our confirmation of Havenite involvement at Candor, Klein Station, and Zuckerman.

"Nonetheless, Your Grace," she said, looking straight at Cromarty, "it is ONI's considered opinion that we're looking at a pattern of deliberately engineered and orchestrated provocations. The timing is too tight, and they're too widespread, to be anything else, and the differences between them are far surpassed by the single thread common to them all: each of them has inflicted damage upon or underscored a threat to a star system which has been at the center of at least one confrontation between the Kingdom and the People's Republic over the past four to five years. Assuming that the same people planned and executed all of them—and I think we must—then the only possible suspect is the PRH. Only the Peeps have both the resources to manage something like this and any conceivable motive for provoking us in this fashion."

The brown-haired admiral switched off her wand and resumed her seat while the holo wall glowed behind her. Cromarty studied it with hooded eyes, and silence stretched out for a few seconds before the Prime Minister tugged at an earlobe and sighed.

"Thank you, Admiral Givens." He cocked his head at Caparelli. "Just how serious a threat do these incidents pose, Admiral?"

"Not much of one, in themselves, Your Grace. The loss of life involved is more than just painful, but our casualties might have been far heavier, and our strategic position remains unchanged. In addition, none of the forces we've seen has been powerful enough to pose more than a purely local threat. Admittedly, they could have taken Zuckerman out had they chosen to, but that was far and away the heaviest force they've committed anywhere."

"Then what are they up to?" Baroness Morncreek asked. "What's the point of it all?"

"They're crowding us, Milady," Caparelli said bluntly. "They're deliberately turning up the pressure."

"Then they're playing with fire," William Alexander observed.

"Exactly, Lord Alexander," Givens said. "Both sides have settled down in what we know have to be our final pre-war positions. We've developed 'bunker' mentalities on both sides of the line, and given the tension and suspicion that's provoked, 'playing with fire' is *exactly* what they're doing."

"But why?" Cromarty asked. "What does it gain for them?"

"Admiral Givens?" Caparelli invited heavily, and Givens sighed.

"I'm afraid, Your Grace, that their current activities indicate ONI's assessment of the Peep political leadership's intentions was fundamentally in error. The consensus of my analysts—and my own personal opinion—was that they had too many domestic problems to consider any sort of foreign adventures. We were wrong, and Commander Hale, our attaché on Haven, was right. They're actively seeking a confrontation, possibly as a means to divert Dolist attention from internal concerns to an external enemy."

"Then why the covert nature of the majority of the incidents?" Alexander asked.

"It could be a sort of double-blind, my lord. We know it's them, but if they demand we prove it, we can't. They may want us to accuse them of responsibility while they maintain their innocence for the benefit of their propaganda. That way they can have their cake and eat it, too; they get their incident, but we look like the crisis-mongers."

"Do you think that's all there is to it, Admiral?" Cromarty asked.

"There's too little evidence to know, Sir," Givens said frankly. "All we can do is guess, and guessing about an enemy's intentions is an excellent way to stumble right into a confrontation neither side can back out of."

"What do you recommend we do, then, Admiral Caparelli?"

"We have three main options, Your Grace." Caparelli squared his shoulders and met the Prime Minister's eyes. "The first is to refuse to play their game—whatever it is. Given that they've hit our merchantmen and destroyed two of our warships, plus the damage they've done our allies, I see no option but to strengthen our convoy escorts and patrols. Beyond that, however, we can refuse to react in any way. We can't deny them a confrontation if they really want one, but we can make them come out into the open to get it. If we pursue that option, however, we voluntarily surrender the initiative. If they're willing to commit an overt act of war, our frontier forces will be too light to stop them from hurting us badly wherever they finally do so.

"The second option is to give them the incident they want by formally accusing them of responsibility and warning them that we will hold them accountable for any future aggression. If we follow that route, then my staff and I feel we must simultaneously reinforce the covering forces for our more important and/or exposed bases and allies. Such a redeployment would both underscore the fact that we're serious and constitute a prudent adjustment of our stance to protect ourselves against future frontier violations.

"Third, we can say nothing but carry out the same reinforcement. That leaves the ball in their court. They can still have their confrontation, but we'll be in a position to hurt them badly when they reach for it. In addition, of course, it will protect our own subjects and allies, and any incident which does take place will occur in Alliance space, so they can hardly claim that *we* went after *them*."

"I see." Cromarty returned his gaze to the holo wall for a long, silent moment. "And which option do you favor, Admiral?" he asked finally.

"The third, Your Grace." Caparelli didn't hesitate. "As I say, we can't stop them from pushing it if they really want to, but I see no reason to help them do it. If we make our frontier detachments powerful enough, they'd have to commit heavy forces of their own—and quite possibly kick off a full-fledged war—if they decide to keep pushing. That might cause them to back off entirely if this is no more than an effort to divert Dolist attention from domestic complaints. Even if it doesn't have that effect, we'll give our local commanders the strength to stand a fighting chance when they come in."

"I see," the Prime Minister replied, then glanced up the conference table at Admiral White Haven. The earl had sat silent throughout, thoughtful blue eyes studying each speaker in turn. He showed no disposition to speak up now, and Cromarty was fully aware of the awkward position he'd put him in. But he hadn't brought the admiral along for his silence, and he cleared his throat. "Which option do you favor, Earl White Haven?"

Caparelli's eyes flashed, and one fist clenched under the table, but he said nothing. He simply turned to look at White Haven.

"I think," the earl said quietly, "that before we recommend any of them, we might ask ourselves exactly why the PRH has chosen this particular pattern of provocations."

"Meaning?" Cromarty prompted.

"Meaning that they could have achieved the same degree of tension without spreading their efforts all up and down the frontier," White Haven replied in the same, quiet voice. "They've hit us—or prodded us, at least—all the way from Minorca to Grendelsbane, but aside from Yeltsin, they *haven't* hit any of our nodal fleet stations like Hancock, Reevesport, or Talbot. Any of those are more important than someplace like Zuckerman or Quentin, yet they've stayed well away from them, again with the exception of Yeltsin, even though they must know how much more sensitive we'd be to any threat to them. Why?"

"Because those *are* our nodal positions." Caparelli's voice was a bit harsh, but he made himself pull his tone back to normal. "Our mobile forces are enormously stronger in those systems. That's why they got in and out so fast at Yeltsin. They knew that if they'd poked their noses deeper in the way they did at Zuckerman or Candor, we'd have sawed them right off at the ankles."

"Agreed." White Haven nodded. "But what if they did it for another reason? A specific purpose, not simply to minimize their risk?"

"A bait? Something they want *us* to do in response?" Givens murmured, her eyes thoughtful as she turned in her chair to study the holo wall afresh, and White Haven nodded again.

"Exactly. As Admiral Caparelli says, they've virtually left us no choice but to reinforce the frontier. Certainly they have to know that increases their risk in any future incident . . . but they also know those reinforcements will have to come from somewhere."

Caparelli grunted unhappily, his own eyes clinging to the display, and felt an acid burn of agreement as he realized White Haven might just have a point . . . again.

"You're suggesting that they're trying to pull us into strategic dispersal," he said flatly.

"I'm saying that *may* be what they want. They know we won't reduce our strength at our major frontier nodes. That means any meaningful reinforcement has to come from Home Fleet, and anything we send to, say, Grendelsbane or Minorca, will be far beyond support range of Manticore. If someone pushes the button, it would take them almost as long to get back to the home system as it would take a Peep task force to make the same trip—and they couldn't even know to start home until we got a courier to them with orders to return."

"But that only makes sense if they really are considering pushing the button." There was a new note in Caparelli's voice, a combination of devil's advocate and an unwillingness to believe Haven might actually do that after so long. Yet his eyes said the idea *did* make sense, and silence hovered once more in the wake of his words.

"Admiral Givens," Cromarty broke the stillness at length, "is there any intelligence to support the possibility Admiral White Haven and Sir Thomas have raised?"

"No, Your Grace. But I'm afraid there isn't anything to *dismiss* it, either. There may be some pointers that are simply buried in the sheer mass of data coming at us, and I'll certainly try to find them if there are, but if the Peeps are finally getting ready to attack, none of our sources in the PRH have picked up on it. That doesn't mean they aren't doing it—their government's had a lot of experience in security, and they thoroughly understand the advantage of surprise after a half-century of conquest—but there's simply no way to get inside their heads and know what they're thinking."

The Second Space Lord studied the display a moment longer, then turned back to face the Prime Minister.

"Having said that, however, I don't think it's a possibility we can afford to ignore, Sir," she said quietly. "The first principle of the military analyst is to figure out how the enemy can hurt you worst with his known capabilities and then plan to stop him, not hope he won't try it."

"Admiral Givens is right, Your Grace." Part of Caparelli still wanted to glower at White Haven just for being there, but his own integrity wouldn't let him reject the earl's analysis. "You can't avoid running risks, sometimes, where military operations are concerned, but prudence is a powerful military virtue. And prudence suggests that you err on the side of pessimism, especially *before* the shooting starts."

"Which means what, in terms of deployments?" Baroness Morncreek asked.

"I'm not certain yet, Milady," Caparelli admitted. He looked at White Haven with opaque eyes. "I don't think there's much question that, whatever they're up to, at least some redeployment of our forces to strengthen the frontier is in order," he said in a toneless voice, and his shoulders relaxed minutely at White Haven's firm nod of agreement.

"Even if they are seeking no more than a confrontation short of war," the First Space Lord continued more naturally, "we have no choice but to increase the forces that may have to respond to it. At the same time, any major dispersion of our wall of battle clearly constitutes an unwarrantable risk." He paused and rubbed his right temple for a moment, then shrugged.

"I'll want to do some very careful force analyses before making a formal recommendation, Your Grace," he told the Prime Minister. "Despite our buildup, our margin for error is slim. Their wall of battle has an advantage of almost fifty percent in hulls, and their tonnage advantage is even higher, since our fleet has a much higher percentage of dreadnoughts.

"Most of our ships are bigger and more powerful than theirs on a class-for-class basis, but their edge in *super*-dreadnoughts means we not only have less hulls but that our ships of the wall actually average smaller. That means each battle squadron we remove from Home Fleet will weaken us more than diverting the same number of ships would weaken *them*, both proportionately and absolutely."

He shook his head, powerful shoulders hunching as he considered the unpalatable numbers, then sighed.

"With your permission, Your Grace, I'd like to ask Admiral White Haven to join me and Admiral Givens at Admiralty House." He made the admission with only a trace of his earlier resentment as his mind grappled with the problem. "Let the three of us take a very close look at our commitments, and I'll try to have a recommendation for you by sometime tomorrow morning."

"That will be more than satisfactory, Sir Thomas," Cromarty told him.

"In the meantime," White Haven said in his quiet voice, "I think it would be a good idea to send a formal war warning—and the reasoning behind it—to all our station commanders."

The tension in the room clicked back up at the suggestion, but Caparelli nodded with another sigh.

"I don't see any option," he agreed. "I don't like the potential to increase anxieties. A nervous CO is a lot more likely to make a mistake we'll all regret, but they deserve our confidence . . . and the warning. The communication lag's always meant we had to trust them to act on their own initiative, and they can't do that intelligently without information that's as complete as we can give them. I'll instruct them to be on the alert for provocations, as well, and to do their best to hold any confrontation to a minimum, but we've got to warn them."

"Agreed—and may God be with us all," the Prime Minister said softly.

• CHAPTER TWELVE

"Thank you, Mac. That was delicious—as always," Honor said as the steward poured the wine. Commander Henke made a replete sound of agreement from the other side of the table, and MacGuiness shrugged with a smile.

"Will you be needing anything else, Ma'am?"

"No, we're fine." He started to gather up the dessert dishes, but she waved a hand. "Leave them for now, Mac. I'll buzz you."

"Of course, Ma'am." MacGuiness gave a small half-bow and vanished, and Honor leaned back with a sigh.

"If he stuffs you like this every night, you're going to start looking like one of those old pre-space blimps," Henke warned her, and she chuckled.

"Nimitz, maybe." Honor smiled fondly at the treecat. He lay belly-down, stretched full length along the perch above her desk with all six limbs dangling, and his soft, buzzing snores were those of a well-stuffed 'cat at peace with the universe.

"But *me* get fat?" she went on with a headshake. "Not with Paul throwing me around the salle! Or with the Admiral running me ragged, for that matter."

"Amen to that," Henke agreed fervently. Water flowed downhill, and with Honor so immersed in squadron activities, an ever mounting flood of paper-work had inundated the exec. She started to say something else, then paused with a frown and leaned back in her own chair while she toyed with the stem of her wineglass.

"Still, we're making progress," Honor pointed out, "and the yard will have *Nike* back up in another week or so. I think things are actually going to get a bit easier once we can form the entire squadron in space with proper division organizations and buckle down to blow the last of the rust off."

"Um." Henke nodded absently, still looking down into her wine, then raised her head and cocked an eyebrow. "And Admiral Parks?"

"What about him?" Honor's tone was guarded, and Henke snorted.

"I happen to know you're the only flag captain in this task force who's *never* been invited to a conference aboard *Gryphon*. Why don't I think that's a simple oversight?"

"There hasn't been any real reason for him to call me on board," Honor said uncomfortably, and Henke's snort was even louder.

"It's odd enough when an admiral doesn't even invite a newly arrived battlecruiser captain aboard for a courtesy call, Honor. When that captain is also the flag captain of his primary screening formation and she isn't invited to a single flagship conference, it goes beyond odd."

"Perhaps." Honor sipped her wine, then sighed and set the glass aside. "No, not 'perhaps,'" she admitted. "I thought at first I was in the doghouse over Fusion Three, but that stopped making sense weeks ago."

"Exactly. I don't know what his problem is, but it's obvious there is one. And our people are beginning to notice. They're not happy that their captain seems to be being snubbed by their admiral."

"It doesn't reflect on them!" Honor said sharply.

"It's not the reflection on *them* they're worried about," Henke replied quietly, and Honor shifted uncomfortably.

"Well, there's not much I can do about it. He outranks me by a few light-months, if you recall."

"Have you spoken to Admiral Sarnow about it?"

"No—and I'm not going to, either! If Admiral Parks

has some sort of problem with me, it's my problem, not the Admiral's."

Henke nodded. Not in agreement, but because she'd already known what Honor would say.

"In that case, what's on the schedule for tomorrow?" she asked.

"More sims," Honor replied, accepting the change of subject with a small, grateful smile. "A convoy exercise. First we get to defend it against 'raiders operating in unknown strength,' then we get to turn around and attack it—against a dreadnought division escort."

"Ouch! I hope this 'convoy's' going to be carrying something to make our lumps worthwhile."

"Ours not to reason why," Honor said solemnly, and Henke chuckled.

"Well, if we're going to be invited to make the supreme sacrifice for Queen and Kingdom tomorrow, I'd better emulate Nimitz and get some sleep." She started to rise, but Honor's raised hand stopped her. "Something else?" she asked in surprise.

"As a matter of fact . . ." Honor began, but then her voice trailed off. She lowered her eyes to the linen tablecloth and fidgeted with a fork, and Henke leaned back in her chair in sudden speculation as her commanding officer's face turned bright, hot pink.

"You remember when I needed advice back at Saganami Island?" Honor said after a moment.

"What sort of advice? Multi-dee math?"

"No." Honor's blush darkened. "Personal advice."

Henke managed to keep her eyes from widening and nodded with only a brief hesitation, and Honor shrugged.

"Well, I need some more of it. There are some . . . things I never learned, and now I wish I had."

"What sorts of things?" Henke asked cautiously.

"All sorts!" Honor surprised her yet again with a breathless little laugh and dropped the fork to fling up her hands. Her face was still flushed, but it was as if the laugh had demolished some internal barrier, and she smiled. "As a matter of fact, I need some help with makeup, Mike."

"Makeup?" The word started to come out sharp with astonishment, but Henke choked the incredulity out of her voice just in time. And she was thankful she had when she saw the sparkle in Honor's dark eyes.

"I could have asked my mom about it anytime, and she would've been delighted to teach me. Maybe that was part of the problem. She would have decided the 'ice maiden' had finally melted, and God only knows where that would've ended!" Honor laughed again. "Did I ever tell you what she wanted to give me as a graduation present?"

"No, I don't think you did," Henke said, and deep inside she felt a sense of wonder. For all their closeness, there'd always been a guarded core to Honor Harrington—one Henke suspected only Nimitz had ever managed to breach—and this bright-eyed, almost breathless Honor was a stranger to her.

"She wanted to buy me an evening with one of the best male 'escorts' in Landing." Honor shook her head and chuckled at Henke's expression. "Can't you just see it? A great big, towering gawk of an ensign with fuzz for hair out on the town with some glamorous hunk! Lord, I would have *died*! And just imagine what the neighbors would've thought if they'd ever found out!"

Henke began to chuckle herself as she pictured it, for Sphinx was far and away the most straight-laced of the Kingdom's planets. Professional, licensed courtesans were a fact of life on Manticore. It might not be considered quite the thing to seek their services, but everyone knew "someone else" who had. They weren't particularly unusual on Gryphon, either, but they were very rare birds indeed on Sphinx. Yet she could easily believe Allison Harrington would have done just that. Honor's mother was an immigrant from the Sigma Draconis System's Beowulf, and the sexual mores which prevailed there would have curled a native born Manticoran's hair, much less a Sphinxian's!

The women faced one another across the table, and their chuckles turned into full-throated laughter as each saw the almost fiendish delight in the other's face. But then Honor's laughter slowly ebbed, and she leaned back once more with a sigh.

"Sometimes I wish I'd let her go ahead and do it," she said wistfully. "I could have trusted her to pick the best for me, and maybe then—"

She broke off and waved her hand, and Henke nodded. She'd known Honor for almost thirty T-years, and in all that time, there had never been a man in her life. Never even a hint of one, which seemed even odder somehow in light of her easy relationships and often close friendships with male officers.

And yet, perhaps it wasn't so strange. Honor didn't seem to have any problem regarding herself as "one of the guys," but it was painfully obvious she still thought of herself as the "towering gawk" and "hatchet-faced horse" of her girlhood. She was wrong, of course, but Henke understood how little right or wrong mattered in terms of self-image. Then there'd been Pavel Young, the only man on Saganami Island ever to express an interest in Ms. Midshipman Harrington—and the man who'd tried to rape her when she wasn't interested in return. Honor had kept that whole episode locked inside, but Lord only knew how it had affected a girl who already thought she was ugly.

Yet Henke suspected there was another reason, as well—one Honor herself wasn't aware of—and that reason was Nimitz. Mike Henke remembered the desperately lonely girl who'd been assigned as her dorm mate at Saganami Island, but that loneliness had extended only to other people. Whatever else happened to her, Honor had always had the assurance—not just the belief, but the *proof*—that one creature in the universe loved her . . . and that creature was an empath. Henke had known several people who'd been adopted by treecats, and every one of them seemed to demand more from personal relationships. They demanded trust.

Absolute, total trust, and very few human beings were prepared to extend that to *anyone*. Henke had always known that. It was one reason she was so immensely flattered to possess Honor's friendship, but she sensed, if only dimly, how that need for trust could cripple anything more than friendship, for a treecat's companion *knew* when another's trust—and trustworthiness—were less than absolute. In a sense, the price they paid for their bonds with their 'cats was a certain coolness, a distance, from other humans. Especially lovers, with their bottomless capacity to hurt them.

Some of them dealt with it through casual affairs, surface flings intentionally kept too superficial to ever get past their guards, but Honor couldn't do that. More importantly, she *wouldn't* do it. Despite her mother, there was too much Sphinxian in her . . . and too much stubborn integrity.

"Well, the past is past." Honor sighed, breaking the train of the commander's thoughts. "I can't get it back or do it over again, but I'm afraid it's left me without some of the skills other people take for granted." She touched her face—the left side of her face, Henke noted—and smiled wryly. "Like makeup."

"You don't really need it, you know," Henke said gently, and it was true. She'd never seen Honor wear even lip gloss, but that didn't detract from her clean cut, knife-edged attractiveness.

"Lady," Honor disagreed with half-embarrassed, half-laughing vehemence, "*this* face needs all the help it can get!"

"You're wrong, but I won't argue with you about it." Henke cocked her head, then smiled slightly. "May I take it you want me to help you repair the, um, deficiencies in your education?" Honor nodded, and Henke's eyes gleamed with fond mockery. "Or should I say, the deficiencies in your *arsenal*?" she teased, and chuckled as Honor blushed afresh.

"Whatever," she said with all the dignity she could muster.

"Well . . ." Henke pursed her lips thoughtfully, then shrugged. "Our coloring is just a *bit* different, you know."

"Does that matter?"

"Oh, *Lord*!" Henke moaned, rolling her eyes heavenward at the simple innocence—and abysmal ignorance—that question betrayed. Honor looked surprised, and Henke shook her head.

"Trust me, it matters. On the other hand, Mother always insisted that all her daughters be well instructed in the fundamental hunting skills. I think I can probably do a little something with you, but I'll have to make a raid on the ship's store, first. Nothing *I* use would work on you, that's for sure." She frowned and ran through a mental checklist of all she'd need, for one thing was certain; there were no cosmetics in *Honor's* medicine cabinet.

"How soon do you want to achieve the desired result?" she asked.

"Within the next week or so?" Honor suggested almost hesitantly, and Henke, to her credit, managed not to smile.

"I think we can manage that. Tell you what, this is Thursday—how about I drop by before supper next Wednesday and educate you in Drop Dead Gorgeous 101 then?"

"Wednesday?" Honor's blush was back. She looked away, studying the Queen's painting on the bulkhead, and Henke fought an urge to laugh, for Honor had dined regularly with Paul Tankersley on Wednesday nights for over six weeks now. "Wednesday would be good," she agreed after a moment, and Henke nodded.

"Done. In the meantime, however—" she rose "—I really do need to get some sack time for tomorrow. Meet to discuss the sim at zero-six-thirty?"

"That sounds about right." Honor sounded relieved by the return to a professional topic, but she dragged her eyes back from Queen Elizabeth's portrait and smiled. "And . . . thanks, Mike. Thanks a lot."

"Hey! What are friends for?" Henke laughed, then straightened her shoulders and clicked to a sort of abbreviated attention. "And on that note, good night, Ma'am."

"Good night, Mike," Honor said, and her smile followed the commander out the hatch.

" . . . and I believe that covers just about everything, ladies and gentlemen," Sir Yancey Parks said. "Thank you, and good night."

His assembled squadron commanders stood at his dismissal and departed with courteous nods. All but one of them, and Parks' eyebrows rose as Rear Admiral Mark Sarnow retained his seat.

"Is something on your mind, Admiral?" he asked.

"Yes, Sir, I'm afraid something is," Sarnow said quietly. "I wonder if I might speak with you a moment." His eyes flicked to Commodore Capra and Captain Hurston, then back to Parks. "In private, Sir."

Parks inhaled sharply and felt the matching surprise in Capra and Hurston. Sarnow's tone was diffident and respectful yet firm, and his green eyes were very level. Capra started to say something, but the admiral raised a hand and stopped him.

"Vincent? Mark? If you'd excuse us for a moment? I'll join you in my chart room to finish reexamining those deployment changes when Admiral Sarnow and I are finished."

"Of course, Sir." Capra rose, gathering up the ops officer with his eyes, and the two of them left. The hatch sighed shut behind them, and Parks tilted his chair back and raised one hand, palm uppermost, at Sarnow.

"What was it you wished to speak to me about, Admiral?"

"Captain Harrington, Sir," Sarnow replied, and Parks' eyes narrowed.

"What about Captain Harrington? Is there a problem?"

"Not with her, Sir. I'm delighted with her performance. In fact, that's the reason I asked to speak to you."

"Oh?"

"Yes, Sir." Sarnow met his CO's gaze with an edge of challenge. "May I ask, Sir, why Captain Harrington is the only flag captain never to be invited to a conference aboard *Gryphon*?"

Parks leaned further back, his face expressionless, and his fingers drummed on the arm of his chair.

"Captain Harrington," he said after a moment, "has been fully occupied getting her ship back on-line and learning her responsibilities *as* a flag captain, Admiral. I saw no reason to take her away from those more pressing duties to attend routine conferences."

"With all due respect, Sir Yancey, I don't believe that's true," Sarnow said, and Parks flushed.

"Are you calling me a liar, Admiral Sarnow?" he asked very softly. The younger man shook his head, but his eyes never flinched.

"No, Sir. Perhaps I should have said I don't believe her pressing schedule is the *sole* reason you've excluded her from your confidence."

Air hissed between Parks' teeth as he inhaled, and his eyes were as icy as his voice.

"Even assuming that statement to be true, I fail to see precisely how my relationship with Captain Harrington concerns you, Admiral."

"She's my flag captain, Sir, and a damned fine one," Sarnow replied in those same, level tones. "In the past eleven weeks, she has not only mastered her squadron duties to my complete—my *total*—satisfaction, but done so while simultaneously overseeing major repairs to her own command. She's demonstrated an almost uncanny knack for tactical evolutions, earned the respect of all of my other captains, and taken a considerable portion of Captain Corell's headaches onto her own shoulders. More than that, she's an outstanding officer with a record and depth of experience any captain could be proud of and very few can match, but her pointed exclusion from task force conferences can only be taken as an indication that you lack confidence in her."

"I have never said or even hinted that I lack confidence in Captain Harrington," Parks said frigidly.

"Perhaps you've never said so, Sir, but you have certainly, whether intentionally or unintentionally, indicated that you *do*."

Parks' chair snapped upright, and his face tightened. He was clearly furious, yet there was something more than simple fury in his eyes as he leaned toward Sarnow.

"Let me make one thing plain, Admiral. I will not tolerate insubordination. Is that clear?"

"It isn't my intention to be insubordinate, Sir Yancey." Sarnow's normally melodious tenor was flat, almost painfully neutral but unflinching. "As the commander of a battlecruiser squadron attached to your command, however, it is my duty to support my officers. And if I feel one of them is being treated unfairly or unjustly, it's my responsibility to seek an explanation of his or her treatment."

"I see." Parks pushed himself back in his chair and took a firm grip on his seething temper. "In that case, Admiral, I'll be perfectly frank. I wasn't pleased when Captain Harrington was assigned to this task force. I have a less than lively faith in her judgment, you see."

"No, Sir, again with all due respect, I *don't* see how you could form an opinion of her judgment without ever even meeting her."

Parks right hand clenched on the conference table, and his eyes were dangerous.

"Her record clearly demonstrates that she's both hotheaded and impulsive," he said coldly. "She personally antagonized Klaus Hauptman, and I need hardly tell you how powerful the Hauptman Cartel is. Or how rocky Hauptman's relationship with the Fleet has been for years. Given the tension with the PRH, setting him at loggerheads—*further* at loggerheads, I should say—with Her Majesty's Navy was a stupid thing for any officer to do. Then there was her insubordination to Admiral Hemphill when she addressed the Weapons Development Board after Basilisk. What she said needed saying, granted, but it should have been said in private and with at least a modicum of proper military respect. Certainly she showed gross misjudgment by using a vital service board to publicly embarrass a flag officer in the Queen's service!

"Not content with that, she *assaulted* a diplomatic envoy of Her Majesty's Government in Yeltsin, and then issued an *ultimatum* to a friendly head of state. And while no charges were ever filed, it is a matter of common knowledge that she had to be physically restrained from murdering POWs in her custody after the Battle of Blackbird! However splendid her combat record, that behavior indicates a clear pattern of instability. The woman is a loose warhead, Admiral, and I don't want her under my command!"

Parks made his hands unclench and leaned back, breathing heavily, but Sarnow refused to retreat a centimeter.

"I disagree, Sir," he said softly. "Klaus Hauptman went to Basilisk to browbeat her into abandoning her duty as a Queen's officer. She refused, and her subsequent actions—for which she received this Kingdom's second highest award for valor—are the only reason Basilisk does not now belong to the People's Republic. As for her appearance before the WDB, she addressed herself solely to the issues the Board had invited her there to discuss, and did so in a rational, respectful fashion. If the conclusions of the Board embarrassed its chairwoman, that certainly wasn't her fault.

"In Yeltsin," Sarnow went on in a voice whose calm fooled neither man, "she found herself, as Her Majesty's senior officer, in a near hopeless position. No one could have realistically blamed her for obeying Mr. Houseman's *illegal* order to abandon Grayson to the Masadans—and Haven. Instead, she chose to fight, despite the odds. I don't condone her physical attack on him, but I certainly understand it. And as for the 'prisoners of war' she allegedly attempted to murder, may I remind you that the POW in question was the senior officer of Blackbird

Base, who had not simply permitted but *ordered* the murder and mass rape of *Manticoran* prisoners. Under the circumstances, I *would* have shot the bastard—unlike Captain Harrington, who allowed her allies to talk her out of it so that he could be legally tried and sentenced to death. Moreover, the judgment of Her Majesty's Government on her actions in Yeltsin is plain. May I remind you that Captain Harrington was not only knighted and admitted to the peerage as Countess Harrington but is the only non-Grayson ever to be awarded the Star of Grayson for heroism?"

"*Countess!*" Parks snorted. "That was no more than a political gesture to please the Graysons by acknowledging all the awards *they* piled on her!"

"With respect, Sir, it was much more than a 'political gesture,' though I don't deny it pleased the Graysons. Of course, if she'd been given the precedence actually due a steadholder under Grayson Law—or, for that matter, commensurate with the size of her estates on Grayson or their probable eventual income—she wouldn't have been made a countess. She'd be *Duchess* Harrington."

Parks glared at him but bit his lip in silence, for Sarnow was right and he knew it. The younger admiral waited a moment, then continued.

"Finally, Sir, there is no record, anywhere, of her ever acting with less than total professionalism and courtesy to any individual who had not offered nearly intolerable provocation to her. Nor is there any record of her ever having done one millimeter less than her duty.

"As for your judgment that you don't want her under your command, I can only say that I am delighted to have her under *mine*. And if she remains as my flag captain, then both her position and her record require that she be accorded the respect they deserve."

Silence stretched out between them, and Parks felt his anger like slow, churning lava as he recognized the ultimatum in Sarnow's eyes. The only way to get rid of Harrington was to get rid of Sarnow, and he couldn't. He'd known that from the start, given the Admiralty's decision to assign both of them here—and, for that matter, to give Harrington *Nike*. Worse, Sarnow was just likely to lodge an official protest if he tried to sack Harrington, and except for her obvious inability or unwillingness to restrain her temper, he had no overt justification for doing so—especially with Sarnow so obviously poised to write an outstanding fitness report on her for any board of inquiry.

He wanted to snarl at the rear admiral, to relieve him for his insubordination and send *both* of them packing, but he couldn't. And deep inside he knew part of it was his own temper, his own anger and frustration. Not just at having to put up with Harrington, but for having put himself in a position which allowed this arrogant sprig to lecture him on military propriety . . . and be right, damn him!

"All right, Admiral Sarnow," he asked after endless minutes of fulminating silence, "just what is it you want me to do?"

"All I ask, Sir, is that you accord Captain Harrington the same respect and opportunity for input into task force operations that you accord every other flag captain under your command."

"I see." Parks made his muscles unclench and regarded the rear admiral with a cold lack of liking, then inhaled. "Very well, Admiral. I'll give Captain Harrington the opportunity to prove me wrong about her. And for both your sakes, I hope she does."

• CHAPTER THIRTEEN

Three of President Harris' bodyguards stepped out of the elevator to scan the corridor beyond, and he waited with the patience of long practice. To be born a Legislaturalist—and especially a Harris—meant one was surrounded by security people from birth. He'd never lived any other way, and the only changes when he inherited the presidency had been the intensity of the effort and who provided it, for the well-being of the People's Republic's presidents was too important to entrust to the Republic's citizens.

The Presidential Security Force's personnel were mercenaries, hired from the planet of New Geneva in regimental strength. New Geneva's soldiers and security personnel were professional, highly trained, and noted for their loyalty to their employers. That loyalty was their true stock in trade, the real reason governments paid their high fees rather than rely on their own citizenries—and the fact that they were regarded as outsiders, both by themselves and by the citizens of the PRH, neatly eliminated the possibility that any countervailing source of loyalty might turn the PSF against the president they were sworn to guard with their lives.

Unfortunately, it also meant the PSF wasn't especially popular with the PRH's homegrown military who believed (correctly) that the New Genevans' presence meant *they* weren't quite trusted by their own government.

The head of Harris' personal detachment listened to his earbug until his point men reported the corridor secure, then nodded his charge respectfully forward, and a Marine brigadier saluted as Harris emerged from the elevator. The brigadier's expression was courteous, but Harris felt his simmering subsurface dislike for the PSF people who'd invaded his domain. And, he supposed, the brigadier had a point. The towering black spire of The Octagon, the nerve center of the PRH's military operations, seemed an unlikely place for assassins to lurk. On the other hand, Harris could stand much worse than a single Marine officer's resentment, and, especially since the Frankel assassination, the PSF refused to leave anything to chance. Which didn't mean he needed to rub the man's nose in it; he reached out in a greeting handshake as the brigadier lowered his own hand from the salute.

"Welcome, Mr. President," the Marine said a bit stiffly.

"Thank you, Brigadier . . . Simpkins, isn't it?"

"Yes, Sir." Brigadier Simpkins smiled, pleased to be remembered by his head of state, and Harris smiled back. As if the PSF would have let him encounter, however casually, anyone he *wasn't* thoroughly briefed upon! But the gesture soothed Simpkins' resentment, and his invitation for Harris to accompany him down the corridor seemed much more natural.

"Admiral Parnell is waiting for you, Sir. If you'll come this way?"

"Of course, Brigadier. Lead on."

It was a short trip, and the door at the end didn't look exceptionally important—aside from the armed guards who flanked it. One of them opened the door for the President, and the people already gathered in the small conference room rose as he walked in.

He stopped his security people at the threshold with a small wave. They gave him the pained look they always did when he went *anywhere* without them, but they obeyed his silent order with the resignation of experience. As far as President Harris was concerned, any secret known to more than one person was automatically compromised, whether or not the enemy had discovered it yet, and he intended to compromise *this* information as little as possible. That was why there were only three other people in the room. The rest of the cabinet would no doubt be peeved when they discovered they'd been excluded, but that, too, was something he could live with.

"Mr. President," Admiral Parnell greeted him.

"Amos." Harris shook the CNO's hand, then glanced at his secretaries of war and foreign affairs. "Elaine. Ron. Good to see you all." His civilian colleagues returned his nod of greeting, and he looked back to Parnell. "My time's short, Amos. My appointments secretary's done a little creative scheduling to prove I'm somewhere else right now if anyone asks, but I have to resurface soon to make that stick, so let's get right to it."

"Of course, Sir." The admiral waved his guests into chairs and stood at the end of the conference table to face them.

"Actually, Mr. President, I can keep this extremely brief, since I can speak only in general terms, anyway. The distances involved mean that getting dispatches back and forth takes too long for me to try any sort of detailed coordination from here. That's why I need to relocate to Barnett."

Harris nodded in understanding. Haven was almost three hundred light-years from Manticore—and over a hundred and fifty from its own western border, for that matter. Even for courier boats, who routinely rode the risky upper edge of hyper-space's theta band, it would take something like sixteen days to get a message one-way between Haven and the Barnett fleet base across the hundred and twenty-seven light-years between them.

"I suppose I really just wanted to touch base before you go," he said.

"Of course, Sir." Parnell touched a control panel, and a huge holo map appeared above the table. Its volume was dotted with the tiny sparks of color-coded stars and other icons, but what drew the eye were the glaring red pinpricks all along the frontier between the PRH and the Manticoran Alliance.

"The red data codes indicate the sites of our intended

provocations, Mr. President." He touched another button, and a few red dots were suddenly circled by green bands. "These are the systems in which we have confirmation initial operations have been successfully completed. We've scheduled follow-up intrusions in many cases, of course, so even an initial success doesn't guarantee something still won't go wrong, but so far things look very good. The time and money we've invested in the Argus net have paid off handsomely in the data our planners had to work with when we set things up. At the moment, we appear to be almost exactly on schedule, and we've suffered no reported losses. At the same time, Mr. President, it's important to remember that somewhere along the line we *will* get hurt, however good our intelligence and planning. That's inevitable, given the scale and scope of our operations."

"Understood, Amos." Harris studied the holo map, savoring the wide dispersion of incidents, then glanced at Ron Bergren. "Do we have any indications they're jumping the way we want, Ron?"

"Not really, Sid." Bergren gave a small shrug and stroked his mustache. "Our intelligence conduits have a lower data transmission speed than the Navy's dispatches, not to mention the fact that it's harder for spies to get the information we need than it is for an admiral to debrief his COs. I'm afraid Naval Intelligence and my own people were essentially correct when they pointed out that we couldn't count on independent confirmation, but it does appear the Manticoran media have begun to twig to the fact that something is going on. They don't know exactly what, which indicates a fairly severe government clampdown for someone with their press traditions. Given that and my own reading of Cromarty and his government, I'd say we've got a better than even chance that they are. A lot depends on what their military recommends."

The foreign secretary raised an eyebrow at Elaine Dumarest, and it was the secretary of war's turn to shrug.

"I can only repeat what NavInt said at the outset. Caparelli's replacement of Webster as their First Space Lord is a very hopeful sign. From his dossier, he's more of a bull in the china shop than Webster was. He's well thought of by his colleagues as a tactician, but he's both less capable of delegation than Webster and weaker on the analysis side. That makes him less likely to seek advice and more prone to prefer quick, direct solutions, which certainly suggests his recommendations will follow the general pattern we're hoping for."

"I'm afraid that's the best we can say at this point, Mr. President," Parnell said in respectful support of his superior. "We're showing him a bait we hope he'll take, but no one can guarantee he will. Left to his own devices, I'm almost certain of how he'd respond, but he doesn't work in a vacuum. There's always the possibility that someone—like their Admiral Givens, who, unfortunately, is very good at her job from all reports—will see something he didn't and convince him to take note of it. At the same time, they'll *have* to do some of what we want, whoever calls the shots on their side of the fence."

"I was afraid you were all going to insist on qualifiers." Harris' wry smile took the potential sting from his words, and he sighed. "That's what I hate most about my job. Things would be so much simpler if other people would just be nice and predictable all the time!"

His subordinates smiled dutifully, and he looked at his chrono.

"All right, I'm going to have to wrap this up fairly quickly. Amos," he gave the CNO a level look, "we're going to rely on you to handle the final timing from Barnett. Give us all the advance warning you can so we can tie up the final prep work at this end, but I realize there may not be time for you to check with us. That's why I'm authorizing you right now to activate the final phase when you think the situation is most ripe. Don't let us down."

"I'll give it everything I've got, Mr. President," Parnell promised.

"I know you will, Amos." Harris moved his eyes to Bergren. "Ron, double-check everything from your end. Once the shooting starts, our relations with neutral powers, especially the Solarian League, may be critical. We can't risk giving the show away, but do all the pump-priming you can—and once things actually break, use our ambassadors and attachés to be sure *our* version of what's going on reaches the neutral media before any of their damned correspondents get into the area for 'independent' reports. I'll bring Jessup into the picture next week so his people at Information can start putting together the initial releases for your embassy people to hand out."

Bergren nodded, and the President turned to Dumarest.

"You said you were still thinking over whether or not to accompany Amos to Barnett, Elaine. Have you made up your mind?"

"Yes." Dumarest plucked at her lower lip and frowned. "My emotions say I should go, but he doesn't really need me looking over his shoulder. And if both of us vanish, somebody's a lot more likely to wonder where we are and put two and two together. Under the circumstances, I think I'd better stay home."

"I was thinking the same thing myself," Harris agreed. "And I can certainly use you. Sit down with Jessup and Ron to help them put the right spin on our news releases. I want to restrict this to the cabinet level until we launch actual operations, so the release preparation time is going to be short. The more thought we can put into giving the writers detailed guidelines and official data when we dump it on them, the better."

"Of course, Mr. President."

"Then that's about it, I think. Except—" he turned his eyes back to Parnell "—for one other point."

"Another point, Mr. President?" Parnell sounded surprised, and Harris laughed without undue humor.

"It's not really about operations, Amos. It's about Rob Pierre."

"What about Mr. Pierre, Sir?" Parnell didn't quite

succeed in keeping his distaste out of his voice, and Harris laughed again, more naturally.

"He *can* be a pain in the ass, can't he? Unfortunately, he's got too much Quorum influence for me to ignore him—and, I'm sorry to say, he knows it. At the moment, he's badgering me about several letters to his son which were returned undelivered by NavSec."

Parnell and Dumarest exchanged speaking glances, but there was a trace of unwilling sympathy in the admiral's eyes. People, even prominent people, had been known to vanish in the People's Republic, and relatives started sweating the instant they heard the word "security." Naval Security had a better reputation than most of the PRH's security organs (the Mental Hygiene Police had far and away the worst), but they were still security. And much though Parnell personally detested both Rob Pierre and his son Edward, the elder Pierre's love for his only child was as intense as it was well known.

But whatever sympathy Parnell might feel, he was still chief of naval operations, and Pierre the Younger was still an officer, officially like any other, under his command.

"I hadn't been informed of it, Mr. President," he said after a moment, "but Admiral Pierre's squadron is involved in our current operations, and we've clamped down a communications blackout to maintain operational security."

"I don't suppose you could make an exception in this case?" Harris asked, but his tone said he didn't intend to push it if Parnell turned him down, and the admiral shook his head with a clear conscience.

"I'd really prefer not to, Sir. First, because keeping this operation secret really is important, but secondly, if I may be completely honest, because there's already a great deal of resentment against Admiral Pierre over his father's blatant use of his influence to further his career. It's unfortunate, because while I personally dislike Admiral Pierre, he actually is a very competent officer, despite a certain hotheadedness and arrogance. But if I make a special exception in his case, it's going to cause resentment among our other officers."

Harris nodded without surprise. Legislaturalists might use influence to promote their children's careers, but they were jealous of that prerogative. The President was too much a part of the system to condemn it—after all, look what family interest had done for *him*—but he considered it a pity that it worked against even the most competent of outsiders. Still, he would shed no tears, not even crocodile ones, for Rob Pierre. The man was exactly what he'd called him: a monumental pain in the ass. Worse, Palmer-Levy's moles in the Citizens' Rights Union were picking up more and more rumbles that he was buttering both sides of his bread by cozying up to the CRU's leadership. He was being careful to limit his contacts to the "legitimate" CRP splinter in the People's Quorum, but the President rather looked forward, all things considered, to remorsefully informing him that "operational security considerations" made it impossible to meet his requests.

"All right, I'll tell him it's no go." Harris rose and extended his hand once more. "And on that note, I'll be going. Good luck, Amos. We're depending on you."

"Yes, Sir, Mr. President." Parnell took the proffered hand. "Thank you—both for the good wishes and your confidence."

Harris gave his cabinet secretaries another nod and turned back to the door and his waiting security people.

• CHAPTER FOURTEEN

Captain Brentworth accepted the message board without leaving his command chair. It was quiet on *Jason Alvarez's* bridge, but there was a tension under the surface, like silently snarling marsh cats, and he wondered how much longer it would take the waiting to dull the raw, sharp edges.

He finished the routine dispatch, fingerprinted his receipt on the scan panel, and handed it back to the yeoman with a nod of thanks, then looked automatically into his tactical display.

Virtually every ship in the Grayson Navy—a small force, by galactic standards, but infinitely more powerful than just a year before—formed a huge, tenuous sphere fourteen light-minutes from Yeltsin's Star and a hundred and fifteen light-minutes in circumference. Their Manticore-designed sensors reached out far beyond that, yet their presence was a deception measure.

Manty intelligence was positive the Peeps still hadn't realized that Manticore had finally found a way for remotely deployed tactical sensors to transmit messages at FTL speeds. Their range remained limited to less than twelve light-hours, but the specially designed generators aboard the latest Manticoran sensor platforms and recon drones could produce directional grav pulses. And since grav waves were faster than light, so were their transmission speeds across their range.

The Grayson Navy knew about them, for their existence had been Lady Harrington's trump card in her epic defense of their world, but Manticore and her allies had gone to enormous lengths to deny the Peeps any evidence of their existence. Which, in no small part, explained the Graysons' present deployment.

By spreading themselves so thin, they virtually guaranteed they would be unable to intercept any intruders with more than one or two ships, but their purpose wasn't to intercept. Their job was to serve as obvious bird dogs for the heavy Manty battle squadrons behind them. Any Peep captain who poked his nose into Yeltsin would see their thin screen well before he saw any Manticoran ships of the wall, and the obvious assumption would be that it was the *Graysons* who'd picked him up and reported him to their allies. No doubt he would curse the luck which had placed an RMN battle squadron or two— purely fortuitously, undoubtedly as the result of some routine training maneuver—in a position to generate an intercept vector once the Graysons warned him.

Brentworth smiled unpleasantly at the thought. The sensor platforms would pick up any normal space approach at well over thirty light-hours and relay complete data back to Command Central by grav pulse, and with that data, High Admiral Matthews and Admiral D'Orville, the Manty commander, would pre-position their forces to meet the intruders at a time and place of their own choosing . . . and in whatever strength seemed required.

Of course, it was probable the Peeps would break and run the moment they saw capital ships, and that far out from Yeltsin they could pop straight into h-space, assuming their velocity was under .3 *c*. Still, if their velocity was higher than that, they'd have to decelerate to a safe translation speed. Under *those* circumstances, they were likely to run into a tiny bit of trouble before they could hyper out . . . and wouldn't that just be too bad?

A mere captain wasn't supposed to know about the inner deliberations of his supreme commanders, but Brentworth had connections few captains had. He knew Matthews and D'Orville would deliberately put together a force heavy enough to leave the Peeps no option but to run . . . but he also knew that if their approach vector made evasion impossible, the Alliance admirals intended to annihilate their entire force.

And that was why, after the murder of Convoy MG-19, Captain Mark Brentworth asked God each night to send the bastards in at too high a base velocity to hyper out before the superdreadnoughts caught them.

"—attle stations! Battle stations! All hands man battle stations! This is not a drill! Repeat, this is not a drill!"

The raucous, recorded voice and shrill, atonal alarm filled HMS *Star Knight* as her crew thundered to their stations. Captain Seamus O'Donnell sidestepped quickly to avoid a missile tech as the woman disappeared down the access tube to her station, then vaulted into the lift and punched the button. He was still sealing his skin suit when the doors opened on the bridge, and his exec looked up, then scrambled from the command chair with obvious relief.

O'Donnell dropped into the chair almost before Commander Rogers was clear. He racked his helmet by feel and familiarity alone, for his eyes were already busy absorbing the information on his tactical repeaters, and his mouth tightened.

Star Knight was the lead ship of the Manticoran Navy's most powerful heavy cruiser class. At three hundred thousand tons, she was fit to take on anything smaller than a battlecruiser, and, under the right conditions, she might even engage a battlecruiser with a chance of victory. It had been done, after all. Once.

But she wasn't the equal of the force coming at her today.

"IDs?" he snapped at his tac officer.

"None definite, Sir, but preliminary signature analysis says they're Peeps." The tac officer's reply was tight with anxiety, and O'Donnell grunted an acknowledgment.

"No response to our challenges, Com?"

"No, Sir."

O'Donnell grunted again, and his mind raced. The Poicters System was hardly crucial in military terms.

The powerful base built at Talbot had reduced Poicters to little more than a flank guard for the task force stationed there, but it was still an inhabited system, with a total population of almost a billion, and the Star Kingdom was committed to defend those people. That was why *Star Knight* and the other ships of her squadron were here, but none of her consorts were within light-minutes of her at the moment.

"Positive ID from CIC, Sir," his tac officer said suddenly. "They're Peeps, all right. *Sultan* class."

"Damn," O'Donnell said softly. He tapped on a command chair arm for a moment, then looked across at the tac officer. "Enemy vector?"

"They're on an almost exact reciprocal, Sir—one-seven-three zero-one-eight relative. Their base velocity is point-zero-four-three cee, and their current acceleration is four-seven-zero gees. Range one-point-three-zero-eight light-minutes. They just popped out of hyper less than two minutes ago, Sir. We didn't have a clue they were coming."

O'Donnell nodded, silently cursing the luck which had put him in such a position. Or *was* it luck? The squadron had maintained the same patrol schedule for months now. Had the Peeps slipped a scout into range to analyze their movements? He hoped not, because if they had, this was a deliberate interception, and there was no way *Star Knight* could face four battlecruisers.

He laid maneuvering cursors on his display and looked for some way out. His ship was headed almost straight down their throats at a closing speed of over 33,000 KPS, and the powered missile envelope would be close to 19,000,000 kilometers under those conditions. That meant he'd enter it in less than two and a half minutes unless he found some way to avoid it. But the maneuvering computers told him what he'd already known: there was no way he could. He had little more than a 50 g acceleration advantage; even if he turned directly away, it would take him over seventeen hours to begin pulling away from them, and he'd overshoot their present position in less than thirteen minutes, even at max decel. If they *were* here to attack, their broadsides would rip his ship apart long before he did.

"Helm, roll ship and bring us to zero-niner-zero by zero-niner-zero at maximum acceleration," he ordered.

"Aye, aye, Sir. Coming to zero-niner-zero zero-niner-zero at five-two-three gravities acceleration," his coxswain responded, and O'Donnell watched his display for the Peeps' reaction as *Star Knight* rolled up on her side, presenting the impenetrable belly of her impeller wedge to them, and snapped through a skew turn down and away to starboard. It was a clear bid to avoid action, and it would work . . . unless the Peeps chose to split their formation and go in pursuit.

"Com, get a report off to Commodore Weaver," O'Donnell said, his eyes glued to his display. "Inform him we have positively identified four Havenite *Sultan*-class battlecruisers in violation of Poicters space. Include our position, tac analysis, and current vectors. Request assistance and inform him I am attempting to avoid action."

"Aye, aye, Sir."

O'Donnell nodded absently, still staring at his display, and then his hands clenched. The glaring dots of hostile impeller wedges were shifting their vectors—not simply relative to *Star Knight*, but to one another, as well. They were altering course to intercept . . . and splitting their formation to come at him from so many angles he could never interpose his wedge against all of them.

"Amend that signal, Com," he said quietly. "Inform Commodore Weaver I do not expect to be able to avoid action. Tell him we'll do our best."

Rear Admiral Edward Pierre leaned back in his command chair with a hungry smile as his four ships swept towards the hyper limit of the Talbot System. He'd heard for years how good the Manticorans were—how they had a tradition of victory, how hard they trained, how good their tactics were, how their analysts and planners were up to every trick—and it had always irritated him immensely. *He* hadn't seen any of their graveyards, and if they were so damned good, why was the People's Republic of Haven gobbling up every choice bit of stellar real estate in sight, not them? And why were they so damned scared to pull the trigger themselves, if their superiority was so great?

Pierre wasn't like the majority of the People's Navy's senior flag officers, and he both resented the distinction and took immense pride in it. His father's political power helped explain Pierre's rapid rise, but Rob Pierre's fight to claw his way off the Dole as a young man had imbued him with a burning contempt for "his" government, and his son had inherited that contempt along with the benefits of his power. That was one of the several reasons Admiral Pierre belonged to the Navy's "war now" faction.

There was an invisible wall in the People's Navy. If you wanted rank above a rear admiral's, then you had to be born a Legislaturalist. That alone would have made Pierre hate most of his superiors—not that he didn't have other reasons. The Legislaturalist admirals, safe from competition behind their wall of privilege, had gotten fat and lazy. They'd had it too good for too long, and the guts had gone out of them, until they were afraid to risk their power and wealth and comfort even against a two-for-a-credit single-system threat like Manticore. Pierre despised them for that, and he'd been delighted when he was picked for this mission and the chance to show them how groundless their fears were.

He rechecked the chrono and nodded mentally. His ships were right on schedule, and for all their overinflated reputation, the Manticorans were as blind-drunk stupid as a Prole on BLS day. Pierre didn't know the details—he wasn't senior enough for that, he thought sourly—but he knew the People's Navy had sneaked powered-down scout ships into and through the Manties' outer systems on ballistic courses for over two years now, plotting their patrols' movements, and the idiots didn't even seem aware of the possibility. If they had been, their patrols wouldn't have followed clockwork schedules that left them wide open for the sort of pounce Pierre planned today. For *both* pounces, actually; Commodore Yuranovich and the other half of the squadron should be killing themselves a Manty cruiser about now.

Just as Pierre intended to do in the next—he checked the chronometer again—two and a half hours or so.

Commander Gregory, captain of the light cruiser HMS *Athena*, stood by his tactical officer's shoulder and shook his head at the image on the visual display. The dreadnought *Bellerophon* was coming up fast from astern, overtaking Gregory's cruiser as she eased along on another long, slow leg of her patrol.

Gregory had known *Bellerophon* was due to rotate home, but he hadn't known she was leaving today, and she certainly made an impressive sight to break up the monotony of patrol duty.

The six-and-a-half-megaton leviathan swam closer and closer, dwarfing the light cruiser into minnow insignificance as she rode up five thousand kilometers off *Athena*'s port quarter. Even a ship her size was no more than a dot of reflected sunlight to the naked eye at that range, but the visual display brought her into needle-sharp focus, and Gregory shook his head again as he watched her sweep up on *Athena*'s beam. She outmassed his ship by over sixty to one, and the difference between her broadside and *Athena*'s was quite literally inconceivable. The commander wouldn't have traded his lithe, beautiful ship for a dozen clumsy dreadnoughts, yet it felt reassuring to see that much firepower and know it was on his side.

Bellerophon overtook *Athena* and forged past with a velocity advantage of twelve thousand KPS on her way to the hyper limit, and Gregory grinned as he nodded to his com officer to flash *Athena*'s running lights in the close-range visual salute starships seldom got a chance to exchange in deep space. *Bellerophon* returned it; then she was gone, roaring ahead under a steady 350 g's acceleration, and the commander sighed.

"Well, that was exciting," he told his tac officer. "Too bad it's the *only* excitement we're going to get today."

"Hyper limit in thirty seconds, Admiral Pierre."

"Thank you." Pierre nodded to acknowledge the information, and the battlecruiser *Selim*'s GQ alarm whooped once to warn her crew.

"Hyper transit! I'm reading an unidentified hyper footprint!" *Athena*'s tac officer snapped. His surprise showed in his voice, but he was already bent over his panel, working the contact.

"Where?" Commander Gregory demanded sharply.

"Bearing zero-zero-five, zero-one-one. Range one-eight-zero million klicks. Christ, Skipper! It's right on top of *Bellerophon*!"

"Contact! Enemy vessel bearing oh-five-three, oh-oh-six, range five-seven-four thousand kilometers!"

Pierre jerked in his command chair and twisted toward his ops officer's sudden, unanticipated report. They should be eleven *light-minutes* from their target! What the *hell* was the woman talking about?!

"Contact confirmed!" *Selim*'s tac officer called out, and then— "Oh, my God! *It's a dreadnought!*"

Disbelief froze the admiral's mind. It *couldn't* be—not way the hell out here! But he was already turning back to his own display, and his heart lurched as it showed him CIC's confirming identification.

"Put us back into hyper!"

"We can't translate for another eight minutes, Sir," *Selim*'s white-faced captain said. "The generators are still cycling."

Pierre stared at the captain, and his mind whirled like a ground-looping air car. The man's words seemed to take forever to register, while his ships closed with the enemy at over forty thousand kilometers per second, and the admiral swallowed around an icy lump of panic. They were dead. They were all dead, unless, just possibly, that dreadnought's crew was as shocked as he was. He had a clear shot down the front of her wedge if he could get his ships around to clear their broadsides, and they couldn't possibly have been expecting him to appear in their face. If they took long enough reacting, long enough getting to battle stations—

"Hard a port!" he barked. "All batteries, fire as you bear!"

"Sweet Jesus, they're *Peeps!*" *Bellerophon's* junior tactical officer whispered. The Book didn't like enemy reports like that, but Lieutenant Commander Avshari felt no inclination to criticize. After all, The Book didn't envision this lunatic sort of situation, either.

The lieutenant commander watched his status boards' green lights turn amber and red and wished to hell the Captain would get here. Or the Exec. Or *anybody* senior to him, because he didn't have a clue and he knew it. This was supposed to be a milk run, a good opportunity for junior watch keepers to get a little bridge time on their logs, but he was a *communications* officer, for God's sake—and one whose Academy tactical scores had been a disaster, to boot! What the *hell* was he supposed to do next?

"Sidewalls active! Starboard energy batteries closed up on computer override, Sir!" the youthful lieutenant at Tactical said, and Avshari nodded in relief. That decided which way to turn, anyway.

"Bring us hard to port, Helm."

"Aye, aye, Sir. Coming hard to port."

The dreadnought began her turn, and fresh alarms whooped even as she swung.

"Incoming fire!" the tac officer snapped, and lasers and grasers ripped at *Bellerophon's* suddenly interposed sidewall. Most of them achieved absolutely nothing as the sidewall bent and degraded them, but red lights bloomed on Avshari's damage control display as half a

dozen minor hits cratered her massive armor, and this
time he knew exactly what to do.

"Ms. Wolversham, you are authorized to return fire!"
Bellerophon's com officer barked the order straight from
The Book, and Lieutenant Arlene Wolversham punched
the button.

Admiral Pierre swallowed a groan as the dreadnought
snapped around and her sidewall swatted his broadsides
contemptuously aside. He'd never seen a ship that size
maneuver so rapidly and confidently. She'd taken barely
ten seconds to bring her sidewalls up and get around—
her captain must have the instincts and reactions of a
cat!

He could see his intended prey's impeller signature in
his display now, millions of kilometers astern of the
dreadnought, and realized intuitively what had happened.
His intelligence had been perfect, but he'd blundered
into an unscheduled departure. A stupid, routine transit
there'd been no way to predict. And now there was no
way to evade the consequences.

"All units, roll ship!" he barked, but even as he
snapped out the order, he knew it was futile this deep
into the enemy's missile envelope. Even if his ships
rolled up behind their wedges in time to evade the
dreadnought's beams, it would only delay the inevitable,
require her to kill them with laser heads, instead. . . .

And then he realized they weren't going to manage
even that much.

HMS *Bellerophon's* broadside opened fire, and enough
energy to shatter a small moon flashed through the
"gunports" in her starboard sidewall.

A quarter-second later, Battlecruiser Divisions 141 and
142 of the People's Navy ceased to exist.

• CHAPTER FIFTEEN

Honor smiled a sleepy little smile into the darkness, listening to the slow, even breathing behind her, and her hand crept up to caress the wrist and forearm draped over her ribs. It was a shy caress, almost an incredulous one, and amusement at her own sense of wonder deepened her smile.

A soft noise came out of the dark, and her eyes turned unerringly to its source. The sleeping cabin's hatch had been closed when she dozed off. Now it stood ajar, and a thin edge of light leaked through it. It was dim, barely lightening the blackness, but it was enough. Two green eyes sparkled at her from the bedside desk, and she felt the deep, gentle approval behind them.

She touched the wrist again, smile trembling with mingled echoes of present joy and remembered pain as old memories stabbed, and, for the first time in years, she let herself face the things she'd chosen to suppress for so long.

Being Allison Harrington's daughter had been hard for a girl who knew she was ugly. Honor loved her mother and knew her mother loved her. Despite a career at least as demanding as a naval officer's, Allison had never been "too busy" to give her daughter warmth and love and support . . . but she'd also been petite and beautiful. And there Honor had been, knowing she would never match her beauty, that she would always be the out-sized freak, and secretly loathing the part of herself that couldn't quite forgive her mother for making her *feel* her plain-faced gawkiness.

And then there'd been Pavel Young.

Her smile disappeared as she bared her teeth in automatic reflex. Pavel Young, who'd done his hateful best to destroy what little illusion of attractiveness she'd somehow nourished and turn her wistful dreams of what might have been into something ugly and disgusting. But at least she'd known he was the enemy, known his attack had been born of hate and outraged ego, not something she'd somehow deserved. He'd left her feeling dirtied and defiled, but he hadn't quite finished her off. No, *that* had been left to a "friend."

The remembered sorrow and crushing shame of a long-ago afternoon poured through her. It had been an agonizing thing, the most deeply hidden secret of an often desperately unhappy adolescence, for she hadn't realized until it was too late why Nimitz had taken such a dislike to Cal Panokulous. Not until she'd come smilingly, without knocking, into the dorm room of someone she thought loved her . . . and overheard the man who'd washed away the foulness of Young's touch chuckling over the com with an Academy classmate who knew them both over how "clumsy" she was.

She closed her eyes against the flood of long-denied anguish. Even after all these years, she'd never been able to admit how savagely that had wounded her. Not just the betrayal, but the terrible, cutting blow to a teen-aged girl who'd already been shamed by a would-be rapist. A girl whose mother was beautiful and who knew *she* was ugly. Who'd been so desperate for someone to prove she wasn't that she'd ignored Nimitz's warning only to discover how horribly one human being could wound another.

Never again. She'd sworn to herself that it would never happen again, just as she would never let him know she'd overheard. She'd simply fled, for if she'd confronted him, he would either have lied and denied it or laughed and admitted it . . . and in either case, she would have killed him with her bare hands. Yet, in a way, she'd been almost grateful. He'd warned her what could happen, shown her that no man would ever have more than a crude and casual interest in bedding someone as clumsy and ugly as she, and so she'd put any thought of its ever happening out of her mind.

She touched that warm, gentle hand again, pressing it to her ribs, absorbing its warmth like some pagan charm against devils, and her eyes closed tighter. She'd always known most men were decent. No one could be adopted by a 'cat and not know that, but she'd built her walls anyway. She'd hidden not just a part of herself but the *reason* she hid that part, even from the best of them, for she'd had to. Friends, yes; friends she would die with or for, but never lovers. Never. She'd cut herself off from that risk—cut herself off so completely she'd actually been content, never consciously realizing what she'd done—because she couldn't let anyone, especially herself, know how deeply the shamed girl still hiding within the determined naval officer had been wounded. Because she couldn't let anyone guess that one thing, at least, in the universe hurt so much, frightened her so completely, that she dared not confront it.

And so she'd gone her own way, cool and disengaged, faintly amused by the romantic entanglements she saw about her but totally untouched by them. She'd known it worried her mother, but her mother was the last person she could ever have discussed it with, and Allison Harrington didn't know what had happened to her daughter at Saganami Island. Without that knowledge and with a set of cultural baggage so different from that of a typical Sphinxian, there was no way she could have guessed what Honor chose not to admit even to herself, and Honor had been glad it was so. She'd actually been content, in a wistful sort of way, for she'd had Nimitz, and she'd accepted that she would never have—or need, or even truly want—anyone else.

Until now.

Paul Tankersley's slow breathing didn't change, but his hand responded even in his sleep. It slipped up her ribs and cupped her breast like a warm, friendly little animal.

Not passionately, only tenderly. His warmth pressed against her spine, his breath gusted on the back of her neck, and her fingers clasped his hand against her as her nerves recalled the smooth, incredible heat of his skin, the silken fineness of his hair.

She'd wanted to come here tonight, yet she'd been terrified, as well. It seemed silly now, but the decorated war hero, the captain whose tunic sparkled with ribbons for valor, had been *afraid*, and she'd agonized over bringing Nimitz. She'd *needed* the 'cat. Much as she'd trusted Paul, as much as she'd wanted him, she'd needed Nimitz's ability to protect her, less against Paul than against her own fear of still more betrayal. Her insecurity had shamed her, but she couldn't simply reject it, even though she'd known how few humans realized how utterly disinterested 'cats were in human sexuality and feared Paul might feel as if she'd brought a voyeur.

Yet Paul hadn't objected to Nimitz any more than he'd commented on her cosmetics, though his eyes had lit at the sight of Mike's efforts. She'd felt his emotions through Nimitz while they ate, and this time she'd clung to that awareness rather than discourage the 'cat from linking them. She'd tasted the pleasant, somehow tingling edge of his desire, like the smoky lightning of old whiskey, but there'd been so much more behind it. Things she had known with absolute certainty no man would ever feel for her.

Her pulse had calmed—or perhaps simply raced for another reason—and, for the first time she could recall, she'd been glad to let someone else take charge. Someone who understood the mysteries which had always confused and frightened her. And when the meal was over, she'd actually grinned when Paul informed the 'cat that bedroom doors were intended to assure privacy.

That was the moment, she thought now, luxuriating in the comfortable darkness, when she knew, absolutely and beyond doubt, that she'd been right about Paul Tankersley, for Nimitz had simply risen high on his true-feet with a flirt of his tail to reach the door button. He'd opened the hatch and walked unconcernedly out into the main cabin, leaving her alone with Paul in the clearest possible proof that *he* trusted this man.

Yet for all that, she'd been stiff and wooden at first. The old inadequacies had cut too deep, made her too aware of her ignorance. She was forty-five T-years old, and she didn't know what to do. Didn't even know where to begin! The courage it took to reveal that to a man had dwarfed what it had taken to sail *Fearless* into *Saladin's* broadsides at Yeltsin, but she'd known, somehow, that if she didn't risk herself now, she never would.

Even without Nimitz, she'd felt his surprise at her inexperienced responses, but there'd been none of Cal Panokulous' shallow adolescent scorn, none of Pavel Young's contempt and need to punish. There'd been only wonder and gentleness, slowness and laughter, and after that—

She smiled again, eyes prickling with tears, and lifted his hand in the darkness. Not very far. Just far enough to brush a soft kiss across its back before she returned it to her breast and closed her eyes.

The sharp, musical chime cut through the stillness, and Honor tried to roll out of bed even as she reached for her bedside terminal in a captain's sheer spinal reflex. But something was wrong. She was tangled up in someone else's limbs, and she wiggled against them for a second before her eyes popped back open and her mind snapped into focus with the realization that it wasn't *her* com after all.

She blinked, then giggled. Lord! She could just imagine the reaction of Paul's caller if *she'd* answered—especially since pajamas would definitely have been in the way tonight!

The chime sounded again, and Paul muttered something irritable in his sleep. He snorted and tried to snuggle closer to her back, and the com chimed a third time.

Well, one thing was certain. He was a *much* sounder sleeper than she was. Which was no doubt worth knowing, but wouldn't get the ship out of the docking slip.

She jabbed him gently in the ribs as the chime turned into a higher, continuous buzz. He snorted again, louder, then rose on one elbow in a rush.

"What—?" He began, then cut himself off as the buzz registered. "Oh, *hell*!" he muttered. "I *told* the switchboard—"

He shook his head, the ends of his long hair sweeping her bare shoulder like tickling silk, and shook himself into full awareness.

"Sorry." He pressed a kiss to her shoulder blade, and she wanted to purr like Nimitz. But then he sat up quickly. "They wouldn't have put it through unless they thought it was important," he went on. "And they'd damned well better be right! When I think of all the time and effort I put into getting tonight just right. . . ."

His deep voice trailed off suggestively, and she smiled.

"You'd better answer before someone starts on the hatch with a laser cutter," she said, and he laughed and reached across her, accepting the call voice-only without bringing the video up.

"Tankersley," he said.

"Captain, this is Commander Henke," a furry contralto said, and Honor sat up even more quickly than he had as the formality of Mike's words and tone registered and she heard Admiral Sarnow issuing crisp, rapid orders to his staff behind her exec's voice.

"Yes, Commander?" Paul sounded as surprised as Honor, but he'd picked up on the formal cue. "What can I do for you?"

"I'm trying to track down Captain Harrington, Sir. I understand she intended to dine with you tonight. Would she still be there by any chance?" Mike asked in that same cool, professionally impersonal voice—bless her!

Honor rolled out of bed and began collecting her

scattered uniform from the cabin carpet, blushing in strangely delighted embarrassment as Paul brought up the cabin lights and watched her with an appreciative eye.

"Why, yes," he told his cousin innocently. "In fact, I believe she's getting ready to leave right now." Honor paused in just her briefs, one foot inserted into a trouser leg, to make a rude gesture, and his face crinkled in delight. "Would you like to speak to her?"

"Yes, please."

It was remarkable how repressive Mike could sound without changing her tone in any identifiable way, Honor thought. She pulled her trousers the rest of the way on and sat before the com, swatting Paul out of her way with her hip, and a smile quivered on her mouth as he stretched himself in shameless, luxurious nakedness and his eyes laughed at her.

"Yes, Mike?" She couldn't quite keep an edge of laughter out of her own voice, but it vanished with Henke's next sentence.

"Captain, Admiral Sarnow requested me, with his compliments, to ask you to return aboard immediately."

"Of course." Honor's eyes narrowed. "Is there a problem?"

"We've just received a general signal from the fleet flagship, Ma'am. All flag officers and flag captains are to repair aboard immediately."

Henke was waiting when Honor swam hurriedly out of the repair base docking tube into *Nike*'s entry port. MacGuiness stood at the exec's shoulder, a garment bag draped over his arm, and both of them wore harried expressions. The rating manning the tube's inboard end started to come to attention, but Honor waved for him to stand easy and started for the lift with her quick, long-legged stride while her henchpeople scurried after her.

"Admiral Sarnow is holding his pinnace in the forward boat bay," Henke said as the three of them stepped aboard the lift. The doors closed, and Honor keyed their destination, then blinked in surprise as Henke reached out right behind her and locked the lift between decks.

"I thought you said the Admiral was waiting, Mike!"

"I did, but before you go aboard *Gryphon*—" The exec's hand darted into the small belt purse under her tunic for a cleaning tissue, and Honor's face turned crimson as Henke reached out to whisk away the remnants of eye shadow and lip gloss. The commander didn't even smile, but her eyes twinkled, and Honor's own eyes cut sideways to MacGuiness.

The steward wore no expression at all. Or, no, that wasn't quite right. He looked like a man who was both insufferably pleased and afraid of what might happen if he admitted it. Honor captured his gaze and held it for a single, fulminating moment while Henke worked on her face, and he cleared his throat and looked away quickly, busying himself with the garment bag.

It opened to reveal Honor's best dress tunic and trousers, and she cocked an imperious eyebrow at him.

"Commander Henke said you might require a change, Ma'am. And, of course, I knew—" MacGuiness hit the verb just a bit too hard "—you'd want to look your best tonight."

"I do *not* need a pair of mother hens! And I'll thank—"

"Hold still!" A ruthless hand gripped her chin, tilting her head to the side, and the tissue muffled her voice as it made a final swipe across her lips. Henke cocked her own head to consider her work, then nodded. "There! Uniform, Mac?"

"Of course, Ma'am."

Honor gave up and shoved Nimitz into the crook of MacGuiness's elbow, then shed her undress tunic even as she toed off her boots. For the first time, she felt an edge of body consciousness in MacGuiness's presence, but he seemed unaware of any reason she should be remotely uncomfortable, and she grinned wryly to herself. All those years in gyms and dressing rooms, working out with men, throwing them around the salle—and being thrown *by* them—and tonight she was suddenly aware that she wasn't just "one of the guys" after all!

She stepped out of her trousers, suppressing an urge to turn her back on MacGuiness, and accepted the fresh pair with the gold stripes up their outer seams.

"Oh, *damn!*" Henke sighed as she sealed the trousers. "There's makeup on your collar, Honor. Hold still!"

Honor froze, and Henke's fingers worked busily with the soft roll of her white blouse's turtleneck.

"There!" the exec said again. "Just be careful not to fuss with it and disarrange anything."

"Yes, Ma'am," Honor murmured meekly, and Henke's lips quivered as she took the tunic from MacGuiness' unencumbered hand and helped her into it.

"Get us moving again," Honor went on, pulling her boots back on. She bloused her trouser legs properly and sealed the tunic, and the lift began to move once more. She accepted a comb from MacGuiness and dragged it through her hair with ruthless dispatch while she watched the steward stuff her discarded clothing into the garment bag, and laughter glinted in her eyes.

A soft tone warned of their impending arrival, and she jammed the comb into a pocket and tugged the hem of her tunic down. Nimitz leapt up onto her shoulder and purred in her ear while she adjusted her beret, and there was just time for a quick, approving inspection of her reflection in the polished lift wall before the words "BOAT BAY ONE" flashed on the location display.

"Thank you—both of you," she said from the side of her mouth, and stepped through the door as it opened.

"Ah, there you are, Dame Honor!" The shadow of tension on Sarnow's dark face betrayed his own surprise at their abrupt summons to the flagship, and Honor wondered for a moment if he was being sarcastic. But he smiled, and his next words took any possible rebuke out of his comment. "I'm surprised you managed to get back aboard so quickly with so little warning."

He nodded towards the open pinnace hatch, and Captain Corell ducked through it. Honor followed the chief of staff, and Sarnow was hard on her heels. They settled into their seats while the flight engineer closed the hatch, made a quick but thorough visual inspection of the seal, and spoke into the boom mike of her com headset.

"Hatch secure," she told the flight deck, and Honor settled Nimitz in her lap as the departure light flashed on the cabin's forward bulkhead. The mechanical latches retracted, a puff of thrusters drifted them clear of the buffers, and then a harder surge of power—imperceptible through the pinnace's onboard grav generator—sent them streaking out of the bay like a scalded cat.

Auxiliary thrusters carried the pinnace's impeller safety perimeter clear of the ship, the pilot lit off his main drive, and Sarnow gave a tiny sigh of relief as the small craft went instantly to over two hundred gravities of acceleration.

Honor glanced across at him, and he smiled and tapped his chrono.

"I always hate being the last to arrive for a conference," he admitted, "but unless Admiral Konstanzakis' pilot's figured out how to take a pinnace into hyper, we should beat her by at least five minutes. Good work, Captain. I never thought you'd make it back aboard in time."

"I tried not to let any snow melt under my feet, Sir," she said with a small, answering smile, and he chuckled.

"So I noticed." He cocked an eye at his chief of staff, but Captain Corell was busy consulting a memo pad in her lap, and he leaned a bit closer to his flag captain and lowered his voice.

"And may I also say, Lady Harrington," he went on in an admirably grave tone, "that I've never seen you look more becoming."

Honor's eyebrows flew up at the totally unexpected—and unprecedented—compliment, and his smile turned into a mustache-quivering grin.

"I see supper agreed with you," he said even more softly . . . and winked at her.

• CHAPTER SIXTEEN

Honor's own sense of urgency echoed around her as she stepped into the late-night bustle of HMS *Gryphon*. No warship ever truly shuts down, but even spacers tend to retain a sense of "day" and "night" as dictated by their clocks. It may not make much difference to the people who actually have the watch at any given moment, but it is too easy for the human animal to lose its temporal place without some sort of agreed upon referent. And as a general rule, a flagship's "day" is defined as "the Admiral is up." When he retires, so do most of his staff and its myriad attachments, and the entire tempo of the flagship seems to relax with an appreciable breath of gratitude.

But no one was relaxed tonight. *Gryphon's* boat bays were brilliant with light and busy with side parties as flag officer after flag officer arrived aboard, and Honor didn't envy her boat bay control officer. Juggling that many small craft was a herculean task, even with the docking capacity of a superdreadnought.

She led Captain Corell out the hatch of *Nike's* pinnace behind Sarnow and hid a smile, despite her own tension, as the lieutenant assigned to greet them snapped to attention. The side party followed her example, bosun's pipes trilled, Marines saluted—nothing could have been more punctilious, but the lieutenant's harassed expression suggested another pinnace was coming in right behind them . . . as soon as *their* boat got out of the way, that was.

"Welcome aboard, Admiral Sarnow. Lady Harrington. Captain Corell. I'm Lieutenant Eisenbrei. Admiral Parks extends his compliments and asks you to follow me to the briefing room, please."

"Thank you, Lieutenant." Sarnow gestured for her to lead the way, and Honor could almost hear Eisenbrei's sigh of relief as she shepherded them out of the boat bay gallery. Another lieutenant tried not to hover too obviously to one side, and Eisenbrei gave her colleague a nod and made a small shooing gesture towards the gallery even as *Nike*'s pinnace undocked. The other lieutenant vanished at a trot, Eisenbrei led her charges briskly away, and Honor managed—somehow—not to laugh as Corell looked her way and rolled her eyes heavenward.

Gryphon's main briefing room was crowded, despite its size, and heads turned to glance at the newcomers as Honor and Corell followed Sarnow through the hatch. There were dozens of admirals, commodores, and senior captains, all glittering with braid, and Honor extended a silent but profound thanks to Henke and MacGuiness as she took in the hectares of dress uniforms awaiting her.

She brought her cybernetic eye's magnification up slightly, studying the assembly while they walked toward it, and she saw her own puzzlement and curiosity on most of those faces. Most but not all—and those which didn't look puzzled wore masked expressions that looked ominously like anxiety. Even fear.

Admiral Parks was bent over a holo display with a commodore—probably Commodore Capra, the chief of staff, she thought, noting the braided aiguilette hanging from his left shoulder—but he, too, looked up at their entry. Looked up and raised a hand, interrupting Capra in mid-sentence.

His eyes narrowed as he straightened. The distance was too great for anyone without the advantage of Honor's enhanced vision to notice it, but those cold, blue eyes clung to her for just a moment, and the lips below them tightened. Then Parks moved his gaze to Sarnow, and his mouth tightened still further before he made it relax.

Honor snapped her eye back into normal vision and schooled her own face into careful nonexpression, but mental warning signals buzzed, and Nimitz shifted uneasily. That wasn't the way an admiral looked at someone he was happy to see, and her memory replayed her week-old supper conversation with Henke. Parks didn't seem any too pleased with Admiral Sarnow, either, but he'd looked at Honor first. Did that mean she was somehow the source of his unhappiness with the admiral?

Sarnow, at least, seemed unfazed by any potential hostility. He led Honor and Corell across the deck to Parks, and his voice was respectful but relaxed when he spoke.

"Admiral Parks."

"Admiral Sarnow." Parks returned the greeting in a tone which sounded just a bit too normal against the background of an emergency fleet conference, but he extended his hand. Sarnow shook it, then nodded to his subordinates.

"Allow me to introduce Captain Harrington, Sir. I believe you've already met Captain Corell."

"Yes, I have," Parks replied, nodding at Corell, but his eyes were on Honor, and she sensed a tiny hesitation before he extended his hand to her turn. "Welcome aboard *Gryphon*, Lady Harrington."

"Thank, you, Sir."

"Please, find your seats," Parks went on, returning his attention to Sarnow. "I expect Admirals Konstanzakis and Miazawa momentarily, and I'd like to get started as soon as they arrive."

"Of course, Sir." Sarnow nodded, but waved his subordinates on toward the huge conference table while he paused for a word with an admiral Honor didn't recognize. She and Corell found the chairs marked with their names, and Honor glanced around to confirm that no one was immediately at hand.

"What was that all about, Ernie?" she murmured softly, and Corell mirrored her own precaution with a quick glance, then shrugged.

"I don't know," she replied. Honor cocked an eyebrow,

and the other captain shrugged again. "Really, Honor, I *don't* know. All I know for sure is that the Admiral was getting upset with Admiral Parks ab—"

She broke off as another officer slid into the chair beside hers, and her silent eyes begged Honor not to pursue it.

Honor nodded. This was neither the time nor the place, but if there *was* a problem, she intended to find out what it was. And soon.

At that moment, Admiral Konstanzakis walked—jogged, really—through the hatch with Admiral Miazawa. Konstanzakis was barely shorter than Honor, and she was also much heavier-boned and stockier. She probably out-massed Honor by at least fifty percent, whereas Miazawa was barely a hundred and sixty centimeters tall and couldn't have weighed much more than fifty kilos. They looked like a mastiff and a Pekingese, but the sudden increase in background tension as their peers realized everyone had now arrived depressed any temptation to humor.

Admiral Parks moved to his own place and watched the late arrivals find their chairs, then rapped lightly—and superfluously—on the tabletop and cleared his throat.

"Thank you all for coming so promptly, ladies and gentlemen. I apologize for summoning you on such short notice. As you've no doubt surmised, I wouldn't have done so without a most pressing reason. Vincent?"

He nodded to Commodore Capra, and the chief of staff stood.

"Ladies and gentlemen, we've just received an urgent priority dispatch from the Admiralty." The tension clicked even higher, and he keyed a message board to life and began to read.

"To Commanding Officer, Hancock Station, repeated to all station and task force commanders. From Admiral Sir Thomas Caparelli, First Space Lord. Reports have been received here of widespread and apparently orchestrated incidents along the outer arc of the Alliance's frontline systems. While PRH involvement cannot be confirmed in all instances, units of the People's Navy have been positively—repeat, positively—identified in three incursions into Alliance space at Candor, Klein Station, and Zuckerman."

A soft sound ran around the table, a sound of collectively indrawn breath, but Capra continued reading in the same level voice.

"At this time, we have no confirmed reports of exchanges of fire between RMN and PN units, but the PN force which violated Zuckerman's territorial limit extensively damaged one quadrant's outer sensor platforms before withdrawing. In addition, member systems of the Alliance have suffered both material and personnel losses in incidents which cannot be attributed to any positively identified force. To date, confirmed RMN losses to parties unknown consist of destroyers *Turbulent* and *Havoc* and the complete destruction of Convoy Mike-Golf-Nineteen."

This time the sound wasn't of indrawn breath. It was a growl, throaty and ugly, and Admiral Parks' face tightened as he heard it.

"At this moment, ONI is unable to suggest with any confidence a motive which might lead the People's Republic to seek a deliberate confrontation," Capra went on. "Nonetheless, in light of positive identification of PN involvement at Candor, Klein, and Zuckerman, we see no alternative but to assume at least the possibility—repeat, possibility—of PRH responsibility for all such incidents. Accordingly, you are instructed to take all reasonable and prudent precautions within your area of responsibility. You are cautioned to avoid any actions which might unilaterally escalate or exacerbate the situation, but your primary concern must be the security of your command area and the protection of our allies."

The commodore paused for just a moment, then continued in a flatter, deeper voice.

"This dispatch is to be considered a war warning. You are authorized and directed to go to Readiness State Alpha Two under Rules of Engagement Baker. God bless

you all. Signed, Admiral Sir Thomas Caparelli, First
Space Lord, Royal Manticoran Navy, for Her Majesty
the Queen."

Capra switched off the message board and laid it gently on
the conference table as he sank back into his chair amid an
absolute silence. Alpha Two was only one step short of open
hostilities, and ROE Baker authorized any squadron commander to open fire, even preemptively, if he believed his
command was under threat. By repeating those orders to
every station commander, Admiral Caparelli had just formally put the trigger to the war every RMN officer had
feared for decades in the hands of some junior grade captain
commanding a light cruiser flotilla picketing some nameless
star system in the back of beyond, and an icy chill danced up
and down Honor's spine.

She swallowed and felt the cold, hollow fear deep in
her belly. Unlike the majority of the officers at this table,
she'd seen recent, brutal combat. She understood exactly
what that message meant; they didn't. Not really. They
couldn't without her own experience.

"Under the circumstances," Admiral Parks' voice broke
the hush, "an immediate reconsideration of our own posture and responsibilities is in order. Particularly since at
least some of the incursions by 'unknown forces' almost
certainly account for the Caliphate Navy's losses in
Zanzibar." He gazed around the table, then leaned back
and folded his arms with deliberate calm.

"Along with the message Commodore Capra just read,
we've received a dispatch detailing additional forces
which Admiral Caparelli is deploying to Hancock. In
addition to sufficient heavy and light cruisers to bring all
of our screening squadrons and flotillas up to full
strength, the Admiralty is sending us the Eighteenth
Battle Squadron under Admiral Danislav." One or two
faces showed a tinge of relief, and Parks smiled thinly.

"Unfortunately, it will require time to concentrate
Admiral Danislav's dreadnoughts. Admiral Caparelli estimates that we cannot expect their arrival here for a
minimum of three weeks.

"At the same time," the admiral went on, ignoring any fresh signs of dismay among his listeners, "our light cruisers have continued to picket the Seaford Nine approaches. While our patrols have reported the recent arrival of a third superdreadnought squadron there, they have *not* reported any major changes in the PN's operational patterns. Since the only reported incidents in this region have been the attacks on Zanzibaran naval units, in the course of which the Peeps—if, indeed, they're responsible—have very carefully hidden any sign of complicity, the lack of any activity on Admiral Rollins' part may indicate they aren't yet ready for precipitate action in our command area. Or—" he bared his teeth in a humorless smile "—those same signs *could* indicate they plan to launch a major attack in our area and are simply being careful to deny us any clue as to their intentions."

Someone made a sound that was more than a sigh but not quite a groan, and Parks' grim smile flickered with a hint of true amusement.

"Come now, ladies and gentlemen! If the answer were easy to guess, anyone could play." That won an uneasy mutter of laughter, and he unfolded his arms and propped an elbow on the conference table.

"Better. Now, we're all aware of the sensitivity of our command area. I'm certain the Admiralty is, as well. Unfortunately, we're here, and Their Lordships *aren't*. Moreover, they're going to have to cope with all the *other* 'sensitive' areas, so I think we must assume that what we have now, plus BatRon Eighteen, are all we're going to have if the missile goes up. Assuming that to be the case, what are our options?"

He raised his eyebrows and scanned his flag officers. There was another moment of silence, and then Mark Sarnow raised an index finger in an attention-gathering gesture. Parks' mouth might have tightened just a bit, but he nodded to the rear admiral.

"I'd like to renew my suggestion for a forward deployment against Seaford, Sir Yancey." Sarnow picked his words—and tone—with care. "While it's true our cruiser pickets should spot any movement of their forces out of the system, they'll still have to report to us before we can act. That probably won't matter if the Peeps move against Hancock, since our cruisers should get here first and alert us. But if they strike at one of our allies in the region, our interception window will be much narrower. In fact, if they move against Yorik, we'd have virtually no chance of intercepting them short of the system."

Parks started to reply, but Admiral Konstanzakis spoke up first.

"With all due respect, Sir Yancey, I still feel that's the wrong move," she said bluntly. "Admiral Caparelli specifically instructed us to avoid any unilateral escalation. I hardly see what else we could call moving the entire task force to the edge of the Seaford territorial limit!"

"Admiral Caparelli's dispatch took a week to get here, Dame Christa, and the information on which it's based is older still." Sarnow turned his head to meet the admiral's brown eyes. "It's entirely possible—even probable—that the situation has worsened in that time. Under the circumstances, I believe the need to adopt 'reasonable and prudent' measures by insuring Admiral Rollins and his ships can't leave Seaford without our being able to intercept them outweighs the possibility that our actions might be seen as provocative, especially by the people who seem to be pushing the crisis in the first place."

"But you're talking about blockading Seaford," Admiral Miazawa protested. "That's not just a provocation; it's an outright act of war."

"I'm not suggesting a blockade." Sarnow kept his mellow tenor reasonable, but a certain undeniable edge crept into it. "What I *am* suggesting, Sir, is that we concentrate our force in company with the pickets already watching the system, not that we interfere with their movements in any way. But the unpalatable fact is that once a fleet goes into hyper, we can only guess where it's going to come out again. In my opinion, the only way to be positive that we can deliver our entire wall of battle, concentrated and ready for action at need, is to keep it in such close proximity to *their* wall that they can't possibly elude us."

"Calmly, ladies and gentlemen." Admiral Parks held Sarnow's eyes for a moment, then continued.

"Admiral Sarnow has made an excellent point. So, unfortunately, have Admiral Konstanzakis and Admiral Miazawa, which illustrates the impossibility of forming detailed plans in the absence of concrete information. By the same token, however, our out-system sensor platforms have detected no sign that the Peeps have been picketing Hancock, so it would seem Admiral Rollins doesn't have such information on *us*—and the fact that they can't see our main force sitting on their doorstep leaves Rollins ignorant of our dispositions. In which case, he's probably playing the same sort of guessing game *I* am."

He smiled another wintry smile, and Konstanzakis snorted in wry agreement.

"If we adopt your forward deployment, Admiral Sarnow, we'll have the advantage of knowing exactly what their force *at Seaford Nine* may do and being in position to engage it at a time of our choice. That's a major plus. On the debit side, Admiral Konstanzakis is correct about the potential for escalation. Perhaps even more importantly, concentrating to watch the force we *know* about would leave nothing here to protect Hancock—or any of our allies in the region—should the Peeps run in a *second* force. If all of our ships of the wall are tied down watching Seaford Nine, they could snap up any or all of our allies with relatively light forces, in which case Seaford would have become a magnet to suck us out of position at the critical moment. Correct?"

"The possibility would certainly exist, Sir," Sarnow conceded. "But if the Peeps committed weak forces to such an operation, they'd face almost certain destruction if they *were* intercepted. If they pay the kind of attention to Murphy's Law I'd expect of someone with their experience, I strongly doubt they'll try for finesse or fancy coordination across that many light-years."

"So you believe that if they move in this region at all, they'll do so in force from Seaford."

"More or less, Sir. I won't deny that they might choose to do otherwise, but if they do, I believe they'll commit a force which in their opinion would be sufficient to take us on in its own right. Under those circumstances, I feel it would still be better to cover our allies with light pickets while we concentrate off Seaford. If word of an attack elsewhere comes in, we should then move in and crush the Seaford force *before* responding to any other threats. In the long run, the crucial objective must be to eliminate or whittle down their overall tonnage advantage by bringing them to action on terms most advantageous to us as quickly and decisively as possible."

"You sound like we're already at war, Admiral!" Miazawa snapped.

"For all we know, Sir, by now we *are*," Sarnow replied, and Miazawa's nostrils flared.

"That will be all, gentlemen," Parks said softly. He regarded both men for some seconds, then sighed and rubbed his forehead.

"In many ways, Admiral Sarnow, I would actually prefer to adopt your proposal." He sounded as if the admission surprised him, but then he shook his head. "Unfortunately, I believe the suggestion that we avoid further escalation also has merit. And unlike you, I can't quite free myself of the suspicion that, Murphy's Law or no, they might be attempting to suck us out of position to strike with light forces behind us. Moreover, my first and foremost responsibility is to protect the civilian populations and territorial integrity of our allies. For all of those reasons, I'm afraid the idea of a forward deployment is out of the question."

Sarnow's mouth tightened briefly, but then he nodded and leaned back in his chair. Admiral Parks gazed at him a moment longer, then let his eyes trail across Honor's face before he continued.

"At the moment, and barring any further reinforcement of Seaford Nine, we have at least parity with the known enemy forces in our area. As Admiral Sarnow points out, however, a sudden lunge against Yorik could slip past us unintercepted, which would make our margin of superiority moot. An attack against Alizon or Zanzibar, on the other hand, would have to move almost directly across us here, giving us an excellent opportunity to intercept it short of its objective.

"Accordingly," he drew a deep breath and committed himself, "I intend to dispatch Admiral Konstanzakis' and Admiral Miazawa's superdreadnought squadrons and Admiral Tolliver's dreadnoughts to Yorik. That will preposition twenty-four ships of the wall to cover our most vulnerable responsibility in the event that someone does slip past us, and will also protect Yorik against an attack by lighter forces inserted into the area for that purpose.

"Admiral Kostmeyer," he turned to the CO of Battle Squadron Nine, "you'll take your dreadnoughts to Zanzibar. I'm not comfortable about the losses the Caliph's units have been taking, and with so much of our strength at Yorik, they'll be the next most exposed target."

Kostmeyer nodded, not entirely happily, and Parks smiled thinly.

"I won't leave you quite alone out at the end of your limb, Admiral. I intend to recall and reassemble Admiral Tyrel's battlecruisers and send them all to join you there as quickly as possible. Deploy your sensor platforms and use those battlecruisers to patrol as aggressively as you like. If an attack comes at you in overwhelming force, yield the system but remain concentrated and in contact with them if at all possible until the remainder of the task force can come to your assistance."

"*Yield* the system, Sir?" Kostmeyer couldn't quite keep the surprise out of her voice, and Parks smiled frostily.

"It's our responsibility to protect Zanzibar, Admiral, and we will. But, as Admiral Sarnow says, we must engage them as a coherent whole, and moving back in to retake the system with our full strength would probably result in less actual damage to its people and infrastructure than would a desperate but unsuccessful defense of it."

Honor chewed the inside of her lip and reached up to stroke Nimitz's ears. She could not but respect the moral courage it took for any commander to order one of his admirals to voluntarily surrender an allied star system to the enemy. Even if Parks was correct and his concentrated forces sufficed to take it back undamaged, his actions would provoke a furor, and the consequences to his career could be catastrophic. But resolution or no, the idea of splitting their forces in the face of potential attack appalled her. All her instincts insisted that Sarnow was right and Parks was wrong about the best way to bring the enemy to action, but perhaps even more frighteningly, that disposed of all thirty-two of Hancock Station's ships of the wall. In fact, it disposed of *everything* . . . except Battlecruiser Squadron Five.

"In the meantime," Parks continued evenly, as if he'd heard her thoughts, "you, Admiral Sarnow, will remain here in Hancock with your squadron as the core of a light task group. Your function will be to cover this base against attack, but, even more importantly, Hancock will continue to function as the linchpin of our entire deployment. I'll leave detailed orders for Admiral Danislav, but for your planning information, I intend to hold his battle squadron here, as well. The two of you will be well placed as our central information relay and to cover Alizon against direct attack, and I'll detach another light cruiser flotilla to thicken up our Seaford pickets. That should enable them both to retain sufficient strength to shadow the enemy as a precaution against deception course changes and to alert you in time for you to move to reinforce Admiral Kostmeyer should Haven attack Zanzibar. I realize Admiral Kostmeyer will be much more poorly placed to come to *your* assistance, but so long as Admiral Rollins doesn't know we've pulled any substantial forces out of Hancock, he'll have to scout the system before committing himself to attack it, and that should alert us in time to bring one or both of the detached forces back to Hancock."

He paused, watching Sarnow's face, then went on quietly.

"I realize I'm leaving you exposed here, Admiral. Even after Admiral Danislav's arrival, you'll be heavily outnumbered if Admiral Rollins' units slip by us before we can redeploy to cover you, and I'd prefer not to put you in that kind of position. But I don't think I can avoid risking you. The overriding function of this base is to protect our allies and maintain control of this general area. If we lose Zanzibar, Alizon, and Yorik, Hancock will be effectively isolated and cut off from relief, in which case it loses both its value and its viability, anyway."

"I understand, Sir." Sarnow's clipped voice was free of rancor, yet Honor noted that he hadn't said he *agreed* with Parks.

"Very well, then." Parks pinched the bridge of his nose and looked at his staff ops officer. "All right, Mark, let's look at the nuts and bolts."

"Yes, Sir. First, Admiral, I think we have to consider how best to distribute our available screening units between Admiral Kostmeyer and the rest of our wall. After that—"

Captain Hurston went on speaking in crisp, professional tones, but Honor hardly noticed. She sat back in her chair, hearing the details and recording them for future reference but not really listening to them, and she felt Captain Corell's matching stiffness beside her.

Parks was making a mistake. For the best of reasons and not without the support of logic, but a mistake. She felt it, sensed it the same way she sensed the sudden fusion of a complicated tactical problem into a single, coherent unity.

She could be wrong. In fact, she hoped—prayed—that she was. But it didn't feel that way. And, she wondered, just how much of Admiral Parks' final decision was based on logic and how much on the desire, conscious or unconscious, to leave Admiral Mark Sarnow and his bothersome flag captain safely on a back burner, unable to upset his peace of mind?

• CHAPTER SEVENTEEN

The faces in *Nike's* briefing room were unhappy, and Honor leaned back in her chair as Commander Houseman unburdened himself.

" . . . realize the gravity of the situation, Admiral Sarnow, but surely Sir Yancey must realize we can't possibly hold this system against an attack in force! We don't *begin* to have the firepower, and—"

"That's enough, Commander." There was no expression at all in Mark Sarnow's voice, but Houseman closed his mouth with a snap, and the admiral bestowed a wintry smile upon the assembled commodores, captains, and staff officers of what was about to become Task Group Hancock 001.

"I asked for your frank opinions, ladies and gentlemen, and I want them. But let us stick to the relevant, if you please. Whether or not our orders are the best possible ones is beside the point. Our concern has to be making them *work*. Correct?"

"Absolutely, Sir." Commodore Van Slyke gave his chief of staff a rare public look of disapproval and nodded emphatically.

"Good." Sarnow ignored Houseman's flush and looked at Commodore Banton, his senior divisional commander. "Have you and Commander Turner completed that study Ernie and I discussed with you Monday, Isabella?"

"Just about, Sir, and it looks like Captain Corell and Dame Honor are right. The sims say it should work, anyway, but we've got to nail down exactly what fire control modifications will be required, and the availability numbers are still up in the air. I'm afraid

Gryphon has other things on her mind than our data requests just now." Banton allowed herself a smile that matched her admiral's, and one or two people actually chuckled.

"At the moment, Sir, I'd have to say that, unless Admiral Parks changes his mind and takes them with him, there should be enough pods to pull it off. I gave Captain Corell our latest figures when we came aboard this evening, and Commander Turner is working out the software changes now."

Sarnow glanced at Corell, who nodded in confirmation. A few people—notably Commander Houseman—looked skeptical, but Honor felt a trickle of satisfaction. The concept might be a tactical antique, yet its very outdatedness should keep the Peeps from expecting it in the first place.

A parasite pod was nothing more than a drone slaved to the fire control of the ship towing it astern on a tractor. Each pod mounted several, usually a half-dozen or so, single-shot missile launchers similar to those LACs used. The idea was simple—to link the pod with the ship's internal tubes and launch a greater number of birds in a single salvo in order to saturate an opponent's defenses—but they hadn't been used in a fleet engagement for eighty T-years because advances in antimissile defenses had rendered them ineffective.

The old pods' launchers had lacked the powerful mass-drivers which gave warships' missiles their initial impetus. That, in turn, gave them a lower initial velocity, and since their missiles had exactly the same drives as any other missile, they couldn't make up the velocity differential unless the ship-launched birds were stepped down to less than optimal power settings. If you didn't step your shipboard missiles down, you lost much of the saturation effect because the velocity discrepancy effectively split your launch into two separate salvos. Yet if you *did* step them down, the slower speed of your entire launch not only gave the enemy more time to evade and adjust his ECM, but also gave his active defenses extra tracking and engagement time.

It was the tracking time that was the real killer, for point defense had improved enormously over the last century. Neither LAC launchers nor the old-style pods had been able to overcome the advantage it now held (which was one reason the Admiralty had stopped all new LAC construction twenty Manticoran years ago). Moreover, the RMN's data on the People's Navy's point defense, available in no small part thanks to Captain Dame Honor Harrington, indicated that the Peeps' missile defenses, while poorer than Manticore's, were still more than sufficient to eat old-style pod salvos for breakfast.

But the Weapons Development Board, not without opposition from its then head, Lady Sonja Hemphill, had resurrected the pods and given them a new and heavier punch. Hemphill rejected the entire concept as "retrograde," but her successor at the WDB had pushed the project energetically, and Honor couldn't quite see the logic behind Hemphill's objections. Given her vocal advocacy of material-based tactics, Honor would have expected her to embrace the pods with enthusiasm . . . unless it was simply that something inside the admiral equated "old" weapon systems with "inherently inferior" ones.

As far as Honor was concerned, an idea's age didn't necessarily invalidate it—especially not with the new launchers, whose development Hemphill herself had overseen. Of course, Hemphill hadn't intended them to be used in something as ancient as pods. She'd been looking for a way to make LACs effective once more as part of the tactical approach her critics called the "Sonja Swarm." The new launchers were far more expensive than traditional LAC launchers, which was the official core of Hemphill's opposition to "wasting" them in pods, but expense hadn't bothered her where the LACs were concerned. Building one with the new launchers pushed its price tag up to about a quarter of a destroyer's, especially with the fire control upgrades to take full advantage of the launchers' capabilities, yet Hemphill had lobbied hard for the resumption of LAC construction, and she'd succeeded.

Like most of her *jeune école* fellows, she still regarded LACs as expendable, single-salvo assets (which didn't endear her to their crews), but at least she'd seen the virtue in increasing their effectiveness while they lasted. The fact that it also gave them a better chance of survival was probably immaterial to her thinking, but that was all right with Honor. She didn't care why Horrible Hemphill did something, on the rare occasions when it was the *right* something. And however loudly the cost effectiveness analysts might complain, Honor had a pretty shrewd notion how LAC skippers felt about the notion of living through an engagement.

But the point at hand was that the same improvements could be applied to parasite pods, and, despite Hemphill's objections, they had been. Of course, the new pods—with ten tubes each, not six—were intended for ships of the wall, which had plenty of redundant fire control to manage them, not battlecruisers. But it sounded like Turner was finding the answer to that, and their missiles were actually heavier than the standard ship-to-ship birds. With the new lightweight mass-drivers BuShips had perfected, their performance could equal or even exceed that of normal, ship-launched missiles, and their warheads were more destructive to boot. The pods were clumsy, of course, and towing them did unfortunate things to a warship's inertial compensator field, which held down maximum accelerations by twenty-five percent or so. They were also vulnerable to proximity soft kills, since they carried neither sidewalls nor radiation shielding of their own, but if they got their shots off before they were killed, that hardly mattered.

"Good, Isabella." Sarnow's voice recalled Honor to the conversation at hand. "If we can get him to leave them here, we can put at least five on tow behind each of our battlecruisers—six, for the newer ships. Even the heavy cruisers can manage two or three." He smiled thinly. "It may not help in a long engagement, but our initial salvos should make anyone on the other side wonder if they've run into dreadnoughts instead of battlecruisers!"

Unpleasant smiles were shared about the table, but Houseman wasn't quite finished, though he was careful about his tone when he spoke up again.

"No doubt you're correct, Admiral, but it's the idea of a long engagement that worries me. With the repair base to protect, we won't be able to mount a real mobile defense—they can always pin us down by going straight for the base—and once the pods are exhausted, your battlecruisers are going to find themselves hard-pressed by ships of the wall, Sir."

Honor's eyes narrowed as she examined Houseman's face. It took nerve for a commander to keep arguing after two different flag officers, one his own immediate CO, had just more or less told him to shut up. What bothered her was where Houseman's nerve came from. Was it the courage of his convictions, or was it arrogance? The fact that she disliked the man made it hard to be objective, and she warned herself to give him the benefit of the doubt.

Sarnow seemed less charitably inclined.

"I realize that, Mr. Houseman," he replied. "But at the possible expense of boring you, let me repeat that the purpose of this conference is to *solve* our problems, not simply to recapitulate them."

Houseman seemed to shrink into himself, hunching down in his chair with a total lack of expression as Van Slyke gave him an even colder glance, and someone cleared his throat.

"Admiral Sarnow?"

"Yes, Commodore Prentis?"

"We do have one other major advantage, Sir," Battlecruiser Division 53's CO pointed out. "All our sensor platforms have the new FTL systems, and with *Nike* and *Achilles* to coordinate—"

The commodore shrugged, and Sarnow nodded sharply. *Nike* was one of the first ships built with the new grav pulse technology from the keel out, but *Achilles* had received the same system in her last refit, and their pulse transmitters gave both battlecruisers the ability to send FTL messages to any ship with gravitic sensors. They had to shut down their own wedges long enough to complete any transmission, since no sensor could pick message pulses out of the background "noise" of a warship's drive signature, but they would give Sarnow a command and control "reach" the Peeps couldn't hope to match.

"Jack has an excellent point, Admiral, if you'll pardon my saying so." This time Van Slyke didn't even glance at Houseman as he spoke—which suggested there was going to be a lively discussion when they returned to Van Slyke's flagship. "If we can't match them toe-to-toe, we'll just have to use our footwork to make up the difference."

"Agreed." Sarnow leaned back and rubbed his mustache. "Do any other advantages we've got—or that we can create—spring to mind?"

Honor cleared her throat quietly, and Sarnow cocked an eyebrow at her.

"Yes, Dame Honor?"

"One thing that's occurred to me, Sir, is those *Erebus*-class minelayers. Do we know what Admiral Parks intends to do with them?"

"Ernie?" Sarnow passed the question to his chief of staff, and Captain Corell ran one fine-boned hand through her hair while she scrolled through data on her memo pad. She reached the end and looked up with a headshake.

"There's nothing in the flagship's current download, Sir. Of course, we haven't received their finalized dump yet. They're still thinking things over, just like us."

"It might be a good idea to ask about them, Sir," Honor suggested, and Sarnow nodded in agreement. The minelayers weren't officially assigned to Hancock—they'd simply been passing through on their way to Reevesport when Parks read Admiral Caparelli's dispatch and short-stopped them. It was probably little more than an instinctive reaction, but if he could be convinced to hold them here indefinitely . . .

"Assuming we can get Admiral Parks to steal them for us, how were you thinking of using them, Captain?" Commodore Banton asked. "I suppose we could mine the approaches to the base, but how effective would it really be? Surely the Peeps would be watching for mines when they finally closed on the base."

The objection made sense, since the mines were simply old-fashioned bomb-pumped lasers. They were cheap but good for only a single shot each, and their accuracy was less than outstanding, which made them most effective when employed en masse against ships moving at low velocities. That meant they were usually emplaced for area coverage of relatively immobile targets like wormhole junctions, planets, or orbital bases . . . where, as Banton had just pointed out, the Peeps would expect to see them. But putting them where the Peeps expected wasn't what Honor had in mind.

"Actually, Ma'am, I've been looking at the drive specs on the layers, and we might be able to use them more advantageously than that."

"Oh?" Banton cocked her head—consideringly, not in challenge—and Honor nodded.

"Yes, Ma'am. The *Erebus*-class ships are fast—almost as fast as a battlecruiser—and they're configured for rapid, mass mine emplacement. If we could make the Peeps think they *are* battlecruisers and operate them with the rest of our force, then kick the mines out in the Peeps' path. . ."

She let her voice trail off suggestively, and Banton gave a sudden, fierce snort of laughter.

"I like it, Admiral!" she told Sarnow. "It's sneaky as hell, and it might just work."

"Assuming the Peeps don't shoot at them and give the show away," Commodore Prentis observed. "Minelayers don't have much in the way of point defense, and their sidewalls aren't much, either. You'd be asking their captains to run an awful risk, Dame Honor."

"We could cover them fairly well against missile attack by tying them into our divisional tac nets, Sir," Honor countered. "There are only five of them. We could include one in each division's net and hook the odd man out into *Nike*'s and *Agamemnon*'s net. The Peeps won't be able to tell exactly where our defensive fire is coming from, so they shouldn't be able to ID them at any extended range. And for us to make the mines work, we'd have to use them before we got to beam range, anyway."

"And if they spot the mines?" Prentis was thinking aloud, not arguing, and Honor allowed herself a small shrug.

"Their fire control's a hundred percent passive, Sir. They don't have active emission signatures, and they're mighty small radar targets. I doubt the Peeps could spot them at much more than a million klicks, especially if they're busy chasing *us*."

Prentis nodded with growing enthusiasm, and Sarnow gestured to Corell.

"Make a note of Dame Honor's suggestion, Ernie. I'll float the idea to Sir Yancey; you get hold of Commodore Capra. Bug the hell out of him if you have to, but I want authorization to use those ships in the event of an attack on Hancock."

"Yes, Sir." Corell tapped at her memo pad, and the admiral tilted his chair back and swiveled slowly from side to side.

"All right. Let's assume we can steal the minelayers from Reevesport and that we can talk Admiral Parks into leaving us enough parasite pods for at least the opening broadsides. I don't see any option but to hold our main striking power in a central position—right here with the base, probably—to allow us to respond to a threat from any direction. At the same time, I want to go on concealing the existence of our pulse transmitter technology. I'm sure—" he allowed himself a wry smile "—Their Lordships would appreciate it if we can manage it, at any rate. But that means we've got to give the Peeps something they can see to explain how we can know where they are. We're not going to have as many light units as I'd like for that, but I think we're going to have to split them up as pickets."

Heads nodded, and he let his chair snap back upright.

"Commodore Van Slyke, your squadron's our next heaviest tactical unit, so we'll have to keep you concentrated with the battlecruisers. Ernie," he turned to his chief of staff once more, "I want you and Joe to figure the most economical way to use the light cruisers and tin-cans for perimeter coverage."

"Yes, Sir. We'll do our best, but there's no way we can get complete coverage with so few units for a sphere that size."

"I know. Do your best, and concentrate on the most likely approach vectors from Seaford. Even if we don't have anyone in position to 'spot' them the minute they arrive, we may be able to maneuver someone into position using the pulse transmitters."

Corell nodded and punched more notes into her pad, and the admiral smiled at his subordinates.

"I'm beginning to feel a little better about this," he announced. "Not a lot, you understand, but a little. Now I want you to make me feel even better by suggesting the best possible way to use the tactical resources we hope to have available. The floor is open, ladies and gentlemen."

It was quiet on *Nike*'s flag bridge. Twenty-six hours of frantic conferences and frenzied staff work had translated intentions into reality, and now Vice Admiral Sir Yancey Parks' forces moved to execute his orders.

No one seemed inclined to casual conversation as Admiral Sarnow and his staff watched the massive dreadnoughts and superdreadnoughts form up in their loose cruising formations, each ship well clear of her sisters' impeller wedges. The flag deck holo sphere blazed with the crawling fire of their light codes as their drives came on-line, and far flung necklaces of light cruisers and destroyers glowed ahead of them and on either flank, sensors probing the endless dark as they guarded their massive charges. The stronger drive signatures of heavy cruisers, still infinitely lighter than the ships of the wall, formed closer, tighter necklaces about each squadron, and the whole, enormous formation began to move, like a newborn constellation crawling across the sphere.

It was impressive, Honor thought, standing at Sarnow's elbow and staring down into the display with him. Very impressive. But all that ponderous firepower was headed *away* from them, and Battlecruiser Squadron Five's handful of emission sources seemed shrunken and forlorn as they were left to defend Hancock Station alone. She felt the chill of abandonment in her heart, and took herself sternly to task for it.

"Well, there they go," Captain Corell said quietly, and Commander Cartwright grunted agreement beside her.

"At least he left us the pods and the minelayers," the ops officer remarked after a moment, and it was Sarnow's turn to grunt. The admiral brooded down on the sphere for a long, silent minute, then sighed.

"Yes, he left them, Joe, but I don't know how much good they're going to do." He turned his back on the display, the gesture somehow deliberate and almost defiant, and looked at Honor. His mustache twitched as he smiled, but his face looked wearier and far more worn than she'd ever seen it before.

"I'm not knocking your input, Honor," he said quietly, and she nodded. He didn't omit the honorific "Dame" often. Whenever he did, she listened very carefully, for she'd learned it meant he was speaking to his tactical alter ego, not simply his flag captain.

"That was a brilliant idea about the minelayers," he went on, "and you and Ernie were right to suggest we might be able to modify our fire control to handle the pods, too. But even though Houseman may be an asshole—hell, even though he *is* an asshole—he was right, too. We may dazzle them with our footwork at the start, even get in a few good licks they don't expect. But if they bring in ships of the wall and keep coming, we're dead meat."

"We could always abandon the system, Sir," Cartwright suggested wryly. "After all, if Admiral Parks is willing to give up Zanzibar, he shouldn't have much room to complain if we make an, um, tactical withdrawal from Hancock."

"Mutinous sentiments if ever I heard them, Joe." Sarnow smiled again, tiredly, and shook his head. "And I'm afraid it's just not on. The Admiral overlooked a couple of points, you see—like how we evacuate the base personnel if we withdraw."

A deeper, colder chill touched Honor's heart, for that was a thought she'd tried hard not to consider. The ongoing expansion of Hancock's facilities had swelled the station's work force enormously, and the ungainly repair base was home to almost eleven thousand men and women. The squadron and its screening units might squeeze sixty or seventy percent of them aboard—assuming none of the ships were lost or badly damaged in action first—but only at the expense of ruinously overloading their environmental services. And even if they did, thirty or forty percent of the yard dogs would simply *have* to be left behind. And she knew one officer who would insist that it was his duty to remain if any of his people did.

"He did sort of miss out on that one, didn't he?" Captain Corell murmured, and this time Sarnow chuckled. It wasn't a very pleasant sound, but there was a germ of true humor in it, and Honor felt strangely moved after the confident front he'd projected at the squadron meetings.

"I noticed that," he agreed, and stretched his arms in an enormous yawn. "On the other hand, he had a point about the relative value of Hancock. If we lose all our allies in the area, there's not much need for a base here. More to the point, there's no way we could hold it if they set up strong blocking positions to cut us off from the rear and come at us full bore. Besides, he has to balance the possible loss of thirty or forty thousand

Manticorans in Hancock against the risk to billions of civilians in the inhabited systems we're here to defend." He shook his head. "No, I can't fault *that* part of his reasoning. It's cold, I grant you, but sometimes an admiral *has* to be cold."

"But he could have avoided it, Sir." Deferential stubbornness edged Corell's voice, and Sarnow looked her way.

"Now, now, Ernie. I'm his most junior admiral. It's easy for the low man on the totem pole to urge an aggressive response—after all, it's not his head that'll roll if his CO takes his advice and screws up. And Dame Christa was right about the potential for a collision neither side really wants."

"Maybe. But what would *you* have done in his place?" Cartwright challenged.

"Unfair supposition. I'm *not* in his place. I'd like to think I'd have taken my own advice if I were, but I can't be sure of it. Heavy lies the head that wears a vice admiral's beret, Joe."

"Nice evasive action, Sir," Cartwright said sourly, and Sarnow shrugged.

"Part of the job description, Joe. Part of the job description." He yawned again and waved a weary hand at Corell. "I need some rack time, Ernie. You and Dame Honor mind the store for me for a few hours, okay? I'll have my steward haul me out in time for that conference on defensive exercises."

"Certainly, Sir," Corell said, and Honor seconded her with a nod.

The admiral walked from the bridge without the usual springy energy Honor associated with him, and his three subordinates exchanged glances.

"There," Captain The Honorable Ernestine Corell said softly, "goes a man who just got royally screwed by his own CO."

Vice Admiral Parks stood watching his display as his detachments' vectors began to diverge, and his face was grim. He didn't like what he'd just done. If the Peeps came at Sarnow before Danislav arrived—

He suppressed the thought with a mental shudder. The nagging possibility that Sarnow had been right, that he'd persuaded himself into less than the optimal response, worried at him, but there were too many imponderables, too many variables. And Sarnow was too damned aggressive. Parks allowed himself a small snort. No wonder the rear admiral got along so well with Harrington! Well, at least if he had to delegate a possible fight to the death to one of his squadrons, he'd just picked the one with the command team best suited to the task.

Not that he expected it to help him sleep any better if it turned out he'd been wrong.

"Admiral Kostmeyer will hit the hyper limit on her vector in another twenty minutes, Sir. We'll hit it seventy-three minutes after she does."

Parks glanced up at his chief of staff's report. Capra looked even more exhausted than the admiral felt after dealing with the tidal wave of last-minute details. His dark eyes were rimmed with red, but he was freshly shaved and his uniform looked as if he'd donned it ten minutes before.

"Tell me," Parks said softly. "Do you think I made the right call?"

"Frankly, Sir?"

"Always, Vincent."

"In that case, Sir, I have to say that . . . I don't know. I just don't know." The commodore's own weariness showed in his headshake. "If the Peeps do run forces in behind Hancock to take out Yeltsin, Zanzibar, and Alizon, we'd have a hell of a time kicking them back out with Seaford threatening our rear. But by the same token, we've surrendered the initiative. We're reacting, not pushing *them*." He shrugged. "Maybe if we knew more about what's going on elsewhere we'd be in a better position to judge, but I have to tell you, Sir, I'm not happy about stripping Hancock so clean."

"Neither am I." Parks turned away from the master

display and sank into his command chair with a sigh. "But worst case, Rollins is still going to have to assume we're concentrated here until he scouts Hancock and learns positively that we're not, and he's been mighty slack about that for months. He can't move his main force out to support his scouting elements without our pickets picking up on it, and if he sends them out unsupported, Sarnow may just be able to pick them off before they get close enough to confirm that we aren't there. Even if he can't, they'll take at least three T-days each way to make the run and report back, then another three or four days for Rollins to move. We can be back from Yorik in just over three—seven from the minute one of our pickets hypers out of Seaford space to tell us his fleet is moving."

"Eight, Sir," Capra corrected quietly. "They'll have to shadow him long enough to confirm he isn't headed for Yorik before we can move."

"All right, eight." Parks shook his head wearily. "If Sarnow can just keep them occupied for four days . . . "

His voice trailed off, and he met his chief of staff's gaze almost pleadingly. Four days. It didn't sound like all that much—unless you were a squadron of battlecruisers up against four squadrons of ships of the wall.

"It's my decision," Parks said at last. "Maybe it *is* the wrong one. I hope not, but right or wrong, I've got to live with it. And at least the Peeps don't know what we're up to yet. If Danislav expedites his movement and gets here before they figure it out, he and Sarnow will have a fair chance."

"And at least they'll have the capacity to lift the construction workers out if they have to run," Capra said in that same quiet voice.

"And lift the workers out if they have to run," Parks agreed, and closed his eyes with a sigh.

The massive squadrons vanished into the trackless wastes of hyper-space, and in their wake, a frail handful of battlecruisers took up the task they'd just abandoned.

● CHAPTER EIGHTEEN

Admiral Parnell gazed out a view port as his shuttle touched down at DuQuesne Central, the main landing facility for the PRH's third largest naval base. The sprawling military facility named for the master architect of the Republic's march to empire was the primary—indeed, the only real—industry of Enki, the Barnett System's single habitable planet. Well over a million Marines and navy personnel were permanently stationed on Enki, and the system seethed with warships of every size, all guarded by massive fixed fortifications.

Parnell had studied those warships from the bridge of the heavy cruiser which delivered him to Barnett, and he'd been impressed. Yet that wasn't all he'd been, for he recognized the risk he was committing his navy to accept, and he didn't like it.

As he'd told President Harris months ago, he didn't really want to take Manticore on at all. Unlike Haven's other victims, the Star Kingdom had had both the time and the leadership to prepare. Despite the confused pacifism of some of its politicians, its people were generally united behind their stiff-necked, almost obsessively determined queen, its wealth had let it amass a frightening amount of firepower, and the sheer breadth of its alliance system faced the People's Navy with a whole new dimension of threat. Unlike Haven's past, single-system conquests, there was no quick, clean way to take the Alliance out, short of a direct thrust to its heart, and driving clear to Manticore without protecting the Fleet's flanks and rear invited catastrophe.

No, if they wanted the Star Kingdom, they had to fight for it. And, as the very first step, they had to break its frontier defenses and annihilate a sizable chunk of its navy in the process.

The admiral climbed out of his seat as the landing gear engaged. He scooped up his briefcase, nodded to the security team which accompanied him everywhere, and made his way down the shuttle ramp with a smile that hid his inner apprehension.

DuQuesne Base's huge war room was even more lavishly appointed than Central Planning back home in the Octagon, and Parnell's staff stood in a silent arc behind him as he studied the status boards. It was a habit of his to absorb the raw data for himself. He knew it irked some of his staffers, but he didn't do it because he distrusted their competence. If he hadn't trusted them, they wouldn't be here in the first place, but even the best people made mistakes. He'd caught more than a few of them in his time, and while he knew he couldn't possibly assimilate that much detail, he'd trained himself over the decades to absorb a general overview.

The confirmed reports on Manty naval deployments were scantier than he'd hoped for, but what there were of them looked hopeful. There were signs of movement all along the frontier, and Operation Argus had done better than he'd ever expected when the notion was first proposed to him. Argus was hardly a speedy way to amass information, but the data it *did* bring in was surprisingly detailed, and that insight into normal Manty ops patterns was all that had made this entire operation workable. Besides, he admitted, Argus made him feel better. Manticore's persistently better hardware had begun to assume Sisyphean proportions for Parnell, and it pleased him to see the Manties' faith in their technological superiority boomeranging on them.

He noted with satisfaction the arrival of fresh Manticoran forces in Zuckerman, Dorcas, and Minette, and other reports indicated that the RMN had substantially reinforced its escort and frontier patrol forces. That was good. Every ship committed to any of those areas was one less he'd have to worry about when the ball actually opened.

He was less pleased by the information from Seaford Nine. The sheer spatial volume of the cursed Alliance meant it was out of date, of course, but it was also unfortunately vague. Well, Rollins knew how critical the situation was; undoubtedly he was working to refine his data even now, assuming he hadn't already done so.

The CNO let his eyes run down Nav Int's latest estimates (guesstimates, he corrected himself wryly) of the current strength of Manticore's Home Fleet. There was no possible way to confirm the accuracy of *that*, but it wasn't really vital at this moment, anyway.

He turned to the tally boards listing the planned first and second phase incursions and the results so far reported, and, for the first time since entering the command center, he frowned and glanced over his shoulder.

"Commodore Perot."

"Sir?" His chief of staff replied.

"What went wrong in Talbot?" Parnell asked, and Perot grimaced.

"We don't know, Sir. The Manties haven't said a word about it, but Admiral Pierre's ships must have run into some sort of trap."

"Something nasty enough to get *all* of them?" Parnell murmured, half to himself, and Perot nodded even less happily.

"Must have been, Sir."

"But how in hell could they have pulled it off?" Parnell rubbed his chin and frowned at the bland "UNKNOWN" glowing beside the names of four of the PN's best battlecruisers. "He should have been able to avoid anything he couldn't fight. Could they have known when and where he was coming in?"

"The possibility can't be completely ruled out, Sir, but even Admiral Pierre didn't know his objective until he opened his sealed orders. And the Poicters side of the operation went off without a hitch. Commodore Yuranovich nailed a *Star Knight*-class cruiser right where he expected to find her. As you can see," Perot pointed at the information displayed below the names of the ships committed to the Poicters raid, "he took more damage than we'd hoped—I'm afraid *Barbarossa* and *Sinjar* are going to be in yard hands for some time—but there was no sign they'd suspected anything. Since both halves of the mission were covered by exactly the same security, our best guess is that they didn't know Pierre was coming, either."

"You're putting it down to coincidence, then," Parnell said flatly, and Perot gave a tiny shrug.

"At the moment, there's nothing else we *can* put it down to, Sir. We're due for another Argus dump from Talbot late next week, and we should get at least some information then. The birds cover the area where the interception was supposed to take place, anyway."

"Um." Parnell rubbed his chin harder. "Any response from Manticore over the *Star Knight*?"

"Not in so many words, but they've closed the Junction to our shipping, ejected all our diplomatic courier boats from Alliance space without any formal explanation, and begun shadowing and harassing our convoys moving through Alliance territory. There was an incident in Casca, but we're not sure who started it. Casca may be officially nonaligned, but they've always leaned a bit towards Manticore, and some of my analysts think our Phase One operations may have pushed the Cascans themselves into pressing the panic button and asking for Manticoran protection. Our local CO exchanged long-range fire with a Manty cruiser squadron, then hauled ass." Perot shrugged again. "Hard to blame him, Sir. He didn't have anything heavier than a destroyer, and they would've eaten him for lunch if he'd stood and fought."

Parnell's nod was calmer than he felt. The situation was heating up, and Manticore was starting to push back, but they weren't lodging any formal diplomatic protests. That could be good or bad. It might mean they knew exactly what was happening and chose to keep silent in order to keep him in the dark about their response till they had it in position. But it could just as well indicate they *didn't* know what was going on . . . or just how much crap was about to fall on top of them. If they'd simply decided the incidents and provocations *might* be the start of some larger operation, they could be holding their protests until they figured out what that operation was.

In either case, they'd obviously decided protests would serve no purpose, and the way their forces were pushing back across the board, not just in a few local instances, certainly argued that new orders had gone out to their station commanders. And his fragmentary reports on their ship movements suggested they were also repositioning their units to support whatever those orders were. Now if they'd just do enough of that. . . .

His eyes returned to the total lack of new data from Seaford Nine, and he grimaced.

"All right, ladies and gentlemen," he said finally, turning to regard his staff, "let's get down to it."

He led the way to the conference room, followed by his subordinates, and Commodore Perot began the detailed brief. Parnell listened closely, nodding occasionally, and deep inside he felt the moment of final decision rushing closer with every heartbeat.

On the face of it, the possibility of locating and attacking someone else's commerce in hyper shouldn't even exist. Maximum reliable scanner range is barely twenty light-minutes, hyper-space is vast, and even knowing a convoy's planned arrival and departure times shouldn't help much.

But appearances can be deceiving. To be sure, hyper-space *is* vast, yet virtually all its traffic moves down the highways of its grav waves, drawing both its power and absurdly high acceleration from its Warshawski sails. There are only so many efficient grav wave connections from one star system to another, and the optimum points of interchange are known to most navies. So are the points which must be avoided because of high levels of grav turbulence. If a raider knows a given ship's schedule, he doesn't really need its route. He can work through the same astro tables as his target's skipper and project its probable course closely enough to intercept it.

For those not blessed with such foreknowledge, there are still ways. Merchant skippers, for example, vastly prefer to ride a grav wave clear through their final hyper translation. Power costs are lower, and riding the wave through the hyper wall reduces both the structural and physiological stresses. Which means raiders often lurk at points where inbound grav waves intersect a star's hyper limit, waiting for prey to amble up to them.

And, if all else fails, there is always the blind chance method. Ships are at their most vulnerable at and shortly after they translate back into normal space. Their base velocities are low, their sensor systems are still sorting out the sudden influx of n-space information, and for at least ten minutes or so, while their hyper generators recycle, they can't even dodge back into hyper and run away if something comes at them. A translation right on the system ecliptic is the norm, if not the inviolable rule, so a patient raider might put his ship into a solar orbit right on the hyper limit, run his power (and emissions) down to minimum levels, and simply wait until some fat and unwary freighter translates within his interception envelope. With no emissions to betray it, something as tiny as a warship is extremely difficult to spot, and many an unfortunate merchant skipper's first intimation of trouble has been the arrival of the leading missile salvo.

But the heavy cruiser PNS *Sword* and her consorts had no need for such hit-or-miss hunting techniques, Captain Theisman thought. Thanks to Nav Int's spies, Commodore Reichman knew her prey's exact schedule. In fact, Theisman's tac officer had spotted the five-ship convoy and its escort hours ago as *Sword*'s squadron lay doggo in a handy "bubble" in the local grav wave, letting them pass without being spotted in return before emerging in pursuit.

Theisman didn't like his present mission, partly because he disliked both Commodore Annette Reichman and her proposed tactics. Given his druthers, he would have moved to catch the convoy six light-years further along, when it would have to transition between grav waves under impeller drive. Reichman had decided differently—and stupidly, in his opinion—yet that explained only a part of his dislike. He was also a naval officer, with a naval officer's innate instinct to *protect* merchantmen, and the fact that two of the squadron's targets weren't really freighters at all only made it worse. But he'd been asked to do a lot of things he didn't like in his career, and if he had to do it, he might as well do it right . . . assuming Reichman would let him.

He stood on *Sword's* command deck, studying his plot, and frowned silently while he awaited the commodore's next order. The Manties were good, as he could attest from painful personal experience, yet Reichman seemed confident. Possibly more confident than the situation merited. True, the convoy escort consisted of only two light cruisers and a trio of tin-cans, but hyper-space combat wasn't like an n-space engagement. Much of a heavier ship's normal defensive advantage was negated here, and Reichman's unconcern over her squadron's increased vulnerability worried Theisman.

Still, the tactical situation was developing much as the commodore had predicted. With so few ships, the escort commander had opted to sweep ahead of the merchies against the greater danger of a head-on interception while only a single escort watched their rear to cover what should have been the vector of minimum threat. Only Reichman didn't need a head-on intercept. The maximum safe velocity in hyper for any merchantman was barely .5 c. That translated to an effective normal-space velocity of many hundreds of times light-speed, but all that mattered were *relative* speeds, and their better particle and radiation shielding let Reichman's ships attain a velocity twenty percent greater than that. Which meant that she was currently overtaking the convoy at just under thirty thousand KPS and that the trailing destroyer ought to see them just . . . about . . . now.

Lieutenant Commander MacAllister jerked upright in his command chair as threat sources sparkled suddenly in his plot. His destroyer's sensors should have read them sooner, even under the conditions of hyper-space, but the count was tentative, and the identifying data codes shifted and flowed as he watched them. Someone back there had some pretty decent electronic warfare capabilities, and they were using them.

His eyes darted to the vector readouts, and he swallowed a curse. They were barely three hundred million klicks back. At their closing speed, they'd overtake the convoy in under three hours, and there was no way in hell merchantmen could outrun them.

He swore softly, rubbing his palms up and down the chair arms. Whoever was sneaking up on them had to have military-grade shielding to generate that much overtake velocity, so they had to be warships. A fact, he thought grimly, their EW activity had already confirmed. Just as that activity confirmed their hostile intent. But who were they? Were there more of them back there than he could see yet? And how powerful were they?

There was only one way to find out.

"Battle stations," MacAllister told his tactical officer grimly, and alarms began to whoop as he turned to his com officer. "Ruth, get a signal off to Captain Zilwicki. Tell her we have bogies coming up from astern—append Tactical's present data—and that I'm turning for a positive ID."

"Aye, aye, Sir."

"Helm, bring us around one-eight-zero degrees. Maximum deceleration."

"Aye, aye, Sir."

"Manny," MacAllister looked at his astrogator, "I want a turnover that puts us back at our present closure rate at ten light-minutes. We may not be able to fingerprint them from there, but we can sure as hell figure out what size they are."

"Yes, Sir." The astrogator bent over his console just as MacAllister's vacsuited exec appeared on the bridge with the lieutenant commander's skin suit slung over her shoulder. He smiled at her in grim thanks and nodded to the display as he took the suit.

"It seems we're invited to a party, Marge." He started for his minuscule briefing room to change. "Hold the fort while I get suited up."

"The tin-can's coming back at us, Sir," Theisman's tac officer reported, and the captain glanced at Reichman. The commodore didn't even blink. No doubt she'd expected it, just as Theisman had. In fact, he'd expected it sooner, and he felt a dull sense of sympathy for the crew of that ship.

"Well, they see us, Ma'am," he said after a moment. "Any orders?"

"No. I doubt he'll come all the way into range before he gets an accurate read on us, but we can hope. Besides," the commodore smiled without humor, "it's not like the bastards can get away from us, now is it?"

"No, Ma'am," Theisman said softly, "I don't suppose it is."

HMS *Hotspur* decelerated towards the bogies at over 51 KPS^2 as her Warshawski sails channeled the grav wave's power. Nineteen minutes later, she flipped end for end, accelerating away from them until their overtake speed had dropped once more to thirty thousand KPS at a range of just under a hundred and fifty-eight million kilometers, and Lieutenant Commander MacAllister's face tightened as *Hotspur*'s sensors penetrated their ECM at last.

"Get another message off to the Old Lady, Ruth," he said very quietly. "Tell her we have six Peep heavy cruisers—they look like *Scimitars*. I estimate they'll enter range of the convoy in—" he glanced back down at his plot "—two hours and thirty-six minutes."

* * *

Captain Helen Zilwicki's face was stone as she listened to MacAllister's analysis of the threat thirteen and a half light-minutes behind her tiny squadron. Six of them to her five, and all of them bigger and far more heavily armed. Even the technical edge her ships might have exploited in normal space would hardly matter here, for it paid its biggest dividends in missile engagements, and missiles were useless within a grav wave. No impeller drive could function there; the wave's powerful gravitational forces would burn it out instantly. Which meant any missile vaporized the second its drive kicked in—and that none of her ships had the protection of their own impeller wedges . . . or sidewalls.

She didn't even consider the possibility of breaking free of the wave. It would have restored her sidewalls and let her use her missiles, but her charges were four light-hours into the wave. They'd need *eight* hours to get clear, and they didn't have eight hours.

She felt her bridge crew's tension, smelled their fear like her own, but no one said a word, and she closed her eyes in anguish. Two of her huge, clumsy ships were combination freighter-transports, bound for Grendelsbane Station with vitally needed machine tools, shipyard mechs and remotes . . . and over six thousand priceless civilian and Navy technicians and their families.

Including Captain (Junior Grade) Anton Zilwicki and their daughter.

She tried not to think about that. She couldn't afford to. Not if she was going to do anything to save them. But there was only one thing she *could* do, and she felt a terrible stab of guilt as she looked up at her officers at last.

"General message to all units, Com." Her voice sounded rusty and strained in her own ears. "Message begins: From CO escort to all ships. We have detected six warships, apparently Havenite heavy cruisers, closing from astern. Present range one-three-point-six light-minutes, closing velocity three-zero thousand KPS. On present course, they will overtake us in two hours and fourteen minutes." She drew a deep breath, staring down into her display. "In view of Admiralty warnings, I must assume their intention is to attack. All escorts will form on me and turn to engage the enemy. The convoy will scatter and proceed independently. Zilwicki clear."

"Recorded, Ma'am." The com officer's voice was flat.

"Transmit." The word came out fogged with tears, and the captain cleared her throat harshly. "Helm, prepare to bring us around."

"Aye, aye, Ma'am."

She kept her eyes on the display, trying not to think of the two most important people in her universe or how they would react to her last cold, official message, and someone touched her shoulder. She looked up, blinking to clear her vision. It was her exec.

"Tell them you love them, Helen," he said very softly, and she clenched her fists in agony.

"I can't," she whispered. "Not when none of the rest of you can tell *your*—"

Her voice broke, and his hand tightened painfully on her shoulder.

"Don't be stupid!" His voice was harsh, almost fierce. "There's not a soul on this ship who doesn't know your family's over there—or who thinks for one minute they're the only reason you're doing this! Now get on the com and tell them you love them, goddamn it!"

He shook her in her command chair, and she ripped her eyes from his, staring almost desperately at the other officers and ratings on her bridge, pleading for their forgiveness.

But there was no need to plead. She saw it in their eyes, read it in their faces, and she drew a deep breath.

"Helm," her voice was suddenly clear, "bring us about. Jeff," she looked at the com officer, "please get me a personal link to *Carnarvon*. I'll take it in my briefing room."

"Yes, Ma'am," the com officer said gently, and Helen Zilwicki pushed herself out of her chair and walked to the hatch with her head high.

*   *   *

Thomas Theisman's jaw clenched as the drive sources came back toward him in attack formation. He folded his hands tightly behind his back and made himself look at Commodore Reichman without expression. She'd been so sure the Manty commander would order the entire convoy, escorts and merchantmen alike, to scatter. After all, she'd pointed out, the grav wave would strip them of the long-range missile advantage, which might have given them the chance to achieve anything worthwhile. That was the whole reason for intercepting here rather than between waves, as Theisman had suggested. No commander would throw his ships away for nothing when scattering meant at least four of his ten ships would survive.

Thomas Theisman had known better, but Annette Reichman had never fought Manticorans before. And because Theisman had lost when *he* fought them, she'd ignored his warnings with barely veiled patronization.

"Orders, Ma'am?" he asked now, and Reichman swallowed.

"We'll take them head-on," she said after a moment. As if she had a choice, Theisman thought in disgust.

"Yes, Ma'am. Do you wish to change our formation?" He kept his tone as neutral as possible, but her nostrils flared.

"No!" she snapped.

Theisman raised his eyes over her shoulder. His cold glance sent her staff and his own bridge officers sidling out of earshot, and he leaned toward her and spoke quietly.

"Commodore, if you fight a conventional closing engagement with your chase armaments, they're going to turn to open their broadsides and give us everything they've got at optimum range."

"Nonsense! That would be suicide!" Reichman snapped. "We'll tear them apart if they come out from behind their sails!"

"Ma'am," he spoke softly, as if to a child, "we out-mass

those ships seven to one, and they *have* to close to energy range. They know what that means as well as we do. So they'll do the only thing they can. They'll open their broadsides to bring every beam they can to bear, and they'll go for our forward alpha nodes. If they take out even one, our own foresail will go down, and this deep into a grav wave—"

He didn't have to complete the sentence. With no forward sail to balance her after sail, it was impossible for any starship to maneuver in a grav wave. They would be trapped on the same vector, at the same velocity. They couldn't even drop out of hyper, because they couldn't control their translation attitude until and unless they could make repairs, and even the tiniest patch of turbulence would tear them apart. Which meant the loss of a single sail would cost Reichman at least two ships, because any ship which lost a sail would have to be towed clear of the wave on a consort's tractors.

"But—" She stopped and swallowed again. "What do you recommend, Captain?" she asked after a moment.

"That we do the same thing. We'll get hurt, probably lose a few ships, but it'll actually reduce our sails' exposure and give us far heavier broadsides and a better chance to take them out before they gut our sails."

He met her gaze levelly, strangling the desire to scream at her that he'd *told* her this would happen, and her eyes fell.

"Very well, Captain Theisman," she said. "Make it so."

Anton Zilwicki sat on the padded decksole, eyes closed, arms tight around the four-year-old girl weeping into his tunic. She was too young to understand it all, but she understood enough, he thought emptily as he listened to the voices behind him: the voices of *Carnarvon*'s taut-faced bridge officers, clustered around the huge transport's main display.

"My God," the exec whispered. "*Look* at that!"

"There goes another one," someone else said harshly. "Was that one of the cruisers?"

"No, I think it was another can, and—"

"Look—*look!* That was one of the Peep bastards! And there goes another one!"

"Oh, *Jesus!* That *was* a cruiser!" someone groaned, and Zilwicki closed his eyes tighter, fighting his own tears for his daughter's sake. He knew *Carnarvon* was piling on every scrap of drive power she had, running madly away from her sisters, seeking the elusive safety of dispersal. If two of the Peeps were gone, then at least one merchantman would live . . . but which one?

"My God, she got another one!" a voice gasped, and his arms tightened about his child.

"What about that one?" someone asked.

"No, he's still there. It's just his sail, but that should— Oh, God!"

The voices cut off with knifelike suddenness, and his heart twisted within him. He knew what that silence meant, and he raised his head slowly. Most of the officers looked away, but not *Carnarvon's* skipper. Tears ran down the woman's face, yet she met his gaze without flinching.

"She's gone," she said softly. "They all are. But she killed three of them first, and at least one survivor's lost a sail. I . . . don't think they'll continue the pursuit with just one ship, even if she's undamaged. Not with a cripple to tow clear."

Zilwicki nodded, and wondered vaguely how the universe could hold so much pain. His shoulders began to shake as his own tears came at last, and his daughter threw her arms around his neck and clung tightly.

"W-what's happening, Daddy?" she whispered. "Are . . . are the Peeps gonna hurt Mommy? Are they gonna get *us?*"

"Shsssh, Helen," he got out through his tears. He pressed his cheek into her hair, smelling the fresh, little-girl smell of her, and closed his eyes once more as he rocked her gently.

"The Peeps won't get us, baby," he whispered. "We're safe now." He drew a ragged breath. "Mommy made it safe."

• CHAPTER NINETEEN

Nike altered course for home, and Mike Henke hid a grin as she glanced across the bridge at her captain. Honor seldom displayed satisfaction with her own efforts, especially on the bridge. Satisfaction with the performance of her officers and crew, yes; yet her own competence was something to be taken for granted. But today she leaned back against her command chair's contoured cushions, legs crossed, and a small smile played about her lips while Nimitz preened shamelessly on the chair's back.

Henke chuckled and looked over to Tactical to bestow a wink of triumph on Eve Chandler. The diminutive redhead grinned back and raised her clasped hands over her head, and Henke heard someone else snort with laughter behind her.

Well, they had every excuse to be insufferably pleased with themselves—and their captain, Henke reflected. The squadron had worked hard in the week since Vice Admiral Parks' departure. Its steadily developing snap and precision had actually brought smiles of approval from Admiral Sarnow, and *Nike*'s escape from the repair slip couldn't have come at a better time.

Henke wasn't the only one of Honor's officers who'd heard about Captain Dournet's concern that the flagship's enforced inactivity might have made her rusty enough to embarrass his own *Agamemnon*, but she'd been better placed than most to do something about it. Honor had been too submerged in squadron affairs to take on *Nike*'s day-to-day training efforts. Besides, that sort of ongoing activity was really the exec's responsibility, and all the long, grueling simulator hours Henke had inflicted on *Nike*'s crew had paid off handsomely in yesterday's maneuvers. *Nike* hadn't embarrassed *Agamemnon*. In point of fact, Dournet's ship had had all she could handle just to stay in shouting distance of her division mate, and Henke looked forward to her next meeting with *Agamemnon*'s exec.

Nike had turned in the best gunnery performance of the exercise, as well, outshooting Captain Daumier's *Invincible* by a clear eight percent, much to the disgust of Daumier's crew, but that hadn't been the best part. No, Henke thought with a lazy smile, the *best* part had come when Admiral Sarnow divided his small task group in half for war games.

Commodore Banton had commanded the squadron's second and third divisions and their screen while Sarnow commanded the first and fourth, but that was only for the record. In fact, Sarnow had informed Honor five minutes into the exercise that both he and Captain Rubenstein, Division 54's senior officer, had just become casualties and that *she* was in command.

That was all the warning she'd gotten, but it was obvious she'd been thinking ahead, for her own orders had come without any hesitation at all. She'd used the FTL sensor platforms to locate Banton's ships, split her own force into two two-ship divisions, accelerated to intercept velocity, then killed her drives and gone to the electronic and gravitic equivalent of "silent running." But she hadn't stopped there, for she'd known Banton's *Achilles* had the same ability to spot and track her. And since Honor knew the commodore had plotted her base course before she closed down her emissions, she'd launched electronic warfare drones, programmed to mimic her battlecruisers' drives, on a course designed with malice aforethought to draw Banton into a position of *her* choice.

The commodore had taken the bait—partly, perhaps, because she didn't expect anyone to use up EW drones (at eight million dollars a pop) in an exercise—and altered course to intercept them. By the time she realized what was really going on, Honor had brought both her own divisions slashing in on purely ballistic courses, wedges and sidewalls down to the very last instant and still operating separately in blatant disregard of conventional tactical wisdom. She'd hit Banton's surprised formation from widely divergent bearings, and her unorthodox approach had used Banton's more traditional formation against her, pounding her lead ships with fire from two directions, confusing her point defense, and using her own lead division to block the return fire of her rearmost ships for almost two full minutes. And, just to make it even better, she'd had Commander Chandler reprogram their screen's antimissile decoys so that the heavy cruisers suddenly looked like battlecruisers.

The decoys had come on-line at the worst possible moment for Banton's tac officer. With no running plot on Honor's "invisible" ships until their drives suddenly came back up, he'd had to sort out who was who before he engaged, and the decoys had confused him just long enough for *Nike*, *Agamemnon*, *Onslaught*, and *Invincible* to "kill" Banton's flagship and "cripple" her division mate *Cassandra* with no damage of their own. *Defiant* and *Intolerant* had done their best after that—indeed, Captain Trinh's stellar performance had gone far to redeem his earlier problems—but they'd never had a chance. The final score had shown the complete destruction of Banton's force, moderate damage to *Agamemnon* and *Invincible*, and a mere two laser hits on *Nike*. *Onslaught* had escaped completely unscathed and even recovered all but two of the EW drones Honor had used. The drones would require overhaul before they could be reused, but their recovery had saved the Navy something like forty-eight million dollars, and Henke suspected Rubenstein's crew was going to do even more gloating than her own people.

Admiral Sarnow hadn't said a word, but his grin when he ambled onto *Nike*'s bridge for the closing phase of the "battle" had been eloquent. Besides, Commodore

Banton was a fair-minded woman. She knew she and her people had been had, and she'd commed her personal congratulations to Honor even before the computers finished calculating the final damage estimates.

A *most* satisfactory two days, taken all together, Henke decided. A whole week had passed without incident since Admiral Parks disappeared over the hyper limit, which had produced a deep sense of relief but hadn't lessened the squadron's determination to disprove any reservations Parks might entertain about their admiral and his flag captain . . . and the last couple of days' successes looked like an excellent first step.

Of course, she thought smugly, it had been an even better step for some than for others. Eve Chandler was already licking her chops in anticipation of her next conversation with *Invincible's* tac officer. Queen's Cup for gunnery, indeed! And Ivan Ravicz was as happy as a treecat with his own celery patch. His new fusion plant had performed flawlessly, and *Agamemnon* had been pushed to the limit matching the acceleration of *Nike's* superbly tuned drive. Even George Monet had been seen to crack a smile or two, and that constituted an historic first for the com officer.

Besides, Commodore Banton had already promised that her ships' companies were buying the beer.

Honor noted the gleam in Henke's eyes and smiled fondly as her exec turned back to her own panel. Mike had a right to be pleased. It was her training programs which had kept *Nike* in such top-notch fighting trim, after all.

But there was more to it than training alone. Exercises and simulations could do many things, but they couldn't provide that indefinable something more that separated a crack crew from one that was simply good. *Nike* had that something more. Perhaps it came from the mysterious esprit de corps which always seemed to infuse the ships of her name, the sense that they had a special tradition to maintain. Or perhaps it came from somewhere else entirely. Honor didn't know, but she'd felt it crackling about her like latent lightning, begging her to use it, and she had. She hadn't even thought about her maneuvers—not on a conscious level; they'd simply come to her with a smooth, flawless precision. Her people had executed them the same way, and they had every right to feel pleased with themselves.

It helped that Commodore Banton was a good sort, of course. Honor could think of several flag officers who would have reacted far less cheerfully to the drubbing Banton had just taken, especially when they discovered they'd been beaten not by their admiral but by his flag captain. But she suspected Banton shared her own suspicions about the Admiral's motive for declaring himself a casualty. Honor might be his flag captain, yet she was also junior to six of the seven other battlecruiser captains under his command, and it was the first chance she'd had to show her stuff anywhere but in the simulators. Sarnow had deliberately stepped aside to let her win her spurs in the squadron's eyes, and she wanted to preen like Nimitz at how well it had gone.

In fact, she thought, leaning back to steeple her fingers under her pointed chin, "preen" was exactly what she intended to be doing very shortly . . . among other things. It was Wednesday, and the squadron was going to rendezvous with the repair base well before supper. She intended to arrive in Paul's quarters with a bottle of her father's precious Delacourt and find out just what his laughing hints about hot oil rubdowns were all about.

The corners of her mouth quirked at the thought, her right cheek dimpled, and she felt her face heating up, and she didn't care at all.

"Captain, I'm picking up a hyper footprint at two-zero-six," Commander Chandler announced. "One drive source, range six-point-niner-five light-minutes. It's too heavy for a courier boat, Ma'am."

Honor looked at the tac officer in faint surprise, but Chandler didn't notice as she queried her computers and worked the contact. Several seconds passed, and then she straightened with a satisfied nod.

"Definitely a Manticoran drive pattern, Ma'am. Looks like a heavy cruiser. I won't know for sure till the light-speed sensors have her."

"Understood. Keep an eye on her, Eve."

"Aye, aye, Ma'am."

A cruiser, hmmm? Honor leaned back in her chair once more. One cruiser wouldn't make much difference, but Van Slyke would be happy to see her. She would bring his squadron up to full strength at last, and the rest of the task group would probably see her as a harbinger of the far more powerful reinforcements they'd been promised. Besides, she'd probably have dispatches on board, and even the tiniest scrap of fresh information would be a vast relief.

She reached up and drew Nimitz down into her lap, rubbing his ears and considering the com conference the Admiral had scheduled for tomorrow morning. There were several points she wanted to make—not least how lucky she'd been to get away with that EW drone trick—and she slid further down in the chair as she considered the best (and most tactful) way to express them.

Several minutes ticked away, and the quiet, orderly routine of her bridge murmured to her like some soothing mantra. Her mind toyed with phrases and sentences, maneuvering them with a sort of languid, catlike pleasure. Yet her dreamy eyes were deceptive. The soft chime of an incoming signal from the com section brought her instantly back to full awareness, and her gaze moved to Lieutenant Commander Monet's narrow back.

The com officer depressed a button and listened to his earbug for a moment, and Honor's eyes narrowed when his shoulders twitched. If she hadn't known what an utterly reliable, totally humorless sort he was, she might actually have thought he was chuckling.

He pressed another sequence of buttons, then swiveled his chair to face her. His face was admirably grave, but his brown eyes twinkled slightly as he cleared his throat.

"Burst transmission for you, Captain." He paused just a moment. "It's from Captain Tankersley, Ma'am."

Faint, pink heat tingled along Honor's cheekbones. Did *every* member of her crew know about her . . . relationship with Paul?! It was none of their business, even if they did, darn it! It wasn't as if there were anything shady or underhanded about it—Paul was a yard dog, so even the prohibition against affairs with officers in the same chain of command didn't come into it!

But even as she prepared to glower at the com officer, her own sense of the ridiculous came to her rescue. Of course they knew—even Admiral Sarnow knew! She'd never realized her nonexistent love life was so widely noticed, but if she'd wanted to keep a low profile she should have thought of it sooner. And the twinkle in Monet's eyes wasn't the smutty thing it could have been. In fact, she realized as she sensed the same gentle amusement from the rest of her silent bridge crew, he actually seemed pleased for her.

"Ah, switch it to my screen," she said, suddenly realizing she'd been silent just a bit too long.

"It's a private signal, Ma'am." Monet's voice was so bland Honor's mouth twitched in response. She shoved herself up out of her chair, cradling Nimitz in her arms and fighting her rebellious dimple.

"In that case, I'll take it on my briefing room terminal."

"Of course, Ma'am. I'll switch it over."

"Thank you," Honor said with all the dignity she could muster, and crossed to the briefing room hatch.

It slid open for her, and as she stepped through it, she suddenly wondered why Paul was screening her at all. *Nike* would reach the base in another thirty minutes or so, but the transmission lag at this range was still something like seventeen seconds. That ruled out any practical real-time conversation, so why hadn't he waited another fifteen minutes to avoid it?

An eyebrow arched in speculation, and she deposited

Nimitz on the briefing room table as she sat in the captain's chair at its head and keyed the terminal. The screen flashed a ready signal, and then Paul's face appeared.

"Hi, Honor. Sorry to disturb you, but I thought you'd better know." Her eyebrows knitted in a frown as his grim expression registered. "We just got an arrival signal from a heavy cruiser," his recorded voice continued, then paused. "It's *Warlock*, Honor," he said, and she went rigid in her chair.

Paul looked out of the screen as if he could see her reaction, and there was compassion in his eyes—and warning—as his image nodded.

"Young's still in command," he said softly, "and he's still senior to you. Watch yourself, okay?"

PNS *Napoleon* drifted through blackness, far from the dim beacon of the system's red dwarf primary. The light cruiser's drive was down, her active sensors dead, and her captain sat tensely on her bridge as she coasted along her silent course, well inside the orbit of Hancock's frozen outermost planet. He could see two different Manty destroyers' impeller signatures in his display, but the nearest was over twelve light-minutes from *Napoleon*, and he had absolutely no intention of attracting its attention.

Commander Ogilve hadn't thought much of Operation Argus when he was first briefed for it. The whole idea had struck him as an excellent way to start a war and get his ship fried in the process, yet it had worked out far better than he'd expected. It was horribly time-consuming, and the fact that none of the ships involved had been caught yet didn't mean none of them ever would be, but it only had to go on working for a little longer. Just long enough for Admiral Rollins to receive the data he needed . . . and for PNS *Napoleon* to get the hell out of Hancock in one piece.

"Coming up on the first relay, Sir." His com officer sounded as unhappy as Ogilve felt, and the commander took pains to exude calm as he withdrew his gaze from the display and nodded in response. Wouldn't do to let the troops know their captain was as scared as they were, he thought dryly.

"Prepare to initiate data dump," he said.

"Yes, Sir."

The bridge was silent as the com officer brought his communication lasers up from standby. Any sort of emission was extremely dangerous under the circumstances, but the relay's position had been plotted with painstaking care. The people who'd planned Operation Argus had known the perimeters of all Manticoran star systems were guarded by sensor platforms whose reach and sensitivity the People's Republic couldn't match, but no surveillance net could cover everything. Their deployment patterns and plans had taken that into consideration, and—so far, at least—they'd been right on the money.

Ogilve snorted at his own choice of cliché, for Argus had cost billions. The heavily stealthed sensor platforms had been inserted from over two light-months out, coasting in out of the silence of interstellar space with all power locked down to absolute minimum. They'd slid through the Manties' sensors like any other bits of space debris, and the tiny trickle of power which had braked them and aligned them in their final, carefully chosen positions had been so small as to be utterly indetectable at anything over a few thousand kilometers.

In point of fact, getting the platforms in had been the easy part. Laymen tended to forget just how huge—and empty—any given star system was. Even the largest starship was less than a mote on such a scale; as long as it radiated no betraying energy signature to attract attention it might as well be invisible, and the sensor arrays were tinier still and equipped with the best stealth systems Haven could produce. Or, Ogilve amended, in this case buy clandestinely from the Solarian League. The biggest risk came from the low-powered, hair-thin lasers that tied them to the central storage relays, but even there the risk had been reduced to absolute minimum.

The platforms communicated only via ultra high-speed burst transmissions. Even if someone strayed into their path, it would require an enormous stroke of bad luck for him to realize he'd heard something, and the platforms' programming restricted them from sending if their sensors picked up *anything* in a position to intercept their messages.

No, there was very little chance of the Manties tumbling to the tiny robotic spies—it was the mailmen who collected their data who had to sweat. Because small as it might be, a starship was larger than any sensor array, and harvesting that information meant a ship *had* to radiate, however stealthily.

"Tight beam standing by, Sir. Coming up on transmission point in . . . nineteen seconds."

"Initiate when we reach the bearing."

"Aye, Sir. Standing by." The seconds ticked past, and then the com officer licked his lips. "Initiating now, Sir."

Ogilve tensed, and his eyes returned to his display with unseemly haste. He watched the Manty destroyers with painful intensity, but they continued along their blissfully unobservant way, and then—

"Dump completed, Sir!" The com officer didn't quite wipe his brow as he killed the laser, and Ogilve smiled despite his own tension.

"Well done, Jamie." He rubbed his hands and grinned at his tac officer. "Well, Ms. Austell, shall we see what we've caught?"

"An excellent idea, Sir." The tac officer returned his grin, then began querying the data dump. Several minutes passed in silence, for the last Argus collection had been a month and a half earlier. That left a great deal of information to sort through, but then she stiffened and looked up sharply.

"I've got something very interesting here, Sir."

The suppressed excitement in her voice drew Ogilve out of his chair without conscious thought. He crossed the bridge in a few, quick strides and leaned over her shoulder as she tapped keys. Her display flickered for a moment, then settled, and a date and time readout glowed in one corner.

Ogilve sucked in sharply as the data before him registered. A score of heavy capital ships—no, more than that. By God, there were over thirty of the bastards! Jesus, it was the Manties' *entire* wall of battle!

He stared at the display, holding his breath, unable to believe what he was seeing as the massive fleet movement played itself out. The time scale was enormously compressed, and the incredible mass of impeller signatures slid across the star system at breakneck speed.

It had to be some sort of maneuver. That was the only thing it *could* be. Ogilve told himself that over and over, like some sort of mental incantation against the disappointment that had to come.

But it didn't come. The stupendous dreadnoughts and superdreadnoughts went right on moving, sweeping out from Hancock until they hit the hyper limit.

And then they vanished. Every goddamned one of them simply *vanished*, and Ogilve straightened with slow, almost painful caution.

"Did they come back, Midge?" he half-whispered, and the tac officer shook her head, eyes huge. "Would this sector's platforms necessarily have spotted them if they *had* come back?" the commander pressed.

"Not automatically, Sir. The Manties could have come back on a course outside their search envelope. But unless they knew about the sensors and deliberately set this up to fake us out, they would've come back in from any maneuvers on roughly reciprocal headings. If they'd done that, the platforms *would* have seen them . . . and they've been gone for over a week, Sir."

Ogilve nodded and pinched the bridge of his nose. It was incredible. The idea that the Manties would conduct some sort of exercise that took them away from Hancock at a time of such tension was ridiculous on the face of it. But impossible as it seemed, they'd done something even stupider. They'd pulled out entirely. Hancock Station was wide open!

He drew another deep breath and looked at his astrogator.

"How soon can we get the hell out of here?"

"Without our hyper footprint being detected?"

"Of *course* without being detected!"

"Um." The astrogator's fingers flew as he worked through the problem. "On this vector, niner-four-point-eight hours to clear known Manty sensor arrays, Sir."

"*Damn*," Ogilve whispered. He rubbed his hands up and down the seams of his trousers and forced his impatience back under control. This was too important to risk blowing. He was going to have to wait. To make himself sit on it for another four days before he could head home with the unbelievable news. But once they reached Seaford—

"All right," he said crisply. "I want a complete shutdown. *Nothing* goes out from this ship. Jamie, abort the remainder of the data dumps. Midge, I want you to damned well *live* up here with your passive sensors. If anything even *looks* like it could be coming our way, I want to know it. This data just paid the entire cost of this operation from day one, and we're getting it home if we have to hyper out of here right under some Manty's nose!"

"But what about operational security, Sir?" his exec protested.

"I'm not going to call any attention to us," Ogilve said tightly. "But this is too important to risk losing, so if it looks like they *may* be going to spot us, we're out of here, and the hell with the rest of Operation Argus. This is *exactly* what Admiral Rollins has been waiting for, and we, by God, are going to tell him about it!"

• CHAPTER TWENTY

Honor nodded to her Marine sentry and stepped through her cabin hatch without a word. Her face showed no emotion at all, but Nimitz was tense on her shoulder, and MacGuiness' welcoming smile congealed into nonexpression the moment he saw her.

"Good evening, Ma'am," he said.

She turned her head at the sound of his voice, and her eyes flickered, as if only now noting his presence. He watched her lips tighten for just an instant, but then she drew a deep breath and smiled at him. To someone who didn't know her, that smile might have looked almost natural.

"Good evening, Mac." She crossed to her desk and dropped her beret on it, then ran her hands through her hair, looking away from him for a moment, before she moved Nimitz from her shoulder to his padded perch, sat in her chair, and swiveled back to face the steward.

"I've got to finish my report on the maneuvers," she said. "Screen my calls while I deal with it, will you? Put anything from Commander Henke, Admiral Sarnow or his staff, or any of the other skippers through, but ask anyone else if the Exec can handle it."

"Of course, Ma'am." MacGuiness hid his concern at the unusual order, and she smiled again, gratefully, at his neutral tone.

"Thank you." She booted her terminal, and he cleared his throat.

"Would you like a cup of cocoa, Ma'am?"

"No, thank you," she said without raising her eyes from the screen. MacGuiness looked at the crown of her head, then exchanged silent glances with Nimitz. The 'cat's body language radiated his own tension, but he flicked his ears and turned his head, pointing his muzzle at the hatch to the captain's pantry, and the steward relaxed slightly. He nodded back and withdrew like a puff of breeze.

Honor continued to stare at the characters on her screen until she heard the hatch close behind him, then shut her eyes and covered them with her hands. She hadn't missed the silent exchange between MacGuiness and Nimitz. A part of her hunkered petulantly down deep inside, resenting it, but most of her was intensely grateful.

She lowered her hands and tipped her chair back with a sigh. Nimitz crooned to her from his perch, and she looked up at him with a weary, bittersweet smile.

"I know," she said quietly.

He hopped down onto her desk and sat upright, holding her dark eyes with his grass-green gaze, and she reached out to caress his soft cream and gray fur. Her fingers were light, barely brushing him, but he didn't push her for more energetic petting, and she felt his concern reaching out to her.

For as long as Nimitz had been with her, Honor had always known he did *something* to help her through spasms of anger or depression, yet she'd never been able to figure out what it was. As far as she knew, no one who'd been adopted by a 'cat had ever been able to do so, but the strange intensification of their link since Grayson was at work now. She felt his touch, like a loving mental hand reaching deep inside her to soothe the raw edges of her emotions. He wasn't taking them away. Perhaps that was beyond his ability—or perhaps he knew how she would have resented it. Perhaps it was even simpler than that, something which would have been against his own principles. She didn't know, but she closed her eyes once more, hands gentle on his fur while his equally gentle caress comforted her inner hurt.

It was bitterly unfair. She'd been so happy, despite the tension of the Havenite crisis, and now this. It was as if Young had known how well things were going and deliberately gotten himself sent here just to ruin them. She wanted to scream and break things, to storm and rage at a universe that let things like this happen.

But the universe wasn't really unfair, she thought, and her mouth quirked. It just didn't give much of a damn one way or the other.

A strong, delicate true-hand touched her right cheek like a feather, and her eyes reopened. Nimitz crooned to her again, and her smile turned real. She drew him into her arms, hugging him to her breasts, feeling his relief as her inner pain ebbed.

"Thanks," she said softly, burying her face in his furry warmth. He bleeked gently to her, and she gave him another, tighter hug, then lifted him back to his perch. "Okay, Stinker. I'm on top of it, now." He flipped his tail in agreement, and her smile became a grin. "And the truth is, I *do* have to finish that report before I can run off to supper. So you just sit up there and keep an eye on me, right?"

He nodded and arranged himself comfortably, watching over her while she began scrolling through the paragraphs she'd already written.

Minutes passed, then a half hour, and there was no sound except the hum of Honor's terminal and the soft brush of fingers on a keyboard. She was so deep into her work she hardly noticed the soft com chime.

It sounded again, and she made a face and opened a window to accept the call at her workstation. The lines of her report vanished, and MacGuiness' face replaced them.

"Sorry to disturb you, Ma'am," he said formally, "but the Admiral is screening."

"Thank you, Mac." Honor straightened and brushed her fingers through her hair once more. It might be a good idea to let it grow long enough to braid, she thought absently, and keyed an "ACCEPT" code.

"Good evening, Honor." Admiral Sarnow's tenor was a bit deeper than usual, and she suppressed an ironic smile. She'd wondered if he'd heard the stories about her and Young.

"Good evening, Sir. What can I do for you?"

"I've been working my way through the dispatches *Warlock* delivered." He watched her face as he named Young's ship, but her eyes didn't even flicker, and he gave a sort of subliminal nod, more felt than seen, at the confirmation that she'd already known.

"There are several items we're going to have to cover in our squadron conference," he went on in a neutral tone, "but before that, I need to welcome Captain Young to the task group."

Honor nodded. The thought of inviting Young aboard her ship sickened her, but she'd known it was coming. Mark Sarnow would never pull a Sir Yancey Parks and freeze *any* captain out. Not until that captain had given him some specific reason to do so.

"I understand, Sir," she said after a moment. "Has *Warlock* rendezvoused with the base yet?"

"Yes, she has."

"Then I'll see to the invitation, Sir," she said flatly.

Sarnow started to open his mouth, then closed it. She saw the temptation to send the request through his own communication channels in his eyes and willed him not to make the offer.

"Thank you, Honor. I appreciate it," he said after a moment.

"No problem, Sir," she lied, and the words of her report returned as she cut the link.

She gazed at the report sightlessly for some seconds, then sighed. She'd finished it anyway, she told herself, and saved it to memory. She spent a few minutes routing copies to Sarnow and Ernestine Corell, knowing as she did that she was simply delaying the inevitable, then keyed a com combination. An instant later, the screen lit with Mike Henke's face.

"Bridge, Exec speaking," the commander began, then smiled. "Hello, Skipper. What can I do for you?"

"Please have George contact the repair base, Mike.

Ask them to relay a message to the heavy cruiser *Warlock*." Honor saw Henke's eyes widen and continued in the same, flat voice. "She's just arrived as part of our reinforcements. Please extend my and Admiral Sarnow's compliments to her captain—" the courteous formula was bitter on her tongue "—and invite him to repair on board immediately to confer with the Admiral."

"Yes, Ma'am," Henke said quietly.

"After George passes the message, inform the Bosun we're going to need a side party. And as soon as you hear back from *Warlock*, let me know when we can expect him aboard."

"Yes, Ma'am. Would you like me to greet him, Ma'am?"

"That won't be necessary, Mike. Just let me know when he's getting here."

"Of course, Ma'am. I'll get right on it."

"Thank you," Honor said, and cut the circuit.

Captain Lord Pavel Young stood stiff and silent in the repair base personnel capsule, watching the position display flicker as the capsule hurtled through the tube. He wore his best mess dress uniform, complete with the ornate golden sash and anachronistic dress sword, and his reflection looked back at him from the polished capsule wall.

He studied himself silently, eyes bitter despite his gorgeous appearance. Skillful (and expensive) tailoring deemphasized the steady thickening of his middle without *quite* becoming nonregulation, just as his neatly trimmed beard disguised his double chin. His appearance was satisfyingly perfect, but it took every gram of over-stressed self-control not to snarl at his reflected image.

The gall of the bitch. The sheer *gall* of her! Her "compliments," indeed! Yes, and oh-so-incidentally linked with Admiral Sarnow's!

This time he did snarl, but he rammed his self-control back into place and banished the expression even while his nerves tingled and spasmed with hatred. Honor Harrington. *Lady* Harrington. The commonborn slut who'd ruined his career—and now the task group flag captain.

His teeth ground together as he remembered. He hadn't thought much of her the first time he saw her at Saganami Island. She'd been a full form behind him, which should have put her beneath his notice even if she'd been more than some dirt-grubber from Sphinx. And she'd been plain-faced and unsophisticated with her almost shaven hair and beak of a nose, as well. Hardly worth a second look, and certainly not up to his usual standards. But there'd been something about the way she moved, something in the grace of her carriage, which had piqued his interest.

He'd watched her after that. She'd been the pet of the Academy, of course, her and her damned treecat. Oh, she'd pretended she didn't know how the instructors made her their favorite or how everyone fawned over her filthy little beast, but he'd seen it. Even Chief MacDougal, that lout of a phys ed instructor, had doted on her, and Mr. Midshipman Lord Young's interest had grown until he finally made it known.

And the baseborn bitch had turned him down. She'd *snubbed* him—snubbed *him!*—in front of his friends.. She'd tried to make it seem she didn't know what she was doing, but she had, and when he'd started to put her in her place with a few well-chosen words, that *bastard* MacDougal had appeared out of nowhere and put *him* on report for "harassing" her!

No one had turned him down, not since his father's yacht pilot when he was sixteen T-years old, and he'd fixed *her* ass the next time he caught her alone. Yes, and his father had seen to it she kept her mouth shut about it, too. It should have been the same with Harrington, but it hadn't. Oh, no, not with Harrington.

A low, harsh, hating sound quivered deep in his throat as he remembered his humiliation. He'd planned it so carefully. He'd spent days timing her schedule, until he learned about those private late-night exercise sessions of hers. She liked to turn the grav plates up, and she could have the gym to herself that late, and he'd smiled as he realized he could catch her alone in the showers. He'd even taken the precaution of slipping cotanine into the celery one of her friends kept feeding to her damned treecat. He hadn't got enough into it to kill the little monster, damn it, but it had made him so sleepy she'd left him in her dorm room.

It had been perfect. He'd caught her actually in the shower, naked, and seen the shock and shame in her eyes. He'd savored her panic as he stalked her through the spray, watching her back away while her hands tried ridiculously to cover herself, already tasting his revenge . . . but then something changed. The panic in her eyes had turned into something else when he reached for her to throw her up against the shower wall, and her slippery-wet skin had twisted out of his grasp.

He'd been surprised by her strength as she broke his grip. That was his first thought. And then he'd whooped in anguish as the heel of her right hand slammed into his belly. He'd doubled up, retching with hurt, and her knee had driven up into his crotch like a battering ram.

He'd screamed. Sweat beaded his forehead as he remembered the shame of that moment, the searing agony in his groin and, behind it, the sick, terrible humiliation of defeat. But just stopping him hadn't been enough for the bitch. Her savage, unfair blow had surprised and paralyzed him, and she'd followed through with brutal efficiency.

An elbow had smashed his lips to paste. The edge of a chopping hand had broken his nose. Another crushing blow snapped his collarbone, and her knee ripped up again—this time into his face—as he went down. She'd snapped off two incisors at the gum-line, broken six of his ribs, and left him sobbing in bloody-mouthed agony and terror under the pounding shower as she snatched up her clothing and fled.

God only knew how he'd gotten to the infirmary. He

couldn't even remember staggering out of the gym or how he'd run into Reardon and Cavendish, but they'd put some sort of story together. Not enough for anyone to believe, but enough, coupled with his name, to deflect official retribution. Or most of it, anyway. That sanctimonious prig Hartley had still dragged him into his office and made him apologize—*apologize!*—to the bitch in front of him and the Adjutant.

They'd had to settle for reprimanding him for the "harassment" episode. Young didn't doubt the slut had spilled her guts, but no one had dared do anything about it. Not with no more than her word against that of the Earl of North Hollow's son. But he'd still had to "apologize" to her. And infinitely worse, he'd been afraid of her. He'd tasted his own terror that she might hurt him again, and he'd hated her for that even more than for the beating itself.

He bared his teeth viciously at his reflection. He'd done his best to get her after that, used all his family's influence to destroy her career the way she deserved. But the bitch always had too many friends, like that asshole Courvosier. Of course, Young had always understood *that* relationship. He'd never been able to prove it, despite the time and money he'd invested in the effort, but he'd known she was spreading for Courvosier. It was the only explanation for the way the old bastard had watched over her career, and—his smile turned ugly with triumph—at least Courvosier had finally gotten *his*. Too bad the Masadans hadn't gotten their hands on Harrington, too!

He shook himself free of that sweet daydream and back to the drear reality of his repeated failures to deal with her once and for all. He and his father had managed to throw out enough roadblocks to slow her promotions, but the slut had a way of being there whenever the shit hit the fan, and somehow *she* always got the credit. Like the power room disaster when she'd been tac office on *Manticore*. She'd gotten the CGM and Monarch's Thanks for pulling three worthless ratings out of that one, then gotten herself mentioned in dispatches for rescuing assholes too stupid to get out of the way when the Attica Avalanche hit Gryphon in 275. Every goddamned time he turned around, there was Harrington, with everyone telling him how *wonderful* she was.

He'd thought he finally had her in Basilisk, but then she stumbled over the Peep attempt to seize the system. Blind fucking luck again, but did it matter? Hell, no! *She* got all the kudos, and *he* got officially censured for "failing to properly assess the threat to his assigned station"! And while *she* went off to fresh glory in Yeltsin, those motherless bastards at the Admiralty had shuffled him off into oblivion escorting convoys to the Silesian Confederacy, running routine grav wave surveys to update BuAstro's charts—every scut job they could think of. In fact, he'd been due to take still another convoy to Silesia when the growing crisis forced the Admiralty to pull *Warlock* at the last minute to reinforce Hancock.

And now this. She was flag captain. He was going to have to take the conniving bitch's *orders*, and he couldn't even use his superior birth to put her in her place. She actually took *social* precedence, as well! He might be heir to one of the Kingdom's oldest earldoms, but *she* was a "countess" in her own right. The newest parvenu in the peerage, perhaps, but a countess.

The flicker of the location display slowed as the tube capsule neared its destination, and he managed—somehow—to get the snarl off his face. Four years. Four long, endless T-years he'd endured his shame, the humiliating smirks of his inferiors as he toiled under the Admiralty's displeasure over Basilisk. He owed the bitch for that, too, and someday, somehow, he'd see to it that she paid in full. But for now, he had to endure one more humiliation and pretend nothing had ever happened between them.

The doors slid open, and he drew a deep breath as he stepped out into the spacedock gallery. Fresh, bitter hatred glittered briefly in his eyes as he saw the magnificent ship floating in the dock. HMS *Nike*, pride of the

Fleet. She should have been *his*, not Harrington's, but the bitch had taken that away from him, as well.

He settled his sword on his hip and walked stiffly towards the Marine sentries at *Nike's* boarding tube.

Honor stood with the side party in the entry port, waiting while Young swam the tube, and her palms were damp. Sick loathing boiled in her belly, and she wanted to dry her hands. But she didn't. She simply stood there, face calm, shoulder feeling unnaturally light and oddly vulnerable without Nimitz's warm weight. She hadn't even considered bringing the 'cat to *this* meeting.

Young appeared around the final bend, sliding through the tube's zero-gee, and her mouth tightened almost imperceptibly as she saw his mess uniform. Just like him to overdress, she thought scornfully. He always had to impress lesser beings with his family's power and wealth.

He reached the scarlet warning line and grasped the grab bar to swing across the interface into *Nike's* internal gravity, and the scabbard of his sword caught between his legs. He stumbled awkwardly, almost falling, even as the bosun's pipe's shrilled and the wooden-faced side party snapped to attention, and Honor's eyes glowed with brief, vicious pleasure as his face went scarlet in humiliation. But he got himself back on balance, and she'd banished satisfaction from her expression, if not her emotions, by the time he'd settled the sword properly back into place.

He saluted her, his face still red, and she didn't need Nimitz to feel his hatred. He might be senior to her, but he was visiting *her* ship, and she knew exactly how bitter that had to taste to him as she returned the salute.

"Permission to come aboard, Captain?" The tenor voice, so like and yet so unlike Admiral Sarnow's, was utterly without inflection.

"Permission granted, Captain," she replied with equal formality, and he stepped through the entry port hatch. "If you'll come with me, Captain, the Admiral is waiting for you in his briefing room."

Young nodded a curt acknowledgment and followed her into the lift. He stood on the opposite side of the car, back to the wall, while she punched their destination into the panel, and silence hung between them like poison.

He watched her, savoring his hate like some rare vintage, its bitter bouquet touched with a sweet, hot promise that his day would come. She seemed unaware of his gaze, standing completely at ease with her hands clasped behind her while she watched the location display and ignored him, and his hand tightened on the hilt of his sword like a claw.

The plain-faced slut he remembered from Saganami Island had vanished, and he realized he hated the tall, beautiful woman who'd replaced her even more than he'd hated that self-conscious girl. The understated elegance of artfully applied cosmetics emphasized her beauty, and even through his hatred and the residual fear of finding himself within her physical reach, he felt the tug of desire. The hunger to have her and reduce her to one more notch on his bedpost to put her in her place forever.

The lift stopped, the door opened, and her graceful wave gestured him out. He accompanied her down the passage to the flag briefing room, and Admiral Sarnow looked up as they stepped into the compartment.

"Captain Young, Sir," Harrington said quietly, and he came to attention.

Sarnow looked at him for a long, silent moment, then rose from his chair. Young met his gaze expressionlessly, but something about the admiral's green eyes warned him that this was yet another of the flag officers who sided with the bitch. Was she putting out for him on the side, too?

"Captain." Sarnow nodded, and Young's jaw clenched behind the cover of his beard at the omission of his peerage title.

"Admiral," he replied in an equally toneless voice.

"I imagine you've got a lot to tell me about the situation as seen from Manticore," Sarnow went on, "and I'm eager to hear it. Be seated, please."

Young slid into the chair, adjusting his sword carefully. It was awkward, but it also gave him a flicker of superiority as he compared his own sartorial splendor to the plain undress uniform the admiral wore. Sarnow glanced at him, then looked back at Harrington.

"I understand you have a previous engagement aboard the base, Dame Honor." Young's jaw clenched tighter as he used *her* title. "Captain Young and I will undoubtedly be tied up here for some time, so I won't keep you. Don't forget the com conference." Something like a small smile touched his lips. "It won't be necessary for you to return aboard if that will be inconvenient. Feel free to use a com aboard the base, if you like."

"Thank you, Sir." Harrington braced to attention, then glanced at Young. "Good evening, Captain," she said emotionlessly, and vanished.

"And now, Captain Young—" Sarnow sat back down and leaned back in his chair "—to business. You brought me a dispatch from Admiral Caparelli, and he says you and he discussed the situation at some length before he sent you out. So suppose you start by letting me hear exactly what His Lordship had to say."

"Of course, Admiral." Young leaned back and crossed his legs. "First of all . . ."

• CHAPTER TWENTY-ONE

Robert Stanton Pierre eased the small, nondescript air car out of the main traffic pattern and turned his flight computer over to Hoskins Tower's approach control. He sat back in his seat, looking out and down at the twinkling oceans and mountains of light which were Nouveau Paris, capital city of the People's Republic, and his face wore the grim, harsh expression he did not allow himself in daylight.

There wasn't much traffic this late at night. In a way, Pierre wished there were; he could have used the rush and flow of other vehicles to hide his own. But his official schedule was too busy for him to slip away during the day, especially with Palmer-Levy's Security goons watching him like hawks.

Of course, they weren't very *bright* hawks. His tight mouth twitched wryly, despite the pain locked deep within him. If you showed them what they expected to see, you could count on them to see it—and to stop looking for anything else. That was why he'd made sure they knew about his meetings with the CRP. The Citizens' Rights Party had been part of the system for so long its leadership, with a very few exceptions, couldn't find its ass with both hands, an incapacity which reduced it to little more than a convenient blind for his real activities. Not that the CRP wouldn't prove useful if— *when*—the time came. It just wouldn't be the CRP Palmer-Levy (or, for that matter, most of the present CRP's leaders) knew anything about.

Approach control nudged his air car closer to the pinnacle of the tower, and he turned his attention fully to it.

Hoskins Tower was just over four hundred stories tall
and a kilometer in diameter—a huge, hollow hexagon of
steel and ceramacrete, dotted with air traffic access
points and thrusting up from the greenery so far below.
There'd been a time when Nouveau Paris' towers, each a
small city in its own right, were its pride, but Hoskins
Tower's supposedly near-indestructible ceramacrete was
already beginning to crack and scale after barely thirty
years. Seen close at hand, the tower's skin was leprous
with slap-dash patches and repairs, and though it wasn't
evident from the outside, Pierre knew its upper twenty-
three floors had been closed off and abandoned over five
T-years ago because of massive plumbing failures.
Hoskins was still on the waiting list for repair crews
who, probably, would get around to its pipes someday.
Assuming, of course, that the bureaucrats didn't end up
diverting them to some more urgent "emergency" (like
repairs to President Harris' swimming pool) . . . or that
the repair crews didn't decide life would be easier on
the Dole and simply quit.

Pierre didn't like Hoskins Tower. It reminded him of
too many things from his own past, and the fact that
even a Dolist Manager with his clout hadn't been able to
get its plumbing fixed infuriated him. But this was "his"
district of the capital. He controlled the votes of the
people who lived in Hoskins, and it was to him they
looked for their share of the welfare system's spoils. That
made him a very important man to them—and gave him
a security screen here that even Palmer-Levy couldn't
match . . . or breach.

Pierre's lips curled back from his teeth as approach control inserted him into the tower's hollow top and his air
car began drifting down the patchily lit bore. Despite the
physical youth prolong conferred, he was ninety-one
T-years old, and he remembered other days. Days when
he'd fought his way off the Dole, before the rot had set so
deep. There'd been a time when Hoskins Tower's plumbing would have been fixed within days—when the
discovery that the bureaucrats in charge of its construction

had used substandard materials and evaded building codes throughout the massive structure in order to pocket enormous profits would have led to indictments and prison time. Now, no one even cared.

He punched an inconspicuous button, and the air car withdrew itself from approach control's grip. It was illegal—and supposedly impossible—to do that, but like everything else in the People's Republic, there were ways around that for anyone with the money to buy them and the will to use them.

He slid the air car sideways, sidling up to an abandoned apartment on the three hundred and ninety-third floor, and settled it onto a terrace. The terrace hadn't been designed for such landings, but that was why the air car was so small and light.

It was time, Pierre thought as he powered down the systems, for someone to fix Hoskins Tower. Among other things.

Wallace Canning raised his head, the movement quick and nervous. Heels clacked sharply on the bare floor, echoing and resounding down the hollow, empty corridors until it seemed an entire, unseen legion was converging upon him, but he'd been to plenty of meetings like this over the last three years, if not any under quite such outré conditions. He was no longer prone to panic, and his pulse trickled back to normal as his ears sorted out the single pair of feet at the heart of the murmuring echoes and a patch of light appeared.

He leaned back against the wall, watching the patch become a beam that swung from side to side as the walker picked his way down the steps from the mezzanine. Halfway down, the beam flicked up, pinning Canning to the wall while he screwed up his eyes against its intensity. It held on him for an instant, then swiveled back down to the bits and pieces of fallen ceiling littering the stairs. It reached their bottom at last and crossed to Canning, and then Rob Pierre shifted the light to his left hand and extended his right.

"Good to see you, Wallace," Pierre said, and Canning nodded with a smile that was no longer forced.

"Good to see you, too, Sir," he said. There'd been a time when saying "Sir" to a Prole, even one who was also a Dolist Manager, would have choked him. But those days were gone, for Wallace Canning had fallen from grace. His diplomatic career had ended in humiliation and failure, and not even his Legislaturalist family had been able to save him from the consequences. Worse, they hadn't even tried.

Canning had become an object lesson, a warning for those who failed. They'd stripped him of place and position, banished him into Prole housing like Hoskins Tower and into the monthly lines that gathered for their Basic Living Stipend checks. They'd turned him into a Dolist, but not like other Dolists. His accent and speech patterns, even the way he walked or looked at others, all singled him out as "different" in the eyes of his new fellows. Rejected by everyone he'd ever known, he'd found himself shunned by those whose equal he'd become, and it had seemed hate and self-pity were all that was left to him.

"Have the others arrived?" Pierre asked.

"Yes, Sir. Once I looked the site over, I decided to use the tennis court instead of the main concourse because the court doesn't have any skylights and I only had to black out two sections of windows."

"Good, Wallace." Pierre nodded and clapped the younger man on the shoulder. Quite a few of the so-called "leaders" Pierre was about to meet with tonight would have dithered for hours over something as simple as moving the meeting site a distance of forty or fifty meters. Canning had simply gone ahead and done it. It was a small thing, perhaps, but leadership and initiative were always made up of small things.

Canning turned to lead the way, but the hand on his shoulder stopped him. He turned back to Pierre, and not even the strange shadows across the other man's bottom-lit face could hide his concern.

"Are you certain you're ready for this, Wallace?" His voice was soft, almost gentle, but there was urgency in it. "I can't completely guarantee all these people are exactly what they seem."

"I trust your judgment, Sir." It was hard for Canning to say that, and even harder to mean it, but it was also true. There were many points upon which he still differed with this man, but he trusted him implicitly, and he made himself grin. "After all, I know you caught at least one InSec plant. I'd like to think that means you caught *all* of them."

"I'm afraid there's only one way to find out," Pierre sighed, and laid his arm across the ex-Legislaturalist's shoulders. "Oh, well! Let's go do it."

Canning nodded and swept aside the thick sheet of fabric which had been hung across an out-sized arch. The arch gave access to a short, broad passage between turnstiles and ticket-taker's windows, and Pierre followed his guide down it to the matching fabric barrier hung at its far end.

Canning thrust it aside in turn, and the politician switched off his handlight as they stepped into dim illumination. Their feet were loud on the bare floor, and the air smelled of musty disuse and abandonment. It was as if the building were the corpse of some mighty tree, rotting from the inside out, but the wan glow of widely spaced light tubes guided them across the back of the echoing concourse, past the basketball court and swimming pools thick in dust, to the central element of the long-dead sports complex.

Canning pushed another draped cloth barrier aside, and Pierre blinked. Clearly Canning had managed to replace most of the overhead lights that had been scavenged by tenants since the tennis court was abandoned, and the result of his labors was all Pierre could have wished. The blacked-out windows confined the light, hiding it from any outside eye, but it transformed the spacious tennis court into an illuminated stage. There was a powerful symbolism in meeting in this decaying monument to mismanagement and corruption, but Canning's work crew had created a pocket of light and order in its midst. They'd even swept and mopped, dusted the spectators' seats and cleared away the cobwebs, and there was an equally powerful symbolism in *that*. Despite the risk every person in this chamber ran, there was no aura of furtive concealment, none of the paranoiac stealthiness with which other clandestine groups met.

To be sure, he reflected as they walked down a seat aisle to the level of the court, paranoia and stealth had their places, especially in an operation like this, but decisive moments required their own psychologies. If he brought this off tonight, it would be worth every risk he and Canning had run to establish the setting and mood to make that possible.

And if he *didn't* bring it off, of course, he and Canning would probably "disappear" very shortly.

He reached the court itself and crossed to the small table Canning had set up at its center. Seventy-odd men and women looked back at him from the rows of seats facing it, and each face carried its own, unique blend of anxiety and excitement. The twelve people in the front row looked particularly tense, for they were the sole members of the CRP's eighty-person Central Committee whom he'd trusted enough to invite.

Pierre seated himself in the waiting chair, Canning standing behind him, and folded his hands on the tabletop. He sat silently, letting his eyes move slowly over all those faces, pausing briefly on each of them, until he reached the very end. Then he cleared his throat.

"Thank you for coming." His voice echoed in the huge chamber, and he smiled wryly. "I realize this isn't the most convenient possible spot, and I also recognize the risk in gathering all of us together in one place, yet I felt it was necessary. Some of you have never met before, but I assure you that *I* have met with each of the people you do not know. If I didn't trust them, they wouldn't be here. Of course, my judgment could be at fault, but—"

He shrugged, and one or two members of his audience managed to smile. But then he leaned forward, and all temptation to levity faded as his face hardened.

"The reason I invited you here tonight is simple. The time has come for us to stop talking about change and begin making it happen."

A soft sigh of indrawn breath answered him, and he nodded slowly.

"Each of us has his or her own reasons for being here. I warn you all now that not all of your fellows are motivated by altruism or principle—quite frankly, those qualities make poor revolutionaries." One or two people flinched at his choice of noun, and he smiled frostily. "To succeed at something like this requires an intense personal commitment. Principle is all very well, but something more is needed, and I've selected you because each of you *has* that something more. Whether it's personal outrage, anger over something done to you or yours, or simple ambition matters far less than that you have the strength of your motivation and the wit to make it effective. I believe all of you do."

He leaned back, hands still on the table, and let silence linger for a moment. When he spoke again, his voice was cold and harsh.

"For the record, ladies and gentlemen, I won't pretend *I* felt noble or altruistic when I began my contacts with the CRP and CRU. Quite the contrary, in fact. I was looking to protect my own power base, and why shouldn't I have? I've spent sixty years securing my present position in the Quorum. It was only natural for me to look to my flanks, and I did.

"But that wasn't my entire motive. Anyone with eyes can see the PRH is in trouble. Our economy might as well not exist, our productivity's fallen steadily for over two T-centuries—we exist only as a parasite, drawing our sustenance from the star systems our 'government' conquers to fill the treasury. Yet the bigger we become, the more ramshackle we grow. The Legislaturalists are riddled by factions, each protecting its own little piece of turf, and the Navy is equally politicized. Our so-called 'leaders' are fighting over the choicest cuts of the pie while the Republic's infrastructure rots out from under them—like this very tower around us—and no one seems to care. Or, at least, no one seems to know how to stop it."

He fell silent, letting them listen to his words, then resumed in a quieter but somehow sharper voice.

"I'm older than most of you. I remember times when the government was accountable, at least to the People's Quorum. Now it isn't. I'm considered a power within the Quorum, and I tell you that it's become nothing more than a rubber stamp. We do what we're told, when we're told. In return, we get our own piece of the pie, and because we do, we let the Legislaturalists make plans and formulate policies shaped by *their* interests, not ours. Plans which are leading the entire Republic straight into disaster."

"Disaster, Mr. Pierre?"

He looked up at the question. It came from a petite, golden-haired woman in the first row of chairs. She wore the gaudy clothing of a Dolist, but there was something subtly less baroque than usual about its cut, and her face bore none of the exaggerated face paint currently in vogue.

"Disaster, Ms. Ransom," Pierre repeated quietly. "Look around you. As long as the government keeps the BLS ahead of inflation, people are happy, but look at the underlying structure. Buildings crumble, the utilities are less and less reliable, our education system is a shambles, gang violence is a daily fact of life in the Prole towers—and *still* the money goes to the BLS, public entertainments . . . and Internal Security. It goes into keeping us all fat and happy and the Legislaturalists in power, not into reinvestment and repair.

"But even aside from the civilian economy, look at the military. The Navy sucks up an enormous percentage of our total budget, and the admirals are just as corrupt and self-seeking as our political lords and masters. Worse, they're incompetent."

The last sentence came out harsh and grating, and several people looked at one another as his hands fisted. But Ransom wasn't quite done.

"Are you suggesting that the solution is to dismantle the entire system?" she asked, and he snorted.

"We can't," he said, and sensed a wave of relaxation in his audience. "No one can. This system took over two centuries to evolve. Even if we wanted to, we couldn't possibly disassemble it overnight. The BLS is a fact of life; it must remain one for the foreseeable future. The need to loot other planets—and let's be honest; that's precisely what we do—to keep *something* in the treasury will be with us for decades, whatever changes we initiate in our economy. If we try pulling out too many bricks too quickly, the whole structure will come crashing down on us. This planet can't even *feed* itself without outside food sources! What do you think would happen if we suddenly found ourselves without the foreign exchange to buy that food?"

Silence answered him, and he nodded grimly.

"Exactly. Those of us who want radical reform had better understand right now that accomplishing it is going to be a long and difficult task. And those of us who are less interested in reform and more in power— and there are people like that in this room right now," he added with a thin smile, "had better understand that without at least some reform, there won't be anything to hold power *in* within another ten years. Reformers need power to act; power-seekers need reform to survive. Remember that, all of you. The time to fight over policy decisions will come *after* the Legislaturalists are toppled, not before. Is that understood?"

He swept them with cold eyes, and nodding murmurs of agreement came back to him.

"Very well." He pinched the bridge of his nose, then went on speaking past his raised hand. "No doubt you're all wondering why I called you together to say these things to you *now*. Well," he lowered his hand, and his eyes were hard, "there's a reason. All of you have heard reports about incidents between us and the Manties, right?" Heads nodded once more, and he snorted bitterly. "Of course you have. Public Information is playing them for all they're worth, drumming up a sense of crisis to keep people quiet. But what Information isn't telling you is that the Manties aren't responsible for them. *We're* deliberately orchestrating those incidents as the preliminary to an all-out attack on the Manticoran Alliance."

Someone gasped aloud, and Pierre nodded again.

"That's right, they're finally going to do it—after letting the Manties get stronger and stronger, dig in deeper and deeper. This isn't going to be like any of our other 'wars.' The Manties are too tough for that, and frankly, our own admirals are too gutless and incompetent." Pain wrenched at his expression, but he smoothed it back out and leaned over the table.

"The idiots in the Octagon have put together a 'campaign' and sold it to the cabinet. I don't have all the details, but even if it were the best plan ever written, I wouldn't trust *our* Navy to execute it. Not against someone as good as the Manties. And I *do* know that they've already had several disasters in the early phases—disasters they're concealing even from the Quorum."

He gazed grimly at his audience, and his voice was more than harsh when he resumed. It was ugly with hate, and his eyes blazed.

"Among those disasters was one that concerned me personally. My son and half his squadron were destroyed—annihilated—carrying out one of their 'minor provocations.' They were thrown away, *wasted* for no return at all, and the bastards refuse even to acknowledge that anything happened to them! If I didn't have my own sources in the military—"

He chopped himself off and glared down at the fists clenched on the table before him, and the room was deathly silent.

"So there you have *my* motive, ladies and gentlemen," he said finally, the depths of his voice cold and still.

"The last thing needed to push me from planning and thinking into action. But however personal my reasons may be, they've neither invalidated anything I've said nor pushed me into a wild, reckless adventure. I want the bastards who killed my son for *nothing* to pay, and for that to happen, I have to succeed. Which means you all have to succeed with me. Are you interested?"

He raised his eyes to his listeners, watching their expressions as his challenge hit them. He saw their fear and anxiety—and their temptation—and knew he had them.

"Very well," he said softly, pushing the pain out of his voice. "Between us, and coupled with my other contacts, including those I've mentioned in the military, we have the ability to bring it off. Not immediately. We need the proper conditions, the right sequence of events, but they're coming. I can *feel* them coming. And when they do, we have an ace in the hole."

"An ace in the hole?" someone said, and Pierre snorted a laugh.

"Several of them, actually, but I had one particular ace in mind." He nodded to Canning, still standing at his shoulder. "Those of you who didn't know Mr. Canning before tonight have all met him now. What you don't know about him—and what he's agreed to let me tell you—is that he works for Constance Palmer-Levy as a spy for Internal Security."

A dozen people exploded to their feet in a sudden, babbling tumult of shock. Two people actually bolted for the exit, but Pierre's voice cracked across the confusion like a whip.

"*Sit back down!*" His sheer, cold authority stunned them back into stillness, and he glowered at them in the sudden hush.

"Do you think Wallace would've agreed to let me tell you if he meant to betray us? For that matter, do you think InSec wouldn't have been waiting when we arrived? For God's sake, *he* made all the arrangements for tonight!"

He held them with his glare, radiating contempt for their doubts, without mentioning that letting Canning make the arrangements had been his own final test of the ex-Legislaturalist's reliability.

The people who'd risen resumed their seats, and the two who'd bolted returned sheepishly to the others. Pierre waited until they were all seated once more, then nodded.

"Better. Of course he was inserted into the CRP as a mole. Can you blame him for agreeing to be? They took everything away from him, disgraced and humiliated him, then offered him a way to get it all back, and why should he have felt any loyalty to *you*? You were the enemy, weren't you? Traitors and troublemakers out to destroy the world he was raised in!

"But they hadn't counted on what might happen once he was in place." He looked up at Canning, seeing his tension and the hard set of his jaw. "He knew exactly how he was being manipulated, and they hadn't left him any reason to be loyal to *them*, either.

"So he listened and reported like a good little spy, but even while he did, he thought about what he was reporting—and who he was reporting it to. Not one of the people whose help he'd had a right to expect had lifted a finger for him. How do you think that made him feel about the system?"

Everyone was staring at Canning, and the ex-diplomat raised his chin, returning their gaze with fiery eyes.

"And then, one night, he saw *me* meet with two CRU cell leaders, and he didn't report it. I know he didn't report it, because I saw what he *did* report." He smiled thinly as one or two people looked at him in surprise. "Oh, yes. Wallace isn't my only InSec contact. So when he decided to tell me who—and what—he was, I knew he was telling the truth, at least about his relationship with InSec.

"That was over three T-years ago, ladies and gentlemen. In all that time, I've never caught him in a lie or a deception. Of course he knew he was being tested. No doubt if he had been a plant, he would have gone to great lengths to maintain his cover from me, but he couldn't have done it this long. Not with the prizes I've offered over the years to tempt him into betraying me. Like all of us, he has his own motives, but I have complete faith in him, and he's a large part of what can make this work."

"How?" someone asked, and Pierre shrugged.

"He's gotten deeper and closer to me and my contacts with the CRP than any other spy Palmer-Levy ever planted on me. As of last month, he's actually become one of my staff aides. They *know* he has the inside track on my actions, and we've been very careful to see to it that anything he reports to them is accurate. Of course," the thin smile flashed again, "they don't realize quite how much he *doesn't* report."

Someone laughed in sudden understanding, and Pierre nodded.

"Precisely. They have so much faith in him that they've made him their primary information source on me, and he's telling them precisely what I *want* them to hear. Not everyone who works for InSec is an idiot, and maintaining our own security will be as important as ever, but we have an invaluable resource here—and one with intimate personal knowledge of our 'government's' internal workings, as well. Now do you see why I called him an ace in the hole?"

A soft murmur of assent answered him. He let it fade, then leaned over the table once more, and his voice was soft.

"All right, it's time to commit ourselves. War with Manticore is coming. There's no way we could stop it even if we wanted to, but if the Navy continues to screw up, it's going to turn into a disaster. And disasters, ladies and gentlemen, are a revolution's opportunities. But if we're going to take advantage of them, we have to mobilize and plan *now*. Among you, and with the addition of my military and security contacts, you represent all the elements we need for success—*if* you all commit yourself to work with me from this moment on and mean it."

He reached into his jacket and extracted a sheet of paper. He unfolded it and looked at them with cold, challenging eyes.

"This is an oath to do just that, ladies and gentlemen." He held it up, letting them see the few neatly printed lines—and the two signatures beneath them—and bared his teeth.

"Wallace and I have already signed it," he said quietly. "If InSec gets hold of this, he and I are dead men, but it proves our commitment. Now it's time for you to prove yours." He laid the sheet of paper on the table and uncapped a stylus. "Once you sign this, there's no backing out. I have every reason to keep it safely concealed, and I assure you I will. But if one of us betrays the others—if one of us even screws up and accidentally leads InSec to us—it will be found. But by the same token, each of us will know we all know that. That we *are* committed to see it through to the end."

He laid the stylus on the document and leaned back, watching them silently. Sweat beaded more than one pale face, and the silence stretched out intolerably, but then a chair scraped on the bare floor.

Cordelia Ransom was the first to walk to the table and sign.

• CHAPTER TWENTY-TWO

Honor lay face-down and sighed into the pillow as strong, skillful fingers kneaded her shoulders and worked down the hollow of her spine. She'd enjoyed her share of rubdowns and massages over the years, but Paul was one of the most skilled masseurs she'd ever encountered . . . even if his touch *was* a bit unprofessional.

She giggled at the thought, then arched with a soft, throaty purr as those delicious fingers dipped under to caress her breasts. *Definitely* unprofessional, she thought blissfully, luxuriating in his touch, and breath puffed on the back of her neck just before his lips touched.

"Feeling a bit better, are we?" he murmured, digging his thumbs gently into the small of her back while his fingers spanned and massaged her waist.

"Ummmmmm, *lots* better," she sighed, then chuckled deep in her throat. "You're really an awful person, Paul Tankersley."

"Awful?" he repeated in injured tones, and she nodded.

"Awful. Just look at the way you distract me from my duty."

"Ah, yes," he whispered, sliding his hands down over her hips and bending to kiss her spine. "Sweet distraction, that knits up the raveled sleeve of care."

"I don't think you've got that quite right," she said, turning on her back and reaching up her arms to him. "On the other hand, who cares?"

"Well, now." Paul poured fresh wine and handed her a glass, then lounged back beside her. She angled forward

246

for him to slide his arm around her, then leaned back into his embrace. He might be shorter than she, but a lot of her height was in her legs, and at moments like this he was *exactly* the right height.

"Well, what?" she asked.

"Well, do you want to talk about a certain pain in the ass captain?"

She turned her head, eyes darkening, but his understanding smile softened the sudden stab of resurgent tension. She started to open her mouth, then paused as Nimitz hopped up onto the foot of the bed.

"I see someone else wants to put in his two cents worth," Paul said dryly. He hadn't ejected Nimitz from his bedroom since that first night, and Honor often wondered if he'd done it the first time more for himself or for her. Whatever his reason had been, he'd come further faster in accepting the 'cat for who he was than most people ever managed. Now he simply nodded to the newcomer, then grinned as Nimitz stalked delicately up Honor's sheet-covered body to sprawl across *both* their laps.

"Hedonist!" he accused, and chuckled as the 'cat bleeked in contented agreement. Then his smile faded and he looked back at Honor. "As I was saying before a certain party intervened, are you ready to talk about it?"

"What's to talk about?" Honor lowered her gaze to her fingers and plucked at the edge of the sheet. "He's here. I'm here. Somehow I have to put up with him." She shrugged. "If I have to, I will."

"So cut and dried!" he chided, and she looked back up with a wan smile.

"Maybe not entirely. But—" She shrugged again, and Paul frowned.

"Honor, does he still scare you?" he asked very gently.

She flushed, but she didn't look away, and Nimitz's purr of support vibrated into her lap.

"I don't—" she began, then sighed. "Yes, I suppose he does," she admitted, still plucking at the sheet. "Not of what he might try to *do* this time, so much as what he reminds me of, I guess. I had nightmares about him for years, and every time I think of him, it all comes back. Besides," she lowered her eyes at last, "it frightens me to know I hate *anyone* as much as I hate him."

"That's more or less what I thought." His arm tightened, easing her head down on his shoulder, and his voice rumbled in her ear. "On the other hand, you might want to think about how *he* feels right now."

"I really don't *care* how he feels!" she said tartly, and he laughed.

"Oh, but you should! Honor, Pavel Young has to be one of the most miserable officers in the Fleet right now—and it's your fault."

She sat up straight, sheet slipping down to cover Nimitz, and turned to stare at him in surprise.

"Believe it, Honor. Look at it. His career's been frozen since Basilisk, while *your* career's taken off like a missile. He's been off escorting merchantmen in the back of beyond or updating star charts, but you've been at the center of the action. Worse, everyone in the Fleet knows what he tried to do to you—*and* the way you shoved his face down in it. And where does he find himself now? Attached to a task group that *you're* flag captain of!" He shook his head wryly. "I can't think of *anything* he'd find more humiliating."

"Well, yes, but—"

"But me no buts." He covered her mouth with his fingers. "Besides, there's another side to it. Don't you realize what a coward he is?"

"Coward?"

"Absolutely. Honor, I was his exec for damned near two T-years. You get to know someone in that long, and Pavel Young is a *toad*. He enjoys all the perquisites of his rank, but he'd never in a million years risk his career like you risked yours in Basilisk. And if *he'd* been in Yeltsin, he would've set a new hyper speed record pulling out. In short, my sweet, he's got the moral—and physical—courage of a beetle, and you beat the hell out of him when you were only nineteen T-years old. Believe me, his worst nightmare is finding himself in arm's reach of you for a repeat performance!"

Honor realized her mouth was hanging open and snapped it shut, and he laughed again at her expression. She stared into his eyes, trying to see how much of what he'd just said he really meant and how much was intended only to comfort her, and her expression slowly eased as she realized it was *all* true. He might be wrong, but he wasn't just saying it to make her feel better.

She snuggled back down against him, grappling with a vision of Pavel Young she'd never before entertained, and Paul left her to it. She studied the hideous memory of that night in the showers from a different perspective, and this time she saw the fear—the *terror*—under his hatred as she took him down. And she remembered other things, as well. Remembered Pavel Young avoiding contact sports, the way he backed down on the rare occasions when one of his social equals challenged his petty cruelties. . . .

It had never occurred to her that Young might be frightened of her. She'd certainly never been frightened of *him* after that night. Not in a physical sense, anyway. But if he was . . .

"You may be right," she said wonderingly.

"Of course I am. I'm *always* right," he said with studied pomposity, then *oofed* as a finger rammed into his ribs. "Maybe *I* should be scared of you, you violent woman!" he gasped, rubbing the injured spot, and grinned as she laughed. "That's better. Just remember that every time he has to look at you or take an order from the flagship he's going to be remembering what you did to him—and what happened when he tried to backstab you. Someone once said the best revenge is living well, so enjoy it."

"I'll try," she said seriously, then sighed. "But the truth is that knowing *he's* unhappy doesn't really make *me* much happier to have him around."

"There'd be something wrong with you if it did," he said, equally seriously, then bounced his hips to tumble

Nimitz off the edge of the bed. The 'cat twisted agilely in midair to hit the floor on all six feet with a solid thud, and Paul's eyes laughed at Honor. "In the meantime, if you're looking for something that *will* make you feel happier, I'm game if you are," he purred.

"I believe we're all here now, so let's get started." Mark Sarnow nodded from the com screen at his assembled captains and flag officers. The terminal in Paul's quarters was too small to display all the others at anything like a normal image size, but it was big enough for Honor to tell who was who. The admiral's screen, of course, was big enough to show him every detail, and she was happy her uniform hadn't gotten rumpled last night.

"The first item, of course, is a critique of yesterday's exercise," Sarnow went on. "An exercise which, I might note in passing, seemed to go better for some of us than for others." His cheerful tone took the potential sting from his words, and Commodore Banton grinned wryly.

"What you mean, Sir, is that some of us got taken to the cleaners," she replied. Her eyes moved to Honor's image, and she shook her head. "That was some major league sneakiness, Dame Honor. You suckered me completely."

"I was lucky, Ma'am."

"Lucky!" Banton snorted, then shrugged. "Well, I suppose you were, but some people seem to make their own luck. Mind you, I intend to pin your ears back next time, but don't sell yourself short."

Two or three other voices murmured agreement, and Honor's face heated.

"I agree with Commodore Banton's assessment," Sarnow said firmly, "which brings me to one of the points I wanted to raise. We're already planning to use the parasite pods to thicken up our missile salvos. What if we used the EW drones in the same way Dame Honor did, as well?"

"You mean to sneak into missile range on a powered-down intercept while they look the other way?" Commodore Prentis said with a thoughtful frown. "Be a bit risky against a real wall of battle, wouldn't it, Sir? If they picked up our fire control before we let fly—"

"Hold it, Jack," Banton cut in. "The Admiral may be onto something. Even if they do spot us, at optimum missile range we'd have two or three minutes to bring our impellers up. If we hold them at maximum readiness, we can get them up in ninety seconds. Sidewalls, too—and we'd still get our launch off."

"True," Captain Rubenstein said, "but there's still—"

The debate was off and running, and Honor sat back, content to listen to the others. Personally, she liked the idea, at least as one possible option. Too much would depend on the actual tactical situation to lay detailed plans in advance, but she certainly approved of the way Sarnow involved his officers in his skull sessions. If his captains knew how he thought ahead of time, they were far more likely to react quickly rather than wait for detailed orders.

The discussion moved on to finer details of the maneuvers and ended with an update from Ernestine Corell and Commander Turner on the fire control modifications for the parasite pods. Things were looking good all around, Honor decided. There was still an undertone of anxiety, for the task group was only too well aware of how naked it was out here by itself, but it was taking its cue from Sarnow's battlecruiser skippers and digging in to do something about its situation.

" . . . that just about ties everything up, then," Sarnow said finally. "Captain Corell will have those new targeting patterns to all of you by lunch, and I'd like to go over the final version of the parasite firing codes with you and Commander Turner, Isabella. Can you screen me at, oh, thirteen hundred?"

"Of course, Sir."

"In that case, ladies and gentlemen, good morning. Go have your breakfasts." Faces smiled at him as people prepared to cut the circuit, but Honor paused, her finger already on the key, as he looked straight at her

"Hold on just a moment, Dame Honor," he requested, and she sat back, eyes curious, as the other faces disappeared. Then they were alone, and she raised an eyebrow.

"Was there something special, Sir?"

"Yes, Honor, there was." He leaned back and brushed a finger over his mustache, then sighed. "I thought you should know that there's been a change in Commodore Van Slyke's chain of command."

"Indeed, Sir?" She managed to hang onto her natural tone.

"Yes. Captain Young is senior to any of his other COs. That makes him Van Slyke's second in command."

"I see," Honor said quietly.

"I thought you would." Sarnow frowned for a moment, then shrugged. "I'm not entirely happy about it, but there's no way to change it. I'm afraid, however, that it may involve us in helping Van Slyke bring him up to speed, and I wanted you to hear about it from me."

"Thank you, Sir. I appreciate that."

"Yes." Sarnow shrugged again, then straightened. "Well, so much for the unpleasant news. Will you join me for lunch? Bring Commander Henke with you, and we'll make it a working meal."

"Of course, Sir. We'll be there."

"Good." Sarnow nodded to her and killed the circuit, and she leaned back and gathered Nimitz in her arms.

"Time for breakfast before you go?" Paul called from the tiny attached dining cabin, and she shook herself.

"Always," she told him, "and I hope you've got some celery for a certain furry bandit."

Pavel Young stepped through the tube from his cutter into HMS *Crusader*'s boat bay. *Crusader* was older and smaller than his own *Warlock*, but even Young could find nothing to fault in the sharpness of the side party or the spotlessness of the boat bay gallery, and he nodded approvingly, for a neat ship was an efficient ship.

"Welcome aboard, Lord Young. I'm Commander Lovat, the Exec. The Commodore asked me to escort you to his briefing room."

"Of course, Commander." Young took in the slender commander's intricately-braided chestnut hair and attractively curved figure and gave her a gracious smile. He wouldn't mind having her for *his* exec, and he let his eyes linger unobtrusively on her hips and nicely filled trousers as he followed her to the lift.

Lovat led him to the flag briefing room without conversation and pressed the hatch admittance key for him.

"Here we are, Sir." Her voice was pleasant but cool, and Young gave her an even more gracious smile as the hatch opened.

"Thank you, Commander. I hope we meet again." He brushed against her as he stepped past her into the briefing room, then paused as he saw not the commodore but another commander with the aiguilette of a staff officer.

"Good morning, Lord Young," the commander said. "I'm Arthur Houseman, Commodore Van Slyke's chief of staff. I'm afraid the Commodore ran into a last-minute delay after you were already in transit. He asked me to assure you that he'll be here as soon as he can and to make you welcome until he arrives."

"I see." Young advanced across the compartment and took one of the chairs at the table with a suppressed frown. It always irritated him to be fobbed off with some junior officer, but he supposed it wasn't really Houseman's fault. "Please, sit down, Commander," he said, indicating another chair, and Houseman sat.

Young leaned back, considering the staff officer from under lowered lids. Houseman. One of the Waldsheim Housemans from New Bavaria, no doubt—he had the look. Young curled a mental lip in contempt. The Housemans were notorious for their extreme Liberal politics, always whining about "the little man" and "social responsibility." Which, Young had noticed, didn't prevent any of them from enjoying every advantage their own lofty birth and wealth provided. It only gave them a smug sense of complacency when they looked down their noses at other people who did the same things without mouthing pious platitudes to proclaim their own worthiness.

"I imagine you didn't get much notice when they sent you out here, Sir," Houseman said in the tone of one making polite conversation.

"No, I didn't." Young shrugged. "But when the Admiralty cuts you urgent priority orders, you don't complain. You just execute them."

"So I've noticed. But at least your arrival spared you what the rest of us had to endure yesterday, Sir."

"Yesterday?" Young cocked his head, and Houseman smiled humorlessly.

"We were part of Commodore Banton's screening element," he explained. Young still looked blank, and the commander's smile turned even more sour. "*Crusader* got wiped out along with her battlecruisers when our gallant flag captain pulled her little surprise, Sir."

Young sat very still, mental antennae quivering at Houseman's acid tone. He wondered if the commander realized how much he'd just given away, and another corner of his mind wondered why Houseman hated Harrington.

And then it clicked. *Houseman.*

"No," he leaned casually back, crossing his legs, "I missed the exercise. Of course, I've known Captain Harrington a long time. Since the Academy, in fact."

"You have, Sir?" The lack of surprise in Houseman's voice suggested his earlier revelation had been intentional, and his next words confirmed it. "I've only known her for a few months, myself. Of course, I've heard about her. One does hear things, you know, Sir."

"I do indeed." Young showed his teeth in an almost-smile. "I understand she's made quite a name for herself in the last few years." He shrugged. "She always was . . .

determined, one might say. I always thought she was a bit hot-tempered, myself, but I don't suppose that's a drawback in combat. Not as long as you don't lose your head, of course."

"I agree, Sir. On the other hand, I'm not certain 'hot-tempered' is exactly the way I'd describe the flag captain. It's too . . . too *mild*, if you see what I mean."

"Perhaps it is." Young bared his teeth again. It wasn't quite the thing to encourage an officer to criticize one of his superiors, but Houseman wasn't just any officer. He was chief of staff to a commodore Harrington would have to deal with on a regular basis, and Van Slyke would have to be superhuman not to be influenced by his chief of staff's opinion of the flag captain.

"Actually, you may have a point, Commander," he said, settling in for a long—and profitable—conversation. "I remember back at Saganami Island she had a tendency to push people. Always within the letter of the regs, of course, but I always thought . . ."

• CHAPTER TWENTY-THREE

A quiet signal chirped through the eye-soothing dimness of the Central War Room, known to its inhabitants as "the Pit." Admiral Caparelli raised his head to check the master display at the far end of the Pit for the new incident's location, then punched up the details on his terminal, and his eyes flicked over the data.

"Bad?" Admiral Givens asked quietly across the smaller quadrant plot holo, and he shrugged.

"More irritating than serious—I think. Another in-and-out at Talbot. Of course—" he smiled without mirth "—the report *is* eleven days old. Things may have gotten a bit more than 'irritating' since."

"Um." Givens pursed her lips and brooded down at the holo between them. Her eyes were focused on something only she could see, and Caparelli waited patiently for her to hunt down whatever it was. Several seconds passed, then a full minute, while he listened to the Pit's quiet background sounds before she shook herself and looked back across the tiny stars at him.

"A thought, I take it?"

"More of a general observation, really."

"Well, don't sit on it till it hatches, Pat."

"Yes, Sir." She gave him a fleeting smile, then turned serious. "The thing that just occurred to me—something that's *been* occurring to me for several days now—is that the Peeps are being too cute for their own good."

"Ah?" Caparelli tilted his chair back and raised an eyebrow. "How so?"

"I think they're trying for too fine a degree of coordination." Givens waved at the display. "They've been turning the pressure up for weeks now. At first it was just 'mystery' raiders we couldn't positively ID, and when we *knew* they were Peeps, there was no combat. Then they started actively harassing our patrols. Now they're pouncing on convoys and system pickets with hunt-and-kill tactics. But every time they do something to up the ante, it starts at one point, then ripples out north and south."

"Indicating what?"

"Indicating that each increase in pressure is the result of a specific authorization from some central command node. Look at the timing, Sir." She reached into the holo, running her fingers up and down the frontier. "If you assume each fresh escalation was authorized from someplace fifty or sixty light-years inside the Peep border—like Barnett, for example—the delay in the incidents to either side of the first incident in the new pattern is just about right for the difference in the flight times to those points from Barnett."

She withdrew her hand and frowned at the display, worrying her lower lip between her teeth.

"So they're coordinating from a central node," Caparelli agreed. "But we figured that all along, Pat. In fact, we're doing the same thing. So how does that constitute 'too cute for their own good'?"

"We're *not* doing the same thing, Sir. We're channeling information and authorizing general deployments, but we're trusting local COs to use their own judgments because of the com lag. It looks to me like the Peeps are authorizing each successive wave of activity from Barnett, which implies a two-way command and control link, not just information flow. They're waiting until they hear back, then sending out orders to begin the next stage, then waiting for fresh reports before authorizing the *next* step. They're playing brontosaurus—that's why this whole thing seems to be building up so ponderously."

"Um." It was Caparelli's turn to stare into the holo. Givens' theory was certainly one explanation for the

Peeps' increasing heavy-handedness. What had started out as a series of lightning pinpricks was becoming a chain of steadily heavier blows spaced out over longer periods of time. It felt undeniably clumsier, but then again, any strategist would try to build in cutouts: points at which he could abort the operation if he had to. It was quite possible Pat was right, that the coordination for this phase was emanating from Barnett, but it didn't follow that the same pattern would apply after they actually pulled the trigger. Once you were committed, there was no more point in cutouts; it was all or nothing, and if you had a clue as to what you were doing, you went for the most flexible possible command arrangements.

If you had a clue.

He turned his chair slowly from side to side, then raised his eyes once more to Givens.

"You're suggesting they may continue to operate this way once the shooting starts in earnest?"

"I don't know. It's possible, given their past operational patterns. Remember, Sir, we're the first multi-system opponent they've gone after. All their previous ops plans have involved closely controlled converging thrusts on relatively small targets, spatially speaking, and even the best staffs get into habits of thought. They may have overlooked some of the implications of the difference in scale.

"But my real point is that whatever they plan to do *after* the shooting starts, they're running under tight central control in the opening game. They have to have a detailed ops plan for when they finally move in strength, and after studying their previous campaigns, I'm willing to bet this one involves some careful—and cumbersome—timing constraints. Even if I'm wrong about that, at the moment they're going to react and respond to anything *we* do on the basis and within the limitations of that two-way traffic flow to Barnett."

"Assuming they haven't sent out orders for the next phase even as we sit here."

"Assuming that," Givens agreed. "But if they *haven't* reached that point yet, it could be useful to consider inserting information we'd like them to have into that command loop."

"Such as?"

"I don't know," Givens admitted. "I just hate the thought of losing any opportunity to throw them off stride. The worst thing we could do is let them steamroller us on *their* timetable. I'd like to shake them up, draw them off balance."

Caparelli nodded and joined her in pondering the holo afresh.

His eyes flitted automatically back to the three most worrisome points: Yeltsin, Hancock Station, and the Talbot-Poicters area. Although the pace and violence of Haven's war of nerves had increased steadily, Manticore had held its own in actual encounters to date. The loss of *Star Knight* with all hands was more than offset, albeit fortuitously, by *Bellerophon's* destruction of two entire Peep battlecruiser divisions in Talbot. By the same token, the tragic loss of Captain Zilwicki's entire squadron had not only earned her the Parliamentary Medal of Valor, the Kingdom's highest award for heroism, but saved every ship in the convoy under her protection . . . and cost the People's Navy almost twice her own ships' combined tonnage. Other Peep attacks had been more successful, of course, for they had the advantage of the initiative. And, he conceded unhappily, they also seemed to have fiendishly good intelligence on supposedly secure star systems. But by and large, their successes were outweighed, in the cold, brutal logic of war, by their less numerous but more spectacular failures.

Unfortunately, that didn't mean their operation *as a whole* was failing. Although his redeployments to face the threat had been much less drastic than he'd originally envisioned, there was still a general shift and flow of task forces and squadrons all throughout the volume of the Alliance. That left him feeling off balance and defensive-minded, driven into passive reaction, not initiation, and some of his local commanders seemed similarly afflicted. They were making decisions which looked more than a little questionable from his own vantage point, at any rate.

He tapped his fingertips on his console, and his frown deepened. Talbot-Poicters worried him because there'd been so much Peep activity in the area. Both star systems were exposed, and the incidents within them *could* simply be classic probing missions. Reconnaissances in force which happened to run into local pickets—or over them, he thought grimly—in the course of pre-attack scouting missions. Except that their timing argued that the Peeps already *had* detailed intelligence.

Yeltsin and Hancock, on the other hand, worried him because there'd been *no* action in their areas, other than the original convoy raid in Yeltsin and the Caliph's mystery losses in Zanzibar. Perhaps it was because he viewed them as his most vulnerable points, but the lack of activity around either star made him wonder why the Peeps didn't want him worrying about them.

Added to which, Admiral Parks' decision to uncover Hancock was enough to give any First Space Lord ulcers. He understood Parks' reasoning, but he wasn't at all certain he shared it. In fact, he'd gone so far as to draft a dispatch ordering Parks back to Hancock only to file it unsent and settle for ordering Admiral Danislav to expedite his own movements. The RMN tradition was that the Admiralty didn't override the man on the spot unless it had very specific intelligence that he didn't have . . . and the one thing Sir Thomas Caparelli currently had in abundance was a *lack* of specific intelligence.

"They're going to do it, Pat," he murmured, eyes still fixed on the display. "They're really going to do it."

It was the first time either of them had said so in so many words, but Givens only nodded.

"Yes, Sir, they are," she agreed, her voice equally soft.

"There has *got* to be some way to pull them off balance," the First Space Lord muttered, drumming his fingers harder on the console. "Some way to turn this thing around so it bites them on the ass."

Givens gnawed her lower lip a moment longer, then drew a deep breath and reached back into the display. She cupped her palm around Yeltsin's Star, and Caparelli's eyes narrowed as he raised his head to look at her.

"I believe there may be, Sir," she said quietly.

"Let me be certain I understand this correctly, Sir Thomas." The Duke of Cromarty's voice was very quiet. "You're suggesting that we deliberately *entice* the PRH into attacking Yeltsin's Star?"

"Yes, Sir." Caparelli met the Prime Minister's gaze levelly.

"And your reasoning for this is?" Cromarty prompted.

"In essence, Sir, we hope to set a trap for the Peeps." Caparelli cleared his throat and activated a small-scale holo display of the Yeltsin System in the high-security conference room just off Cromarty's office.

"At present, Yeltsin's Star represents our most powerful concentration short of Home Fleet itself, Your Grace," he explained. "We've taken pains to keep our exact strength in the system a secret. Given the intelligence the Peeps seem to have on our routine movements elsewhere, it's quite possible they know much more about Yeltsin than we'd like, but Admiral Givens' plan offers us at least the possibility of turning that around on them."

He manipulated controls, and the tiny star system above the table was suddenly lit by tinier flecks of bright green light.

"The Graysons have spent the last year fortifying their system with our assistance, Your Grace. We're still a long, long way from completing our plans, but as you can see, we've made considerable progress and Grayson itself is well covered by orbital forts. They're small, by our standards, because they're left over from the Grayson-Masada cold war, but there are a lot of them, and they've been heavily refitted and rearmed. In addition, the Grayson

Navy itself must now be considered equivalent to at least a heavy task group of our own Navy—a truly enormous accomplishment for a seventeen-month effort from their beginning tech base—and Admiral D'Orville's Second Fleet is an extremely powerful formation. All in all, Sir, this system has turned into an excellent place for an attacker to break his teeth."

"But it also happens to belong to a sovereign ally of the Star Kingdom, Admiral." Concern and more than a hint of disapproval tinged Cromarty's voice. "You're suggesting that we deliberately draw the enemy into attacking one of our friends—without consulting them."

"I fully realize the implications of my suggestion, Your Grace, but I'm afraid we've reached a point at which we don't have time for consultations. If Admiral Givens is correct—and I think she is—the Peeps are counting down against a timetable they may have spent years perfecting. We have our own defensive plans, but allowing them to begin a war on their terms, at a time of their choice, against a target of their choice, is extremely dangerous. If at all possible, we need to draw them into a false start or, at least, into attacking a target of our choice. But to do that, Your Grace, we have to get the information we want them to have into their hands in time for them to rethink their operations and send out new orders from their central command node *before* their scheduled 'X' hour.

"The key to the plan is one of Admiral Givens' communication officers at BuPlan. The Havenite ambassador's gone to great pains to suborn him. He's been working for them for almost two T-years now, but what they don't know—we hope—is that he's *actually* working for Admiral Givens. To date, his reports have been one hundred percent accurate, but he's reported only information which couldn't hurt us or which we were reasonably certain the Peeps could obtain by other means.

"What we propose is to use him to inform the Peeps, through Ambassador Gowan, that the activity around

Talbot Station has concerned us so deeply that we're transferring several of D'Orville's battle squadrons there as reinforcements. We'll be sending replacements to Yeltsin, of course, but not for two or three weeks. At the same time as he passes the information off to Gowan, we'll send the same instructions to Admiral D'Orville through regular channels. As far as anyone will know, it will be an absolutely genuine order . . . but the same courier boat will carry *separate* orders under a diplomatic cover instructing Admiral D'Orville to disregard the redeployment instructions. If the Peeps have sources in our communications sections that we *don't* know about, they may pick up the 'official' orders as confirmation of our double agent's report.

"If our present analysis of Peep operations is accurate, they're probably coordinating from their base in the Barnett System. If we can get this false information to Barnett quickly enough, whoever's in command there will have a window to hit Yeltsin before our 'replacements' arrive. Only when he does, he'll find out none of D'Orville's ships ever left."

"I understand that, Sir Thomas, but what if he hits Yeltsin hard enough to take the system *despite* Admiral D'Orville's strength? Bad enough that we're asking our allies to take the brunt of the first blow, but what if that blow is heavy enough to conquer them despite all we can do?"

Caparelli leaned back in his chair, his face like stone. He was silent for several seconds. When he spoke again, his voice was heavy.

"Your Grace, they're going to attack us. Neither I nor any member of my staff doubts that, and when they do, Yeltsin will be a primary target. It *has* to be, given the shallowness of our frontier at that point. I realize the risk I'm suggesting we expose the Graysons to, but it's my opinion that drawing the Peeps into attacking us there on our terms is our most effective option. In a best-case scenario, they'll underestimate D'Orville's strength and attack in insufficient force, in which case officers like D'Orville and High Admiral Matthews will hand them their heads. And even if we lose D'Orville's entire fleet *and* Yeltsin, we'll hurt them very, very badly, and a prompt counterattack from Manticore should retake the system with an overall loss rate which will be heavily in our favor."

"I see." Cromarty rubbed his chin, eyes dark, then drew a deep breath. "How quickly do you need a decision, Sir Thomas?"

"Frankly, Your Grace, the sooner the better. We don't know that we still have enough time to bring this off— assuming it works at all—before they launch an attack elsewhere. If we *do* have time, we don't have a lot of it."

"I see," the duke repeated. "Very well, Admiral. I'll give you my decision, one way or the other, as quickly as possible."

"Thank you, Your Grace."

Caparelli withdrew from the conference room, and the Prime Minister leaned his elbows on the table and propped his chin in his cupped palms while he stared at the holo for long, silent moments. His was a politician's well-trained face, yet his expression mirrored his internal struggle, and, at last, he reached for his com terminal and pressed a key.

"Yes, Your Grace?" a voice asked.

"I need a high-security scrambled link to Admiral White Haven's flagship, Janet," he said quietly.

Hamish Alexander paced back and forth across his briefing room aboard HMS *Sphinx*, hands folded behind him, and scowled as he listened to the Prime Minister's voice from the com.

" . . . and that's about the size of it, Hamish. What do you think?"

"I *think*, Allen, that you shouldn't be asking me that," the Earl of White Haven said testily. "You're undercutting Caparelli's authority by asking me to second-guess him. Especially by ignoring official channels to go behind his back this way!"

"I realize that. Unfortunately—or fortunately, depending on one's viewpoint—you're my best source for a second opinion. I've known you and Willie for years. If I can't ask you, who *can* I ask?"

"You're putting me in a hell of a spot," White Haven muttered. "And if Caparelli finds out about it, I wouldn't blame him for resigning."

"A risk I'm willing to take." Cromarty's voice hardened. "What he's proposing comes very close to betraying an ally, Hamish, and you happen to be not only a respected strategist but the officer who conquered Endicott and finalized our alliance with Grayson. You know the people involved, not just the military situation. So give me an opinion, one way or the other."

White Haven clenched his teeth, then sighed and stopped pacing. He recognized an order, however distasteful, when he heard one.

"All right, Allen." He sank into a chair in front of the terminal and thought deeply for a few moments, then shrugged. "I think he's right," he said, and smiled crookedly at Cromarty's obvious surprise.

"Would you care to elaborate?" the duke asked after a moment.

"Or, put another way, why am I backing a man I don't like?" White Haven's smile grew broader, and he waved a hand. "If it works, it does exactly what Caparelli says it will—let's us call the opening shot and, probably, hit them with a much heavier force than they're expecting. He's also right that they're going to hit Yeltsin anyway, and this gives us our best chance to hold the system. At the very least, we should tear a real hole in their attack force, and that makes it exactly the sort of battle we *need* to fight. One that gives us an excellent chance at an outright victory—which would be of incalculable psychological importance at the outset of a war—and inflicts severe losses on them even if we lose. As for the Graysons, they're tough people, Allen. They knew they were making themselves targets the day they signed up with us, and they still thought it was worth it."

"But doing it without even warning them. . . ." Cromarty's voice trailed off, but his acute unhappiness was evident.

"I know," White Haven murmured, then paused.

"You know," he went on after a moment, "I've just had a couple of thoughts. First, you might want to suggest to Caparelli that there's a way to make his strategy even more effective." Cromarty looked a question, and the admiral shrugged. "I know I've opposed dispersing Home Fleet, but suppose that at the same time as we leak the information that we're stripping Yeltsin's Star we actually pull three or four squadrons out of Home Fleet and send them in to reinforce D'Orville. If the Peeps think we pulled, say, four squadrons *out* of Yeltsin when in fact we've just put four additional squadrons *into* the system, their force estimate is going to be very badly off."

"And if they're watching Home Fleet? I'm no admiral, but even I know it's not too hard for even merchantmen to track impeller drives for a force of that magnitude. And it's virtually certain that at least some of our 'neutral' merchant traffic is actively spying for Haven."

"True, but we can set it up as a training exercise for, say, two squadrons, and cut the other two official orders for Grendelsbane, then do the same sort of trick Caparelli's already talking about for D'Orville. Not even the admirals involved would know where they were actually headed until they opened their sealed orders after going into hyper, and any taps the Peeps have on us would show them departing on the proper headings for their official orders. You might even ask Pat Givens whether she thinks a reference to their movements could be added to her leak without making the bait too obvious."

"Um." Cromarty frowned at the other end of the com link, his eyes thoughtful. Clearly the idea of reinforcing Yeltsin appealed to him, and he pondered it for several seconds, then nodded. "All right, I think I *will* suggest it. But you said you had 'a couple of thoughts.' What's the other one?"

"Unless I'm mistaken, Michael Mayhew's right here on Manticore. I know he's enrolled for graduate work at King's College—has he left because of the crisis?"

The Prime Minister stiffened, then shook his head, and White Haven shrugged. "In that case, you've got access to Protector Benjamin's heir, effectively the crown prince of Grayson. It wouldn't be the same as talking to their head of state, but it would certainly be the next best thing."

" . . . so I'm sure you can see why I asked you to visit me, Lord Mayhew," the Duke of Cromarty said quietly. "My senior officers all agree that this represents our best strategic option, but it necessarily means exposing your homeworld to enormous risk. And because of the time pressures involved, there is quite literally no time to discuss it with Protector Benjamin."

Michael Mayhew nodded. He looked (and was) absurdly young for a graduate student, even on Manticore. In fact, he was young enough his body could still accept the original, first-generation prolong treatments, something which had been unavailable to Grayson's isolated people before they joined the Alliance. Now Cromarty watched that youthful face frown in thought and wondered if Grayson was ready for the longevity its children were about to inherit.

"I see the problem, Sir," Mayhew said at last. He exchanged glances with the Grayson ambassador and shrugged. "I don't see that we have a lot of choice, Andrew."

"I wish we could speak directly to the Protector about it," the ambassador worried, and Mayhew shrugged again.

"I do, too, but I think I know what he'd say." He turned back to Cromarty, and his young eyes were level. "Your Grace, my brother knew what he was getting into when he chose to ally with Manticore rather than be digested by Haven—or, worse yet, Masada. We've always known that when the showdown finally came we'd be caught in the middle, so if we're going to be attacked anyway, anything that improves our chances of winning has to be worth trying. Besides," he finished simply, a flash of genuine warmth lighting those steady eyes, "we owe you."

"So you think we should go ahead?"

"I do. In fact, as Steadholder Mayhew and heir to the Protectorship, I formally *request* that you do so, Mr. Prime Minister."

"I don't believe it," Sir Thomas Caparelli murmured. He folded the short, terse, handwritten directive, and slid it back into the envelope with the bright yellow and black security flashes. He dropped them both into the disposal slot on his desk, then looked up at Patricia Givens. "Less than five hours, and we've got the go-ahead."

"We do?" Even Givens sounded surprised, and Caparelli snorted a laugh.

"More than that, he's directed us to up the stakes." He slid a sketched out deployment order across the desk to her and tipped back his chair as she scanned it.

"Four squadrons?" Givens murmured, absently twisting a lock of brown hair around an index finger. "That's quite a diversion."

"You can say that again—and all superdreadnoughts." Caparelli smiled a bit sourly. "That's twenty-six percent of Home Fleet's superdreadnoughts. If we get hit here while they're out there—" He broke off and waved both hands in a throwaway gesture, and Givens pursed her lips.

"Maybe, Sir. Then again, maybe not. It won't exactly leave us uncovered, and if the Peeps buy our fake redeployments, they'll run into over sixty superdreadnoughts they think are somewhere else."

"I know." Caparelli frowned a moment longer, then nodded. "All right, let's get this set up. And I guess we'd better send along a flag officer with the seniority for that big a reinforcement."

"Who did you have in mind, Sir?"

"Who else?" Caparelli's sour smile was back. "It'll almost have to be White Haven, won't it?"

"White Haven?" Givens couldn't quite hide her surprise. Not only did she know Caparelli and White Haven disliked one another, but White Haven was currently second in command of Home Fleet, as well.

"White Haven," Caparelli repeated. "I know it'll make a hole in Webster's command structure, but so will the squadrons we're taking away from him. And White Haven not only has the seniority and the savvy to command them, he's also our most popular officer—after Harrington—in Grayson eyes."

"True, Sir. But he's senior to Admiral D'Orville, as well. That means he'll supersede the man on the spot when he arrives. Will that cause problems?"

"I don't think so." Caparelli thought for a moment, then shook his head. "No, I'm certain it won't. He and D'Orville have been friends for years, and they both know how critical the situation is. Besides—" the First Space Lord bared his teeth in a mirthless smile "—there ought to be plenty of crap to fall on both of them, even if this works."

• CHAPTER TWENTY-FOUR

Admiral Parnell entered the DuQuesne war room briskly despite the late hour. No one looking at him would have thought he'd had less than three hours sleep, but Parnell himself was naggingly aware of his fatigue. He considered—again—taking a stim tab, but if he did that he'd never get back to sleep again. Better to see what hot coffee could accomplish first.

Commodore Perot was already there, and he turned quickly, a message board tucked under his arm, at his boss's approach.

"This better be important, Russell." Parnell's tone was only half joking, and Perot nodded.

"I know, Sir. I wouldn't have bothered you if I didn't think it was." Perot's voice was calm, but he tilted his head to one side, inviting the admiral into one of the high-security briefing rooms, and surprise raised Parnell's eyebrows before he could stop them.

Perot closed the door behind them, shutting out the war room's background murmur, and punched a complicated security code into the message board before pressing his thumb to the scanner. The display blinked obediently to life, and he passed it to the admiral without a word.

Parnell frowned at the diplomatic corps header, then glanced at the text and stiffened. He sank into a chair, running his eyes slowly back over the terse sentences, and felt the rags of weariness blowing away from his brain.

"My God, Sir. They've done it," Perot said softly.

"Maybe," Parnell said more warily, but his own exultation warred with his caution. He laid the message board on the desk and rubbed his temple. "How reliable is this source of Ambassador Gowan's?"

"No intelligence source can ever be absolutely guaranteed, Sir, but everything this one's ever given us has panned out, and—"

"Which could mean they know all about him and they've been setting us up for the big one," Parnell interrupted dryly.

"That's always the problem with spies, Sir," Perot agreed. "In this case, however, we have some additional intelligence to support him." Parnell raised an eyebrow, and Perot shrugged. "If you scroll to the next page of the Ambassador's dispatch, you'll see that both of the Home Fleet detachments mentioned in his source's initial report departed almost exactly on the schedule he gave us, and their headings matched his version of their orders. Gowan had a day or two to work his other contacts, too, and some of the personnel involved were fairly loose-lipped. Three of his people—two restaurant workers and a barber, all on *Hephaestus*—report overhearing customers complaining about being ordered clear out to Grendelsbane."

"What sort of customers?" Parnell asked intently.

"Enlisted and noncom, Sir—not officers. And they were all regular patrons." Perot shook his head. "They certainly weren't ringers brought in for the occasion, so unless we want to assume Gowan's entire network's been broken and Manty intelligence knew exactly who to have gossip in front of who—" The chief of staff broke off with a shrug.

"Um." Parnell stared back down at the message board, wanting to believe and fighting his own desires. If only they'd been able to extend the Argus net to Yeltsin! But there hadn't been enough time to set it up—even assuming the seething deep-space activity in Yeltsin hadn't ruled it out. The Graysons seemed intent on smelting down every asteroid in the system for their orbital and planetary projects, and Nav Int had decided they were too likely to stumble over one of the sensor platforms, however heavily stealthed, and blow the entire Argus operation. Which meant he didn't have the same "look" into Yeltsin. Maybe that was his problem. He'd gotten used to more detailed intelligence than he had any right to expect.

"Anything from Rollins?" he asked.

"No, Sir." Perot glanced at the time and date display on the wall and made a face. "The Argus ships can't maintain a guaranteed schedule, but if they're running as close as they usually do, he should have gotten the latest dump from Hancock no later than yesterday."

"Which means seventeen more days before *we* get it," Parnell grunted.

He leaned back, nibbling on his lower lip. Seventeen days was far too long to wait. Barnett was a hundred and forty-six light-years from Yeltsin, a three-week trip for superdreadnoughts, and his window was barely twenty-six days wide. He couldn't possibly delay his decision until he had Rollins' report, and, by the same token, if he went, he'd have to go in without Admiral Ruiz's three battle squadrons, still en route to Barnett. He could substitute the two squadrons his original deployment plan had assigned to reinforce Seaford, then send all of Ruiz's to Seaford to replace them . . . but if Ruiz was delayed, Rollins might come up painfully short against *his* objective.

He nibbled harder. The master plan envisioned hitting Yeltsin in overwhelming force for the express purpose of isolating and destroying any Manty units stationed there as the first step in demoralizing and grinding away the RMN. If Caparelli really had pulled four squadrons out, then the size of the prize had been cut roughly in half, assuming their original estimates of the Yeltsin deployment were accurate, and he hated to give up the extra kills. On the other hand, the morale effect might be even greater, since a smaller force might well be completely annihilated without any substantial Havenite losses. And a part of him would actually prefer to go in against relatively weaker opposition until he'd had a chance to evaluate the technical differential firsthand.

Available combat reports indicated it was at least as bad as he'd feared, possibly even worse, which made it tempting to stack the numerical odds as heavily in his favor as he could until he knew for certain.

The worst part was that it would mean reshuffling the entire operation on very short notice. His own forces and those at Seaford had been intended to act in concert, moving simultaneously in accordance with final attack orders issued from Barnett. If he moved now, the war would begin the instant he entered Yeltsin space, and he was too ignorant of the situation in the Seaford-Hancock area to be *certain* Rollins had sufficient superiority—even with Ruiz—to carry out his part of the plan.

He sighed and rubbed his temple again. This was the entire reason he'd moved his HQ to DuQuesne Base in the first place, he told himself—and also the reason President Harris had authorized him to use his own judgment for the final timing. But he'd expected a more gradual buildup, not this last minute, lightning-bolt change in the data available to him.

He closed his eyes for a moment, then inhaled sharply and let his chair snap upright.

"We'll go for it," he said crisply.

"Yes, Sir." Suppressed excitement quivered in Perot's voice, but he, too, was a professional. "And Admiral Rollins, Sir?"

"Get a courier boat to him. Send two, in case something happens to one of them. Tell him we'll be departing with our full available strength within forty-eight hours."

"Our full strength, Sir?"

"Less Admiral Coatsworth's Seaford task group," Parnell amended. He plucked at his chin, then nodded. "If they've pulled that much out, we don't need to raid the Seaford detachment to take them at better than two-to-one odds. On the other hand, we don't know the exact situation in Rollins' sector. He may need more muscle than we originally assumed, so tell him the originally assigned elements will depart from Barnett to join him within eight days or as soon as Admiral Ruiz arrives, whichever is sooner. I'll leave orders attaching Ruiz to Coatsworth—that'll thicken up Rollins' order of battle, just in case."

"Yes, Sir." Perot was punching notes into his memo pad at a furious rate.

"As soon as you get those dispatches off, dig out Base Ops. I'll give them forty-eight hours if I have to, but don't tell them that. If at all possible, I want to be ready to roll within twenty-four. Make sure they copy all of our Yeltsin simulations to each battle squadron. I want to run them backwards and forwards on our way to the target."

"Yes, Sir."

"And be sure to specifically instruct Admiral Coatsworth to send a courier to Rollins before he actually departs. I know he'll do it anyway, but make it official. Rollins has to know his schedule—and whether or not Ruiz is with him—to coordinate his own movements, and we can't afford any screw-ups when we're changing plans on the fly this way."

"Yes, Sir."

"After that, we'll have to inform the President. I'll record the dispatch while you start everything else in motion, and I'll need another courier to get it back to Haven."

This time Perot merely nodded, fingers still tapping notes into his memo pad, and the admiral smiled thinly.

"I suppose I ought to think up some dramatic, quotable phrase for Public Information and the history books, but I'm damned if any of them come to mind. Besides, admitting the truth wouldn't sound too good."

"The truth, Sir?"

"The truth, Russell, is that now the moment's here, I'm scared shitless. Somehow I don't think even Public Information could turn that into good copy."

"Maybe not, Sir . . . but it certainly sums up *my* feelings nicely. On the other hand—"

"On the other hand, we've got them by the short and curlies, assuming our data's reliable," Parnell agreed. He shook himself and stood. "Well, even if it isn't, we should see them in time to hyper the hell out. In any case, we've got to go find out one way or the other."

• CHAPTER TWENTY-FIVE

The small, nondescript man in Robert Pierre's office didn't look like an ogre. Oscar Saint-Just was a mild-mannered man who neither raised his voice, drank, nor swore. He had a wife and two lovely children, and he dressed like some low-level bureaucrat.

He was also First Undersecretary for Internal Security, Constance Palmer-Levy's second in command, and his mild voice had sent more people than even he could count into oblivion.

"I take it no one knows you're here?" Pierre leaned back behind his desk, raising his eyebrows in question as he waved at an empty chair.

"You should have more faith in me, Rob," Saint-Just said reprovingly.

"At this particular moment, my faith in people runs a poor second to my growing paranoia." Pierre's tone was dry, but an edge of humor flickered deep within it, and Saint-Just smiled.

"Understandable, understandable," he murmured. He settled back and crossed his legs. "May I assume you invited me over to tell me things are more or less on schedule?"

"Considerably more than less. Commodore Danton's come through with the weapons and the shuttles right on schedule."

"Excellent!" Saint-Just allowed himself to smile, then cocked his head to one side. "And the manpower to use them?"

"Cordelia Ransom's picked the CRU cells we need and cut them out of the normal CRU loop. She's got them running sims now, but I don't intend to release any actual hardware until we're closer to moving."

"And does Ransom understand the need for the, ah, cleanup details? Her InSec dossier suggests she's genuinely committed, Rob. Are we going to have to clean her up, too?"

"No." Pierre shook his head, and his mouth tightened in distaste for the essentials of his own plan. "She understands how it has to work, and, as you say, she's committed. She's willing to make sacrifices to bring this off, but I suspect we're going to have to give her the Treasury afterward."

"I can live with that," Saint-Just observed.

"So can I—at least as long as she really does understand the need for gradualism, and I think she does."

"If you're satisfied, I'm satisfied." Saint-Just rubbed his upper lip thoughtfully. "And Constance?"

"That part of the plan is ready to go right now— thanks, again, to Cordelia." Pierre smiled. "She didn't have to work around anyone to bring it off, either. The CRU's Central Action Committee jumped at the thought of it, crisis or no crisis. I'm afraid Constance hasn't made herself as popular with them as she could have since Frankel's assassination."

"Neither have I," Saint-Just said quietly. "I do trust they won't try for a double-header in an excess of enthusiasm?"

"If I thought there was any chance of that, I would've intervened personally." Pierre shook his head. "No, Cordelia's stressing the need to give 'InSec's storm-troopers'—that's you, Oscar—'time to reflect on the People's object lesson.' She's really quite good at agit-prop, you know. Perhaps we can convince her to take Public Information instead of the Treasury."

"I'll leave the political maneuvers up to you. Security and tactics I understand, politics—" Saint-Just shrugged and raised his hands, palms up, and Pierre bared his teeth.

"Politics, as practiced in the People's Republic, are

about to change quite drastically, Oscar. For the foreseeable future, I think you may understand the new rules much better than President Harris ever would have."

Kevin Usher slithered quietly across the roof of Rochelle Tower, trying not to wince as the rest of his team followed him. The imagery of his low-light goggles gave the tower's top a shimmery surrealism, but he'd trained with them long enough to be comfortable with that. It was the ungodly—and unavoidable—racket of the rest of his team that worried him.

He circled the last ventilator head and peered out at the open stretch between him and the edge of the tower. Wind flapped his clothing, and that was another cause for worry. Their primary escape plan called for a counter-grav free-fall leap off the tower roof, and with this much wind to blow them back into the tower as they fell—

He pushed the thought aside and eased his sidearm out of its holster. The People's Marines had trained him well during his conscripted term of service, and the pulser felt comforting and familiar in his hand as he looked for the InSec man watching this particular roof. He didn't particularly like this part, but the CRU couldn't afford any witnesses to *this* operation.

There. Usher's enhanced vision found his target, and he went down on one knee, leveling the long-barreled military weapon across his forearm in textbook style. He acquired the sight picture exactly as his instructors had trained him ten years before, and his finger tightened on the stud.

A five-shot burst of nonexplosive darts tore through the InSec man in a spray of blood. He didn't even have time to scream, and Usher grunted in satisfaction as he glided further out onto the roof, head swiveling from side to side and pulser poised in a two-handed combat grip. Their briefing had insisted there was only the one guard, but Usher had seen too many operations blow up from faulty intelligence to take that for granted.

Only this time it seemed the briefing was correct, and he waved the others forward while he stepped to the edge of the roof to check the sight line. Perfect, he thought, and turned to watch the rest of the team set up.

Two of the Viper crew knelt on the roof, and spike-guns thudded with brief, pneumatic violence as they secured the launcher's feet. Two others lifted the tube and guidance unit onto the tripod, and the crew chief's hands were busy with her data pad as she ran the self-test sequence on the first bird. She cocked her head as a minor malfunction light flickered, then put the missile aside and nodded in satisfaction as the backup bird passed its tests.

Usher turned back to his own responsibilities, waving his three-man security team into its perimeter positions. He beckoned the spotter over beside him and pointed at the tower on the far side of the green belt.

"Make sure you've got the right bay," he said quietly, and the woman nodded. She keyed up the schematic on her own goggles and moved her head carefully, aligning its outlines with the outline of the tower until the position pipper blinked directly atop an air traffic access point.

"Got it," she murmured. "Checked and confirmed."

"Then get comfortable. She's supposed to be along in the next ten minutes, but she may be delayed."

The woman nodded again and settled down, laying the riflelike laser designator across the roof parapet and making herself comfortable.

Usher gave the Viper crew another look. They were ready, and far enough back from the roof edge to be invisible from any cursory examination. The only real worry now was an overflight, and that shouldn't happen if their data on the air sweeps was as accurate as the rest of their brief.

If.

He made a quiet circuit of his perimeter, then found a nook out of the direct force of the wind that still gave him a complete field of view and settled down to wait.

*　　*　　*

"I suppose that's about everything, then—unless you can think of something else we need to look at, Oscar?"

Saint-Just shook his head, and Constance Palmer-Levy stood. Her staff followed suit with obvious relief. Few of them shared her taste for late-night strategy sessions, but people didn't argue when the head of InSec asked them to stay late.

"I'll drop by Statistics and light a fire under them about that correlation of CRU activities before I leave," Saint-Just told her. "I think you may be onto something there. Won't hurt to be sure, anyway."

"Good." Palmer-Levy stretched and yawned, then grinned wryly. "I think I may have stayed up a bit late even for me," she confessed.

"Then go home and get some sleep," Saint-Just advised.

"I will." Palmer-Levy turned away and waved her personal aide after her. The two of them stepped out of the conference room, gathering up her security detail as they went, and headed for the elevators.

The elevator deposited the Security chief and her bodyguards in the air car garage on the tower's four-hundredth floor. A tech team swarmed over her limo, completing the routine check for unpleasant surprises, and Palmer-Levy waited patiently for them to complete their task. Memories of Walter Frankel were far too vivid for her to begrudge the time it took.

"All clear, Ma'am," the senior tech said finally, scrawling his name on the signature pad of a memo board. "You're ready to fly."

"Thank you," she said, and led the way aboard.

The air car looked like a luxury civilian limo and boasted the internal fittings to match, but it was fast, heavily armored, and equipped with a sophisticated sensor suite based on the Marines' forward reconnaissance vehicles, and its pilot was a decorated combat veteran. Palmer-Levy smiled at him as she settled into her seat, and he nodded back respectfully, waiting until the hatch closed before bringing up his turbines and counter-grav. The limousine lifted without even a curtsy, and he sent it gliding along the ramp toward the outer access point.

"Mark!" the spotter's whisper crackled over her com, and Usher and his team tensed in readiness. The spotter shifted position, aligning the passive sights of her designator on the nose of the limousine sliding out of the access point, and tension crackled silently across the roof.

"Painting—now!" she snapped, and squeezed the stud.

An alarm shrieked, and Palmer-Levy's pilot twitched in his seat. One eye dropped to the lurid light on his EW panel, and his face paled.

"We're being lased!" he barked.

The launching charge lit the tower roof like lightning as it spat the Viper missile from the tube. Its tiny impeller drive kicked in almost instantly, accelerating it at over two thousand gravities even as its sensors picked up the glare of reflected laser light from the air car below and in front of it, and its nose dipped.

The pilot twisted the controls in a frantic evasion maneuver, but the Viper had an optical lock now, and his speed was too low to generate a miss. He did his best, but it was too late for his best to be enough.

Constance Palmer-Levy had one fleeting instant to realize what was happening, and then the edge of the Viper's impeller wedge struck.

The air car tore apart in a hurricane of splintered composites. Its hydrogen reservoirs exploded in balls of brilliant blue flame, and the commander of Internal Security and her bodyguards cascaded down across Nouveau Paris in a grisly rain.

• CHAPTER TWENTY-SIX

"Thank God."

Commander Ogilve relaxed at last as PNS *Napoleon* dropped out of hyper and the primary of the Seaford Nine System blazed ahead of her. Realistically, they'd been away and free from the instant they went into hyper, but his sleep had been haunted by nightmares of some disaster that would prevent him from delivering his data.

He glanced at his com officer.

"Record a most immediate to Admiral Rollins' personal attention, Jamie. Message begins: Sir, my latest Argus dump confirms total—repeat, total—withdrawal of Manticoran wall of battle from Hancock. Analysis of data suggests maximum remaining force in Hancock consists of one battlecruiser squadron and screening elements. *Napoleon* is en route to rendezvous with your flagship, ETA—" he glanced at his display "—two-point-two hours, with complete data dump. Ogilve clear. Message ends, Jamie."

"Aye, Sir."

Ogilve nodded and leaned back, letting himself feel his weariness at last even as he envisioned the hive of activity his signal was about to kick off aboard Admiral Rollins' flagship. A footstep sounded beside his chair, and he looked up at his exec.

"Somehow I don't think this is going to hurt our careers, Sir," the exec murmured.

"No, I don't imagine it will," Ogilve agreed unsmilingly. His exec came of prominent Legislaturalist stock, and the commander didn't like him a bit. Worse, he didn't trust his competence. But it sometimes seemed the political game was the only one that counted in the People's Navy, and if that meant Commander Ogilve had to carry his exec on his back, then Commander Ogilve had better just have strong back muscles.

And, he thought sourly as the exec moved back to his own station, if he *did* get promotion out of this, maybe it would mean a new assignment that got him away from at least one incompetent asshole.

Admiral Yuri Rollins shook his head, still suffering the lingering aftereffects of numb disbelief, as the Argus dump's images played themselves out in his flagship's main holo sphere for the third time.

"I can't believe it," he muttered. "Why in hell would Parks do something this stupid? It's got to be a trap."

"With all due respect, Sir, I don't see how it can be," Captain Holcombe disagreed. "For it to be a trap, they'd have to know about Argus, and there's no way they can."

"Nothing is impossible, Captain," Rear Admiral Chin said frostily, and Rollins' chief of staff flushed at her tone.

"I didn't mean to say that they couldn't possibly have detected the birds, Ma'am," he replied a bit stiffly. "What I meant was that *if* they knew about them, they would certainly have taken them out by now."

"Indeed? Suppose they know about them and choose subtlety over brute force? Why destroy them if they can use them to lie to us?"

"Unlikely," Rollins said, almost against his will. "Whatever tactical advantage deceiving us in Hancock might offer would be more than outweighed by the strategic damage they're suffering in other systems. No," he shook his head, "they'd never let the net stay up if they knew it was there."

"And if Admiral Parks is the only one to have noticed the platforms?" Chin asked. "If he's only just become aware of them, he might have chosen to use them in his own case while dispatching couriers to the commanders of other stations to alert them to the danger."

"Possible, but again, unlikely." Rollins turned away from the display and thrust his hands into his tunic pockets. "If he knows about them at all, then presumably he also knows they cover the entire system periphery. That means he can't sneak back in to set any sort of ambush without being picked up. Somehow I don't think he'd deliberately risk letting us in unopposed on the off chance that he could intercept us from some distant position."

"I suppose not." Chin folded her arms and looked accusingly into the sphere. "In that case, though, I have to wonder what he thinks he's up to."

"I think it's another indication he *doesn't* know about Argus, Ma'am," Captain Holcombe offered. She raised an eyebrow at him, and he shrugged. "If he's not in Hancock, he almost has to be picketing the Alliance systems in the area. Assuming that to be the case, I believe he uncovered Hancock precisely because he feels we can't know he's done it. After all, one of Argus' primary objectives was to cut down normal scouting ops to make Manty commanders overconfident in hopes they'd make mistakes just like this."

"True." Chin pursed her lips a moment, then nodded. "I suppose it just seems too convenient for him to suddenly do exactly what we want him to."

"But *do* we want him to?" Rollins said, and both his subordinates turned to him in surprise. "Certainly this offers us a perfect opportunity to smash Hancock, but it also means any attack would close on so much empty space, as far as warships are concerned. Battlecruisers? Piffle!" He took a hand from a pocket to wave it dismissively, then stuffed it back in place. "We wanted battle squadrons, and they're somewhere else now. Besides, how long do you think Parks is going to stay wherever he is? Their Admiralty won't let him leave Hancock uncovered for long, whatever he wants to do, so if we're going to take advantage of his absence, we have to move *now*."

"Without confirming with Admiral Parnell?" Chin's question was a statement, and Rollins nodded.

"Exactly. We're eighteen days' message time from Barnett, even by courier boat. That's thirty-six days for a two-way message. If we wait that long, they're bound to reinforce Hancock."

"Can we wait until the scheduled deadline, Sir?" Chin asked, and Rollins frowned. Officially, only he and his staff were supposed to know the timetable, but he'd invited Chin here, despite her status as his most junior battle squadron commander, because he respected her judgment. And if he wanted her input, she had to know the extent of his problems.

"I don't think so," he said finally. "Assuming Admiral Parnell doesn't postpone, we're supposed to move in another thirty-one days."

Chin nodded, her face showing no sign of triumph at finally learning the date the war was supposed to begin.

"In that case, of course, you're right, Sir. We can't wait that long if we want to hit them before they come to their senses."

"I said from the beginning this whole thing was over-centralized," Holcombe muttered. "Linking ops schedules that tightly with this much distance between operating areas is—"

"Is what we're stuck with," Rollins said a bit sharply. His chief of staff closed his mouth with a snap, and Rollins shrugged. "As a matter of fact, I tend to agree with you, Ed, but we're stuck with the way things are."

"So what do you plan to do, Sir?" Chin asked.

"I don't know." Rollins sighed. "I suppose it comes down to which is more important—Hancock's facilities, or its task force."

He lowered himself into a chair and stretched his legs out before him while he frowned up at the deckhead and considered his options.

The original plan had given good promise of success against Hancock. Admiral Coatsworth's arrival from Barnett would increase his own "official" strength by over fifty percent, and the Manties wouldn't even know Coatsworth was coming until he hit Zanzibar in their rear. With Coatsworth behind them and the Seaford task force in front of them, they'd be caught in a vise.

But if Hancock was empty, the entire ops plan went straight out the lock. There was no telling where the Manties were, or in what strength—not, at least, until the other Argus collectors reported in. Still, Hancock was the only Manty repair facility in this sector. If he was going to have to hunt for them anyway, depriving them of anywhere to repair damages would be an invaluable first step.

He drew a deep breath and straightened, and Holcombe and Chin turned toward him at the movement.

"We'll do it," Rollins said simply. Holcombe nodded in approval, and Chin looked relieved that someone else had had to make the call.

"Shall we wait until we hear from the other Argus nets, Sir?" Holcombe asked. Chin said nothing, but she shook her head in instant, instinctive disagreement, and Rollins agreed with her.

"No." He thrust himself up out of the chair. "Waiting would burn another six or seven days, and if we're going to do this, we don't have the time to spare."

"Yes, Sir."

The admiral paced briefly back and forth, thinking hard, then nodded.

"I want the task force ready to move out within twenty-four hours, Ed. Send a courier to Barnett to advise Admiral Parnell of our intentions. It should still get there before Coatsworth pulls out, so instruct him to rendezvous with us at Hancock. We'll consolidate our forces and then move on Zanzibar together. After that, we can hook up to take out Yorik or Alizon. By that time, we'll probably have picked up enough additional intel to know where Parks went and how he's deployed."

"Yes, Sir."

"Admiral Chin, I'll want your squadron to probe Hancock as we go in." Chin nodded, but her surprise showed, for her dreadnoughts were less powerful than the other battle squadrons.

"I haven't lost my senses, Admiral," Rollins said dryly. "Your ships are lighter, but they should be more than adequate to deal with battlecruisers, and if we're not going to get anything bigger, I at least want to nail as many of them as possible before they run. Besides, if there *is* something nasty waiting for us, you can pull a higher acceleration than superdreadnoughts."

In short, he thought, they could get the hell out of it faster than anything else he had, and he saw understanding in Chin's eyes as she nodded.

"And Admiral West's battlecruisers, Sir?" she asked.

"We'll attach them to you, but don't let him get too far ahead of you. His squadron's understrength to start with—I don't want him tangling with Manties at three-to-two odds while you're too far astern to assist."

"Understood, Sir."

"Good." Rollins shoved his hands back into his pockets and rocked on his heels, staring down into the holo sphere, and his eyes were hard.

"Very well," he said at last, "let's get moving. We've got a lot of details to settle before we pull out."

The three officers turned and strode from the compartment, leaving the display alive behind them, and the empty, quiet image of the Hancock System glowed silently in its depths.

• CHAPTER TWENTY-SEVEN

"Still nothing."

Sir Yancey Parks took another quick turn about his flag bridge, and his staff busied themselves with routine tasks that happened to keep them out of his path. All but Commodore Capra, who watched his admiral with a painstaking lack of expression.

"I hate this kind of waiting for the other shoe," Parks fumed.

"Perhaps that's why they're doing it, Sir." Capra's voice was quiet, and Parks snorted.

"Of course it is! Unfortunately, that doesn't make it any less effective." Parks stopped pacing and turned to glare down at the holo sphere. CIC had switched to astrography mode, showing the sparse stars of his command area and the most recent data on friendly and enemy dispositions, and the admiral jabbed an angry chin at the bland light dot of Seaford Nine.

"That bastard over there knows exactly what he plans to do," he said, pitching his voice for Commodore Capra's ears alone. "He knows when he plans to make his move, what he plans to do, and how he plans to bring it off, and all *I* know is that I *don't* know any of those things."

He fell silent again, chewing his lip while acid churned in his stomach. War games and training exercises, he was discovering, were one thing, with nothing more at stake than one's reputation and career. Actual operations were something else again—life and death, not simply for you, but for your crews and, quite possibly, your kingdom, as well.

It was an unpleasant discovery . . . and one which made him doubt his own competence.

He sighed and made his muscles relax by a sheer act of will, then turned to look Capra squarely in the eye.

"Was Sarnow right?" He voiced his own thoughts, and the commodore shrugged uncomfortably.

"You know my view, Sir. I've never been comfortable about leaving Hancock so weak, but whether our posture should be aggressive or defensive—" He shrugged again, almost helplessly. "I just don't know, Sir. I suppose the waiting is getting to me, too."

"But you're starting to think he was right, aren't you?" Parks pressed. The commodore looked away, then drew a deep breath and nodded.

Parks' mouth twitched, and he turned his back on the sphere, folding his hands behind him.

"If anyone needs me, I'll be in my quarters, Vincent," he said quietly, and walked slowly from the flag bridge.

PNS *Alexander* coasted silently through the outer reaches of the Yorik system on another Argus run. It should have been routine, given the light forces the Manties normally maintained here, but *Alexander*'s tactical display was a blaze of crimson impeller sources, and her captain stood peering down at it in consternation.

"What the hell is all this, Leo?" Commander Trent asked her tac officer.

"I don't have the least idea, Ma'am," the tac officer replied frankly. "It looks like a task force picket shell, but what it's doing here beats me. It's more like something I'd expect to see at Hancock."

"Me, too." Trent's tone was sour, and she looked across at Lieutenant Commander Raven. Her exec was officer of the watch, seated in the command chair at the center of the bridge, but his attention was on his captain rather than his displays.

"What do you think, Yasir?" she asked, and he twitched his shoulders at the question.

"I think I'd like to abort the pickup, Ma'am," he

replied in the careful tone of someone who knew what could happen to both their careers if they did. "There's too much traffic out here, and they're operating mighty aggressively. All it takes is one of them in the wrong place, and—"

He grimaced, and Trent nodded. Raven had a point. But the presence of so many Manty ships argued that something unusual was happening in Yorik, which made the Argus data even more important. That, she knew, would be the verdict of any court of inquiry, anyway.

She propped one shoulder against the tac display's hood and closed her eyes in thought. The risk to *Alexander* herself was minimal; they were still outside the hyper limit, and they could bring their wedge on-line in barely two minutes. The hyper generators would take a little longer—the trace signature from a standby translation field was simply too powerful to damp out—but *Alexander* could still be out of here long before anything got close enough to hurt her. No, the risk was to the Argus net itself. If they were picked up, the Manties were bound to wonder why a PN light cruiser would be skulking around way out here. And if something started them actively looking, not even the sensor arrays' Solarian-built stealth systems could hide them forever.

"We'll continue the operation," she said finally. "We can't bring the wedge up without risking detection, anyway, so we're committed to the run in. But I want our sensor people on their toes. If there's even a hint of anyone in the area when we reach the transmission point, we'll pass up the data dump."

Commander Tribeca lounged comfortably in his command chair and chortled mentally while he watched the displays and thumbed his nose at Captain Sir Roland T. Edwards.

HMS *Arrowhead* and the two other destroyers from her division were cast in the role of aggressors for this particular exercise, and, at the moment, *Arrowhead* and *Attack* were busy pretending to be holes in space and watching the rest of the flotilla look for them. Every system was powered down to a bare trickle while his passive sensors tracked the other nine destroyers and the light cruiser bumbling along astern of them in the role of a "merchantman." Another couple of hours should bring the whole "convoy" within missile range, and, at the moment, every one of those destroyers was looking in exactly the wrong direction. There were going to be some red faces at the exercise debrief, he thought complacently.

Of course, it was always possible one of the other cans would double back and look in his direction, but even if they did, they were unlikely to spot him. If he *was* picked up, he was going to have to go for a high-accel run in and hope he got lucky, yet that was a worst-case scenario, and it didn't look like happening. Captain Edwards had obviously decided Tribeca was outside him—not without a little help from Tribeca. *Ambush*, the third destroyer of Tribeca's division, was somewhere out there, where she'd deliberately leaked a carefully designed scrap of divisional com chatter, and Edwards thought he had a fix on the division's general location.

Tribeca gave a silent snicker at the thought. Edwards was such a pompous ass. It would never occur to him that anyone could out-sneak him, and—

"Excuse me, Skipper, but I just picked up something odd. It— There it is again."

"What?" Tribeca spun his chair toward his tactical officer and frowned. "There *what* is, Becky?"

"I don't know, Sir. It's like . . . " Her voice trailed off and she shook her head, then looked at the com officer. "Hal, sweep zero-eight-zero to one-two-zero. I think it's a com laser."

"On it," the com officer replied, and Tribeca's frown deepened.

"A com laser? From who?"

"That's just it, Skip." The tac officer's fingers redirected her own passive sensors as she replied. "I don't see anything. If it's a com laser, it's awful low power, and I'm just catching a trickle now and then."

"It's intermittent?" Tribeca's brow furrowed, and the tac officer nodded.

"I've got it, too, Sir," the com officer said. "Zero-eight-eight." He frowned and adjusted a rheostat carefully. "It's a com laser, all right. We're just catching the fringe of it. If I had to guess, I'd say there's a glitch in the sender's tracking systems. Not much of one—the beam's only kicking a little—but enough to swing it intermittently our way. It's scrambled, too . . . and I don't recognize the scramble code."

"What?" Tribeca shoved himself out of his chair and moved quickly to the tac station. "You don't see *anything* out there, Becky?"

"No, Sir. Whatever it is, it's running silent and too far out to find on passives. Should I go active?"

"Wait." Tribeca rubbed an eyebrow furiously, the exercise forgotten. *Arrowhead* was over ten light-minutes from the nearest senior officer. If he passed the buck, he'd give whoever was on the other end of that laser at least twenty minutes to coast out of active sensor range while he awaited orders, and he had no idea what the bogey's vector might be. But he *did* know the bogey wasn't Manticoran—not if Hal couldn't ID its scramble code.

He dropped back into his command chair and depressed a stud.

"Engineering, Lieutenant Riceman," a voice said.

"Rice, this is the Captain. We're about to go to battle stations." He heard someone inhale sharply on the bridge and ignored it. "Forget the exercise. How quick can you bring the wedge up for real?"

"Eighty seconds and you're hot, Skipper," Riceman said flatly, and Tribeca nodded.

"Get ready, then," he said, and looked back at the tac officer. "I want you to take us to battle stations on my command, Becky, but leave fire control and sensors on standby. Whatever this is, it's in range for a com laser. It could also be in energy weapon range, so I don't want any active emissions until the wedge and sidewalls come up. Got it?"

"Yes, Sir. What about *Attack*, Sir? She'll be a sitting duck without her wedge if someone takes a shot at her."

"Agreed, but if whoever's out there knew we were here, they wouldn't have been transmitting in the first place, so I don't think they've got *us* on passive, either. If I'm right, they'll be too busy looking at our big, noisy emissions signature to notice *Attack* before she figures out something's going on and gets her own wedge up. Just the same, Hal," he looked at the com officer, "lay a laser on her and order her to action stations as soon as our wedge goes up."

"Aye, aye, Sir."

"All right, then, Becky. Battle stations!"

"Contact!" *Alexander's* tac officer shouted. "I have an impeller wedge, bearing one-three-six by oh-niner-two!" He slapped keys on his console. "Manty destroyer at eighteen million klicks, Captain!"

"Shit!" Commander Trent slammed a fist into the arm of her command chair. "Battle stations, but do not go active! Confirm!"

"Do not go active, aye." The tac officer confirmed the order even as Yasir Raven's thumb jammed down on the battle stations alarm. Staying in passive meant the cruiser couldn't bring up her impeller wedge or sidewalls, but it was still remotely possible that they hadn't been detected, and—

"Radar pulse!" Tactical snapped through the yowl of the alarm. "They've got us, Ma'am!" He paused, then, "Second drive source detected! *Two* destroyers at eighteen million klicks!"

Trent bit back another curse. At that range and on that bearing, there was only one reason for a Manty to suddenly light off his drive. *Damn* the luck! What the *hell* had they been doing lying doggo in just the right place for her com beam to hit them?!

"Vector change," Tactical announced in a taut voice. "They're coming to an intercept course, Ma'am. Acceleration five-two-oh gravities."

"Bring the wedge up." Trent turned to her astrogator. "Plot your translation, Jackie, and execute a random vector change the minute we cross the wall. I want us out of here the instant the generators spin up."

"Aye, Ma'am. Feeding the plot now."

"Impellers nominal, Captain!"

"Helm, turn us away from them. Come to one-two-five level and roll port."

"Aye, Ma'am. Coming to one-two-five level and rolling port."

Trent turned back to her display, glaring at the brilliant dots of the Manticoran destroyers. Barely a light-minute, right in her goddamned lap. They were too far out to engage her—even assuming they were confident enough of their ID to class her as definitely hostile—but the damage was done.

She made herself lean back, mouth tight, and drummed on the chair arms. There was going to be hell to pay for this, and whatever else came of it, all the shit in the galaxy was about to come down squarely on her head.

"She's gone active," Tribeca's tac officer reported, her voice almost dreamy with intensity. "Looks like a *Conqueror*-class light cruiser, Sir. She's altering vector away from us."

"Any chance of engaging her?" There was more hope than expectation in Tribeca's voice, and she shook her head.

"Sorry, Sir, no joy. She's way outside our missile envelope, and she's rolling to bring up her belly bands."

"Damn," the commander murmured. He watched his own display, ignoring the confused questions rattling over the com from *Attack*'s skipper, while the Peep cruiser spun still further away from him. She was piling on the accel, too, and this far out—

The impeller source vanished in the sparkle of a hyper footprint, and he grunted. So much for catching her.

"Cut the accel, Helm." He shoved himself more firmly into his cushioned chair while his brain raced. "Hal, get off a contact report to Captain Edwards with all of Becky's data. Repeat it to Admiral Parks."

"Aye, aye, sir."

The bridge lift hissed open to admit his vacsuited exec. The exec's skin suit looked out of place on the bridge, for there'd been no time for the duty watch to suit up, and Tribeca grinned sourly as he saw his own suit over the exec's arm.

"Thanks, Fred, but I think it's all over."

"*What's* all over?" the exec demanded in exasperation. "I hope you realize we just blew off the whole exercise, Skipper!"

"I know, I know." Tribeca stood and crossed back over to the tac station to watch the entire bizarre incident replay itself. "What do you think that was all about, Becky?"

"Well," the tac officer leaned back and scratched her nose, "the one thing I can tell you for sure, Sir, is that she was way too far out to pick up anything from the inner system on shipboard sensors. Add that to the fact that she was hitting *something* with a com laser, and—" She shrugged.

"But how in hell could they have—?" Tribeca shook his head. He couldn't quite believe the Peeps had some sort of stealth system RMN sensors couldn't penetrate, but as Becky said, that cruiser had been lasing *something*. And since his own sensors still didn't show anything for that something to have been, the empirical evidence said they *did* have a stealth capability far better than ONI had ever guessed.

"Helm," he said, still staring down at the tactical display, "put us back where we were when we picked up the first trickle, then come to zero-eight-eight. Take it slow, I don't want to overrun anything."

"Aye, aye, Sir. Reversing course now."

"Good." He put his hand lightly on the tac officer's shoulder. "If there really is something out here, it's going to be harder than hell to spot, Becky. Don't make any assumptions about Peep systems capabilities. Pretend it's something of ours that doesn't want to be found, then find it."

"Aye, aye, Skipper. If it's there, I'll find it," she promised, and he squeezed her shoulder.

"Skipper, will you *please* tell me what's going on?" his exec pleaded, and Tribeca grinned, despite his tension, as the voice of *Attack*'s skipper, still squawking over the com, echoed the question. Then the grin faded.

"Come on into the briefing room, Fred." He sighed. "I might as well explain it to you and Commander Fargo at the same time."

"My God." Admiral Parks shook his head, staring at the message on his screen. "I wouldn't have believed it if I hadn't seen it. How in hell did *Peeps* pull this off, Vincent?"

"I don't know, Sir." Capra pushed to his feet and prowled restlessly around the briefing room. "Oh, I can think of enough different ways to get the platforms into position; I just can't imagine how they came up with the stealth systems to hide them from us after they did it."

"I'd say Commander Tribeca's probably on the right track, Admiral," Zero O'Malley said. The intelligence officer scrolled back up to the pertinent portion of Tribeca's message and tapped it with a stylus. "We can't be sure till he gets back here with the relay and we tear it apart, but his preliminary description of it certainly suggests the fusion of more than one outfit's tech, and God knows there's enough Havenite trade with the Solarian League."

"But the League's embargoed military technology to both of us," Parks pointed out, and O'Malley nodded. Getting that embargo in place had been one of the Star Kingdom's more effective diplomatic moves, for it certainly favored Manticore's generally superior tech base over Haven's. It had also been hard to achieve, and only Manticore's control of the League's traffic through the Sigma Draconis terminus of the Manticore Worm Hole Junction had given the Foreign Office the clout to bring it off.

"Agreed, Sir, but I'm not suggesting this was an authorized technology transfer. The League's organized on an awful loose, consensual basis, and some of its member planets resent how hard we pushed for the embargo. It's possible one of them, or even a rogue defense contractor or a bribable League Navy officer, would be willing to violate it."

"Zero may be right, Sir," Captain Hurston put in, "but I don't think *how* they did it is as important just now as they fact that they *have* done it." The ops officer ran a hand through his hair, and his voice was worried. "And, of course, there's the question of where *else* they've done it. Yorik isn't anywhere near as critical as other Alliance systems, which suggests that it wouldn't have had overriding priority. Which, in turn, suggests—"

"That they've done it all along the frontier," Parks finished grimly, and Hurston nodded.

The admiral tipped his chair back and scrubbed his eyes with the heels of his hands, wishing he could believe Hurston was wrong. But he couldn't. If the Peeps had bugged Yorik with their damned invisible sensor platforms, then they'd done it elsewhere, as well.

He clenched his jaw and swore silently. Manticore had gotten too confident of its technical edge, refused to contemplate the possibility that the Peeps, equally aware of the differential, might take steps to redress it. And he himself had been as blind as anyone else.

"This changes everything," he said finally. "Our—*my*—belief that Admiral Rollins couldn't know we'd pulled out of Hancock no longer applies. Which," he forced himself to make the admission in a level voice, "means Admiral Sarnow was right all along."

He drew a breath and shook himself, then popped his chair upright, lowered his hands, and spoke crisply.

"All right, people. I screwed up, and it's time to try to fix it. Mark," he looked at Hurston, "I want you to tear every one of our contingency plans apart. Crank in the assumption that the Peeps have been watching our deployments all along the frontier for at least the last six months and find any spots in the plan that need adjustment in light of that capability. Zeb," he turned to the intelligence officer, "I want you to take charge of the relay Tribeca's bringing in. Strip it completely. Find out all you can about it—not just how it works, but anything you can tell me about the components and who made the damned thing initially. And see to it that Tribeca knows I intend to commend him strongly for his initiative."

The intelligence officer nodded, and Parks turned to Captain Beasley.

"Theresa, set up a com conference for—" he glanced at the chrono "—zero nine hundred. I want all squadron commanders, their staffs, and flag captains tied in. Then get courier boats off to Hancock, Zanzibar, and the Admiralty. Inform all of them of our findings, and instruct Admiral Kostmeyer to move immediately from Zanzibar to rendezvous with us at Hancock. See to it that Admiral Sarnow gets an information copy of our dispatch to her, as well."

"Yes, Sir."

"Vincent," Parks swung back to his chief of staff, "I want you to work with Mark on his planning review, but first give me a new deployment here. Assume we'll be leaving a destroyer flotilla and a light cruiser squadron to patrol the system . . . and find the rest of these damned sensor platforms. If the Peeps have been watching us all along, the absolute first priority is to get ourselves concentrated again, so draw up the preliminary orders to get us underway as soon as my conference with the squadron COs is over."

"Yes, Sir."

"Very well." Parks laid his hands on the table and squared his shoulders. "Let's get started, then. And let's just hope to God we're in time."

• CHAPTER TWENTY-EIGHT

Honor closed the message file on her screen, tipped back her chair, and sipped her cocoa with a sense of mingled relief and regret. Yesterday's unexpected arrival of the light cruiser *Anubis* with dispatches from Admiral Danislav had brought Admiral Sarnow (and his flag captain) up to date on the latest information available to the Admiralty, and that information was downright frightening. There was no longer any doubt, in the Admiralty's view, that the PRH intended to launch an all-out attack . . . soon.

Honor agreed, and that agreement left her more worried than ever by Parks' dispersal. But at least Danislav had also confirmed that his dreadnought squadron, reinforced by an extra division the Admiralty had scared up, would arrive in a maximum of seventy-two hours. Unfortunately, Danislav had a reputation as an unimaginative, though determined, tactician . . . and he was senior to Sarnow.

She grimaced at the thought. Even with his ten dreadnoughts, Danislav was going to be far too weak to hold the system against serious attack. He'd need all the imagination he could find, and she hoped he'd have the sense to recognize Sarnow's capabilities and rely upon them.

Unlike Parks.

She grimaced again and rolled another sip of cocoa over her tongue. Nimitz made a soft sound, and she smiled as he yawned, twitched his ears, and stretched along his perch, curling his tail in an oddly disdainful gesture to express his own opinion of Parks.

"My sentiments exactly," she told him with a chuckle. Much though she respected Nimitz's intelligence, she entertained no illusions about his ability to judge an admiral's fitness for command. Except, of course, when his judgment matched hers.

She grinned at herself, then let her chair swing in a gentle arc, and her grin faded. The last few days had carried their own undertone of strain for her as Pavel Young settled in among the task force's officers. She'd been able to avoid much direct contact with him, but simply knowing he was there cast a pall over her spirits that even Paul and Mike had trouble lifting. At least she hadn't had to put up with him outside the bounds of formal conferences, though, and she was guiltily aware that Sarnow had handled Young's necessary background briefs through his staff channels, not her. Ernie Corell had been stuck with most of them, and while the chief of staff had been careful about her choice of words, her tone whenever she mentioned Young spoke volumes about her own opinion of him.

Honor frowned and rubbed the tip of her nose, wondering (far from the first time) how someone like Young had survived so long in the Queen's service. She'd seen Corell's reaction to him mirrored in too many other officers, many of them male, to believe her own opinion of him was unique.

She sighed and tipped her chair further back. In light of her troubles with him, she'd researched his background more carefully than she cared to admit, and what she'd found appalled her. She'd always known a certain segment of the aristocracy (not all of them conservatives, by a long mark) believed the rules didn't apply to them, that they were above the constraints lesser beings had to accept, but the Young family was outstanding even among the scum element of the nobility. From all reports, Pavel's father, the current Earl of North Hollow, was as bad as Pavel himself . . . and the record suggested his grandfather might actually have been worse! Three entire generations of the same family had gone their self-centered way, as if determined to single-handedly prove the depths to which "nobility" could sink, and somehow they'd gotten away with it.

Wealth, birth, and political influence, she thought sourly. Power they took so completely for granted that the responsibilities which went with it had no bearing on their lives. Power they abused with a casual lack of concern that sickened her. That it revolted the majority of their peers, as well, did little to protect less eminent persons from them, and sometimes that made her wonder about her entire society. Yet even at her most depressed, a stubborn part of her insisted that the very reason they stood out so disgustingly was because they were the exceptions, not the rule.

She twitched her shoulders and took herself to task. Why Young acted as he did and how he got away with it were less important than the consequences, and one thing had become clear to her. Paul was right; Young *was* afraid of her. It showed in his eyes, now that she knew to look for it, on the rare occasions when he found himself within her reach, and she was a little ashamed by her intense satisfaction at that discovery. Not even the fact that he and Houseman obviously were doing their best to alienate Commodore Van Slyke from her could impair her grim pleasure—though it might have, she conceded honestly, if Van Slyke had been willing to pay them the least attention.

She smiled again, bleakly, and turned back to her terminal as thoughts of the commodore returned her attention to *important* things. She brought up a display of the system and the task group's current dispositions and felt herself nodding in slow satisfaction as she studied it.

Admiral Sarnow had rethought his deployments in the last week or so, and the task group was no longer clustered tightly about the base. He'd left the minelayers there, for he'd evolved a plan for their use that was both subtler and safer than the one Honor had envisioned, but he'd moved his battlecruisers and heavy cruisers to the far side of the primary from the base to cover the most probable approach vectors from Seaford Nine.

There was an element of risk in that, Honor acknowledged. If the bad guys came at them from the opposite direction, they might find themselves badly placed to meet the threat, but they were close enough in that they should have time to intercept short of the base. It would be tight on the least favorable approach, since towing the pods slowed them to a max accel of less than 359 gees, and the interception would come at a dangerously low range, yet the edge their FTL sensor capability gave them should make it possible. On the other hand, it was unlikely Admiral Rollins would get too tricky. If he believed he had the strength to take the system, he'd feel no real need for sneakiness; if he doubted that he could do it, then he'd have every reason for caution and conservatism in any attack he might launch.

She nodded again, then looked up at the admittance signal's chime. She checked her chrono, and her eyebrows rose as she pressed the stud. She hadn't realized it was quite so late in the morning.

"Yes?" she said.

"Executive Officer, Ma'am," her Marine sentry announced.

"Thank you, Corporal. Come on in, Exec."

The hatch slid open almost instantly, and Mike Henke grinned at her.

"Ready for the weekly reports, Ma'am?" Henke took the memo pad from under her arm and waved it, and Honor groaned.

"As ready as I ever am." She sighed, and pointed to a chair across from her desk. "Take a seat and let's see how quickly we can get through them this time."

"All right, then." Henke nodded and tapped a note into her memo pad. "That takes care of the hardware side of the engineering department. Now—" she scanned a fresh screen of data "—about those promotions. Chief Manton is definitely due for senior chief, but if we bump him up we'll be over establishment in electronics."

"Um." Honor tapped a finger gently on her crossed knee as she leaned back in her chair. The captain of a Queen's ship had broad power to authorize enlisted and noncom promotions, as long as she stayed within the establishment laid down by BuPers for her command. If a promotion exceeded her establishment, she was required to return the "overly senior" personnel to Admiralty control for reassignment as soon as possible. It was a pain in the posterior, but Honor knew it was also intended to prevent captains from showing too much favoritism.

"His efficiency report is top drawer, Mike," she said at last. "And Lord knows he's done an outstanding job ever since we commissioned. I don't want to lose him, but I don't want to hold him back, either. Besides, we'll still be over establishment whenever he gets his rocker, even if we wait until BuPers acts, and he'll spend another ten months in grade, easy. If we bump him now, at least we can get him the salary and seniority he deserves."

"Agreed. The only problem is that regs are going to require that either he or Senior Chief Fanning be reassigned out of *Nike*."

"Unless we get the Admiral to sign off on letting us hang onto him 'in the interests of the Service,'" Honor mused. "After all, he's about the best gravitic tech I've ever seen, and we *do* have the pulse transmitter to worry about. That's been his baby from the outset, so—"

She broke off with a grimace as her terminal chimed.

"'Scuse me a minute, Mike," she said, and swung her chair back upright. She punched the acceptance key, and her terminal flicked to life with Evelyn Chandler's face. Honor took one look at her expression and stiffened.

"Yes, Eve?"

"The outer sensor net's just reported a hyper footprint, Ma'am—a big one, about thirty-five light-minutes out from the primary. It's right on the mark for a least-time approach from Seaford."

"I see." Honor felt Henke's sudden tension and was astounded by how calm her own voice sounded. "How big is 'big,' Eve?"

"We're still getting the preliminary readings, Ma'am. At the moment, it looks like thirty to forty capital ships, plus escorts," Chandler said flatly, and Honor's mouth firmed.

"Does Flag Plot have your data?"

"Yes, Ma'am. CIC is feeding it to them now, but—"

A brilliant scarlet override icon flashed in the corner of Honor's screen, and her raised hand halted the tac officer in mid-sentence.

"This is probably the Admiral now, Eve. Don't go away."

She accepted the emergency call and straightened her shoulders as Mark Sarnow's face replaced Chandler's. His heavy eyebrows were tight, his mouth grim under his mustache, and Honor made herself smile a welcome even though she knew he saw the tension in her own expression.

"Good morning, Sir. I assume you've seen the scanner data?"

"I have, indeed."

"I've just been discussing it with Commander Chandler, Sir. May I bring her back into the circuit?"

"Certainly!" Sarnow agreed, and the screen flickered as Honor brought Chandler into a three-way conference. A moment later, a second flicker split Honor's screen into fifths, not halves, as Captain Corell, Commander Cartwright, and Lieutenant Southman, Sarnow's intelligence officer, plugged into the same circuit.

"All right. Exactly what do we know?" Sarnow's clipped voice was brisk but clear. Chandler cleared her throat, and Honor nodded to her.

"We're getting fairly decent information now, Sir," the tac officer reported. "At the moment, we're calling it thirty-five capital ships. The count's less positive on their screening elements, but CIC's current projection makes it—" Chandler glanced to the side to double-check her display "—roughly seventy destroyers and cruisers. Our best call on the capital ships is twenty-two superdreadnoughts, seven dreadnoughts, and six battlecruisers." Chandler met Sarnow's eyes with a grim expression, and Lieutenant Southman pursed his lips in a silent whistle.

"What, Casper?" the admiral asked, and the lieutenant shrugged.

"That's damned close to everything he's got, Sir. He can't have left more than a couple of ships of the wall home—assuming, of course, that this *is* Admiral Rollins."

"Assuming," Corell half-snorted, and Southman's taut mouth twitched in an almost-smile.

"I think we can surmise it is, Ma'am," he acknowledged, "but my point is that our worst-case estimate only gives him thirty-seven capital ships, and *some* of them almost have to be down for refit. So unless he's been heavily reinforced, he must've stripped Seaford down to the fixed fortifications. And surely our pickets would have reported it if he had been reinforced."

"Oh, really?" Cartwright growled. The ops officer's expression was as grim as his tone. "The point that springs to *my* mind is where the hell our pickets are. They should've gotten here hours ago—at least—to warn us Rollins was moving out!"

"They may have gotten too close, Joe," Honor said quietly. Cartwright's eyes flicked to her, and she raised a hand at the screen. "Our picket commanders know their responsibilities. The only thing that could've prevented them from warning us would be for the Peeps to figure out some way to intercept them, and the most likely way for them to get caught would be to shadow Rollins' main body too closely. I don't see any other way the Peeps could've picked them off, and even if there were one, it wouldn't change Casper's point. This really does look like everything Rollins has, which—"

"Which suggests it's no probe," Admiral Sarnow agreed with a sharp nod. "He wouldn't be here in such strength or leave Seaford uncovered unless he had a decisive operation in mind—and he wouldn't think he could get away with it if he hadn't figured out we've left *Hancock* uncovered."

"But how could he, Sir?" Corell half-protested, and Sarnow shrugged.

"It might be any of a number of things. The first that comes to mind is that he probed one of the other systems and spotted units that should have been *here* somewhere else. But right now how he tumbled to it matters less than what he's likely to do about it. And what we're going to do about him." Sarnow's green eyes switched back to Chandler. "Do we have a projected vector for them, Commander?"

"Not yet, Sir. They made a very low-velocity transit, and they've been sitting more or less at rest relative to the primary ever since."

"At *that* range?" The admiral's eyebrows arched, and he and Honor regarded one another with surprised speculation. No shipboard sensor could see Hancock's inner system from that range, so what were the Peeps waiting for? Assuming they didn't know about the FTL sensor net, they should have started building the highest velocity they could before light-speed transmissions from the out-system sensor platforms warned the defenders of their arrival.

"Yes, Sir. I—" Chandler broke off as a buzzer sounded. She dropped her gaze to her display again, then looked back up at the admiral. "They're moving now, Sir. Looks like they're splitting into two elements and sending the dreadnoughts and battlecruisers in ahead. That could change, but at the moment they're opening a definite gap between them, though both groups are coming in at low acceleration. Their lead element looks like about two KPS squared—call it two-zero-four gees—and the SDs are trailing at about half that."

"Two KPS squared." Sarnow's voice and frown were thoughtful.

"Not very daring of them, Sir," Corell observed dryly. "It's not like *we're* going to be able to stop them."

"Their intelligence may not be definite," Cartwright suggested. "If they only think they've got the edge, they might not want to get in too deep until they're positive they can carry through."

"Maybe. But all we can do is guess," Sarnow pointed out. "What's their course, Commander?"

"Commander Oselli's working it up now, Sir. It looks like they're heading to intercept the repair base." Someone said something behind Chandler, and she nodded. "Confirmed, Sir. Assuming they hold their present acceleration and heading with turnover for the lead element in about five and a half hours, the DNs and BCs will be just about at rest relative to the base at range zero in ten hours and forty minutes."

"I see." Sarnow leaned back, green eyes narrow while his thoughts raced. "All right, let's assume for the moment that Joe's right. They're not certain about their data. Maybe they even think it's some kind of trap. Their lead element can pull a higher accel than their SDs, so that would make them the logical ships to use as a probe. And, of course, they've got more than enough firepower to deal with us if, in fact, we *are* unsupported." He shrugged. "It's the cautious approach, but I'm afraid that doesn't help us a lot."

Heads nodded, and Honor heard the soft tapping of his invisible fingers as they drummed on his console.

"At least their accel gives us time." He raised his voice. "Commander Oselli?"

"Yes, Sir?" Charlotte Oselli's reply came faint but clear from beyond the range of Chandler's visual pickup.

"Unless something changes, we're looking at an ideal opening for Sucker Punch, Commander. Please plot our course on that assumption and get back to me as soon as you've got it."

"Aye, aye, Sir."

Sarnow rubbed his mustache for a minute, then looked back at Honor.

"I'll have Samuel pass the preliminary orders to the minelayers over the pulse transmitter, Honor. Once we've got everyone in motion, we'll shift to the regular command net and run it through your com channels."

"Yes, Sir."

Sarnow turned to look over his shoulder.

"You heard, Samuel?" Honor couldn't hear Webster's acknowledgment, but Sarnow nodded. "Good. As soon as Commander Oselli completes her calculations, I'll give them their base course and coordinates for their field."

"Now," he went on, turning back to the screen, "once they get moving on that—"

"Excuse me, Sir," Oselli's voice interrupted, "but I've got our vector. I assume you want to hold our signatures to a minimum?"

"You assume correctly, assuming we can still make it into position."

"It'll be a little tighter than optimum, Sir," Honor's astrogator said, "but we can make it. If we get underway within ten minutes, we can match courses at one-four-one-zero-eight KPS in three hours and five-two minutes. They'll be approximately three-five minutes past turnover at a velocity of three-four-two-seven-eight KPS."

"Range at course merge?"

"Just over six-point-five light-minutes, Sir. Call it one-zero-zero-point-niner million klicks. We'll be about two-zero-three million from the base at that point."

"I see." Sarnow's expression had tightened as Oselli spoke. Honor kept her own face blank, but she could almost read his thoughts. Six and a half light-minutes was ONI's best estimate for the PNS's detection range against a low-powered impeller wedge covered by Manticoran EW systems. But it was *only* an estimate, and if they were picked up sooner than that . . .

"Assume we maneuver as suggested, Commander Chandler. When do we hit the powered missile envelope?"

"Almost exactly two hours after course merge, Sir." Chandler's instant response indicated she'd already worked the numbers. Sarnow's mouth twitched in a quick smile, and the tac officer went on speaking. "Assuming they maintain their projected vector—and that we aren't detected early, of course—we'll be right on a hundred million klicks from the base when the range hits seven million. That should put them over half a million klicks *inside* our envelope."

"I see." Sarnow rubbed his mustache again, then nodded. "All right, let's do it. Samuel, inform the minelayers' senior officer that I want his field laid ninety-eight million klicks out. And—" the admiral's green eyes slipped, almost against their will, toward Honor "—further inform him that he is to execute Carry Out as soon as he's done that."

"Aye, aye, Sir." This time Webster's response was audible over the com, and Honor caught Sarnow's gaze and nodded slightly, acknowledging the sense of his orders. Operation Carry Out would remove all the noncombatants the minelayers could cram aboard from the base. It would only be about fifty percent of the total base personnel—and wouldn't include Paul Tankersley—but there was no point pretending they had any other option. Eight battlecruisers couldn't possibly stop the firepower accelerating toward them.

"Very well, ladies and gentlemen. I believe that takes care of the preliminaries," Sarnow said, and bared his teeth at the pickup. "Now let's see just how much we can hurt these bastards."

• CHAPTER TWENTY-NINE

Admiral Yuri Rollins paced slowly up and down his flag bridge as PNS *Barnett* moved ponderously in-system. His hands were back in his tunic pockets in his favorite thinking posture, and he clamped an unlit pipe between his teeth. That pipe was one of his few real affectations—smoking had only recently become fashionable once more among Haven's Legislaturalists—but he found it comforting at the moment.

So far, things had gone exactly as planned. They'd been shadowed, as expected, from the moment they pulled out of Seaford, but the three light cruisers watching over his force had gotten just a bit too confident. Commander Ogilve and five of his squadron mates had left ten hours before the rest of the fleet, and, unlike the Manties, they'd already known what course Rollins intended to follow. The Manties had known they were safely outside Rollins' range until *Napoleon* and her consorts suddenly appeared behind them, pinning them against the task force. It had been a massacre; in fact, the first of them had been destroyed without getting off a single answering broadside.

Their destruction had been a satisfying start to the operation, though Rollins didn't deceive himself about what the *other* Manticoran pickets had been doing. They'd hypered out in all directions almost the instant his own ships crossed the alpha wall. By now, they must be arriving wherever Parks had taken his ships, and that meant the Manty admiral would be in motion shortly. Parks might not have exact intelligence on his enemies' course, but an attack on his main forward base had to be high on his threat list. Under the circumstances, Rollins had to assume Parks was already en route, with a probable ETA of no more than seventy-two to eighty-four hours.

Which should still be more than adequate, for one thing was certain: the delay to query the Argus net's latest data had confirmed that Parks *wasn't* here now. The platforms didn't have the reach to see anything within ten light-minutes or so of the primary, but they would certainly have noted anything that came in far enough out to clear Hancock's hyper limit, and nothing heavier than a cruiser had.

He paused in his pacing to gaze into the master display. As planned, his own force lagged well astern of Admiral Chin. In fact, he intended to halt his ships eleven light-minutes from Hancock, right on the hyper limit, for he had no intention of miring his sluggish superdreadnoughts any deeper than he had to. Chin's task group would more than suffice to eliminate any Manty battlecruisers—and their base—and if it turned out after all that this was some sort of subtle trap, he refused to let it close upon the core of his task force's true fighting power.

He nodded to himself and resumed his measured pacing.

Honor finished sealing her skin suit and looked down at Nimitz.

"Time to go, Stinker," she said softly, and the 'cat rose to pat her knee with a gentle true-hand. She thrust her gloves under her harness and scooped him up, hugging him for a long moment before she put him carefully into the life-support module. He made his own check of his surroundings, then curled down in the soft nest. Both of them hated being separated at times like this, but it was something they were getting used to.

Honor gave his ears a last caress, inhaled sharply, and closed the door behind him. She double-checked the seals and failsafes, then picked up her helmet and left the cabin without a backward glance.

*   *   *

The quiet efficiency of *Nike's* command deck enfolded her as she stepped out of the bridge lift. She crossed to her command chair and sat, racking her helmet, and pressed the button to deploy her displays from their storage positions. They surrounded her in a nest of information flow, and she reached back to double-check her waiting shock frame by feel while her eyes flicked over the silent screens of data.

Nike and her squadron mates accelerated at a steady .986 gees, screened by Van Slyke's heavy cruisers and the ten light cruisers Cartwright and Ernie Corell had exempted from their picket deployments. The task group seemed to crawl at such a low accel, yet there were limits to even the best electronic warfare capabilities. While the RMN's stealth systems were highly efficient against active sensors like radar, the only effective way to limit detection range against an impeller wedge was to reduce its power.

But slow or not, Sarnow's main striking force was exactly on Charlotte Oselli's course towards its massive foes, and the Peeps were, indeed, maintaining the separation Eve had noticed. That was good—as good, at least, as they had any right to hope for against such a tremendous weight of metal. Operation Sucker Punch wasn't predicated on any ridiculous assumption that battlecruisers could stop ships of the wall, nor was it without serious risks, but it offered a definite chance to bleed the enemy—especially when the enemy was obliging enough to come in split up this way. And it was remotely possible they could delay the Peeps long enough for Danislav to arrive.

Remotely.

She completed her scan of the displays and leaned back to cross her legs and radiate the calm it was her job to display. She looked around the bridge and noted with satisfaction that none of her people were watching her. They had their eyes where they belonged—on their own displays.

She touched a com stud.

"Auxiliary Control, Commander Henke," a furry contralto answered.

"This is the Captain. I'm on the bridge."

"Aye, aye, Ma'am. You're on the bridge, and you have the con."

"Thank you, Mike. I'll see you later."

"Yes, Ma'am. You owe me a beer, anyway."

"I *always* owe you a beer," Honor complained. "I think there's something wrong with your bookkeeping." Henke chuckled, and Honor shook her head. "Clear," she said, and released the stud.

She would have preferred, in a way, to have Mike on the bridge with her, but unlike any of her earlier ships, *Nike* was big enough for a duplicate command deck at the far end of her core hull. Known informally as Coventry, Auxiliary Control was manned by a complete backup of her own bridge crew under Henke's supervision. It was a chilling thought in some ways, but knowing someone she trusted was waiting to look after her ship for her eased her mind more than she'd once expected it could.

She settled herself more comfortably in her own chair and checked the plot. The minelayers had already completed their part of the initial operation and started back for the base, and she wished with all her heart that Paul were among the people they were about to pick up. But he wasn't, and at least the base wasn't totally helpless. It mounted no offensive weapons, but it was fitted with generators for a spherical sidewall "bubble" almost as strong as *Nike*'s own, and its active antimissile defenses were excellent. They'd been unable to adapt its defensive fire control to handle parasite pods, so it still had no offensive punch, but it could protect itself quite well—until, at least, some Peep capital ship got into beam range.

And that was going to happen. She made herself face it. Sarnow would do his best, but not even *his* best was going to change Paul's fate. Even if the task group succeeded in drawing the Peeps' lead element after it and away from the base, they could only delay the inevitable. Oh, Danislav *might* get here in time, but no one was stupid enough to count on that . . . and even if he did, his own ships would be hopelessly outnumbered.

No, they weren't going to save the base, but at least the Admiral had ordered Paul's CO to surrender once the enemy reached energy range. The thought of losing him to a POW camp—especially a Peep POW camp— was heartbreaking, but he'd be alive. That was the important thing, she told herself. He'd be *alive.*

She allowed herself one more moment of silent anguish, then put all thought of Paul Tankersley into a cupboard in her brain and closed the door upon it as lovingly and gently as she'd closed Nimitz's life-support module. Her face smoothed, and she touched another com stud.

"Flag Bridge, Chief of Staff."

"This is the Captain, Ernie. Please inform the Admiral that I'm on the bridge awaiting his orders."

Rear Admiral Genevieve Chin watched her display on PNS *New Boston*'s flag bridge and tried not to fidget. It wasn't nerves, she told herself. Not in the traditional sense, anyway. The fact that she'd been tapped to lead the first real assault on the enemy despite her relative lack of seniority would be a tremendous feather in her cap, and aside from the pair of tin-cans hovering stubbornly just beyond her missile envelope, there wasn't a sign of the Manties. Of course, those spying destroyers meant the defending CO was getting excellent information on her, wherever he was hiding, but she wasn't too concerned. EW or no, there was no way he was going to sneak into range under power without her seeing him. And unless he'd been in exactly the right position when the first light-speed reports of her arrival came in, there was no way he'd have time to get into an attack position—not, at least, one that wasn't suicidal—*without* coming in under power.

Yet despite her own reasoning, she felt undeniably tense. She was almost to turnover, so where *were* the bastards? They should have shown up by now . . . unless they'd decided to abandon Hancock without offering battle.

Assuming her information on their strength was accurate, that would certainly be a rational move, yet it would also be completely at odds with her own assessment of the Manticoran Navy. Edward Saganami had set the RMN's standards in his final engagement when he died defending a convoy against five-to-one odds. His inheritors had proven themselves worthy of their founder over the centuries, and that sort of tradition wasn't built in a moment; somehow she couldn't picture any Manticoran admiral letting it be torn down without a fight.

No, he was out there somewhere, and he was up to something. She couldn't see him, but she didn't have to see him to know that.

"Drive shutdown in five minutes," Oselli reported.

"Thank you, Charlotte." Honor looked down at the screen, which now showed Mark Sarnow's face, and started to open her mouth.

"I heard," he said, and his expression was less tense than it had been before. In fact, it was almost relaxed, as if he, too, were relieved that the moment was approaching. And, she thought dryly, that they'd gotten this far without being spotted. The Peep dreadnoughts had made turnover twenty-eight minutes ago, and they'd hardly be continuing their deceleration if they knew the enemy was now directly ahead of them.

"Yes, Sir. Any orders?"

"None, thank you."

"Very well, Sir."

She leaned back again, resting her elbows on the arms of her command chair, and looked back at the plot. Six and a quarter hours had passed since the Peeps' arrival; now the crimson data codes of enemy ships of the wall plowed up their wake, decelerating steadily but still overtaking at over twenty thousand KPS, and the fact that that was exactly what Hancock's defenders *wanted* them to do didn't make it any less unnerving.

"Argus is reporting something, Sir."

Rollins stopped pacing to dart a quick look at Captain Holcombe. The chief of staff was bent over Captain Santiago's shoulder, watching the ops officer's display, and the admiral made himself wait without comment while the data coalesced.

"Five ships, Sir," Holcombe said finally. "Acceleration about four-point-niner KPS squared. They're on the far side of the inner system, headed directly away from the Manty base—and Admiral Chin—toward the hyper limit." He glanced at a time readout. "Transmission lag is about thirty-three minutes from the platforms that picked them up, Sir."

"IDs?"

"They're pretty big, Sir," Santiago replied. "Pulling that accel, they're probably battlecruisers, but there's no way to confirm that."

"Escorts?"

"No sign of any, Sir."

"I see." Rollins stuffed his hands deeper into his pockets and resumed his pacing. Five probable battlecruisers headed away. It made sense, especially if the defenders had been completely surprised. They couldn't possibly have crammed the base's entire personnel aboard that few ships, but if they'd had to respond to an emergency and organize an evacuation on the fly to get out what they could, the timing was about right. Only where were their escorts?

He frowned and paced a bit faster. Argus had spotted quite a few destroyers and cruisers clustered to cover the most likely approaches from Seaford, not to mention the tin-cans clinging to Chin's flanks. It was possible the Manties had deployed *all* their light units as pickets, which, in turn, would explain the absence of any screen for the battlecruisers, but even so—

"Ed, signal *New Boston*," he said. "Inform Admiral

Chin that Argus confirms the departure of five enemy units, possibly battlecruisers. Give her their vectors and emphasize that our IDs are only tentative."

"Aye, Sir. Shall I instruct her to go in pursuit?"

"Hell no!" Rollins snorted. "There's no way she could overtake, and if they're up to something sneaky there's no reason to do what they want."

"Yes, Sir."

"Coming up on shutdown . . . *now*," Oselli said, and Chief Constanza killed *Nike*'s drive in instant response.

"Rotate," Honor said quietly. "George, confirm the same order to the rest of the task group."

"Aye, aye, Ma'am." Monet spoke into his pickup, for the task group com net emanated from his panel now, just as Chandler's controlled the tactical net. Admiral Sarnow's com section was tied into *Nike*'s gravitics, reading direct from the FTL sensor platforms and feeding the data to CIC.

"Rotating now, Ma'am," Chief Constanza murmured, and her hands gentled the battlecruiser through an end-for-end turn that left her bows-on to the oncoming Peeps. It wasn't a very quick maneuver, for with her wedge down *Nike* maneuvered like a pig—a *lazy* pig—on attitude thrusters alone. The parasite pods trailing astern didn't help, either, yet they were also the reason for the turn. *Nike*'s stealth systems could do a lot to hide her from the enemy, but the tractor-towed pods extended beyond their effective coverage. The only way to hide *them* was to put them in the ship's shadow.

"All units rotated, Ma'am," Monet announced at length.

"Thank you." Honor looked down at her link to the flag bridge, and Sarnow nodded to her.

"And now," he said quietly, "we wait."

"Another message from the flagship, Ma'am," Chin's com officer said. The admiral quirked an eyebrow at him. "Argus reports the impeller sources departing the base are still holding vector for the hyper limit."

"Thank you."

Chin exchanged glances with her chief of staff and ops officer. Commander Klim's frown was as intent as her own, but Commander DeSoto seemed unconcerned. Which didn't mean much. The ops officer was a good, sound technician, but he lacked the chief of staff's imagination.

She scooted down in her command chair and crossed her ankles as she leaned back to think. She no longer felt any inclination to fidget, as if the appearance of those drive signatures on the far side of the base had erased some of her tension, yet a nagging little spike of doubt jabbed at her mind.

They almost had to be battlecruisers to pull that accel, and they'd been doing it too long for them to be EW drones. Yet she'd been too convinced the Manties would try *something* before tamely surrendering a base they'd spent so much time, money, and effort building to accept it without reservation.

"Range to their base?" she asked DeSoto.

"Coming down on one-oh-eight million kilometers, Ma'am."

"Range to base is now one-zero-one million kilometers, Sir," Honor told Mark Sarnow, and the admiral nodded.

"Stand by to rotate and engage." His tenor's slight harshness was the only sign of the last two hour's nerve-wracking strain, and Honor's respect for him clicked up another notch. The dreadnoughts had closed the range by more than ninety-three million kilometers, and their velocity remained almost fifty-six hundred KPS higher than his own. If they went in pursuit at maximum power now, they could force him into energy range, despite his higher accel. She knew all about the ploys he hoped would slow them down, for she'd helped him devise them, but she also knew what would happen if his stratagems failed. There were too many enemy ships back there for merely scattering to save his battlecruisers if they pressed a resolute pursuit, and he'd deliberately accepted that to maximize the one truly heavy blow he could deliver. It required either immense moral courage or a total lack of imagination to do something like that.

She looked back at her plot and let her thoughts turn to the missile pods. *Nike's* redesigned inertial compensator and more powerful impellers let her tow a total of seven of them; *Achilles*, *Agamemnon*, and *Cassandra* could manage six each, but the older, *Redoubtable*-class ships could tow only five. "Only" five. The right corner of her mouth twitched at the thought.

Tension wound tighter and tighter at Honor's core, the first red claws of anticipation ripping at her professional calm as the kilometers oozed away, and then Mark Sarnow spoke from the screen at her right knee.

"Very well, Dame Honor," he said very formally. "Execute!"

• CHAPTER THIRTY

"Contact!"

Admiral Chin jerked upright in her chair. DeSoto was bent intently over his display, and she frowned as seconds leaked away with no more information.

"I'm not sure what it is, Ma'am," he said finally. "I'm picking up some very small radar targets at about seven million klicks. They're not under power, and they're too small to be warships, even LACs, but they're almost exactly on our base course. We're overtaking them at about five-five-niner-four KPS, and—*Jesus Christ!*"

Admiral Mark Sarnow's task group had completed its turn, presenting its broadsides to the oncoming enemy, and the missile pods streamed astern like lumpy, ungainly tails.

"Stand by," Honor murmured. No active sensors were live, but they'd had literally hours to refine the data from their passive systems, and she felt her lips trying to draw back from her teeth.

The tactical net's hair-thin lasers linked the task group into a single, vast entity, and data codes flashed as each division of battlecruisers and cruisers confirmed acquisition of its assigned target. She waited two more heartbeats, then—

"Engage!" she snapped, and Task Group Hancock 001 belched fire.

Nike and *Agamemnon* alone spat a hundred and seventy-eight missiles at the Peeps, almost five times the broadside of a *Sphinx*-class superdreadnought. The other divisions of her squadron had fewer birds, but even Van Slyke's cruiser divisions had twice a *Bellerophon*-class dreadnought's broadside. Nine *hundred* missiles erupted into Admiral Chin's teeth, and every ship's drive came on line in the same instant. They swerved back onto their original heading, redlining their acceleration, and deployed decoys and jammers to cover themselves as they raced ahead down the Havenites' base course at 4.93 KPS^2.

For one terrible moment, Genevieve Chin's mind froze.

Two superdreadnought squadrons couldn't have spawned that massive salvo, and the Manties only had *battlecruisers!* It was impossible!

But it was also happening, and forty years of training wrenched her brain back to life.

"Starboard ninety! All units roll ship!" she snapped, and her fist pounded the arm of her command chair as her ships began to turn. It was going to be close, for dreadnoughts were slow on the helm, and she cursed the precious seconds her own stunned surprise had lost her.

A hurricane of missiles tore down on Havenite ships whose startled missile defense officers had been slow to start their plots. There'd been no one on their sensors to run plots *on*, and they weren't clairvoyant.

Countermissiles began to fire, sporadically at first, then in greater and greater numbers. Dreadnoughts were lavishly equipped with active defenses, but the Manties had targeted the full fury of their fire on just four dreadnoughts and the same number of battlecruisers . . . and almost a third of the incoming missiles carried neither laser heads nor nukes. They were fitted instead with the best ECM emitters and electronic penaids Manticore could build, and they played hell with Havenite tracking systems. Missile impeller signatures split apart and recombined with insane abandon, jammers scrambled defensive radar, and sheer, howling electronic noise attacked squadron tactical nets that hadn't had the least idea they were about to be assailed. Half of them went down—only for seconds, perhaps, before they recovered, but for those seconds Admiral Chin's ships found themselves suddenly alone in the path of the storm. They were forced back into local control, and without centralized direction, two and even three ships attacked some missiles . . . while no one at all engaged others.

Countermissiles and laser clusters tore dozens—scores—of them apart, but nothing could have stopped them all, and Chin clung to her command chair as her massive flagship heaved in agony. Laser heads stabbed at *New Boston* with x-ray stilettos, people and alloy blew apart and vaporized under their deadly impact, and those were the light hits, the ones that had to get through sidewalls and radiation shielding first.

Nouveau Paris, Chin's lead dreadnought, was slow getting around, and over a dozen missiles detonated almost dead ahead of her. Lethal clusters of lasers ripped straight down the wide-open throat of her wedge, and Chin stared at the visual display in sick horror as she blew apart. One instant she was six megatons of capital ship; the next she was an expanding ball of fire.

The battlecruisers *Walid* and *Sulieman* died with her, and other ships took hit after hit. The dreadnought *Waldensville* staggered as her forward impeller ring was blown apart, and the battlecruiser *Malik* careened out of formation as her wedge went down completely. A heavy cruiser division tried to cover her against Manticoran sensors with their own wedges, but with neither wedge nor sidewalls, *Malik* was doomed. Even as Chin watched, her crew took to their escape pods, fleeing their helpless ship before the Manties localized her despite her screen and blew her apart. *Waldensville*'s impeller damage had cut her maximum acceleration in half, the dreadnought *Kaplan* had lost a quarter of her port broadside, her sister ship *Havensport* was almost as badly damaged, and the battlecruiser *Alp Arslan* trailed atmosphere and debris.

Yet her surviving ships were around at last, presenting their full broadsides to the enemy, and their missiles raced after the Manticorans. It was a feeble response to the massive salvo which had ravaged her command, yet she watched the outgoing missile traces with hungry eyes. The Manties were running straight away from her, giving her birds ideal, up-the-kilt shots, but her hand fisted in rage as decoys sucked her fire wide and countermissiles and lasers knocked down the birds that held lock. Unlike her, the enemy had known they'd be taking fire, and their active defenses were frighteningly effective.

A fresh salvo of Manticoran missiles scorched in on *Malik*. There were only a few dozen of them this time, yet the battlecruiser was a sitting target. Her cruiser screen did its best to stop them, but at least ten got through, and they weren't even laser heads. Megaton-range fireballs enveloped *Malik* in a star-bright boil; when it cleared, another eight hundred and fifty thousand tons of warship had been wiped away, and Chin swore with silent, bitter venom.

A dreadnought and three battlecruisers—all of them *Sultans*—gone just like that. The enemy's targeting had been as deadly as the sheer weight of his fire, and she'd walked straight into it. She made herself accept that, then looked back at the plot, and her teeth showed as she digested the data. She didn't know how battlecruisers had pumped so many missiles at her, but they'd exposed themselves to do it. Despite their higher accelerations, she had more than enough overtake advantage to bring them into beam range, and no battlecruiser could stand up to a dreadnought's energy armament.

"Bring us back around," she grated.

"Aye, Ma'am." DeSoto sounded sick and shaken, but he was regaining his balance, and her wounded command swung back to pursue its tormentors. Then—

"Fresh contact, Admiral. Correction—*multiple* contacts, bearing one-seven-niner by oh-oh-eight, range one-oh-six-point-niner million klicks!"

New light codes appeared in her command chair's tactical repeater, and her jaw clenched. Superdreadnoughts. Sixteen of them—two full battle squadrons—coming at her from the "helpless" repair base at 4.3 KPS^2.

"Reverse course. Maximum deceleration!"

Honor's eyes blazed as the "superdreadnoughts" headed toward the Peeps. The repair base might not be armed, but its gravitic sensors had watched the savagery of the initial exchange, and its traffic control systems had sufficed to activate the preprogrammed electronic warfare drones Sarnow had left in orbit with it. Now the drones raced outward, and the Peeps had no choice but to go to maximum power in the other direction in the faint hope of escaping the "capital ships" lunging to complete their destruction.

Admiral Chin sat motionless for long, silent seconds. A minute passed, then two. Three. Her ships' drives fought desperately to slow their headlong charge toward the Manty superdreadnoughts, but the range fell inexorably and the admiral's eyes burned with frustrated rage as the battlecruisers sped away from her. The missile exchange continued, no less ferocious despite the drop in volume as both sides turned their broadsides away from one another, but the Manties' superior missiles and—especially—defensive EW let them more than hold their own. Worse, they were ignoring everyone else to pound doggedly at *Waldensville*, whose damaged drive, unable to match her consorts' decel, lagged further and further astern—closer and closer to the battlecruisers—as Chin's ships fled the superdreadnoughts.

She stared down at her tactical repeater, then shoved herself out of her chair with a muffled curse and stamped across to the master plot. DeSoto and Klim exchanged unhappy looks as she abandoned the protection of her shock frame and left her helmet racked, but neither dared protest as she glared down into the holo.

"Confirm ID on those SDs!" she snapped.

"Ma'am?" Surprise startled DeSoto into the question, but the ops officer cleared his throat quickly when Chin turned her glare upon him. "Uh, CIC's confidence is high, Ma'am," he said hurriedly, glancing back down at his own display. "Emissions and impeller strength both conform to data base's threat files on *Sphinx*-class super-dreadnoughts across the board."

The admiral made an ugly sound deep in her throat. She folded her hands tightly behind her, and her staff sat silent in the face of her anger as she rocked up and down on her toes. The master plot confirmed the ops officer's report, but now that her instant, instinctive reaction had passed, her own tactical sense warred with the data. It didn't make *sense*. If battlecruisers could pump that many missiles at her—and she was beginning to suspect how they'd done it—surely ships of the wall could have laid down even more fire! Two squadrons of super-dreadnoughts could have annihilated her entire force and come close to evening the odds against Rollins' total task force in a single blow, and if the Manties could get battlecruisers into range undetected, there was no reason they couldn't have done the same thing with SDs.

And if those were superdreadnoughts, why were the battlecruisers still running? They were accelerating away from her at almost five KPS^2; combined with her own deceleration, that produced a cumulative vector change of 9.45 KPS^2. Of course, no battlecruiser wanted to get any closer to a dreadnought than it had to, but their heading also meant they could reply to her ships' after chase armament only with *their* stern chasers. True, their fire was hammering *Waldensville* with ever mounting damage, but they could have turned to open their broadsides and quadrupled the weight of their fire, and with SDs coming to their assistance, Chin couldn't possibly have risked slowing her escape efforts by turning to reply in kind.

Her furious rocking motion slowed and her eyes narrowed as another thought chased itself through her mind. If those *were* SDs, why hadn't the Argus net detected their return to the system?

She glanced at the chrono. Seven minutes since course change. Her velocity had fallen by nineteen hundred KPS and the battlecruisers' had climbed by over two thousand. She'd already lost the chance to bring them into energy range, but if she turned back to pursue them once more, she could hold them in her powered missile range for more than an hour. Except that doing so would also doom her ships by matching them against those SDs. Unless . . .

A trio of Havenite missiles found a gap in the task group's hard-pressed defenses and charged down on HMS *Crusader*. The heavy cruiser's decoys and laser clusters did their best, but the Peeps' fire was too heavy. There were too many threat sources, and the tac net's computers released her systems to self-defense a fraction of a second too late.

The laser heads detonated at less than 13,000 kilometers, and they were capital ship missiles. Their lasers burned through her sidewall as if it didn't exist. Battle steel shattered and vaporized, and a failsafe circuit took a microsecond too long to function.

Commodore Stephen Van Slyke's flagship vanished in the eye-tearing flare of a failing fusion bottle, and Captain Lord Pavel Young suddenly inherited command of Heavy Cruiser Squadron Seventeen.

Admiral Chin barely noticed *Crusader*'s destruction. One heavy cruiser either way hardly mattered against the scale of the engagement . . . or the threat sweeping towards her from the Manty base. If it *was* a threat.

She bit her lip. If those weren't SDs, then they were the best EW drones she'd ever seen, and instinct seemed a frail thing matched against the cold, hard reality of her sensors, but . . .

She inhaled deeply without turning from the display.

"Bring us back around." Her voice was cold and hard. "Pursuit vector, maximum acceleration."

"Admiral Chin is reversing course, Sir!"

Admiral Rollins twitched as Captain Holcombe's report penetrated his sick despair at the trap he'd stumbled into. He twisted in his chair, double-checking his own plot in sheer disbelief, then slumped back and watched Chin's impeller signatures complete their suicidal swing.

"Orders, Sir?" Holcombe asked tautly, and Rollins could only shrug his helplessness. He was over two hundred million kilometers astern of Chin. Any order of his would take over twelve minutes to reach her, and her vector would merge with the Manty SDs' in less than fifty. Her chance of escaping them was already minute; if she accelerated towards them for twelve more minutes, it wouldn't even exist.

"What good would it do?" he asked in a voice of quiet bitterness. "We can't call her off in time, and we couldn't get close enough to help even if she kept running straight towards us. She's on her own."

"They didn't buy it, Sir," Honor said quietly.

"Not completely, no," Sarnow agreed from her com screen. There was no surprise in his voice—not really. They'd both hoped the Peeps might break off their attack when they saw the "superdreadnoughts," yet it had never been more than a hope. "But they know they've been kissed. And they did slow down enough to keep us out of beam range."

Honor nodded silently, and her eyes moved back to her plot and the growing sidebar list of damaged ships. Commodore Prentis' *Defiant* had taken impeller damage, though it wasn't critical yet, and *Onslaught* had also been hit. All her weapons remained in action, but her gravitic sensors had been knocked out, and her communications had been damaged seriously enough for Captain Rubenstein to pass control of his division's tactical net to *Invincible*. The cruisers *Magus* and *Circe* had taken two hits each, as well, but *Crusader* was their only total loss.

A corner of her brain was appalled that she could apply the word "only" to the deaths of nine hundred men and women, but it was the appropriate one, for their casualties were minuscule beside those Sarnow had wreaked in reply. She knew it, yet another corner of her mind still railed at her admiral; for all of his brilliance and audacity he had failed to stop the enemy. They'd hurt the Peeps, but they hadn't saved the base—and Paul—after all.

She stamped a mental foot on her resentment, shamed by its total unfairness, and made herself consider the situation coldly. At least the second Peep element was holding position right on the hyper limit. The contest was still between them and the battered force on their heels, and the glittering icon of the hastily laid minefield blinked in her plot, a bare three million kilometers ahead. Not even *Nike's* sensors could see the mines clearly, despite knowing where they were, and the Peeps should have even poorer luck against their low-signature materials.

"Our time to minefield is two-point-niner-six minutes, Ma'am," Charlotte Oselli said, as if the astrogator had read her mind. "The Peeps should enter attack range in . . . seven-point-five-three minutes."

Honor nodded in acknowledgment, never looking up from her plot. Now if only the mines didn't make a mistake where the task group's IFF was concerned.

"You're right, Ma'am. They've got to be drones."

Genevieve Chin gave Commander Klim a sharp nod and turned from the master display. She stalked back to her command chair and sank into it, locking her shock frame with slow deliberation, then looked at DeSoto.

"Lay in new firing orders. They're concentrating on *Waldensville*; let's give them a little of their own medicine. Pick two BCs and hit them with everything we've got."

"Aye, Ma'am!" Matching hunger sharpened DeSoto's reply, and Chin smiled a thin smile. They'd been suckered and they'd taken their lumps; now it was time to hand out a few in reply.

The sudden shift in fire patterns took Sarnow's missile defense officers by surprise, and the first, concentrated salvo blew a hole through their countermissiles, sweeping into attack range of *Defiant* and *Achilles*. *Defiant* took only three hits, none critical, but a dozen lasers lashed at the open rear of *Achilles'* impeller wedge, and damage alarms screamed as five of them blasted deep into her hull.

"We've lost Graser One-Six and Laser One-Eight, Sir. Five casualties in Radar Eleven. Missile Five-Two's down, but damage control is on it."

"Acknowledged." Captain Oscar Weldon didn't even look up at his exec's report. He only looked at the flag bridge com screen and saw the same awareness in Commodore Banton's eyes. It had been only a matter of time until the Peeps concentrated their fire; now they knew who their targets would be.

Achilles shuddered as another salvo flailed at her, and the battlecruiser writhed into a fresh evasion pattern while two light cruisers closed in tighter on either flank to add their weight to her defense.

"Crossing minefield attack perimeter—now!" Charlotte Oselli snapped, and Honor's eyes darted to Eve Chandler's back. The tac officer said nothing for a second, but then a green light flashed on her boards and her taut shoulders relaxed imperceptibly.

"IFF transponders challenged and accepted, Skipper! We're in clean."

She glanced back over her shoulder, and Honor raised one hand in the ancient thumbs-up gesture. Identification friend or foe circuits could always screw up, especially when ships had taken battle damage that could knock out their onboard transponders or change their emission signatures radically. But the minefield had recognized them; it wouldn't kill their own wounded ships, and, almost more important still, would not reveal its position to the enemy in the process.

Chandler managed a tight answering grin, but then she whipped back around to her display as fresh damage signals shrilled over the task group tactical net. Her grin vanished, and her lips drew back in a snarl.

"They're concentrating on *Achilles* and *Defiant*, Ma'am," Eve Chandler said, and Honor bit her lip, wondering how the Peeps had identified the two divisional flagships.

"Enemy time to minefield?"

"Five-point-two-two minutes, Ma'am."

"That's better," Admiral Chin murmured. According to the emissions signatures, DeSoto had picked himself a *Redoubtable* and a *Homer*-class battlecruiser. The older *Redoubtables* were on the small side, but the *Homers* were every bit as powerful as Haven's later and somewhat larger *Sultans*. She watched a fresh salvo claw at *Achilles'* heels, and her smile was thin and cold.

A *Homer* would make a nice down payment on the revenge Genevieve Chin intended to collect.

"Three minutes to minefield attack range." Lieutenant Commander Oselli's voice was flat and taut.

Honor didn't even bother to nod. Her eyes were glued to the plot as missiles lashed back and forth between the warring ships. The Peep formation had overtaken and passed the crippled dreadnought they'd been pounding, hiding her from Eve Chandler's fire control behind their massed impeller wedges, and the task group shifted to a fresh target. They were getting good hits—a far higher percentage of them than the Peeps—but the enemy was sending in two missiles for every one of theirs, and all of them were targeted on *Achilles* or *Defiant*. *Defiant* seemed to be holding her own, but Banton's flagship had taken at least a dozen hits and lost most of her chase armament. Worse, she'd lost two beta nodes, and the strength of her wedge was falling. She could still match the task group's acceleration, but if she kept taking hits—

"Two minutes to minefield attack range."

Commander DeSoto stiffened as a faint radar return flickered in his display. Adrenaline flared as he remembered the last time his radar had picked something up, and he stabbed a key, interrogating his data base threat files. The computers considered dispassionately, then blinked an obedient reply.

"Minefield dead ahead!" he shouted.

"Roll starboard!" Admiral Chin barked instantly, and her task group swerved once more in the face of a fresh threat.

"They've seen them, Sir," Joseph Cartwright said, and Sarnow grimaced.

He'd hoped they'd come even closer—maybe even straight into the mines' attack—before they spotted them, but the Peeps had gotten a lot sharper since their initial surprise. He watched them slew sideways, and eyes of hard, green flint narrowed as new vector analyses blinked on his plot.

"They see them, but they're not going to avoid them," he said grimly.

The Havenite task group slid into range of the clustered mines like an out-of-control ground car or a ground-looping air car. Chin's lightning-fast response had blunted the threat, yet her velocity was far too high to sidestep it completely. Her ships were up on their sides relative to the field, presenting the bellies of their wedges as they came in, but the people who'd laid that field had known their business. They'd also known the exact vector on which Admiral Sarnow intended to suck her into it, and the mines were a disk perpendicular to her line of approach, stacked as "high" as they were "deep."

Space erupted in a wall of light as the bomb-pumped laser platforms spewed concentrated fury at Chin's ships. Thousands of laser beams, each more powerful than any missile laser head could generate, stabbed and tore at their prey. The vast majority wasted themselves harmlessly against her interposed impeller bands, but there were too many of them and they had too much spread for the wedges to intercept them all.

New Boston shuddered as fresh wounds cratered her

massive armor and wiped away weapons and their crews.
Three beta nodes and an alpha node went with them,
and her flag bridge displays flickered as Fusion Four
went into emergency shutdown, but her other power
plants took the load and damage control and medical
parties charged into her wrecked compartments. *New
Boston* was hurt, but she was still a fighting force as she
cleared the attack zone.

Other ships weren't. *Alp Arslan* broke in half and
vomited flame as her number two fusion plant's contain-
ment bottle failed, and the heavy cruisers *Scimitar*,
Drusus, and *Khopesh* vanished in matching fireballs,
their weaker sidewalls and radiation shielding no match
for the fury that could rip straight through a dreadnought's defenses. Half a dozen destroyers joined them,
and *Waldensville*, already lamed and crippled, reeled out
of the holocaust as a dying hulk.

Genevieve Chin listened to the torrent of loss and
damage reports, and her face was hard, hating stone.
Again. They'd suckered her *again*! But *how*, damn it?!
There was no way a minefield should be sitting way the
hell out here, and she was the one who'd picked her
approach vector! The Manties had matched *her* course,
not lured her onto one of their choosing, so how in *hell*
could they have known exactly where to put their field?

The last of her battered ships—the ones that survived—
streamed out of the attack and rolled back down to engage
the enemy once more, and her mouth was a knife-thin line as
she absorbed her losses. She was down to only two battlecruisers, both old *Tiger*-class ships and both damaged, and
five dreadnoughts, all damaged to greater or lesser degree.
Kaplan's armament had been almost completely gutted, and
Merston had lost half her energy weapons and a third of her
starboard sidewall. *New Boston*, *Havensport*, and *Macrea's
Tor* were hurt less badly, but the lighter ships of her screen
had been devastated. Barely half of them remained combat
effective, and God only knew what *else* the goddamned Manties had waiting for her!

She opened her mouth to order the pursuit broken

off, then froze as the data on her plot changed once more.

A fierce, harsh sound of exultation filled *Nike's* bridge, and Honor's eyes glittered. They were hopelessly outgunned by the ships behind them, but they'd already destroyed more than twice their own total tonnage! If Parks had left even a single battle squadron to support them, they could have annihilated the Peeps' lead element, maybe even saved the entire system, but the task group had nothing to reproach itself for. And maybe, just maybe, their fresh losses would finally convince the Peeps to break off after all.

Then the dreadnoughts rolled back down. Only four of them remained combat effective, but their course change had brought their full broadsides to bear, the range had fallen to little more than five million kilometers, they'd had time to absorb and adjust to the task group's defensive EW patterns, and their furious, humiliated gunners had blood in their eyes.

Two hundred and fifty-eight missiles erupted from the battered dreadnoughts and their surviving escorts, and twenty-two of them broke through everything the task group could throw at them.

HMS *Defiant* staggered sideways under the stunning body blow. Her port sidewall vanished, and half her after impeller ring vaporized. Two of her three fusion plants went into emergency shutdown, and she rolled over on her back, trailing air and shattered plating. There was no one left alive on her bridge, but her executive officer took one look at his displays in Auxiliary Control and knew she was done. The heel of his hand slammed down on a red button, and abandon ship alarms screamed over every speaker and suit com aboard her.

Barely a sixth of *Defiant's* crew escaped before the followup salvo killed her, but she was luckier than *Achilles*, and Honor's face went white as Commodore Isabella Banton's flagship blew up with all hands.

*   *   *

"Yes!"

DeSoto's shout was swallowed in the hungry bray of triumph from Admiral Chin's other officers as the Manticoran battlecruisers died, and her eyes flamed. She swallowed the impulse to break off and threw her ops officer a savage grin.

"Coming up on Point Delta."

Charlotte Oselli's soft voice broke the stunned silence, and Honor had her expression back under control as she looked down at her com screen. Admiral Sarnow had to be as shaken as she was by the loss of his two senior division commanders and a quarter of his squadron, but he met her eyes levelly.

"Course change, Sir?" she asked.

"Bring the task group fifteen degrees to starboard," Sarnow replied, and Honor heard someone inhale sharply.

They'd planned to alter course at Point Delta all along, for the mines had been their last trump card. With no more tricks to play, their sole chance to buy the base—and Admiral Danislav—a few more hours lay in convincing the Peeps to alter their own vector away from it to pursue the task group. But fifteen degrees was the sharpest alteration they'd discussed. It would let the enemy cut inside them, hold them in missile range longer.

She knew what Sarnow was thinking, for the same thought had occurred to her. Coupled with what had just happened, that big a course change would make the temptation to pursue them almost irresistible. His decision was a cold, calculated bid to offer the chance to destroy his entire squadron as bait to win the base time that probably wouldn't matter anyway.

Dame Honor Harrington looked back into her admiral's eyes and nodded.

"Aye, aye, Sir," she said softly.

• CHAPTER THIRTY-ONE

"They're altering course, Ma'am. It's not just an evasion maneuver; their base vector's coming fifteen degrees to starboard."

"I see." Admiral Chin's smile was a hungry wolf's. Those "SDs" *had* to be drones; if they'd been real ships of the wall, the battlecruisers would never have stopped running to meet them. And the course change itself, with its obvious invitation to pursuit, meant only one thing. The Manties had just run out of tricks. They wanted her to chase them in order to keep her out of energy range of their base because they damned well couldn't stop her any other way.

She knew what they were up to. They'd suck her well clear of the base, then scatter. They'd lose the advantage of their massed point defense when they did, but the range would be opening again by then. Only her dreadnoughts would have the weight of fire to get through their individual defenses, and she could only fire at a few of them.

She was tempted to ignore them, but the base wasn't going anywhere, and she might just get lucky. The Manties had lost a quarter of their battlecruisers and one heavy cruiser, and other ships were hurting. If they were willing to let her chase them, she was willing to accept the invitation in hopes of killing a few more of them before they scattered.

"They're taking the bait, Ma'am."

"I see it, Eve." Honor rubbed the tip of her nose and wondered if she were really pleased. The dreadnoughts' fire had eased as their swing back onto a pursuit vector restricted them once more to their chase armament, but their fire control was adapting to the task group's EW. Their targeting remained less effective than Sarnow's, but their warheads were far more powerful and, despite their losses, they still had the edge in launchers. Especially, a grim mental voice told her, now that *Defiant* and *Achilles* were gone.

Nike twisted around, leading her squadron through yet another evasion maneuver, and Honor bit her lip as fresh salvos of missiles tore down on *Agamemnon* and *Cassandra*. The damaged heavy cruiser *Circe* cut across *Cassandra*'s stern as the screen conformed to the battlecruisers' movements, and six of the birds targeted on Captain Quinlan's ship lost lock. They picked up the cruiser, instead, and their sudden swerve to pursue her took them clear of the counter missiles racing to meet them. *Circe*'s laser clusters stopped two of them; the other four got through . . . and shattered the cruiser like a toy.

"Formation Reno, Com—get those cruisers in tighter!"

"Aye, aye, Ma'am. Formation Reno." George Monet's flat voice sounded incongruously calm as he acknowledged and passed the order, and only then did Honor glance at her flag bridge com screen. She'd given the order without thinking about Sarnow, intent only on bringing the escorts in closer to the battlecruisers for mutual support. But Sarnow only nodded in agreement, then turned his head as Cartwright spoke.

"The Peep SDs are starting to move, Sir," the ops officer said. "They're heading for the base."

"Admiral Rollins is moving in, Ma'am," Commander Klim announced.

Admiral Chin merely nodded. It was about time he figured out what those "SDs" were and got his ass in gear, she thought sourly. Not that it would have changed what had already happened to her, but a little psychological support might have been nice.

Of course, it probably meant the Manties would scatter sooner. There'd be no point in their taking any more lumps once they realized Rollins was moving on the base behind her own ships.

HMS *Agamemnon* never even saw the missile coming. It rolled up from astern, slicing through a narrow sensor gap where a previous hit had blinded her radar, and detonated just off her port quarter.

For a moment the damage seemed minor; then her entire after half exploded. The mangled stub of her forward hull lurched to the side, and then it, too, blew up, and her consorts raced away from the fading clouds of gas and heat which had once been a battlecruiser and her crew.

Mark Sarnow's face was bleak and hard. The Peeps' steadily growing accuracy already exceeded his projections, and the task group was still fifteen minutes short of its planned scatter point.

His people had performed superbly—but eight thousand of them had died doing it, and the Peep SDs were coming. There was no point throwing away more lives to protect a base he couldn't save anyway.

He looked at his com screen and saw the same, bitter thought in Honor Harrington's brown eyes. She knew the scatter order was coming, and he opened his mouth to give it.

"Sir! Admiral Sarnow!"

His head snapped around in surprise, for the voice was Lieutenant Commander Samuel Webster's. He'd almost forgotten Webster's presence, but the com officer was pointing at his display—the one tied into the FTL sensor net.

Commander Francis DeSoto bared his teeth as the third Manty battlecruiser died. He didn't need Admiral Chin's orders to look for a replacement target, and he searched his display hungrily. Another *Homer*. That was what he wanted—but then he stiffened as an icon suddenly changed. *Agamemnon's* destruction and a shift in the Manticoran formation had opened a hole in the maze of mutually interfering impeller signatures, and *New Boston's* computers got their first clear look at HMS *Nike*.

The updated plot blinked at DeSoto again, and his eyes glittered. That ship was five percent larger than a *Homer*, and that made her one of the new *Reliant*-class ships.

"It *is* Admiral Danislav, Sir!" Joseph Cartwright's confirmation of Webster's report was jubilant, and Sarnow fought his own elation. The enormous hyper footprint was well beyond *Nike's* onboard sensor range, but there was no question of who it was. The ten dreadnoughts at the formation's core burned sharp and clear, and Danislav must already be querying the sensor net.

The admiral made himself sit still and silent, watching the plot Webster was feeding from the sensor platforms' FTL transmissions. Danislav's ships held their arrival vector for ten seconds, then twenty, coasting without acceleration at the bare 8,000 KPS of their translation into normal space, and then the plot blinked. Danislav's heading changed, his ships went to an acceleration of four hundred and thirty gravities, and a new vector curled out across the display.

Numbers flashed with CIC's analysis. Twenty-six minutes. That was how much longer the Peeps had to keep chasing Sarnow to reach the point of no return. Just twenty-six minutes and they couldn't possibly escape Danislav's oncoming dreadnoughts.

He turned back to his com to give Captain Harrington the news.

Twenty-four missiles sped toward the task group. Five of them lost lock over a million kilometers out as jammers blinded their sensors. Another three locked onto decoys. Two of them couldn't see their primary target and shifted to the secondary, arcing away to strike at the heavy cruiser *Warrior*, and countermissiles smashed six more of them to bits.

Eight of them broke through the outer defense zone and bore in, weaving and bobbing while their own ECM parried and thrust with the systems trying to kill them. They were outclassed . . . but they were also closing at fifty-five thousand KPS. Laser clusters killed one of them, then two more. A fourth. The surviving quartet made their final course correction, two more of them blew apart, and then the last pair of missiles detonated.

HMS *Nike* heaved and twisted as x-ray daggers sank deep into her armored flank. Laser Seven and Graser Five exploded into wreckage. Radar Five went with them, along with Communications Two, Missile Thirteen and Fourteen, Damage Control Three, Boat Bay Two, and ninety-three men and women.

A secondary explosion boiled up out of Com Two and Damage Control Three. Incandescent gas and flying chunks of battle steel erupted into CIC from below, gutting it and killing or wounding twenty-six more people. Fire and smoke filled the compartment, and the massive concussion smashed across it and into its after bulkhead—the one that separated it from *Nike's* flag bridge.

The ruptured bulkhead spat out splinters with deadly velocity. One of them tore Admiral Sarnow's yeoman in half. A second killed three of Joseph Cartwright's ratings. Another shrieked across the flag bridge and decapitated Casper Southman, then ricocheted into Ernestine Corell's console. It missed the chief of staff by centimeters, and she lurched back from her shattered displays in horror, coughing and choking on smoke as the man beside her vanished in an explosion of blood.

And a fourth deadly splinter ripped into the back of Admiral Mark Sarnow's command chair.

It sheared through the chair, spinning end-for-end like a white-hot buzz-saw. The impact snapped the admiral's shock frame and hurled him forward, but the splinter caught him in midair. It severed his right leg just above the knee and mangled his left calf, chunks of the chair itself blasted into his back, and his ribcage shattered like a wicker basket as he impacted on the master plot and bounced back like a broken doll.

Samuel Webster flung himself toward his admiral while slamming blast doors chopped off the cyclone of escaping air. Sarnow's skin suit had already inflated emergency tourniquets on either thigh, and his scream was a faint, thready exhalation as Webster moved him gently to check his life-sign monitors.

The admiral stared up at his com officer, fighting the searing agony. "Don't scatter!" he gasped with all his failing strength, and his hand plucked at Webster's arm like a fevered child's. "Tell them not to scatter!"

Webster's face was white as Sarnow's terrible injuries registered, and his fingers darted across the skin suit's med panel. Blessed relief spread through the admiral, deadening the pain. Unconsciousness beckoned, but he fought it as he had the pain, clinging to awareness, as Ernestine Corell appeared beside him.

"Don't scatter!" he gasped again, and Corell looked at Webster.

"What did he say?" she demanded, and Webster shrugged helplessly.

"I don't know, Ma'am." Grief clogged his voice, and he touched Sarnow's shoulder gently. "I can't make it out."

Corell leaned closer, and Sarnow tried again, desperate to get the order out, but the blackness took him first.

Damage reports flooded into *Nike's* bridge, and Honor heard herself acknowledging them—calm and controlled, like a stranger—while her shocked eyes clung to the blank screen by her right knee.

She tore her gaze from it and looked at her own tactical repeater. CIC was gone, but Tactical's fire control systems had taken over the plot. She saw the cruisers *Sorcerer* and *Merlin* racing into new positions, taking up station on *Nike's* flanks to support her point defense as the task group recognized the Peeps' new target, and her flying thoughts were clear and cold.

She knew what Sarnow had been about to say. She'd been his tactical alter ego too long *not* to know . . . but he hadn't said it.

Command passed with the admiral. She knew that, too, yet there were no flag officers left. Captain Rubenstein was senior officer now, but *Onslaught's* gravitics were gone, her com section heavily damaged; she could neither receive the sensor platforms' transmissions nor pass orders effectively . . . and Rubenstein didn't know Danislav had arrived or what the admiral had intended.

She felt George Monet watching her, knew he was waiting for her order to inform Rubenstein he was in command, and said nothing.

The task group raced onward, flailed by the Havenites' fire, and its return fire grew weaker and more sporadic as laser heads blew away missile tubes and clawed at sidewalls and hulls. The range was opening again, but slowly, and it had dropped to less than three million kilometers first. Mark Sarnow's captains clung grimly to their courses, knowing they'd done all they'd set out to do and waiting for the flagship's order to scatter.

Captain Pavel Young sat white-faced and sweating in his command chair. *Warlock* was untouched, one of the few ships which could say that, and her gravitics had picked up the same information as *Nike's.* He knew the relief force had arrived, and terror gnawed at his vitals as he waited for his ship's unnatural exemption to end.

He stared at the flagship's cursor, tasting blood from a bitten lip as direct hits and near misses lashed at her, their savagery made somehow more terrible by the quiet of *Warlock's* bridge. But even through his near-panic a corner of his brain exulted, for Van Slyke's death had given him squadron command at last, and command experience in a battle like this, however it had come his way, would wash away the Basilisk fiasco's stigma at last!

They reached the prearranged scatter point, and he tensed to order a radical course change at the flagship's command. But no command came. They passed the invisible dot in space, still charging forward, still on course . . . still writhing under the enemy's fire, and his eyes widened in disbelief.

He stared at *Nike*'s data code desperately, almost beseechingly. What the hell was *wrong* with Sarnow? There was no more need for this! The Peeps would spot Danislav's dreadnoughts within twenty minutes—thirty-five at the most! Surely he knew they'd break off the action then anyway. *Why wasn't he letting them save themselves?!*

And then *Warlock*'s immunity ended. The missile wasn't even meant for her, but her port decoy sucked it away from *Invincible*. It detonated at twenty-four thousand kilometers, blasting through her sidewall to blot away Laser Four and rip Magazine Two open to space, and panic roared through Pavel Young's soul on the wail of damage alarms.

"Squadron orders!" His tenor's shrill, raw edges turned every head on his bridge in shock. "All ships scatter! Repeat, all ships scatter!"

Honor Harrington stared at her display as Heavy Cruiser Squadron Seventeen peeled away. It was too soon. They needed another twelve minutes—just twelve more minutes—to insure their pursuers' destruction!

Five of the heavy cruisers swerved away as she watched. Only *Merlin* held her course, glued to *Nike*'s flank like a limpet, her laser clusters firing in desperate defense of the flagship.

"Contact *Warlock*!" she snapped. "Get those ships back in position!"

Pavel Young stared at his com officer.

"Orders, Sir?" His exec's voice was harsh, and Young

wrenched his wild eyes back to his plot. The Peeps were ignoring his fleeing ships to hammer savagely at the battlecruisers exposed by his defection.

"*Orders, Sir?!*" the exec half-shouted, and Captain Lord Pavel Young clenched his jaw in silence. He couldn't go back into that horror. *He couldn't!*

"No response from *Warlock*, Ma'am." *Nike* shook to yet another hit, and Monet's voice quivered with sympathetic vibration, but his stunned surprise at the heavy cruiser's silence came through clearly.

Honor's head whipped up, and Monet flinched back from her expression.

"Give me a direct link to Captain Young!"

"Aye, aye, Ma'am." Monet jabbed keys, and the blank screen at Honor's knee filled with Pavel Young's face. Sweat streaked his cheeks and ran into his beard, and his eyes were a hunted animal's.

"Get back into formation, Captain!" Young only stared at her, his mouth working soundlessly. "*Get back into formation, damn you!*"

The screen went dead as Young killed the circuit. For one stunned second, she couldn't believe it, and in that second a fresh salvo of laser heads slammed at *Nike's* defenses. Her ship heaved and shuddered, frantic damage control reports crackled all around her, and she wrenched her eyes from the com screen to George Monet.

"General signal to all heavy cruisers. Return to formation at once. Repeat, return to formation at once!"

Puzzlement furrowed Admiral Chin's forehead as she watched the Manties' antics. Her fire must have taken out their flagship's communications, she decided. That was the only explanation for their sudden, ragged confusion. Their heavy cruisers dispersed before her eyes, taking themselves out of the antimissile net, and her missiles thundered down on the battlecruisers' weakened defenses. One of them staggered, belching air and debris, but she hauled back onto course and continued to run. Another salvo scorched in, ripping at them, maiming and tearing, and Chin smiled, sensing the kills to come—then snarled as four of the fleeing cruisers suddenly reversed course.

Only one of them continued its flight, and her fire control ignored it to concentrate on the ones who stood to fight.

Honor Harrington spared one last, hating glance for the single data code that continued to streak away from her formation. *Cassandra* had been savagely mauled when Young broke away. Her entire port sidewall was down, leaving her naked and vulnerable, but the other cruisers slotted back into the net, and Honor snapped fresh orders. *Intolerant* and *Invincible* dropped back between *Cassandra* and her enemies, shielding her with their own interposed sidewalls while her crew worked frantically at repairs.

They had nine minutes to get that sidewall back up.

Admiral Yuri Rollins jerked around in his command chair to stare at Captain Holcombe. The chief of staff was white, and Rollins felt the blood drain from his own face as Holcombe's report registered.

He vaulted from his chair and half-ran to the master plot, staring into it in disbelief as the Argus sensors updated the imagery. It had taken over fifteen minutes for the sensor platforms to relay the data to him, and the Manticoran dreadnoughts were already up to twelve thousand KPS.

A blood-red line extended itself from the newly arrived ships, racing out towards Chin's battered squadron, and the admiral's blood turned to ice as CIC's projection flashed before him. Chin would be trapped, unable to evade the threat, in less than ten minutes . . . and it would take any warning from him thirteen minutes to reach her.

"Reverse course—maximum military power!" he

snapped, and turned away as startled responses came back to him. He walked heavily back to his chair and lowered himself into it.

Those fresh ships of the wall weren't enough to stop him—but they could maul him badly before he destroyed them. Nor could he be certain no more were coming . . . and their sudden arrival, coupled with the ambushes through which the Manty battlecruisers had led Chin, argued that they weren't.

It had been a trap after all, he thought dully. He didn't know how they'd managed it. Perhaps they'd had a relay ship waiting out beyond the hyper limit, ready to summon reinforcements at the opportune moment. He didn't know, and it didn't matter. He had to break back out across the hyper limit before anyone *else* turned up—and his course reversal was the only warning he could give Chin. Her gravitics would pick it up . . . and she might even figure out why he'd done it in time.

"Admiral Rollins has gone to maximum decel, Ma'am."

Commander Klim sounded puzzled, and Admiral Chin frowned in surprise. She craned her neck to see the master plot, and her own puzzlement grew.

A light blinked in Honor's display at last as the dispassionate computers confirmed it: her pursuers could no longer escape the retribution of Danislav's reinforced squadron, whatever they did.

She tried to feel exultant, but Mark Sarnow and his people had paid too high a price for that.

"Status on *Cassandra*'s sidewall?"

"Still down, Skipper. She's lost five beta nodes, as well; her max accel's down to four-point-six KPS squared."

Honor inhaled deeply. With the pounding the Peeps had taken, their accel was low enough *Cassandra* could still draw away from them, but she'd never live to get out of range. Not without her sidewall.

"Bring her up on our starboard side. Tuck her in as tight as you can and reduce our accel to match hers.

Instruct her to maintain station on us—then order the rest of the task group to scatter."

Admiral Chin's frown deepened as the Manty task group unraveled. There was no mistake about it this time; each ship spun away from its fellows, scattering far and wide in what was clearly a carefully planned maneuver.

All but two of them. One pair of battlecruisers clung together, so tight her sensors could hardly distinguish one from the other, and she nodded. The closer one was the *Reliant*-class ship, and she was obviously covering a damaged consort, which made the two of them her logical target. But even as she thought that she continued to stare at the decelerating impeller sources of Rollins' superdreadnoughts.

Now why would they be doing that, unless—

The battered Havenite dreadnoughts slowed abruptly, and Honor bared her teeth. They'd figured it out at last. She didn't know how, but they knew . . . only they didn't know it was already too late.

The dreadnoughts completed their turn, decelerating as hard as they could, and she pictured the scene on their flagship's bridge. Their CO couldn't know what bearing the threat was coming from. Until her own sensors picked up Danislav's ships she could only decelerate back the way she'd come, and every second of deceleration increased *Nike's* relative velocity by nine KPS. Which made it time to make the Peeps' targeting problems a little worse.

"Execute Shell Game," she said.

Eve Chandler punched commands into her panel, and eight EW drones erupted away from the two battlecruisers. They scattered in four different directions, each pair tucked in tight, mimicking the signatures of their mother ships, and *Nike* and *Cassandra* altered course sharply to charge off on yet a fifth vector.

The sudden multiplication of targets did exactly what Honor had intended. Unable to be certain which were the real ships, the Peep commander chose not to waste her ammunition on might-have-beens . . . especially when she must have figured out she was going to need every missile she had very shortly.

All fire ceased, and the brutally wounded flagship of TG-H001 and her crippled consort raced for safety.

• CHAPTER THIRTY-TWO

Hereditary President Harris looked around the mag-
nificently decorated dining room and tried not to show
his worry. It was his birthday, and the glittering horde of
well-wishers had gathered as it always did, but this time
there was a difference. The soft clink and clatter of
tableware sounded completely natural; the near total
absence of conversation did not.

His mouth quirked mirthlessly, and he reached for his
wineglass. Of course there was no conversation; no one
wanted to talk about what all of them knew was true.

He drank deep of his wine, hardly noticing its exqui-
site bouquet, and let his eye run over the tables. As it
did on every President's Day, the Republic's government
had virtually shut down for the celebration, since anyone
in government who mattered simply *had* to be here.
Only Ron Bergren and Oscar Saint-Just were absent.
The foreign secretary had departed for the Erewhon
Wormhole Junction, en route to the Solarian League and
a desperate (and probably futile) effort to convince the
League that Manticore had started the war. Saint-Just,
on the other hand, had been working eighteen-hour days
ever since Constance's assassination—without getting any
closer to her killers. But every other cabinet member
was here, as were the heads of all of Haven's most
prominent Legislaturalist clans and their immediate
families.

Harris set the glass back down and stared into its
tawny heart. Despite the forced air of festive normality,
there was a terrible, singing tension in this room, for the
growing fear spawned by Constance's unexpected murder

had been fanned by the disastrous reports from the frontiers.

They'd been mouse-trapped. Harris made himself admit that. They'd set their plans in motion, confident the game was theirs to direct as it always had been, only to discover that, after fifty years of conquest, they had finally met a foe even more cunning than they were.

He'd read the dispatches. Given what Admiral Rollins had known, Harris had to agree he'd had no choice but to move against the Hancock System, yet hindsight proved only too clearly that the Manties had known all about the "secret" Argus net. They'd used it to offer Rollins an irresistible bait by "withdrawing" their ships, and the result had been devastating. The arrival of the dreadnoughts which had compelled Admiral Chin to surrender would have been bad enough, but it hadn't been the end. Oh, no. Not the end.

Harris shuddered. The second jaw of the Manty trap had failed by the thinnest margin when the rest of Admiral Parks' "dispersed" task force dropped out of hyper barely thirty minutes too late to intercept Rollins before he hypered out, yet his escape hadn't saved him in the end. Reinforced to almost a third again of his pre-war strength, Parks had moved instantly against Seaford Nine and Rollins' weakened task force. Seaford's defenders had destroyed a couple of ships of the wall and damaged others, but only three of their own capital ships had survived, and Rollins' flagship hadn't been one of them. PNS *Barnett* had blown up early in the action, killing Rollins and his entire staff, and the command confusion that followed had finished Seaford off.

And then Parks had left one battle squadron to hold Seaford and returned to Hancock . . . just in time to meet Admiral Coatsworth as he moved in, expecting to find Rollins in possession. At least Coatsworth had gotten most of his ships out, yet his lead squadrons had taken a terrible pounding, and without Seaford's repair facilities, he'd been driven clear back to Barnett with his damaged units while his courier boats reported the disaster to Haven.

Public Information had clamped down a total news blackout, but rumors had leaked. That was one reason Harris had gone ahead with his annual birthday celebration, as an effort to convince people of the government's "business as usual" confidence in the face of those rumors. Not, he thought bitterly, that he expected it to do any good. The only thing that could really calm the public would be the news that Admiral Parnell's attack on Yeltsin's Star had succeeded, and it would take at least another week for Parnell's report of victory to reach Haven.

Assuming, of course, that he had a victory to report.

Harris grimaced at his own gloomy thoughts and straightened in his chair. One thing that *wouldn't* help was for the President to look as if his best friend had just died, and—

His thoughts broke off as the head of his security detachment walked quickly across the room towards him. The security man's expression was neutral, but his body language communicated an entirely different message.

"What is it, Eric?" the President asked quietly.

"I'm not certain, Sir." The security man's New Geneva accent was more pronounced—and anxious—than usual. "Capital Traffic Control's just picked up half a dozen Navy shuttles entering city airspace without prior clearance."

"Without clearance?" Harris pushed his chair back and stood. "Where are they headed? What did they say when Control challenged them?"

"They say they're an unscheduled training mission authorized by Naval Security to test CTC's readiness states, Mr. President."

"A security test?" Harris wiped his mouth with his napkin and dropped it beside his plate. "Well, I suppose that makes a degree of sense, under the circumstances, but contact Secretary Saint-Just and get InSec to validate."

"We're trying, Sir, but Secretary Saint-Just is away from his com."

"Then screen Undersecretary Singh. *Someone* must know—"

The Presidential Security Force man stiffened, pressing his hand to his unobtrusive earbug, then paled. His right hand seized the President by the sleeve, and Harris staggered as he was half-flung towards an exit.

"Eric! What the hell—?!"

"Those shuttles just altered course, Mr. President! They're headed straight in our direction, and—"

The PSF man never finished his sentence, for seven assault shuttles of the People's Navy screamed over the People's Palace. Four five-thousand-kilo precision guided warheads scored direct hits on the Presidential Dining Room, and Sidney Harris, his wife, his three children, and his entire cabinet and all of his senior advisors, ceased to exist in a fireball of chemical explosives.

Five seconds later, the Palace itself was little more than flaming rubble strewn across the cratered horror of its once immaculate grounds.

"Ladies and gentlemen of the Quorum, I am appalled by the scale of this act of treason." Speaker Robert Stanton Pierre shook his head sadly as he gazed out over the stunned faces of the People's Quorum and spoke into the dead silence. For all intents and purposes, the entire government of the People's Republic of Haven had been annihilated along with the heads of every Legislaturalist family that really mattered, and the full impact of the disaster was still sinking into the Quorum's minds.

"The fact that Secretary Saint-Just's Internal Security personnel were able to intercept and annihilate the traitors cannot lessen the blow," Pierre went on sadly. "Not only have our leaders and their families been brutally murdered, but the traitors came out of our own military! Commodore Danton has confirmed that the shuttles which carried out the attack were covered by official orders—orders which would have been wiped from his data base by still other traitors if not for the prompt action of loyal members of his staff. I deeply regret the casualties those loyal men and women suffered in the gunfight which wrecked the Commodore's HQ, but the presence of the traitors who provoked it, coupled with their readiness to resort to violence when challenged, must raise the gravest suspicions. Under the circumstances, we have no option but to assume the worst, at least until the most thorough investigation can sift these horrible events in detail."

"Mr. Speaker!" A well-fed, beefy back-bencher stood, and Pierre nodded to him.

"The Chair recognizes Mr. Guzman."

"What do you mean 'assume the worst,' Mr. Speaker?"

"I mean that we face the gravest crisis in our history," Pierre said softly. "This attack was launched by Navy personnel on the heels of the worst defeat our fleet has ever suffered. We must ask ourselves who had the authority to order those shuttles out on their 'exercise.' We must ask ourselves who had reason to fear the government's reaction to their failure against the Hancock System and the loss of Seaford Nine."

"Surely you're not suggesting that senior Navy officers were responsible?!"

"I am suggesting only that until we *know* who was responsible, we must consider every possibility, however terrible," Pierre replied in a level voice. "I hope with all my heart that I am doing our military personnel a grave injustice by even suggesting such a thing, but until we can be certain of that, we owe it to the Republic to guard against the chance that I'm not."

"*We* owe it to the Republic?" someone else asked, without seeking recognition, and Pierre nodded grimly.

"The government has been destroyed, ladies and gentlemen. Secretary Saint-Just and Secretary Bergren are the cabinet's sole survivors, and only Secretary Saint-Just is currently on Haven. He's already informed me that, as no more than Secretary Palmer-Levy's acting successor, he feels neither qualified to nor capable of assuming the burden of government. Which means that *we*, the people's representatives, have no option but to assume

mergency powers until such time as formal government
an be reestablished."

"*Us?*" someone yelped, and Pierre nodded once more.

"I realize our experience is limited, but who else is
here?" He looked at his fellows appealingly. "We are at
var with the Star Kingdom of Manticore and its lackeys.
n a time of such peril, the Republic must not drift
ncontrolled, and until we can know positively that the
nilitary is reliable, we dare not place ourselves at its
nercy. In the face of those inescapable and overriding
oncerns, we have no choice but to face our responsibil-
ty to provide the stability we so desperately need by
rganizing ourselves as a committee of public safety to
ssume direction of the state."

The People's Quorum stared at its speaker in shock.
After so many decades of rubber-stamp approval of
omeone else's policies, barely a fraction of them had the
east idea how to wield effective power. The very
hought of it terrified them, yet none of them could
leny the force of Pierre's logic. *Someone* had to assume
ontrol, and if there was the chance of a full-scale mili-
ary coup . . .

Pierre let the silence linger for long, endless moments,
hen cleared his throat.

"I have, on my own authority, discussed our critical
ituation with Secretary Saint-Just. He has already moved
o secure control of the essential administrative centers
ere on Haven and assures me of the loyalty of his own
nSec personnel, but he has no desire to impose any sort
f one-man rule on the Republic. In fact, he's practically
egged me to explain the realities of our plight to you so
hat we can move quickly to establish the broad-based
ommittee required to reassure our own people and the
alaxy at large that no coup will be permitted to over-
hrow the Republic." Pierre shrugged helplessly.

"I see no option but to honor his request, ladies and
entlemen, and organize ourselves as a caretaker govern-
nent until public safety can be restored."

● CHAPTER THIRTY-THREE

Amos Parnell sat in his office off DuQuesne Base's central war room and stared in sick horror at his terminal. The stocky, powerful CNO seemed shrunken, aged beyond his years, and his face was haggard.

His task force had returned to the Barnett System less than ten hours ago after its agonizingly slow passage from Yeltsin and what he supposed historians would call the Battle of Yeltsin. "Massacre of Yeltsin" would be more appropriate, and it was his fault. He'd taken the Manties' bait hook, line, and sinker.

He closed his eyes, covering his face with his hands, and knew he was a beaten man. Not just by the Manties, but inside. He'd gone into Yeltsin believing he had a three-to-one advantage, only to find himself facing a force even stronger than his own, and somehow the Manties and their allies had been able to preposition their powered-down wall of battle perfectly. It was as if they'd been clairvoyant, as if they'd been able to see every move he made in real time.

Their opening broadsides had taken him totally by surprise. A quarter of his fleet had been crippled or destroyed almost before he knew the enemy was there, and he had no idea how he'd extricated *anything* from the deadly trap. He couldn't remember. No doubt he could replay the com records and flag bridge recorders and reconstruct his orders, but he had absolutely no coherent memory of giving them. It was all a hideous nightmare of lightning-fast decisions and desperate improvisation that had somehow fought clear of Yeltsin with barely half the ships he'd taken into it, and half of *them* had been so battered their return to Barnett had taken more than twice as long as the passage out.

And now this. The President was dead. The entire *government* was dead, as were his own father, his younger sister, his brother, three of his cousins, and virtually their entire families, and *Navy personnel* had done it.

He ground his teeth in agony at the thought. The Manties' Hancock trap had succeeded even more completely against Admiral Rollins than the Yeltsin ambush had against him. Sixteen percent—the *best* sixteen percent—of the Fleet's wall of battle had been wiped out, and even as the Navy bled and died on the frontiers, another faction of its personnel had committed mass murder against its own people. He ached with agonizing, personal shame and thought longingly of the loaded pulser in his desk drawer. All it would take was a single squeeze of the stud . . . but he owed the Republic more than that. He owed it whatever he could do to stem the tide of disaster.

His office door opened, and he snatched his hands down and looked up. Commodore Perot stood in the doorway, and Parnell opened his mouth to demand the reason for the intrusion, then paused.

The commodore wasn't alone, for two men and a woman stood behind him. They wore InSec's uniform, and Perot's face was a sickly, ashen hue.

One of the InSec men touched Perot's shoulder, and he shambled into the office, his eyes stunned. Parnell stiffened and opened his mouth once more, but the woman spoke before he could.

"Admiral Amos Daughtry Parnell?" It came out hard and clipped, an accusation, not a form of address.

"What's the meaning of this?" Parnell tried to put iron into his voice, but he heard its wan, weary quiver.

"Admiral Parnell, I am Special Undersecretary for Security Cordelia Ransom, and it is my duty to inform you that you are under arrest."

"*Arrest?*" Parnell stared at her, feeling anesthetized

and numb, as she drew a crackling sheaf of paper from her pocket. "On what charges?"

"On charges of treason against the people," Ransom said in that same, hard voice. She tossed the sheaf of paper onto his desk, and the admiral stared down at it dazedly, then picked it up in trembling hands.

From its date, the standard InSec detention order must have been written within hours of his Yeltsin dispatch's arrival on Haven, and like all InSec DOs, its wording was vague. The charges were listed in bald, terse sentences, but no amplification or specifics were offered.

He read the charges slowly, unable to believe this was happening, and then he came to the last page. It wasn't a standard detention order after all, for the signature block had been changed. The space which should have contained the Secretary of Internal Security's authorization of Parnell's arrest bore another name and title, and he stared at it numbly.

"By order of Rob S. Pierre, Chairman, Committee of Public Safety," it said.

Dame Honor Harrington stepped into the briefing room. She removed her white beret, and Nimitz swayed gently on her shoulder as she tucked the beret under her left epaulet and looked at the man awaiting her.

Vice Admiral Sir Yancey Parks returned her gaze levelly. She felt his emotions through her link to the treecat, and there was still no liking for her in them. She wasn't surprised. She might not know what had prejudiced Parks against her to start with, but she'd come to the conclusion that it didn't much matter, anyway. They were simply the wrong personalities to like one another.

Yet they were also professionals. They didn't *have* to like each other, and just as she felt Parks' dislike, she felt his stubborn determination to do his duty. It was a pity, she thought, that he couldn't feel *her* emotions. Perhaps that sort of understanding might have overcome their mutual dislike.

And perhaps not.

"I've just been reading your doctor's report on Admiral Sarnow," Parks said a bit abruptly. "I must say, I'm impressed. Very impressed."

"Yes, Sir. Commander Montoya is one of the finest doctors I've ever known—as I can attest from personal experience."

"So I understand." Parks' lips quirked in a dour smile, and he pointed at a chair. "Sit, Captain. Sit!" His voice had a testy edge, and he watched through wintry eyes as she obeyed.

"I owe Admiral Sarnow—and you—a very great vote of thanks." Parks didn't like admitting that, but he did it. "Of course, you were technically in the wrong not to pass command to Captain Rubenstein, but in view of the tactical situation—and the result—I have fully endorsed your decision, and my dispatch to Admiral Caparelli fully approves your conduct and commends your skill and courage."

"Thank you, Sir," Honor said quietly, and reached up to still Nimitz with a touch as the 'cat shifted on her shoulder.

"I've also read your report on the . . . incidents of the engagement," Parks went on in a flat tone, "and taken statements from all surviving captains. In light of those statements and the com records from *Warlock*'s data base, there is no question in my mind that Lord Young first ordered his squadron to scatter without authorization and subsequently withdrew his ship and its support against your specific orders. The situation is complicated by the fact that he was, in fact, senior to you, but he had no way of knowing Admiral Sarnow had been incapacitated. At the moment he made his decision, he did so against what he believed to be Admiral Sarnow's orders and hence in defiance of his lawful superior while in the presence of the enemy. As such, I have had no choice but to remove him from command and assemble a captains' board to consider his actions."

He paused, and Honor watched him in silence. She'd known all about the board of inquiry. She might not like

Parks, but she had to admit he'd acted both promptly and generously where the task group was concerned. Of course, she thought bitterly, there weren't very many people left to be generous *to*. Sarnow's force had suffered over twelve thousand fatal casualties, and none of them had been necessary.

She knew she would never be able to forgive Parks for letting it happen, yet she also knew he'd done the best he could. He'd made a bad call, but he hadn't known about the Peeps' spy satellites when he did it. Once he'd discovered their existence, his actions had been both rapid and decisive. The proof was in the pudding, she supposed, and the conquest of Seaford Nine and the total destruction of the Peeps' military presence in his command area was a very substantial pudding indeed.

But Parks knew how much he owed the task group. He'd been more than generous in his praise, and she'd already seen the honors list he'd proposed to the Queen. She was on it, as were Sarnow, Banton, Van Slyke, and at least a dozen other officers and twice as many ratings and noncoms. Too many of them were mentioned only posthumously, yet Parks had done what he could, and his report on his own actions pulled no punches. He'd fully admitted his mistakes—and been equally explicit in his praise for Admiral Mark Sarnow and the officers and enlisted personnel under his command.

Except for Lord Pavel Young. Young had been relieved from command and placed under open arrest even before Parks moved against Seaford, and Commodore Capra had taken Honor's own testimony in a recorded deposition for the board of inquiry. Now she waited to hear its verdict.

"It is the opinion of the officers of the board," Parks said quietly, "that Lord Young has proven his total lack of fitness to command a Queen's ship. The board has also concluded that the confusion his withdrawal caused in your missile defense net was directly responsible for an indeterminate but substantial number of casualties to other ships of the task group. It is the board's recommendation, which I have endorsed—" Parks looked squarely into Honor's eyes "—that Lord Young be returned to Manticore, there to be tried by court-martial for cowardice and desertion in the face of the enemy."

Honor's nostrils flared, and Nimitz hissed. A savage sense of satisfaction went through her, cold and deadly, not exultant. Parks sat silent, watching her, and she inhaled and squared her shoulders.

"Thank you, Sir. For all of our people."

The admiral shrugged, but her link to Nimitz was still open, and she felt Parks' mixed emotions. His own actions, however successful, left him open to serious criticism. Young's family could be expected to play on them in any defense they mounted, and his endorsement of the board's recommendations would make the Earl of North Hollow his mortal enemy, whatever the trial's outcome. He knew it, and it worried him, but he'd endorsed them anyway.

"At any rate," he went on after a moment, "it's time you took *Nike* home for repairs, Dame Honor."

Honor nodded. The repair base had patched up the most critical of the task group's hurts, but most of its units had already departed for Manticore. There were too many damaged ships for the base's capacity; the worst cripples, the ones needing the most yard time for complete repairs, had to be sent home, and HMS *Nike* would take months to heal.

"You depart for Manticore within the next twelve hours," Parks said, "and I'm sending Lord Young home in your ship under quarters arrest."

Honor stiffened and started to open her mouth, but Parks' gaze pinned her to her chair.

"Yours is the next departing ship. Considering the serious charges against him, he is entitled to the promptest return—and trial—possible, and I will expect you to treat him with proper military courtesy. Until and unless he is tried and convicted, he remains a Queen's officer and your senior. I realize the uncomfortable position in which this places you, but I expect you to do your duty—as you always have."

His eyes softened, somehow, with the final words, and she was puzzled by the surge of genuine apology she sensed through her link to Nimitz. It muted her own angry distaste for sharing the same air as Pavel Young, and she bit her lip for just a moment, then nodded.

"I understand, Sir Yancey."

"I thought you would, Milady." Her eyebrows tried to rise at his totally unexpected form of address, and he smiled. It wasn't an effusive smile, but it was genuine, and he rose and extended his hand.

"Commodore Capra will transmit your formal orders to *Nike*," he said. "I will personally inform Captain Young of the board's recommendations—and my own— before I send him aboard."

"Yes, Sir."

"Then I think that concludes our business, Dame Honor. God speed." He shook her hand firmly, and she braced to attention and turned toward the hatch. It hissed open before her, and she started to step through it, then paused as the admiral spoke again.

"Oh, by the way, Dame Honor. I almost forgot to mention that you'll find another passenger waiting for you when you return to *Nike*."

"Another passenger, Sir?" Honor turned in the open hatch, her expression puzzled, and Parks chuckled with genuine humor.

"It seems Captain Tankersley was promoted from captain junior grade to captain of the list just before the Peep attack. As such, he's too senior to stay on as exec aboard the base here, and since he, um, did such a fine job of dealing with *Nike*'s original engineering difficulties, I thought it only fitting to return him to Manticore for reassignment aboard her."

Honor stared at him, trapped between amazement and sudden joy, and Parks gave her the first completely natural smile she'd ever seen from him.

"I trust the two of you will find something to talk about during the voyage, Captain Harrington."

HONOR HARRINGTON'S NAVY

NAVAL DESIGN AND DOCTRINE

Warship design in the twentieth century of the Diaspora was dictated, as it had been for the past seven hundred T-years, by the limitations and capabilities of starship propulsive systems.

Engagements in hyper-space were far less common than normal-space combat simply because it was so difficult for ships to find one another there. As a result, designs were optimized for normal-space warfare, despite the severe tactical drawbacks this imposed on the rare occasions upon which ships fought one another in hyper.

Normal-space movement depended upon a ship's impeller wedge, the inclined bands of stressed gravity above and below the vessel. The physics of the impeller drive required that this wedge be open both ahead and astern of the ship, although the sternward opening was much shallower. Since no known weapon could penetrate an impeller stress band, this meant no ship could fire at targets directly "above" or "below" it, but it also meant that fire directed *at* a ship from above or below was ineffective.

The sides of the impeller wedge, unlike its ends, could be closed by gravity sidewalls, a much weaker version of the impeller stress band. A warship's sidewalls were its first and primary line of defense, extremely difficult for missiles to penetrate (though there was an unending race between missiles with better sidewall penetrators and defensive designers' efforts to build ever tougher sidewalls) and invulnerable to even the most powerful energy weapons at ranges in excess of 400,000 to 500,000 kilometers (approximately forty percent of effective range against targets *without* sidewalls).

The fact that a ship could no more fire out through its impeller wedge than it could be fired upon also dictated the arrangement of its armament, most of which was grouped on the broadside, with a much weaker "chase" armament arranged for fire ahead and astern. Chase armaments were intended to cover the blind spots in a vessel's broadside firing arcs, but they tended to be much lighter than broadside batteries because there was simply less hull volume in which to mount them.

Although no "holes" could exist in an impeller stress band, portals (known to naval spacers as "gunports") could be opened in a vessel's sidewalls to permit unobstructed fire of its own weapons. In theory, gunports represented dangerous chinks in its defenses; in practice, the targets were too small and fleeting—they were "open" only long enough for a shot to be fired through them—to be deliberately targeted. Nonetheless, it was not unheard of (though it *was* very rare) for a lucky shot to penetrate an open gunport.

Even a freak gunport hit, however, wasn't guaranteed to inflict damage. The maximum safe velocity in n-space was approximately .8 c for a ship with military-grade particle and radiation shielding, whereas merchantmen normally relied on much weaker—and less massive—shield generators, trading lower maximum speeds for greater cargo capacity. But speed wasn't the only reason military shielding was so much more powerful, for it was also used to fill the area between the sidewall and hull and could lessen or even negate the effect of a hit which managed to pierce the primary defense.

The constraints of the impeller drive and the fact that ships were designed for broadside fire also dictated their hull forms.

The nodes which generated the impeller wedge had to be very specifically located relative to the dimensions of a ship. In general, they had to lie within twelve to fifteen percent of the extreme ends of the vessel and well inside the maximum beam which the wedge allowed. Although there were a few idiosyncratic exceptions, this meant virtually all warships were flattened, "hammer-headed" spindles, tapering to their smallest dimensions at their fore and aft impeller rings and then flaring back out to perhaps a quarter of their maximum beam. The fact that starships generated their own internal gravity allowed designers to orient "up" and "down" perpendicular to the long axis of the ship, which both permitted efficient usage of internal volume and gave renewed meaning to the ancient terms "upper" and "lower" decks.

Chase armaments had to be squeezed into the flared ends of the spindle, and there was little room, relatively speaking, into which to fit them. As a general rule, a light warship's chasers might represent as much as a third of the power of its broadsides, but the proportion fell as the size of the ship grew. Truly enormous ships, like superdreadnoughts, might mount broadside weapons on as many as four or five separate decks, and their length was as much as seven or even eight times their maximum beam, which meant that each "gundeck" offered twenty-five to thirty times the weapons volume available to their chasers.

The topsides and bottoms of warships were not armed, though a portion of those areas were used to mount various sensor and communication arrays. Some navies experimented with vertically mounted missile tubes in an effort to recoup that "wasted space," but with generally unsatisfactory results. A capital ship's impeller wedge might be as much as a hundred kilometers "wide," and no missile could activate its own impeller drive inside its mother ship's drive perimeter lest its wedge impinge upon that of the launching ship. Since the interference between them would have vaporized the missile drive (and the rest of the missile with it), any missile's initial flight path had to be a straight line, directly away from the ship and ninety to a hundred kilometers in length, which no practical vertically-launched weapon could attain.

Broadside missile tubes incorporated powerful mass drivers to get the weapon outside the warship's wedge quickly, and, in theory, a vertical launcher could have used a mass driver with an internally curved path to throw a missile out a top-mounted tube at an angle which would clear the wedge. In practice, it was impossible to align the missile flight path precisely enough with a sidewall gunport, and the additional mass required by the longer, curved mass driver was prohibitive, and efforts to devise "swim out" missiles which dispensed with mass drivers and relied on conventional thrusters for their initial acceleration proved universally disappointing.

All normal-space tactics and naval doctrine had evolved around the limitations and capabilities described above. Obviously, the bow or stern of a ship, which could not be protected by a sidewall, represented its most vulnerable aspect, and the ideal of virtually all normal-space tactics was to "cross the enemy's 'T'" and gain a "down the throat" or "up the kilt" shot with one's full broadside while he could reply only with his chase armament. Since both sides knew this, however, opportunities to cross the "T" were rare even in single-ship duels and almost unheard of in fleet engagements.

The most common tactical situation was the broadside duel, in which both ships brought the full power of one broadside to bear upon the other. Even here, however, a canny captain never forgot the impenetrability of his impeller wedge. Whenever possible, he "rolled ship" to take fire—especially missile fire—which he could not avoid against that powerful defense. At close range, lighter ships, which were much faster on the helm due to their lower masses, often resembled whirling dervishes as they spun back and forth in an effort to bring their own weapons to bear and then snap back around to deny their opponent a target for return fire.

Such energetic tactics, however, were less practical for fleet engagements. First, capital ships, which could mass up to 8,500,000 tons, were necessarily slower when it came to rolling ship, but, more important even than that, was the development of the formation known as "the wall of battle."

Since broadside fire was the only practical way to bring maximum fire to bear upon an enemy, admirals evolved the tactic of stacking their capital ships both vertically and in line at the smallest intervals their impeller wedge safety perimeters permitted. This produced the characteristic "wall"—an often enormous formation, one ship wide, which might extend for thousands of kilometers vertically and ahead and astern along the fleet's base vector. This was scarcely a maneuverable formation, but at least it allowed maximum fire to be brought to bear.

Unfortunately, the tactical formalism fostered by the wall of battle also meant that major fleet engagements tended to be frustratingly indecisive unless one side was tied down by the need to defend a target which it simply could not abandon, like a populated star system. If one fleet took the worst of it and had no overriding strategic reason to fight to the death, its commander simply turned the units of his wall up on their sides, presenting only the roofs or floors of their wedges to the enemy, and then bent all his efforts on breaking away. An opponent who turned towards him to close the range and prevent him from disengaging (the only possible counter) might actually cross its own "T," permitting his ships to roll back and fire their broadsides down the throat of the pursuing fleet with deadly effect.

On the rare occasions when warships clashed in hyperspace, the tactical environment was radically different. As a rule, starships in hyper tend to stay within the area of a grav wave, using their Warshawski sails to draw acceleration and deceleration from the wave, and normal impeller drives (including those of missiles) cannot be used within the area of a grav wave.

The Warshawski sail is essentially a highly modified and very powerful impeller stress band projected in the form of a disk at right angles to the hull, not as a wedge above and below it. The sail, which is just as impenetrable as an impeller wedge, extends for three hundred kilometers (as much as five hundred for really large vessels) in all directions. This not only makes chase armaments even more important but also deprives the warship of the protection of its wedge against fire from "above" or "below." Indeed, it deprives a ship even of its sidewalls, for there are no roof and floor for the sidewall to stitch together.

One might expect admirals to avoid grav waves if forced to fight in hyper, but doing so is tantamount to breaking off the action. The reason is simple: a ship under Warshawski sail can pull almost ten times the acceleration it could under impeller drive. Withdrawing from the wave, then, allows a fleet which remains within it to run away with relative impunity.

A few navies have experimented with the idea of mounting the sidewall bubble generators used to generate 360° "sidewalls" around fixed fortifications in their capital ships for use in hyper-space engagements, but the sheer mass of the system is self-defeating. A ship so equipped has an enormous advantage in hyper, but the volume consumed by the generators cuts deeply into that available for weapons, which places the same vessel at an even greater *dis*advantage in normal-space combat. Since n-space combat is the rule and hyper-space combat is the exception, no navy has ever built a major class of warship with bubble generators.

Because warships in hyper are stripped of both their major passive defense against broadside fire and their longest ranged offensive weapons, conventional tactical wisdom calls for a head-on engagement, the exact reverse of n-space warfare. The idea is that the area of the ship ahead or astern of the impenetrable Warshawski sail is much smaller than its unprotected length, and that the reduction in target area (and hence vulnerability) more than compensates for any loss in firepower.

In terms of maneuver once combat is joined in hyper, the advantage of "altitude" can become even more crucial than "crossing the T" in n-space battles. If a portion of one fleet can curl "over" or "under" its opponent, it can fire down (or up) upon the unarmed topsides or bottoms of enemy ships without receiving return fire.

Moreover, rolling ship is not an effective way to break off action under such circumstances, since there is no impeller wedge to hide behind. Obviously, then, any admiral engaged from more than one bearing in hyperspace is in serious trouble.

NAVAL WEAPONRY

The long-range normal-space shipkiller at the beginning of the 20th century of the Diaspora was the impeller-drive missile, capable of maximum accelerations of some 85,000 gravities and fitted with defensive ECM, sidewall penetrators, and laser warheads.

Because even the highest missile velocities are well under that of light, they can be tracked and engaged by antimissile defenses as they close. The ranges at which they can be fired also require that they be capable of active, self-guided homing on their targets, since light-speed transmission limits would quickly render shipboard control arthritic and inaccurate. Because their onboard seeking systems simply can not be as sensitive and capable as those of a full-sized starship, they are particularly susceptible to electronic counter measures, and the fleet whose ECM is superior to its opponent's has a marked edge in combat.

The tracking time enjoyed against missiles also means that a captain can employ evasive maneuvers against them. If nothing else, he can roll ship to take the incoming fire against the impenetrable roof or floor of his wedge. In longer range engagements, the flight time of the missile and the acceleration capability of his ship allow him to maneuver well clear of the position his opponent's fire control had predicted at the moment of fire, imposing a still greater strain on an attacking missile's drive and seekers.

All of this requires that for *effective* missile fire, the missile drive must still be active and capable of terminal attack maneuvers right up to the instant of detonation.

A missile's effective powered flight envelope can be increased by setting it for a lower rate of acceleration, which delays burnout time on its small but powerful impeller drive. Eighty-five thousand gravities represents the maximum attainable acceleration, used for snapshots at closer ranges in order to achieve the shortest possible flight times. At this acceleration rate, the missile has a maximum powered endurance of sixty seconds, which restricts it to a powered engagement envelope (assuming target and firer were at rest relative to one another at the moment of fire) of approximately 1,500,000 kilometers and a terminal velocity of approximately 50,000 KPS. By setting the drive down to 42,500 gravities, time to burnout can be extended to 180 seconds, producing a maximum powered engagement range of 6,755,000 kilometers and a terminal velocity of 75,000 KPS. Lower accelerations are possible, but the maximum range and velocity actually begin to drop as acceleration is further reduced, and most navies adopted hardwired minimum settings in the vicinity of 42,500 g. The RMN, however, had not, as it believed there were instances in which absolute engagement range and velocity were less important than powered flight *time* to follow an opponent's maneuvers. All of these attack envelopes, of course, can be radically extended or reduced by the relative velocities and accelerations of the ships engaged.

Because the chance of knocking a missile down increases geometrically in the last 50,000 or 60,000 kilometers of its run, as it steadies down on its final attack vector, direct hits against modern point defense are virtually unheard of. As a result, the standard megaton-range nuclear warhead was falling into general disuse for ship-to-ship combat by Honor Harrington's time, replaced by the laser head. The terminal bus of a laser head mounts sophisticated targeting systems and powerful attitude thrusters to enable it to align itself so as to direct the greatest number of bomb-pumped laser beams at the target, but it is also designed to have a "porcupine" effect, radiating lasers in all directions. Each laser inflicts less damage than a direct hit could have, but the chances of a hit—even multiple hits—from a single missile are greatly increased. Not only does a laser head's stand-off range lessen point defense's chance to kill it short of detonation, but the cluster effect allows each to cover a much greater volume of space.

Active antimissile defenses consist of countermissiles, laser clusters, and (in navies further from "state of the art" hardware) autocannon. Countermissiles are much smaller versions of shipkillers, with more limited endurance and no warheads but capable of even higher acceleration. Their weapon is their impeller wedge. If any portion of it impinges on an attacking missile's active wedge, both vaporize as their drives burn out; if the target's drive has already burned out, the "grav shear" of the counter missile's wedge is more than adequate to rip it apart. Because of their overpowered drives, however, maximum effective counter missile range is seldom more than 1,000,000 kilometers or so.

If the countermissiles miss their prey, stopping them is up to the computer-commanded laser clusters. Unlike missiles, these require direct hits, but by the time they come into play, their target is normally steadying down for its final attack run, which gives them much simpler fire solutions.

In some navies, the lasers were backed by a last-ditch autocannon defense. The theory was simple: throw so many shells that they built a wall of metal in the missiles' paths. Given missiles' closing velocities, any hit could be counted on to vaporize them, but the development of laser heads made autocannon largely irrelevant. When a missile can attack from 20,000 or 30,000 kilometers, no last-ditch ballistic projectile can reach it in time.

Note that all of the above comments apply only to engagements under *impeller drive*. All normal space combats are, of course, fought out under impeller drive, as are those in hyper-space but outside the boundaries of a grav wave. Within a grav wave, however, where movement is possible only under Warshawski sail, *missiles cannot be used*. Only energy weapons are effective there, and combat under those conditions tends to be very close and extremely brutal.

The energy weapons of choice are the laser and graser, of which the graser has both a longer range and greater effect. But grasers are considerably more massive than lasers, so most ships have mixed batteries, accepting the lower effectiveness of the laser in order to mount greater numbers of weapons (which let them engage greater numbers of *targets*) while retaining the "smashing" ability of the graser. Ships smaller than light cruisers are normally so cramped for weapons space that they have pure laser energy armaments.

Another energy weapon, though seldom used at this period, was the energy torpedo, which fired what were for all intents and purposes packets of plasma confined in electromagnetic bottles. Energy torpedoes moved at near-light speeds, which made them very difficult for point defense to engage, but the energy torpedo had no homing capability. This made it a purely ballistic weapon, so the initial (and only) fire control solution was far more critical than for missiles, and the endurance of its "bottle" was barely more than one second, limiting absolute energy torpedo range to 300,000 kilometers or so. In addition, the fact that they were totally ineffective against an intact sidewall restricted them to down the throat or up the kilt shots, which made them of strictly limited utility. Despite this, some navies' capital ships (the RMN's among them) incorporated light torpedo batteries for use if the enemy's "T" could be crossed or if his sidewall failed due to other battle damage.

A new development, the grav lance, offered the ability to burn out a sidewall by hitting it with a disrupting burst of focused gravitic energy, but this weapon had a maximum effective range of little more than 100,000 kilometers. It was also extremely slow firing, mass intensive, and temperamental, and very few captains were willing to sacrifice displacement which could be used for tried and proven weapons to squeeze in something that *might* work . . . if they could survive to get into its range of the enemy.

THE BALANCE OF NAVAL POWER

The pre-war naval balance between Manticore and Haven was the result of an arms race which had lasted for almost fifty years. Despite the Star Kingdom of Manticore's wealth and the People's Republic of Haven's ramshackle financial structure, the PRH was so much bigger that the smaller percentage of total income it could devote to its military budget was larger in absolute terms. Moreover, the Star Kingdom, the core of the Manticoran Alliance, possessed only three inhabited planets; the PRH contained over a hundred, which provided a far larger pool from which to draw starship crews and support personnel, and it had begun its initial buildup well before Manticore.

The actual strengths of the two sides in 282 A.L. (1904 P.D.) broke down as below:

Comparative Strengths by Class:

CLASS	Royal Manticoran Navy		People's Navy	
	Total #	Tonnage	Total #	Tonnage
SD	188	1318.5 Mt	412	2801.6 Mt
DN	121	694.3 Mt	48	258.3 Mt
BB	—	—	374	1430.6 Mt
BC	199	148.7 Mt	81	59.0 Mt
CA	333	92.0 Mt	210	54.5 Mt
CL	295	30.1 Mt	354	29.8 Mt
DD	485	35.0 Mt	627	40.7 Mt
TOTAL	1,621	2318.6 Mt	1,944	4674.5 Mt

The People's Navy thus had a tonnage advantage of almost exactly two to one, yet its overall advantage in hulls was only 1.2 to 1, despite the fact that the RMN's ships were almost uniformly more massive on a per-class basis. This apparent discrepancy resulted from the *composition* of the two forces. The People's Navy was designed not only for wars of conquest but to police the

enormous sphere the PRH had already conquered. The
large number of battleships in its order of battle were
intended not for the wall of battle, where their smaller
size would place them at a grievous disadvantage against
"proper" ships of the wall, but to cover occupied systems
against anything *smaller* than a wall of battle ship. (This
was of particular importance against Manticore, which
had always favored the battlecruiser. The BC's combination of acceleration and firepower made it ideal for raids
on the orbital industrial infrastructure of enemy star systems, and the RMN had refined these tactics to a fine
art over the centuries.)

The same internal policing requirements explain the
greater numbers of destroyers in the PN fleet mix. In
addition, both navies had large numbers of LACs (light
attack craft) which do not appear in the figures above,
since their individual combat power was slight and they
were not hyper capable, being intended purely for local
defense.

It should also be noted that, once again despite the
greater mass of most classes in the RMN, Haven's total wall of battle (superdreadnoughts and dreadnoughts)
contained forty-nine percent more units than Manticore's but held a tonnage advantage of over fifty-two
percent. This reflected the RMN's need to build a
higher percentage of smaller and less capable dreadnoughts. Not only did each dreadnought use up less of
its smaller budget and require a shorter building time,
but Manticore needed *numbers*, as well as sheer tonnage, for tactical flexibility. Despite this, however, the
Manticoran Admiralty steadfastly rejected all sugges-
tions that it should build still smaller and cheaper
battleships as Haven had done. The RMN's view was
that while some concessions had to be made to bring
numbers up, battleships were simply too small and
weak to lie in the wall of battle, and Manticore, unlike
Haven, could not afford to tie up millions of tons in
"capital ships" unable to bear the brunt of fleet
combat.

The table below shows the relative *average* displacements of the latest generation ships of the two navies, but it should be borne in mind that these are *only* averages.

Average Tonnage by Class:

Class	Manticore	Haven
SD	8,250,000	8,000,000
DN	6,750,495	6,331,818
BB	————	4,500,000
BC	878,894	856,790
CA	325,000	300,000
CL	120,000	98,870
DD	85,000	76,400

The disparity in average hull sizes is evident, but what it actually meant in fighting power can be best illustrated by comparing two ships of nominally equivalent classes: HMS *Nike* and PNS *Sultan*. Both were battlecruisers of the latest generation, but *Nike* massed 879,000 tons with a crew of 2,105 (including Marines) as opposed to *Sultan*'s 858,000 tons and crew of 1,695. Although she was less than three percent more massive overall, *Nike*'s sidewalls were ten percent tougher than *Sultan*'s, and her energy weapons were fifteen percent more massive (and much more powerful) on a mount-for-mount basis.

Offensively, *Sultan* mounted a broadside of nine lasers, six grasers, and twenty missile tubes to *Nike*'s eight lasers, ten grasers, two energy torpedoes, and twenty-five missile tubes. In terms of chase armament, *Sultan* mounted two lasers and five missile tubes ahead and the same astern, while *Nike* mounted four missile tubes, two grasers, and a laser in the same positions.

Part of the Manticoran ship's superior armament was bought at the expense of magazine space, but though *Sultan* actually carried twenty-five percent more missiles, despite her lower number of tubes, this was offset by the RMN's superior electronics and penetration aides, which made *Nike*'s missiles almost thirty percent more accurate (and harder to stop), and a higher rate of fire per launcher.

The two ships also reflected differences in doctrine and design philosophy. The RMN built battlecruisers as screening elements for its battle squadrons, but it also regarded them as raiders and designed them for independent operations, as well. PN doctrine, on the other hand, tied its BCs much more tightly to the wall of battle, regarding them as scaled down, faster elements of the main battle fleet with a sustained combat role in fleet engagements. The RMN believed that any BC's life expectancy against ships of the wall would be brief and that battlecruiser-versus-battlecruiser actions would be short and sharp. As a result, BuShips believed it was better to be able to throw more missiles—especially *better* missiles—faster and incorporate an energy armament heavy enough to make close-range action decisive than to try to outlast an opponent. It is also worth noting that the smaller Manticoran fleet contained well over twice as many BCs as the PN.

Clearly, in any engagement with her opposite number the Manticoran ship's heavier armament, superior electronic warfare capabilities, and generally more efficient point defense gave her a powerful advantage. Indeed, a single *Nike* could engage two *Sultans* with a fair chance of victory.

The personnel of the two fleets showed an almost equally striking disparity. Both officer corps were comprised of long-term volunteer professionals, but Manticore, by and large, hewed to the doctrine established by Commodore Edward Saganami. Its officers were expected to use their own judgment and trained accordingly, whereas Havenite officers were kept on much tighter leashes by their superiors. RMN admirals tended to allow their subordinates considerable freedom of action within broad strategic and tactical parameters; their PN counterparts tied their units into tight, centralized planning and expected them to do as they were told. There were exceptions—some outstanding—to the pattern in each navy, but overall a Manticoran commander was much more comfortable "thinking for himself" than a Havenite CO. Perhaps even more significantly, the People's Republic was not a forgiving master—and it was far more heavily politicized. A Havenite officer dared not deviate (openly, at least) from the "party line," and if he failed to carry out his orders, whether those orders made sense or not, his career was likely to be short. In addition, favoritism and careerism were actually more rampant in the People's Navy than in the RMN, despite Manticoran reformers' understandable concern with their own service's tradition of patronage and family influence.

There was, in addition, a tremendous difference between the enlisted and noncommissioned ranks in the two fleets, for over seventy percent of the People's Navy's lower deck personnel were conscripts. Manticore, on the other hand, had been able to crew her ships entirely with volunteers, many with previous experience in the Star Kingdom's huge merchant fleet, as awareness of "the Havenite threat" grew. Moreover, the RMN's petty officers, the backbone of any navy, averaged almost twice the length of service of their Havenite counterparts because of the higher turnover in a conscript-crewed fleet and the lesser personal incentives the PN offered.

The education levels of the two sides also differed markedly. The progressive "democratization" of the PRH's educational system had emasculated it, while Manticore boasted one of the toughest merit-based systems, especially for university and post-graduate programs, in human space (two facts which largely explain the RMN's pronounced technological superiority). It was sad but true that the best educated enlisted personnel of the PN were conscripts from conquered planets who had largely completed their schooling before the PRH's centralized education policies blighted their teaching establishments.

There was, however, one major offsetting imponderable which neither navy was able to quantify prior to the actual outbreak of war. While the People's Navy might rely on ill-educated (comparatively speaking) conscripts for the bulk of its personnel, it had also been almost continuously at war for over half a Terran century. Admittedly, none of its opponents had been large enough to offer a long or protracted resistance, but the operational experience amassed by the PN was without equal. Inevitably, its crews must have acquired a certain degree of "on the job training" to offset their initial inferiority, and its officers, on the whole, believed in their tradition of victory. It remained to be seen whether these factors overmatched the intensive training and motivation of the RMN's personnel, and only the test of battle could reveal the truth.